Pr

V

"*Vowed in Shadows* _____ intense ride with two complex, comp_____

— *New York Times* bestselling author Nalini Singh

"If you like your stories filled with action and romance,
plus about two wounded souls, then this is a series for you.
This series is wonderful; it has everything you could want
to read about."   — Night Owl Reviews (top pick)

"A solid entry in what is sure to become a classic series in
the genre."   — Fresh Fiction

"Slade's characters are extremely well-developed, with
boundless emotional depth. In this third Marked Souls
novel, the story line is gripping, with plenty of sensual
scenes."   — *Romantic Times*

Forged of Shadows

"Dark, dangerous, and spiced with passion, this is a well-
written tale that will grab your attention from the very beginning."   — Romance Reviews Today

"The wordplay is riveting and the story line is fast and
action-packed."   — Smexy Books Romance Reviews

"The only thing I can say about this series is WOW!!! Ms.
Slade brings the fight against evil from the dark and into
the light. This story is so exciting and action-packed that I
had a hard time putting it down. I ended up reading it in
one night. I can't wait to see what comes next for this great
new romantic urban fantasy series."
                              — Night Owl Reviews (five stars)

"[A] heady mix of philosophy and religion...serves as
part of the framework for this excellent series and sets it
apart from the pack....Be first in line for book three,
Vowed in Shadows."   — Bitten by Books (5 tombstones)

continued ...

"For readers who love J. R. Ward's Black Dagger Brotherhood, the Marked Souls series will hit the spot."
— *Romantic Times* (4 stars)

Seduced by Shadows

"Wonderfully addictive!"
— *New York Times* bestselling author Gena Showalter

"Slade's debut presents a dark and dense supernatural conflict with high stakes in a world where demons and angels possess humans and use them as tools in the unending fight between heaven and hell ... [a] rich crossover urban fantasy."
— *Publishers Weekly*

"A beautiful and inventive new series start, with plenty of action and wonderful characters!"
— Errant Dreams Reviews

"A gripping, suspenseful story, with some hot romantic interactions thrown in for good measure."
— *San Francisco Book Review*

"*Seduced by Shadows* blew me away ... Slade creates a beyond-life-or-death struggle for love and redemption in a chilling, complex, and utterly believable world."
— Jeri Smith-Ready, award-winning author of
Wicked Game

Also by Jessa Slade

Seduced by Shadows
Forged of Shadows
Vowed in Shadows

DARKNESS UNDONE

A NOVEL OF THE MARKED SOULS

JESSA SLADE

A SIGNET ECLIPSE BOOK

SIGNET ECLIPSE
Published by New American Library, a division of
Penguin Group (USA) Inc., 375 Hudson Street,
New York, New York 10014, USA
Penguin Group (Canada), 90 Eglinton Avenue East, Suite 700, Toronto,
Ontario M4P 2Y3, Canada (a division of Pearson Penguin Canada Inc.)
Penguin Books Ltd., 80 Strand, London WC2R 0RL, England
Penguin Ireland, 25 St. Stephen's Green, Dublin 2,
Ireland (a division of Penguin Books Ltd.)
Penguin Group (Australia), 250 Camberwell Road, Camberwell, Victoria 3124,
Australia (a division of Pearson Australia Group Pty. Ltd.)
Penguin Books India Pvt. Ltd., 11 Community Centre, Panchsheel Park,
New Delhi - 110 017, India
Penguin Group (NZ), 67 Apollo Drive, Rosedale, Auckland 0632,
New Zealand (a division of Pearson New Zealand Ltd.)
Penguin Books (South Africa) (Pty.) Ltd., 24 Sturdee Avenue,
Rosebank, Johannesburg 2196, South Africa

Penguin Books Ltd., Registered Offices:
80 Strand, London WC2R 0RL, England

First published by Signet Eclipse, an imprint of New American Library,
a division of Penguin Group (USA) Inc.

First Printing, March 2012
10 9 8 7 6 5 4 3 2 1

To PopPop:
An engineer first, but an artist too. You gave me some good
material, genetics-wise, and some funny stories.
Miss you.

Acknowledgments

My editor, Kerry Donovan, and agent, Becca Stumpf, have been with me from Chapter 1 to glossary, from cover art first-glimpse squees to back cover copyedits. "Thank you" is only two words (can I say anything in two words?) and doesn't even begin to capture my gratitude.

The entire team at NAL brings my books to life—and to bookshelves—and I can't thank them enough, especially Jesse Feldman and Kayleigh Clark; copy editor Jane Steele (who had to put up with all my beloved sentence fragments); and Gene Mollica and Adam Auerbach, who put a chest (if not a face) on my sexy hero.

Mwahs to my cheerleading beta reader, Delilah Marvelle, whose energy in her writing and in her life inspires me endlessly.

As I write this, Book Blogger Appreciation Week is coming to a close, but I want to give them a shout-out here too, considering how their delight in and ardent support of romance has contributed substantially to my to-be-read mountain. Extra special thanks to Bitten by Books, Night Owl Reviews, Errant Dreams Reviews, Romance Reviews Today, and Smexy Books Romance Reviews.

All families put up with craziness in their loved ones, but maybe writers' families sigh more deeply, with a little extra angst. To my family and Scott, much, much thanks and love, love, love.

Dear new Bookkeeper,

Sucks to be you.

You're probably flipping through these mostly blank pages where the notes for the last year should be, wondering why the archives of the Chicago league of demon-possessed male talya warriors haven't been updated lately. Honestly, as the temp secretary, I've been superbusy. Mostly doing my nails.

Hey, sharpened nails come in very handy against the lurking evil of the horde-tenebrae.

Besides, calfskin, goose quills, and illuminated letters went out a long time ago. You Bookkeepers should try Twitter.

So here're the past eleven months—since the demonic possession of the first female in a couple thousand years (that'd be me) and the return of the mated *symballein* bond—condensed to 140 characters with gratuitous emoticons and random misspellings:

More evul than evuh WTF? Djinn-man wants to destroy the world (X_X) But wait! T&A + witty repartee = True Love Saves the Day! <333 The End . . . ?

Well, that pretty much covers it. I can't imagine you'll have any more questions. Now that you're here, I'll be out slaying bad things. Don't worry; just regular ol' bad things—like ratty little malice, huge stinky feralis, and burning salambes—not insanely powerful, straight-up insane djinn-men like Corvus Valerius, who had the nerve to open a portal into hell before we vanquished him three months ago. No thanks to our former Bookkeeper who betrayed us and helped unleash the repentant demon that possessed me and started this whole damn mess. We won't hold that against *you*, though. Really.

We know the ranks of Bookkeeping masters frown on us ~~pulverizing~~ tweaking the traditions the London league has upheld for centuries, but—did I mention?—sucks to be you. Welcome to Chicago.

Sera Littlejohn, Interim Bookkeeper

Chapter I

To human senses, the Chicago night was dark and quiet—at least as dark and quiet as a big city could be. But Sidney Westerbrook knew, somewhere beyond the stark neon and the shouts with the flattened vowels that grated on his merely human eyes and ears, the streets seethed with demonic fury.

And after coming nearly four thousand miles, he wasn't getting the chance to experience any of it.

Sid stuffed his hands to the bottom of his trouser pockets, as if he might find a last kilojoule of warmth down there. His father had warned him London's fog had nothing on Chicago's wind.

Then again, his father had warned him of quite a lot, only some of which had seemed relevant. Sid hunched his shoulders, and his gusty sigh bounced off the upturned collar of his tweed jacket, fogging his spectacles.

Who would've guessed the Chicago talyan would be such contrary blighters? All his Bookkeeper studies had prepared him for the same old, same old: immortal, menacing warriors with preternatural fighting skills and tortured demon-possessed souls, et cetera. But these upstart Yanks—from one of the secondary leagues, no less—had blown apart the theories of generations of Bookkeepers before him. Yet despite their obvious need for objective guidance, they wouldn't give him, their emergency Bookkeeper, even the time of day.

No way in hell were they giving him their nights.

Though Sid didn't have a talya's enhanced vision, the flow of demonic ethers was clearly unsettled in Chicago. He'd hypothesized as much from the sharply refracted energy in every talya iris—purplish glints even an unschooled human would notice. The borderline morbid array of close-quarters weaponry had been another hint. But Liam Niall, the leader of the Chicago league, had refused to let Sid accompany them on patrol.

"It's your first night in town," he'd said. "Kick the jet lag. Then we'll show you . . . everything, as London requested."

Sid hadn't needed enhanced hearing either, to pick up that disdainful pause. Most of the world's major cities had @1 leagues since demonic activity tied into population density and the sorts of upheavals that regularly made the evening news. All the leagues were distinctly autonomous and fighting to hold their burden of darkness at bay. But London, having inherited the position from Rome in the days of expanding empires, held perhaps a "first among equals" distinction, though the other leagues might not readily concede. Probably didn't help matters that Niall had been a victim of the Irish potato famine, which had its rotting roots in British agrarian politics.

That quarrel, in case anyone wanted to consult a calendar, had been dead and buried for a century and a half. Although obviously "dead" meant something different to immortals.

Sid crushed his fists down hard enough to turn pocket

lint to felt. Just what he needed; another old man unwilling to let him in.

He dodged across the street, avoiding a cab that had run the red. He responded to the unwarranted honk with an appropriate American gesture. In some ways, cities were all the same. Certainly he could find common ground with these big, taciturn talya males and their three smaller but equally unnerving females. London might have loaned him to Chicago while his last journeyman Bookkeeper thesis was under review, but if he wanted to prove his mastery—if he wanted all the sacrifices to mean anything—exposing, exploring, and explaining some heretofore unknown talya secret would certainly do the trick.

And the Chicago league had secrets to burn.

He passed an iron stanchion supporting the elevated train, turned the next corner, and came face-to-face with ... fangs.

A squeak of surprise squeezed from his chest.

When his thinking forebrain caught up with his hindbrain, he winced at his instinctive reaction. The rubber monster mask in the shop window wasn't coming for his jugular.

He let out a slow breath, calming the rush of his pulse. He straightened his spectacles and leaned closer to the window. The molded tusks were coated in frightfully realistic gore as if they'd just emerged from someone's thorax. He'd forgotten All Hallows' Eve was less than a fortnight away. Not that the demonic tenebrac scheduled holidays.

He walked on, suddenly thankful he *was* alone tonight. If the talyan had witnessed that squeak, he'd never earn their respect.

But there was no one around.

No one at all.

His heel scuffed the pavement as his steps slowed. The soft scrape repeated down the throat of the dank alley off to his right. He swallowed in disgust at the stench of stewed trash. Really, that costume shop should try bottling the stink for a gag gift—emphasis on gag.

He peered back toward the intersection where the cab had almost sideswiped him. The red flash of brakes and illuminated crosswalk signs blinked with ordinary, reassuring liveliness, but in that moment, bustling humanity seemed strangely far away.

Distance was good. Distance put things in perspective; letting Niall's snub provoke him had been stupid. Well, he'd blame the jet lag and be his own composed Bookkeeper self on the morrow.

Before he could take another step, a disfigured shadow charged out of the alley toward him in a blur of grizzled fur and scabrous gray skin.

Pinched together on a ratlike head, the feralis's bulbous eyes raged with an unholy orange flame. Its tapered jaws gaped wide to expose finger-length incisors. Curiously, the fangs looked sharper on the rubber version....

Sid stumbled back. Adrenaline soaked through him in a hot wash like thin, bitter coffee.

Told you so, said his hindbrain.

He turned to run, but the feralis sprang at him, fiendishly quick on its clawed feet. Its jaws sank into his left shoulder. The shock was literal as well as academic when the teeth sliced through the heavy wool tweed of his coat, into muscle, and—judging by the unpleasant grinding noise—all the way through to bone.

"Bloody hell!" Agony spiked above the adrenaline—the archives never footnoted how much a feralis bite hurt!—and his vision narrowed to brick and blood and darkness.

The feralis shook him once, twice, snapping his head back as if he were nothing more than a chew toy. His spectacles flew off—now the brick, blood, and darkness were blurry—and his spine twisted with a searing streak of pain.

He flailed with his free arm, and something damp crumpled under his fist. Had he smacked its rotting gums? Or its eyeball? His stomach heaved. The talyan never reported squeamishness. Was that a result of indifference or pride?

The rest of him heaved too as the feralis tossed him toward the alley. He hit the pavement and bounced. The brutal blow to his shoulder jolted the breath from him and condensed his vision to a single bloody point.

The red dot winked out. And reappeared. And multiplied to a hundred tiny glittering points. Malice eyes split the darkness like crimson open wounds, not fuzzy at all, despite his nearsightedness. The smoldering, oily smoke of a salambe threaded past the crimson like an evil party streamer.

There were certain times when being a bit on the dim side would be preferable.

Night air leached through the hole in his coat, but he wasn't cold. Between the alarming slick of blood matting the tweed and the singe of the feralis's poisoned bite, he was feeling almost stuffy.

Of course, Bookkeepers were often accused of being stuffy. His father had countered, saying a Bookkeeper was duty-bound to replace nonsensical emotions with the quest for understanding.

As if understanding the inevitability made it any easier to die.

The feralis snapped at a second tenebrae crowding in. Two more of the tenebrae skittered behind them on spidery legs. The mutant quartet shuffled closer, and the air between the brick walls thickened with the stench of decay until Sid's eyes watered.

Bloody marvelous. Now the talyan would find his mangled corpse with tears on his cheeks. Maybe sheer mortification at their comparative weakness was why Bookkeepers were tutored past emotion.

The pain in his shoulder spread in paralyzing waves, but his right hand still worked. He scrabbled along the asphalt for a loose brick, an empty bottle, maybe a rocket launcher. But only pebbles and bits of glass rolled under his desperate fingertips. Not even a dustbin to shelter behind. What sort of evil city kept its alleys so tidy?

"Don't fight, lads," he choked out. How many times had his father chided him with those words? "Run along now."

"They must fight."

The voice—barely a whisper behind him—jerked him around with the force of sharper teeth sunk into his flesh.

From the deepest pool of shadows, a girl, clothed in nothing more than a once-white shift, coalesced like a mist in front of his straining eyes. Her thin arms were bare, and she held herself so tightly, her fingers chased the last of the blood from her skin.

Her hair fell in loose waves over her face and past her shoulders. Between the dark strands, her gaze—eerily pale—was hazy, and a distracted frown arrowed in one line between her arched brows. She took a limping step forward.

What was she doing in the empty alley? Doing drugs or a john? If her moral compass was as unsteady as her steps, she'd be an easy target for the tenebrae evil. He tried to pull himself toward her, and his fingers closed over the smooth frames of his spectacles.

He jerked them on, crookedly. At least now he could see his oncoming demise.

"Get out of here," he hissed. He wouldn't let another innocent die because once again he'd been in the wrong place at a bad time. Whatever or whoever she'd been doing, she didn't deserve this. "Go. Now!"

For a heartbeat, her eyes cleared, but it was like winter clouds clearing the night sky to reveal a moon icy, distant, and dead. "Go where?"

"Away." Fear for her congealed in his throat until he could barely push out the words. "Just go."

Her pale gaze lifted to the ferales. "They have to fight. I have to fight too."

If the feralis attack had been a blur, the girl was a lightning bolt.

One moment she was far enough down the alley that he thought she had a chance to escape. In his next breath, she was amidst the ferales. Her skirt fluttered behind her as she ducked between the two spidery tenebrae, avoiding the stabs of their spearlike legs with artless grace despite her limp.

Shrieking, the salambe shot up in a tight spiral out of the alley. All the malice swarmed after it, like incorporeal rats in the wake of a sinking ship.

That couldn't be a good sign.

God, she wasn't even half their size, and she was so thin, the ferales would snap through her in one unsatisfying bite. She could have gained an inch or two if she had at least been wearing shoes.

He surged upright, determined to throw himself into the fray beside her.

With a roundhouse kick, she slammed her foot into his head and knocked him to the ground again. This might have ticked him off, except his spectacles stayed on this time, so he had a clear view of the feralis that launched over her and landed right where he would have been, had he still been standing.

From his sprawl, he slammed his trainers at the feralis. At least he wasn't wearing tasseled loafers, which his father claimed awarded Bookkeepers a proper visual distinction from the booted talyan.

The feralis hopped sideways with a hiss. From its jaws, slaver dripped, backlit yellow from the streetlights. Those fangs were looking sharper by the second.

The girl grabbed the creature by its fleshy tail and hauled it backward. The lean muscles in her bare arms quivered as the feralis bawled, spraying sulfurous drool. If Sid hadn't known better, he would have said the tenebrae was . . .

afraid. Its claws peeled up curls of asphalt, but it could not resist her relentless force. Her irises gleamed violet.

Sid sucked in a shocked breath. She wasn't human either.

What astounding luck! His first night in Chicago, and he'd found a female talya. She wasn't associated with the league, or Niall would have mentioned her. She must be newly possessed—and unconstrained by the knowledge and rules of the league culture. A tabula rasa, ready for imprinting.

Exhilaration made his head spin. Or maybe that was blood loss.

He winced as she gained traction and heaved the feralis over her shoulder into the remaining trio. Her vise grip tore the tail loose in an arc of ichor. The tenebrae screamed, and the warbling cry hit an octave that iced Sid's spine.

Immortal and inhumanly strong the girl might be, compelled by her repentant demon to fight evil, but she could still be killed. Four marauding ferales—well, three marauding and one that seemed a little shaken—were deadly foes.

He pulled himself upright. He couldn't lose her, not when a journeyman Bookkeeper could write his ticket to London mastery on such a find.

She shoved him back again, and he stumbled into the wall. "Enough!" he shouted, pushing off the bricks. "I want to help you."

She ignored him and lashed out with the tail in her hand. The fleshy whip snaked though the air to drive the ferales back.

Chunks of rot crumbled from the makeshift weapon. Decaying feralis husks never held up well. Sid knew the corrosive ichor congealed within the husks must be burning through the girl's hands, but she never hesitated. With her demon ascendant, she'd feel nothing—not pain, not fear, not loss.

How simple the world must look through the violet eyes of possession. For the merest incomplete contraction of his cardiac musculature—not even a full heartbeat—he wished she could share that simplicity with him.

She cracked the putrid whip again, and one of the ferales shrieked as its limb sheared off. Without the animating etheric energy, the husk fragment putrefied. In minutes it would be only a noxious puddle.

Sid had never quite appreciated just how poorly animated corpses performed under pressure in the field. It was a subject worthy of a paper or two, no doubt.

The wet thud of the feralis's head hitting the asphalt made his gut clench. He realized he wasn't exactly performing up to snuff himself.

The two partially dismembered ferales fled around the corner. The decapitated one tried to follow but kept blundering into the alley wall. In another moment, it would stumble out, and Sid could just imagine its headless-chicken dance down Michigan Avenue.

The girl kicked aside the fourth motionless husk—he hadn't even noticed her destroying that one; what kind of Bookkeeper was he?—and advanced on the hapless feralis.

Her limp was more noticeable, though she hadn't taken a single hit. Had she been wounded earlier in the night, perhaps, and not yet healed despite her demon's power? She was a devoted talya, for which he had reason to be extremely grateful.

The stump where the feralis's ratlike skull had been now spewed ichor and a discomfiting mewl, like an infant's cry. Sid wished it would stop.

The girl jammed both her fists through its sternum and wrenched it asunder in a black gush. The mewling stopped.

His gorge rose up in his throat, choking him. Just as well he'd left the @1 warehouse in a snit and without converting any currency for his supper; otherwise he'd be spewing right about now.

Like some murderous, postapocalyptic librarian spinster, the girl knelt between the decommissioned ferales, her bare toes tucked under the raggedy hem of her old-fashioned gown. How would the talyan, who demonstrated a regrettable morphology tending toward thick-necked gigantism, look in this new dress-for-success? Sid held back a snort.

With a hand on each husk, the girl lowered her head. Her dark hair spread around her shoulders and curtained her face. The orange light in the feralis's protruding eye-stalks faded to white, like a sullen ember smothering in ash, as she drained the animating ether. The energy she took would refresh the demon within her and then . . .

She turned her head just enough to meet his gaze. Violet. So Bookkeeper archives described the glint of nocturnal predator, but that did no justice to the wavelengths of light bending beyond his human perception. He sagged against the bricks as if his marrow had turned to ice water.

She wasn't newly possessed and awkwardly delving into her untested powers.

She was rogue.

He eased back against the wall, letting the bricks support him when his suddenly wobbly knees didn't seem up to the task.

She blinked, and the violet faded to the previous pale haze. "Pardon me." Her voice barely carried across the alley. "No one should have seen that."

The odd cadence of her voice snagged his attention. It sounded like something he'd find on Oxford Street—almost familiar but strangely awry. He realized he was leaning forward to hear her, his muscles canting in her direction, even as the more primitive part of his brain urged him to edge away slowly.

"But you'll forget, won't you?" She tilted her head, and the dark waves of her hair slid to one side, revealing the slender column of her throat. Just above her high collar, a thin black tracery marred her white skin: the mark of her demon. "'Twould be for the best, to forget."

He wondered if "forget" was a euphemism for nipping off his head as she'd done to the feralis. Not much he could do about it, of course. "No doubt most people you save scream more than they say thank you, but . . . thank you."

A violet gleam surfaced in her eyes, spun once, and vanished again. "They *all* scream."

His ever-so-keen powers of observation were starting to tell him his newfound talya had gone a bit off. Not that she seemed handicapped in the butchery department, where a talya truly needed to shine.

He let out a long, nonthreatening sigh. His shoulder was throbbing in earnest, now that the danger seemed to have passed—mostly.

He studied her empty hands where tenebrae gore left scorch marks on her skin. "You have an . . . interesting technique for dispatching ferales. Most talyan use long-handled weapons to keep clear of the ichor."

She didn't move, but something about her stillness became even more still. Apparently the danger hadn't gone very far away at all. "What are these words you use?"

"Ferales." He pointed first at the husks and shifted to the black spill. "Ichor. Talya." He pointed at her.

She shifted onto her haunches, fingers steepled over the asphalt.

"Don't run," he said softly. He hoped she wouldn't leap on him either and rip his heart out, as seemed perfectly possible when he considered her taut white hands. "It's okay."

"Okay? What is okay?"

He pointed to himself.

And then he passed out.

Alyce flattened her palms over the tear in the man's coat. She dared not touch him directly with her filthy hands, but the wound was clotting, and her anxious heartbeat slowed along with his blood loss.

As if in reply, the restless spirits overhead that had lit her way here finally ceased their frantic whirling. Since the luminescent whorls above lacked teeth or claws, she focused on the man. Marshaling her thoughts was like catching clouds; it had been so long since she'd concentrated on anything besides the hunt. Gentling her touch was harder yet. Her fingers trembled with the effort.

The devils had never attacked another person in her presence before—or none she had been able to save. Always, when she appeared, the devils tried to run, and always, the overpowering impulse in her ensured they did not go far. After the first time, when she'd realized the devils didn't leave witnesses, she'd never gone back to sift through their ghastly handiwork.

She had frights enough.

But this man had not screamed when she appeared. The devils had surrounded him, and he had mocked them. He had met her gaze, and he had not run.

Perhaps because he'd swooned. But before his eyes—nice brown eyes, without a flicker of unholy flames—had rolled back in his head, he had stared at evil and not backed down. He mustn't die now, not after he'd chipped a hole in the ice that had frozen her off from the world.

She couldn't take him to a hospital. Once, she had tried to explain to the men in white coats; she had tried to show them. . . . She hadn't tried again. The darkness inside her shifted at the memory.

This man knew everything already. He had no need to come at her with needles and shocks. She removed his eyeglasses and tucked them into his pocket. Determination stiffened her spine, and she lifted the man more gently than she'd dealt with the—what had he called them?—the ferales.

Fresh blood pooled in the tear of his coat and spattered over her. She had to save him. He could tell her what she was; he could tell her why the most horrific monsters in the city cried out and fled from her.

A peculiar warmth trickled through her. Not the pathway of his blood—she was familiar enough with that sensation. This was different and long forgotten.

She was not alone.

A passing vehicle blared at her as she darted across the street, the man an unwieldy weight across her shoulders. Fortunately, the people of the city would notice only that she was small and her burden was large, and they would not imagine she could carry a full-grown man. They would remember, perhaps, a woman carrying a sack of laundry.

Delusions were so lovely.

She had roamed far tonight from her usual haunts. Now she knew why. God had finally taken pity on her and led her to this man who did not scream at monsters—monsters like her.

Fortitude carried her, and she carried the man, although his sliding weight tugged her collar tight until she choked and her limp turned to a stagger by the time she crept down the stairs to her basement hideaway.

She maintained a careful disguise of withered leaves and soft moss on the concrete steps—not so mussed that anyone felt obliged to come down and sweep, but not so tidy that they might think the area in use. The rust on the old lock resisted even a determined tug, but it yielded to her hand. She pulled it into place behind them.

When she faced the room, though, her remaining strength drained away. It was a pit, a cold grave lacking even the comforts of a proper casket. The mattress had been disgusting long before she salvaged it. She couldn't lay him there, but the cracked floor was worse.

Perhaps he would have preferred to bleed to death in the alley.

But since he was insensible, he had no say. With quick, cautious hands, she eased him out of his coat and shirt. His breath caught once, when she slipped the sleeve off his bitten arm, but he did not rouse.

So much blood. In the dark hours of winter, when memories rose chill as hoarfrost out of nothing, she sometimes remembered long-ago sermons on the blandishments of the devil. They'd neglected to mention the piercing teeth.

She ripped the lower panel of her skirt and used the thin fabric to clean him. After, she drained the last of the jug of water she'd stolen from an unwatchful delivery man; the wounds were open and, she saw at last, not fatal.

The thick pad of muscle had protected him. He was not as tall as most men seemed to be these days, which was just as well considering how far she had carried him. But the calculated breadth of his shoulders told her he had considered the shortcoming and compensated.

She realized she'd let her hands linger on those shoulders and forced herself to move on.

With the last unbloodied corner of her shift, she brushed away a thick russet lock of his hair and swabbed his forehead. Her dirty heel had left a smear where she'd kicked him. She wished she'd thought that through first, but the devils—the ferales—had been there, and she hadn't wanted him in the way.

At least she'd made sure to temper the kick so she hadn't lashed his head off his shoulders, which happened sometimes with the ferales. If he complained of a headache, she'd have to tell him that.

She contemplated the man's face. He had labored to make his body hard, but even the slight crookedness of his nose—a natural flaw, she decided; he had never been hit—couldn't disguise his boyish handsomeness. Though tightened with pain, the lines of his mouth arched in a way that beckoned her to touch.

She slowed the stroke of the rag, almost giving in. He wouldn't know. One quick brush of her dirty hand across his lower lip to discover if his lips were as soft and giving as she imagined.

She reached for him, though not with her finger. Instead, she leaned down so her mouth hovered above his. The scent of his bared skin—something both turbulent and steadfast, like the place where the wind over the lake lashed the steel seawalls—roused her senses, and she shivered as if caught in that wild, breathtaking storm.

All night she'd been irresistibly drawn to the alley—to him—and the compulsion ached within her still. So long, so long since she had touched or been touched. One kiss was all she needed; one sweet memory and maybe she would forget the screams, for this night at least. She tilted her head and touched her lips to his.

Just as he opened his eyes.

CHAPTER 2

He was being stalked.

In the pitch blackness, something was after him. Sid braced himself for attack, but the drift of a warm mouth over his stunned him to dumb immobility and submerged his blind fear in a wash of purely physical sensation.

Wits spinning from blood loss and confusion, he struggled to list what he knew. The girl—she was kissing him. He wasn't dead, not if the fervent pounding of his heart was any indication, and his lovely rescuer had awakened him with a kiss.

He'd never had a chance to believe in fairy tales—the monsters in the dark had crowded them out—but for this moment he could make an exception.

Her touch was as light as that of a ghost and her mouth chastely closed. But the faintest quiver of her breath told him she held back so much more. And he wanted it, just for this moment where fairy tale and darkness came together.

He tilted his head and drew her lower lip between his, a

gentle suction that parted her lips and released her gasp of pleasure. He took the chance to rim the inner curve of soft, moist flesh.

The soft sound she made this time was more . . . a growl of low double octaves.

Demonic.

He bolted upright, smacked his forehead into hers, and fell back before his brain had finished fully catching up with his consciousness.

"What am I—?" he stammered, not quite as loud as her "I just wanted to see—"

They both fell silent, and he stared hard into the nothingness.

How could such utter darkness be so alive? Every little puff of air and whisper of sound tingled over his skin.

He struggled to slow his racing pulse. "You just wanted to see what? I can't see a thing."

"'Tis dark." The sibilance of shifting cloth told him she was moving away. "But I can see you."

He reached out, and his fingers brushed some rough material before it twitched beyond his grasp. Exasperation—at himself mostly; how could he have forgotten what she was, even for a moment?—replaced the pain and disquiet. "Of course you can. You are talya, and the teshuva gives you all sorts of advantages."

"Teshuva? You have not said this word before."

"The demon," he snapped, reminding himself why kissing her was stupid, bordering on suicidal. "The demon that possessed you."

When her voice came again, she sounded far away. "So it was a devil."

Remorse at his slapdash introduction and the worry that she might leave him here—wherever *here* was—cramped his belly. He winced, not from his own pain. "You didn't know?"

"I—I knew."

"But didn't want to believe."

"What am I?" Her whisper was sepulchral. In the black, violet flared and guttered.

His hackles prickled at the evidence of her demon's restlessness. "You are still you, with the addition of a repentant teshuva demon seeking redemption via the destruction of the horde-tenebrae in this realm. Those would be the ferales, malice, and the salambe lurking in the alley."

The hush prickled through him, more eerie than her disembodied voice, before she finally spoke. "Am I not damned, then?"

"Ah . . ."

"I knew that too."

Could her voice get any colder? "If by 'damned,' you mean the inexact lay definition of 'condemned to eternal punishment,' then I suppose, yes. Since you are immortal and you are compelled to destroy the tenebrae, that could indeed be construed as eternal punishment. At least until you are killed. But if you're thinking of damned in a more speculative sense as divine seraphic judgment . . . well, then probably still yes, but with ultimate interminable results unsubstantiated and thus subject to some academic dispute."

In the absolute silence, he thought she'd left. The swish of blood through his ears resembled the echo of a mocking laugh, and he wished he'd just kept his mouth shut.

Finally she said, "You make my head hurt."

If only he could see her. Not being able to judge her mood put him at a distinct disadvantage, which was not a place one wanted to be with the demon-ridden. "The tenebrae can kick my ass, and so can you, but I can at least induce headaches."

A breath of air moved against his bare skin, as if she'd taken a few steps closer to him again. "You are not like me? I thought the restless spirits wanted you."

"I'm not possessed by a teshuva as you are, no, but the

demons are drawn to dark emotions, and I've been . . . jet-lagged. The ferales would have made an in-flight snack of me if not for you."

"It wasn't just the . . . the ferales. . . . I don't know what . . ." She blew out a frustrated breath. "It made me come to you, here."

A Bookkeeper could serve in a league for decades before encountering a newly possessed talya in need of guidance. This wasn't her teshuva's virgin ascension, and yet in some ways she was even more innocent—erratic and deadly, but innocent.

And she was his.

Though the taste of her still lingered on his tongue, he tamped down the surge of possessiveness. He spackled over the improper craving with a more respectable crust of impersonal kindness. "I have much I can tell you."

"Can you use fewer words?"

She'd come a little closer yet, judging from the volume of her voice. He'd never understood how someone could *hear* a smile, but in the lightless depths of wherever she'd dragged him, he imagined the relaxing of the tension in her vocal cords, the softening of her lips.

Her lips . . .

A skitter of nerves raced up his arms and down his spine, leaving evidence of its passage in the tiny prickling of goose bumps on his skin—his exposed-to-her-demonically-enhanced-vision skin. He breathed out slowly until the prickles subsided.

"I'll try to keep it simple," he said.

It was a good reminder. He was making a complication of his half nakedness when obviously she'd had no choice but to remove his shirt. While it had been some time since a woman had taken away any of his clothing—the last incident, he supposed, had been his laundress, taking in his dry cleaning—he shouldn't read more into it.

Yet he wished he could remember her touch when she'd

removed his coat and shirt—for his notes, of course. Had she been rough or tentative? Aroused? He meant her te-shuva; had it been ascendant at the time, or had her human emotions of compassion and sympathy guided her?

Any other sort of arousal was . . . incidental.

His shoulder was mangled but manageable, but he wanted to get to a dose of antibiotics. Although ichor might not kill him, the pathogens on a feralis carcass were nasty.

And he wanted to bring the girl with him, back to the @1 warehouse and the male talyan.

This was the chance of a lifetime—to witness the trig-gering of the long-extinct *symballein* bond between two talyan. What Bookkeeper wouldn't risk an inconvenience like sepsis for such a chance? While the leagues held them-selves aloof even from one another, Bookkeepers tried when possible to stay in closer contact to share insights, ad-vance their mission—and claim bragging rights when it came to such amazing finds as this.

He hoped the hectic racing of his pulse didn't scare the girl. "What shall I call you?"

"Hadn't we agreed on damned?"

"A bit awkward to shout across the room at cocktail par-ties, don't you think?"

"More words. Cocktail parties? I have yet to hear even one rooster in this city."

"Rooster?" He swallowed the rest of the question. How long had she been possessed? Most talyan were reluctant to share their origin stories. That was one of the timeless complaints of Bookkeepers trying to keep accurate records. "At a cocktail party, the women wear flattering dresses, and the men drink too much. It's not as much fun as it sounds." He hesitated. "But if, for example, I wanted to leave a bor-ing gathering and I wanted you to come with me, how would I call to you across the room?"

She whispered, so close to his ear that he jerked in sur-prise, "Call me Alyce."

He squinted. Was she that paler patch of darkness? "I appreciate the rescue tonight, Alyce, but I need to get home." Actually, he had a few intervening steps before getting back to London, but he didn't need to bore her with his problems.

The charcoal shape in the black recoiled. "You can't leave. You haven't told me everything yet."

"There's a lot to tell, and it would be easier to explain if I could see you." He tamped down the note of exasperation. "Plus, I could really use a shower."

"A shower?"

He kept his face studiously blank. "A bath." Maybe he couldn't see, but she could, and he didn't want his incredulity undermining their tenuous rapport.

"A bath . . ." Her drawn-out sigh was wistful this time, as if she were imagining the lap of water and bubbles on her skin. Hell, he'd gone only one nonstop flight without bathing, and he shared her yearning.

He did not mean "shared" as in sharing a bath. . . .

He tried to grab the thought, but it spun out of his control—Alyce, lithe and wet, dark hair streaming. . . . A ripple of shivery heat racked him. Could it be the beginnings of the infection, perhaps? "Antibiotics, acetaminophen, reality check," he muttered. "Stat."

Fingers danced across his forehead, her touch cool and fleeting. "You are speaking nonsense again. Are you fevered?"

"Yes." He grasped the excuse even as he edged away from her hand. "Do you have my clothes?"

"Ruined. But here; your eyeglasses are in your pocket." She pressed the frames into his palm. "I think nothing of mine will fit you."

Now she had a sense of humor. He perched the specs on his nose, as if there were something to see besides darkness. "I just need to find a phone without being arrested for public indecency." He'd turned down the league phone Liam had offered. He needed to maintain a certain researcher-subject detachment, after all. It seemed unlikely he'd find a landline in Alyce's lair.

"There is a box of phone very near here."

"You can read?" Ah, and here he'd told himself he wouldn't do incredulous.

"Not as much as you, I am sure." A note of affront stiffened her tone. "But the letters on the side of the box are very large."

He winced. "I didn't mean—"

"Shall I take you there?"

"Please."

He startled at a rusty groan and turned toward the rectangle of lesser-darkness that appeared in the black. She'd opened the door. The trickle of ambient light gave him hardly more information, but there wasn't much to see, anyway.

Next to the mattress he lounged on, a fifteen-liter water jug, like the kind used to fill office water coolers, lay drained on its side. There was nothing else.

Alyce shifted in the doorway. "I have other retreats elsewhere. This was closest."

Damn it again. He knew what had been on his face that time, without even the thin disguise of utter dark. "I'm glad you have a place to get away from the ferales."

"I took this from one of them."

For the first time, a smidgen of anger itched at the back of his jaws. A talya, dedicated to ridding the world of evil, was reduced to hiding in a feralis's burrow? Where had the league been while she struggled with her demon and the passage of years?

She shifted to her other foot. "The devil didn't need it anymore."

His irritation dissolved at the defensiveness in her voice. Half-feral she might be, but she read his every fleeting emotion like the big letters on a phone booth. He gave her an admiring grin, so she didn't think he'd condemned the theft. "I'm sure it didn't need more than a quick sweeping up once you were done with it."

After a long moment, she smiled back, so quick he almost missed it. "Shall I help you dress?"

The hesitant smile touched him, making him realize that was as close as she should get. If he was going to label her as his control group in his emerging female talya study, he couldn't get too involved. "I'm okay."

He wasn't, of course. In the end, she had to help him drape the shredded edges of his coat sleeve over his torn arm. He didn't even bother with the shirt, instead just pressing the wet wad into his wound to catch any spillage.

She gazed at the blood-soaked rag. "Sometimes I can salvage the pieces."

"Don't bother. I have another." He had several more, with access to as many as he chose to buy. He would seem fantastically fortunate to her.

And he was, now that he'd found a rogue female talya of his very own.

Contrary to what she'd said, the pay phone wasn't "very near." Alyce's limp didn't slow her, but a cold slick of sick sweat drenched Sid by the time they'd trekked halfway across the city. At last, the gas station appeared at the end of the block with the box on its steel post clearly labeled PHONE.

Sid reached for his wallet, but his hand found only his empty pocket. "Bloody hell."

Alyce stiffened.

He gritted his teeth. She was like a beaten dog, flinching from a yell. Of course, she could rip his leg off and beat *him* with it if he was the sort to kick a dog. "I don't suppose you have any money on you? A few coins, maybe?"

She stiffened even more, shoulders rounding, though he tried to sound curious rather than reproachful. But damn, it had been a bad night—bad enough that he wasn't going to be able to sulk back to the warehouse under his own power.

This left him only one choice.

He called the toll-free number. "Hugh, it's Sid. I know it's awfully early, but could you do me a favor—" He sighed as the line clicked over to another ring tone before he finished. The London @1 offices served as a finishing school of sorts for the eldest sons of Europe's Bookkeepers, but the leagues' heretofore strictly male definition of good manners hadn't left room for secretarial charm. "No," he muttered, "putting me through to the Bookkeeper was really not the favor I wanted to ask."

"Sidney?"

Sid closed his eyes and reminded himself that routing the call through London kept him from the trouble of having to make a collect call to the Chicago league. Since he wasn't entirely sure they'd accept the charges, it would be easier just to deal with the usual disapproval.

"Hullo, Dad." His father would be at the big mahogany desk with the matching credenza that weighted the room toward Learned Respectability. It was the crack of dawn in London, but his father would be sitting at that desk, which faced away from the gorgeous panorama of the Thames—no sense getting distracted by the view. "How's the weather?"

Over the phone came the thin creak of a chair spinning in place. "Foggy, but not as cold as Chicago."

Sid opened his eyes. Alyce stared down the street away from him. In her thin shift, now minus most of the skirt, she must be freezing. But the only thing less gentlemanly than letting her freeze would be handing her his wadded tweed and bleeding out at her bare feet. "You were right about the cold. Speaking of your being right, I'm in a bit of a bind."

"I'll wire you money for the return flight."

Sid tightened his grip on the phone. The pressure

twanged across to his wounded shoulder. "Nothing so drastic. I just need Hugh to make a call for me."

"Where is your—? Never mind. What's the number?"

"It's nothing you need to bother with, Dad. Hugh can—"

"The number?"

The tension crawled back up Sid's spine to gather at the base of his skull as he rattled off the @1 Chicago phone number. Thank God he'd always been good at memorizing. "If you could ask Niall to send a car to the corner of Ontario and LaSalle, I'd appreciate it."

"What sort of trouble are you in?"

"Dad, I've been here less than forty-eight hours. How bad could it be?" Before his father could enumerate, Sid countered, "How are you doing?"

"I've been here more than seventy years, Sidney. How bad could it be?"

The dry amusement in his father's voice made Sid shut his eyes again. And this time he saw only the empty black. "Right then. I'll check in again later."

"Most likely I'll be here." The rasp of the chair grated through the wires again. "Be careful, Sidney."

"I am, Dad. Take care."

Sid waited until the line disconnected before he hung up.

"Your father is sick," Alyce said.

"I know."

"Then why are you here?"

"Because my father is sick." If the talya could hear cancer over a long-distance call, she could certainly guess from the tone of his voice that she shouldn't ask anything more. "He is my father, but he is also master of my guild. Bookkeeper knowledge passes from father to son to limit our exposure to the general public, but I still need to show him that I'm worth . . . that I've earned my Bookkeeper mastery."

"My master died long ago."

Sid sank down to the sidewalk below the phone. He tipped his head back against the steel post and stared up at the night sky, bleached old-bone gray by the light pollution of the city. Suddenly, he didn't care to poke into her history any more than he cared to poke into the crevice between the slabs of concrete. Yet his damnable curiosity twinged. "How long ago?"

"It's hard to remember," she said.

Sid had read what little information existed on rogues. Psychosis among talyan—unmanageable psychosis, to be precise—happened more than the leagues cared to document. When the etheric energies of a demon's ascension weren't balanced, the newly possessed human slid quickly into insanity. Rogues typically came to bad ends. They wandered off in confusion or flamed out in a fury of tenebrae slaughter.

How would Liam Niall and the rest of the Chicago talyan respond to a rogue in their midst? Certainly they had enough borderline personalities to make room on the fringes for one more. Alyce couldn't keep wandering the streets alone.

Never mind that she'd been doing just that for . . . how long exactly?

Sid pushed himself upright. He hadn't realized he'd slumped sideways against the telephone pole. He was seeping good manners along with his blood. But maybe she hadn't gotten the reserved-silence memo since she missed the new-talya welcome seminar. "What bits do you remember?"

She took a few steps down the sidewalk, her face half averted and her pale gaze fixed on something even farther away. She might not have gotten the memo, but the reserve seemed carved into talya flesh as plainly as the demon's mark that peeked above her high neckline.

"It was cold," she said finally. "And there were lights. Not like candles and not like those." She jerked her chin at the neon over the gas station. "Like lightning behind clouds at night, but unfading. So beautiful . . ."

Sid shook off the mesmerizing drift of her voice. "That's the etheric signature of an unbound demon," he said briskly. "Of course, you couldn't see it until the penultimate moment, but it was coming for you."

She turned abruptly to face him. "Like tonight. Like the one coming—"

"No." He cut off her rising agitation. The redoubled harmony in her voice—the demon's echo—chilled him. Why did she have such trouble focusing on the task of remembering? "The frequencies of the lesser tenebrae you fought tonight are much different from a repentant teshuva. You'll learn."

At his correction, she curled one arm around her belly. The shielding gesture stung him almost more than the feralis bite. But she had so much to know if she was going to join the league and leave her rogue wandering days behind her. It had taken him years to get where he was; she'd have only one chance to prove she wasn't a threat to the league.

Where she clutched at the front of her dress, the neckline had tugged down, and he studied the teshuva's mark. The lines of a *reven* most often lay quiet in the skin, like nothing more than the sketchings of an erratic tattooist. The contours and complexity of the fractal design hinted at both the subspecies and the energy level of the possessing demon.

On Alyce, the *reven* was a simple wheal around her neck. Though she had tried to hide it with the conservative collar, the thin black wave ran just beneath the delicate line of her jaw and peeked out whenever she turned her head. Only a few curls spiraled off the central thread. Not a powerful teshuva, then. Perhaps she had survived so long and yet not thrived precisely because of her weak demon. She'd not been driven to self-destructiveness, but at the same time, she'd been unable to find her way to others like her.

Still, she had demolished two ferales and scared off two more, so weak was relative.

"Sidney?"

He startled. When had she knelt beside him? He hadn't told her his name. But, of course, she had heard his father say his name. "I'm sorry, what?"

"I said, you are losing too much blood. You should not fall asleep or you might not wake up."

"I wasn't falling asleep. I was . . . looking at you." Good God, he'd been less than an hour in her company, and his filters were already on the blink.

"Oh. That explains your fleeting insensibility."

He drew breath to disagree, then peered at her. "Was that a joke of some sort?"

"Yes." She settled on her heels with a frown. "Or perhaps not. I remember that men have looked into my eyes and forgotten how to speak."

Had that been before the demon, or after? He managed to bite his tongue. Time enough to work on her after he got her to his lab.

There was a delicacy to her, though—if one saw beyond the streaks of blood, ichor, and grime—that might very well silence some men. Her skin was smooth, almost luminescent—an advantage of a youthful possession, demonic healing, and an eternal night shift without even fleeting UV damage. And though she was below average in height, she made up for the lack with a pleasing proportionality. When the fretful breeze tugged at the ugly dress, he noted a breast-to-waist-to-hip ratio that might be, in fact, considered something like perfect.

He swallowed and realized he hadn't said anything in quite a long minute.

"Keep me awake then." He cleared his throat of an alarming huskiness.

She tilted toward him a few degrees. "How?"

Her pale eyes glinted violet. Blood trickled at his shoulder with the sudden acceleration of his heart. Was he talking to the girl, or to the demon? No, he shouldn't think of them as separate entities. They were one being, one soul, one dangerous hell-bound killer.

Learning that was his life's work, with no room for error—or for anything else.

A flash of headlights blinded him as a car U-turned in front of them. Before the rust-speckled banger had come to a stop, the passenger door swung open.

Sid squinted against the brightness.

"What the hell, Westerbrook?"

"Something like that." He staggered to his feet, holding back a groan. "Miss Alyce, may I introduce you to one of your fellow talyan, Jonah Walker?" He stumbled in a half circle. "Alyce?"

But in the harsh wash of neon and metal halide lighting, he found nothing. He lifted his gaze to the night beyond.

She was gone.

CHAPTER 3

Alyce folded herself into the shadows to watch the one-armed man help her Sidney into the carriage.

Car, she reminded herself. With no one to share her wonder and fear, she hadn't bothered with the endless changes of the world, but she'd noticed the way Sidney winced at her oddity. At the memory of his expression—as appalled and reluctantly curious as if he'd cracked open the only fresh egg for breakfast to find a half-feathered chick inside—she sank deeper into the darkness.

Across the lighted street, the one-armed man—Jonah, Sidney had named him—lingered beside the car door. The hook where his right hand should have been shone almost as bright as his amethyst eyes while he surveyed the night.

His gaze passed over her. The invasive chill inside that never left her tensed for the attack, but she held herself still. The flares of devilish light that pulsed around the man and the car and Sidney would blind him to her small self.

Jonah climbed into the car beside Sidney and wheeled

the vehicle from the curb with a squeal against the pavement like a temperamental horse.

At least Sidney had said he would have help for his wound. She looked down at the scalds from the devils' blood on her hands and curled her fingers into her frock where congealed blood had glued the folds together. These marks would heal without any help at all, she'd learned.

How long ago had that realization ceased to make her lonely? And why was the terrible feeling—more caustic than ichor—back with a vengeance now?

Memories teased her, as elusive as falling leaves swirled on the autumn wind. She passed through them without pause. Maybe she couldn't grasp the memories, but a clean frock was still within her reach—if she could just remember where she'd left the stash she'd taken from the church charity box.

She followed the flow of cars beneath the raised railroad tracks. The shriek of metal on metal as the train passed overhead was louder than the devils' death knells. Despite the assault on her senses, she stopped when she spied the shadowy presence leaning against a lamppost. Though the lamp was intact and shining brightly, the tall, lean man seemed to stand in a darkness all his own.

"Go away," she said softly, knowing he would hear over the clatter and squeal.

He tilted his head so his long braids swung over the lapels of his coat. In the stuttering light from the train windows above, his hair glinted as shiny black as the leather. "And a good evening to you, Miss Alyce. I saw the fireworks from afar and had to come find you."

"Because you like to watch the devils play."

He stalked toward her. "Because your glow when you vanquish them is irresistible. Like watching a baby stealing candy from the monsters."

He had told her long ago to call him Thorne, and she had remembered, because the name fit him well. His skin was burnished brown, like the cane of some ancient bramble, and his gaze sharper than any barb. Though the sleek blackness of his hair softened the thrust of his cheekbones, the yellow flames in his eyes burned away any chance of mistaking what dwelled within him.

He was a devil.

She stood her ground since she'd never been fast enough to run from him. "Instead of watching, you could fight the monsters too."

"Could I now?" For a fleeting moment, his furrowed brows made him look as lost as she sometimes felt. "And tell me, to fight at your side, all I'd have to do is forget myself?"

She couldn't untangle the threads of puzzlement and scorn in his voice, so she answered simply as she started walking again and he fell into step beside her. "You are stronger than I am; too strong to forget."

"Too bad." The last light of the train gleamed off the sharp spine of his lopsided smile; then the shadows closed in again. "Ah, but that is the point, isn't it? I am too bad, a monster through and through." He bumped her with his hip, not gently, and her weak knee buckled, so she staggered. When she aimed a scowl at him, he laughed. "See? There's the little sparkler I love."

She blinked hard to force down the flicker of the devil in her eyes. "We are not monsters. We can atone. My Sidney will tell you."

His smile faded until his wide mouth curled at only one corner like a snake raising its head to strike. "Your Sidney."

She touched her cheeks, warm under her fingers. "Mine. He knows what I am."

"And don't I know you after all these years together?"

"We aren't together." She stopped and looked at him over her fingertips as he prowled a circle around her.

In the beginning, spurred by the demon, she had tried to destroy him once or twice—perhaps more—and each time he had left her so shattered, she had thought she would finally, finally die. She didn't know why he had never lost patience and finished her, but he did not run from her. And sometimes she thought only that had kept her from sliding at last into madness.

But now she had Sidney. She let her hands drift down from her heated cheeks and drew herself upright. As she straightened her spine, her devil flowed into the spaces between the bones.

Thorne took a step back, eyebrow raised. "This love you've found will break your heart, I bet you."

"Which is the only piece of me you have left unbroken."

Thorne's eyes glittered brighter than the bullet holes in the burning metal drums that warmed the homeless dwellers below the overpasses. "I have left other parts of you untouched. But I'm sure your Sidney will find a way to fill you."

Forgetful she might be, but she did not misunderstand his allusion. "It's not like that," she whispered.

"It's always like that. Older than words, old as evil is *that*." Thorne's laugh cracked like an open slap across her face.

Her cheeks heated, and with that flush of rage, she launched herself at the devil-man. But he only laughed again and struck her aside. The backhanded blow spun her into a parked carriage. Car, she reminded herself viciously as the glass splintered around her elbow and the alarm blared in her ear. If she could not remember "car," how would Sidney ever teach her anything?

By the time she hauled herself out of the broken window, Thorne and his shiny black coat were lost to the night.

She looked down at the fresh smears of blood on her frock. Truly, she needed to find her last stash of clothing.

"Hey, what the fuck'd you do to my car?" A stranger raced toward her. He stabbed one finger at a small black device in his other palm. "I'm calling the cops right now—"

She raised her gaze, and he slid to a halt. The box clattered to the pavement.

"Pardon me," she said. She brushed glass from her skin. "I slipped."

The man screamed, turned, and sprinted away as if for his very life.

From the device, a tinny voice called out. "Nine-one-one. What is the nature of your emergency?"

Alyce retrieved the little box and set it on the front seat of the car, in case he forgot where he'd dropped it. Forgetting was so easy. By the time he stopped running, he wouldn't remember the nature of his emergency, but his white-ringed eyes crystallized her determination.

With the peekaboo moon winking from behind the towers of concrete and steel, she made her way through the streets she haunted. She'd moved so often, over so many years, she wasn't ever sure where she'd last been. The intersections bled together, and the buildings seemed to shift facades before her eyes—from flickering candlelight to the stink of gas to the hum of electric bulbs—as if they couldn't remember who they were either.

She would clothe herself properly. She would find Sidney. She would know what she was. And maybe the blackness in her head would finally go.

Some days were worse than others.

All days were peppered with the buckshot of injustice, banality, and defeat, but evil seemed prone to arm itself in progressively higher calibers of wrongness as the days and decades passed.

Thorne Halfmoon had accepted that truth when his grandmother caught him on the roof of their crappy apartment building after six and a half pointless days of fasting and chanting. Though the *Boys' Life* magazine he'd stolen from the rec center had been a little vague on the particulars of vision quests, in his delirium, he'd seen dark spirits aplenty, but he hadn't found his spirit guide. And as his grandmother—cursing up a Thunderbird-scented storm—dragged his scrawny ten-year-old body down the stairs, he'd realized evil could always get worse and he would always face it alone.

But he preferred not to have to face anyone before, say, coffee. To open the boat's cabin door with his first cup still brimming, unsipped, in his hand and find one of his exceedingly evil brethren standing on his deck, uninvited, was the nadir of bad taste and bad timing.

"You didn't knock," he said.

The djinn-man scrunched his thick features with exaggerated hurt. He tugged at his coat lapels as if soothing his ruffled feathers. "You wouldn'ta answered the door, would ya?"

Thorne spread his empty hand as if displaying a deck of cards. "For you? Never."

"So. I waited. We got the time, am I right?"

"Wait a little longer." Thorne slammed the door.

Too late, of course.

The other man's heather-toned suit said Brooks Brothers, but his footwear was plain shit stomper. He booted open the door, and the heavy wood rebounded against the wall with a thud, rattling the round portal glass.

Thorne sighed in vexation. "You said you'd wait."

"I guess we got the time, but not the patience."

"Why start with virtues now?" Thorne stalked down the narrow stairs to the lower deck, his bare feet silent on the gleaming mahogany floorboards, and left the other man to follow, or not.

In his stateroom, he clunked his coffee cup on the mantel over the empty fireplace and dropped into one of the wing-back chairs framing the hearth. The rose velvet armrest crinkled under his elbow as he slouched, chin in palm, tracking the other man with his eyes. The djinn-man lowered himself to the matching chair and shot his cuffs as if he owned the place.

Thorne dug his elbow into the nap until it squeaked. He really needed to redecorate—something less Colonial. "What do you want, Carlo?"

Carlo crossed one ankle over his knee and steepled his fingers. The managerial pose sent a quiver of annoyance through Thorne like the glass rattling in the door. "Times, they are a-changing." His hard Chicago accent smoothed, as if the voice were no longer his own. "The deadlock that held the war between heaven and hell in balance has cracked. Magdalena is calling an ahāzum."

Thorne smirked when Carlo stumbled over the Akkadian pronunciation. Probably ex–wise guys didn't have much call for mastering extinct Mesopotamian languages. "A gathering of all the djinn-possessed? What is that psychotic bitch thinking?"

Carlo put both feet back on the floor, the better to puff himself up. "Watch your mouth, half-breed." The growl of the street was back in his voice. "My lady hears all."

"Only because you repeat it. Fucking magpie. And what's with the medieval 'my ladying'?"

Carlo's eyes yellowed in outrage. "I owe her my life. I swore her my loyalty."

"You're no knight errant," Thorne scoffed. "You swore that to any slick Chicago mobster who threw you a bone, even before you were possessed."

In contrast, he himself had been too virtuous to ask for the bone, thinking he was fighting for rights, not riches.

Thorne struggled to hold his sneer in place. Was the reproachful voice in his head supposed to be the better angel of his nature? Obviously *that* wasn't possible. Annoyed at his momentary weakness, he let his demon spiral up. "Tell her no, Carlo. For my sake and hers."

"But she wants you. While the sphericanum dicks around, Magdalena is gathering soldati—an army of djinni soldiers, yeah?—and soldati need capos. Men like me and you."

"I want nothing to do with a djinni mob. I want . . ." He

shifted in his chair. The wood, like silky dark hair, and the velvet, pink as flushed cheeks, reminded him of what he desired and yet had not taken. "I want to be left alone."

"Alone ain't a good place to be. Since Corvus Valerius resurrected the *symballein* bond—"

"Corvus the Blackbird? Another fucking birdbrain," Thorne snapped.

Carlo ran his hand over his head without actually touching his hair. "Getting tossed out a high-rise onto one's skull makes for stupid, no doubt. But you ain't thinking right either, Thorne, to defy her." He leaned forward in his chair, as if the cant of his body could add pressure to his words. "You have to fight for the darkness."

"I can fight whomever I choose, or so I've been told." Thorne couldn't keep the wry note from his voice.

"You were told wrong. 'Sides, rumor has it you always pick the losing side. So quit choosing and just give in."

Though every nerve—human and djinni—told him to hold his ground, Thorne surged to his feet. "I had a soft spot for impossible cases. Don't remind me."

"Not much to remember, was there? Magdalena says your little terrorist gang couldn't make a mark with how many pounds of ammonium nitrate?" Carlo claimed smirking rights as he kicked back in his seat. "First *kaboom*, and everyone—even your moll—was fertilizer. Everyone but you."

Thorne stalked to the windows, where the wind lifted whitecapped waves from the lake.

And dropped them again. That was the way of leaders— to whip their followers into a froth, only to leave them roiling over themselves. Corvus the gladiator had despised his masters. He'd wanted to be free.

"The djinn are prohibited from gathering," Thorne said at last. "We stay away from one another. Really, that's the only thing I liked about you all."

Carlo flicked his fingers dismissively. "What I saw, prohi-

bitions are imposed to be broken. Usually in a blotto blaze
of Tommy gunfire." His grin was practically avuncular. "Of
course, you're excused from the drunken part. We never
gathered because we never had the numbers. Since Corvus
punched a hole into hell, there is a way."

"Blackbird failed," Thorne reminded him.

"He died, yeah sure, but the damage he did to the Veil?
That's his legacy to us. Magdalena recovered the notes Corvus kept from his league traitor. If the calculations are
correct—"

"Calculations never are." Thorne leaned his shoulders
against the window with deliberate nonchalance. "If Magdalena is all-knowing, as you seem to think, she'd know
that."

Carlo's gray eyes turned almost as soft as the water
outside—and as implacably pushy. "Don't be so down on
yourself. That explosion wasn't your fault. We checked.
Your bomb was perfect; it was the timer that was off."

The chill from outside leached through the glass to
Thorne's spine. "I know that."

"Anyway, that free lovebird who fucked you into believing in her cause was sleeping with every dumb bastard there. It wasn't your brat in her belly when you blew
her up."

"I know that too." When the djinn-man only gaped at
him, Thorne shook his head. "You should be relieved I
won't be joining your half-assed ahāzum. If I couldn't follow directions in plain English, imagine how much worse I
am in Akkadian."

Carlo gripped the armrests of his chair. "I can't leave
here till I can give my lady the message she wants to hear—
that you will come to her."

Thorne pushed away from the window. The cold stayed
in his skin. "Very well." He walked toward the fireplace
where his coffee waited.

Carlo smiled. "See? That wasn't so hard, now was it? I—"

He stopped talking when Thorne grabbed him by the neck and squeezed.

Mostly puffery though he was, Carlo still bore a djinni, and he put up a not-embarrassing fight.

Both chairs were broken before Thorne had him pinned amidst the mahogany chips of the half-bashed mantel. No great loss—open flame on a boat had always seemed like the depths of wrongness anyway.

Carlo arched away from the fireplace andiron twisted underneath him, but Thorne amped his own djinni higher as he pressed his forearm against the other man's throat and stared him down. Carlo tried to look away, his eyeballs tearing noxious ooze.

With a not-quite sound, an almost tactile sensation, like the tumblers of a lock falling open inside him, Thorne's demon matched itself to the other djinni. He trembled with the surge of stolen energy and pushed harder.

The point of the andiron emerged from Carlo's starched shirt through the gap between the third and fourth buttons. With the next beat of his heart, a gout of blood soaked the cotton, and he choked on a hiccupping cry.

Thorne held him there while the other man's weakened djinni tried frantically to heal the wound. Tender new flesh crept up the blackened iron, withered and died, and was renewed as Carlo writhed. "Stop squirming before you nick something important. I didn't want to hurt you."

Finally, Carlo stilled. "Fooled me," he rasped. The sulfuric tears burned bloody rivulets down his cheeks.

"No, Magdalena did that. Tell her I'll not follow anyone else to the end."

"You think she'll let you stand apart? In the end, there will be no one left alone. No third parties, no watchers, no innocents."

"There's one," Thorne murmured.

Carlo's purpling face contorted in a sneer as his demon's frenzy rippled beneath the dapper gangster facade. "Who? Your half-cracked little talya freak?"

Astonishment slackened Thorne's grip for a heartbeat.

Carlo thrashed like a walleye fished from the lake for dinner but subsided when his struggle gained no headway. "You think Magdalena didn't know about that? I told you she hears all."

"She can hear. She can watch. Just tell her to keep her hands and her ahāzum to herself."

"Gimme a pen so I can write it down." Carlo bared his teeth. "Make it a Sharpie."

"No need to remember the particulars."

With a sharp wrench, Thorne bent the tip of the andiron around to pierce the other side of Carlo's chest. The djinn-man shrieked, and his yellow smoking eyes rolled back in his head. He slumped unconscious, his demon too sapped to rouse him.

A couple more twists and Thorne caged the man's heart in black iron. Magdalena could unwrap him if she chose. Of course, she might adopt the technique.

Thorne stood and plucked his mug from the half of the mantel that had survived the wreckage. The coffee was hot, molecules excited by all the thrashing energies in the room. He took a sip and grunted with satisfaction. The day wasn't looking too bad, after all.

He dashed the rest of the beverage in Carlo's face. The djinn-man sputtered to life. He traced the tangle of iron through his chest with shaking fingers, and his whimper emerged in a bilious froth from the holes.

"Now crawl back to your bitch queen with your tail between your legs," Thorne said, "and hope this time she listens when I say no."

CHAPTER 4

Sid woke in his own bed—well, not his cozy, duvet-covered bed in London, but his assigned synthetic brick, complete with threadbare hobnail spread, at the @1 warehouse—and squinted at the svelte blonde pushing back the noncomplementary curtains. The sudden light did nothing to dispel the cheap motel room ambiance.

He fumbled for his specs, knocking blood-soaked gauze from the bedside table. "Good morning, Scra."

"It was once I flushed all the feralis filth out of your shoulder."

He cleared his raspy throat and grimaced at the lingering chemical sourness of his body's shock on the back of his tongue. With specs in place, he fastened his gaze on the china cup just beyond the flattened tube of antibiotic ointment. "Is that tea?"

"It's my tea." She snagged it and took a sip to demonstrate.

So she'd mend him, but she didn't want him to think that

meant anything—as if their attitude toward him hadn't been made perfectly clear already. He pushed himself upright against the pillows and winced at the piercing twang through his shoulder.

"Don't pull out my stitches," she groused. "Here, have some water."

God, they wouldn't even share their tea bags. And he thought he could tease out the secrets of their unorthodox battles. "Thanks." He took the bottled water she offered and cocked his head to peer at the line of stitches through his flesh. "Thanks for this too."

Sera narrowed her eyes, as if she thought he was being sarcastic. "It's crooked. We don't do much darning here in Chicago." She put an extra twist on the harsh middle *a*.

"I don't do much needlepoint either," he said mildly. "Which is why I said thank you, since I'd still be bleeding otherwise."

Her glare didn't change. "We don't want you dying here."

We don't want you here at all. She didn't have to say it aloud. With Sera Littlejohn serving as interim Bookkeeper for the Chicago league, Sid hadn't realized he'd be stepping on quite so many toes—or toes so capable of kicking his ass. He thought they'd be relieved to have a replacement. Though the leagues strictly maintained their self-sufficiency, London-trained Bookkeepers, renowned for their learning and discipline, were in high demand. Even if he'd been a backwater Bookkeeper from one of the less rigorous, outlying schools, Liam and his crew should have been relieved. Talyan were never interested in books and stats and tests.

But the Chicago league seemed to delight in blasting *never* sky high.

If he could just get through to them, the exclusive research material would prove his merit as Bookkeeper once and for all. Even his father would finally have to concede and could rest easier knowing his life's work would continue. "I need to talk to Liam. Is he still up?"

"Undoubtedly. He won't sleep until he knows everybody survived the night. And since you were passed out in Jonah's car . . ."

Sid gritted his teeth into something like a smile. "How inconvenient my maiming won't heal in minutes."

A spark of violet flared across her hazel iris. "You'd rather be possessed?"

He started to snap back but caught himself. What words had been about to leap off his tongue? Nothing to endear him, certainly. He said only, "I don't want to die here either."

Sera huffed out a breath he couldn't interpret as approving or disappointed. "I'll send Liam in."

How humiliating, to interview the league leader from bed. "No, I'll get up."

"Liam told you to take the night off."

"I did, and look what happened. Where can I find him?"

Sera stood back, neither helping nor hindering as he struggled out of the sloping bed and found a clean shirt. "He'll be down at his forge in the loading bay. He had some things he wanted to pound out."

What brilliant condition he was in to face the league leader. Sid managed to lock his knees enough to stay upright while he eased his aching arm through the sleeve. If he bent over to grab his trainers, he'd faint. That would be almost—not quite, but almost—as bad as grabbing the slip-on loafers out of his duffel.

The bloody bandages, oxidizing to a rusty brown, lay scattered like mute indictments of his vulnerability. He tried to console himself with the excuse of his near death as he left the room barefoot.

When the league's last headquarters had been contaminated in a djinni attack, the warehouse had been remodeled with individual apartments on the second floor for the solitary talyan. Of course, they'd put him at the ass-end of the hall. And most of the fluorescent bars in the ceiling were out since talyan didn't need artificial lighting. Now the distance between the darkened doorways seemed to stretch with spoofed horror-movie absurdity. But he gritted his teeth—though the tension sent a warning pang through his shoulder—and propelled himself forward. If nothing else, momentum would keep him going.

Even the immortal talyan didn't trust the old freight lift that had once delivered architectural salvage to the upper floor, so he took the stairs down. Sera's boot heels clattered out of sync on the metal treads as she paced his slow progression. Was she making sure he didn't keel over, or did she just want a front-row seat while the league leader straightened him out like a bent nail?

With most of the talyan resting from their nightly hunt, their edgy energy blunted by countermeasures invented by Bookkeepers, the interior halls of the warehouse could have housed any business—say, day-sleeping accountants.

Had his life unspooled differently, he could have been an accountant. That was probably true for most people—at least for people who liked their numbers in orderly columns. If he *had* been an accountant . . . No, he wasn't going to start counting those ways.

He shoved open the door to the loading bay hard enough that Sera jumped forward to catch the rebound.

Though the big exterior rolling door was closed, the October cold leaked through the vaultlike room. Despite the icebox temperature reflected by the cinderblock walls, the league leader was stripped down to his jeans and a black vest, his shaggy black hair caught at his nape with an elastic tie. Of course, he had the glowing forge in the corner to warm him.

Liam Niall was a big man, which was not unusual for a talya. The monstrous hammer choked up in his wide palm only exacerbated the impression. He tapped out a delicate rhythm with the tool, belying its blunt force as he hunched over the anvil.

The hammering did get a bit more forceful as Sid approached. "You're still alive," Liam said. "I'm surprised."

Surprised did not necessarily equal glad. Sid twisted his lips. "No doing of mine, I assure you."

Liam smoothed the hammer one last time over the metal, then held up his work. The deer horn knife—two edged crescents interlocked so that the points gleamed outward toward the four cardinal directions—shimmered under the severe fluorescent lights with a stark and dangerous beauty.

Sid blinked. Etheric emanations sank into weapons just as the demonic energies brutally and exquisitely honed the bodies of the previously mortal hosts, much like Liam's hammer worked the metal. Sid had studied printouts of the spectral analyses, but he'd never seen the evidence with his own eyes. Maybe he had never been so aware before, so personally affected by the outcome.

He blinked again, fascinated by the spangles that danced off the blades. How had he never noticed the way a beam of light poured down a finely honed metal edge? Certainly the Bookkeeper side of the equation had nothing so compelling. No dusty, stretched sheepskin, scrawled in ancient warnings, could match that shivery curvature of steel through air.

He blinked a third time and realized Liam was finally watching him, blue eyes steady and impassive.

Sid straightened, and the officious snap of his spine cut off the wayward fascination. "I would have been eaten by that feralis if not for the rogue female talya who came out of nowhere and saved my arse."

While he quickly recapped the encounter, Liam's gaze sharpened to rival the knife in his hand, as if Sid had finally shown himself to be interesting. "A rogue. In my city." The blade glittered as he spun it between his fingers. "And female at that."

Sid tensed at the threatening movement, and his shoulder protested, though he kept his voice level. "An invaluable find."

"For a Bookkeeper," Liam countered. "A potential nightmare for the league. Do you know what that unbalanced energy does to the demons in this city? Repentant demon or tenebrae, it won't matter in the face of such beguiling madness." The teshuva's mark at his temple flared violet with his heartbeat.

Sid averted his gaze before his own pulse could match the violence. From the time his father had inducted him into the Bookkeeper mysteries, he'd been taught not to follow the talyan in their torquing furies. Each had their place in the battle against evil; to confuse their roles was stupid, pointless, and often fatal—at least for the Bookkeepers.

So he tried to knock the sharp edge off his tone. He might have succeeded if he'd had a hammer bigger than Liam's. "I don't see how one woman—and she was tiny—makes things worse."

Genuine amusement crinkled the *reven* next to Liam's eye. "Didn't your father exile you here because of a woman?"

The casual reference sliced through Sid like the multiple points of the deer horn knife, each one sharper than the last.

His father had told someone about that? Told a talya, of all people, even knowing the penalty of indiscretion?

"I would never reveal league confidences." The words peeled from him as rusty and laced with pain as the soiled bandages back in his room.

Revealing himself had been the only thing Maureen asked for. Twenty-three months into their planned two-year pre-engagement cohabitation, they'd both been shocked and appalled to discover that, without divulging the league secrets, he had nothing left to share.

Liam's smile flattened. "As Bookkeeper, you understand how outsiders are so disruptive."

"A rogue is not technically an outsider," Sid pointed out. Not the way he'd always been an outsider, even for those twenty-three months before he'd come to his senses.

"Lucky she was. Any rogue existing under our radar has a highly developed instinct for self-preservation." Liam frowned thoughtfully. "Unless Bookie did know about her."

Sid had gathered the gist of what had happened to his Bookkeeper predecessor. Suffice it to say, embezzlement had been the least of his crimes—not merely crimes, but sins. An image of his own unwritten rap sheet flashed in Sid's brain. The "retired" Bookie might think himself the better man of the two.

"If your last Bookkeeper made note of a rogue, I'll find it," he promised.

"No need." Liam's words dropped to a growl. "Because we'll find her."

The implied menace curled Sid's fingers as if around the haft of some imaginary weapon. "You can't hurt her."

"We do what we have to," Liam said. "You can note that in your archives."

"She's no threat," Sid insisted. In his memory, her pitiless hunter eyes blinked in slow disbelief.

Liam pursed his lips. "Tell that to the feralis she tore apart."

"She's fighting on your side. Every league needs all the weapons it can gather," Sid countered.

"Not if those weapons are double-edged."

Sid looked pointedly at the deer horn knife in the league leader's hand, all its curves treacherously sharp.

Liam sighed. "Right. Most of them do have a regrettable tendency toward slicing off the hand that feeds them."

"You asked for London's help," Sid said.

"No, I asked for access to your archives," Liam corrected.

Sid pushed the specs higher on his nose. "I *am* London's

archives. With Alyce as a baseline, I can do what I came here to do."

"Alyce? You already named her?" Just the corners of Liam's lips curved upward. On a lesser man, it might have been a smirk. "I suppose you have to keep her now."

"If I can find her."

"We're on it."

"You'll be careful? You won't scare her?"

Liam gave him a lowering look. "That fever must be spiking. Get some rest."

Probably it was immortality that gave his voice that paternalistic edge. But Sid already had a disapproving father figure, thanks anyway.

Sera followed him back to his room, like a silent blond wolf watching for him to falter from his path.

He paused in his doorway, trying for a casual lean, though the jamb grated against his aching shoulder. "You wouldn't let them hurt her." When she didn't answer quickly enough for his comfort, he added, "You could *be* her. Imagine possession—the conflicting energies, the impulse to violence, the isolation—without the structure and restraint of the league. Without that, the teshuva is only one long step from being djinni."

Her gaze flickered with violet streaks, pupil and iris submerged beneath the demonic overlay. "You think I don't know that?"

The waves of pain thinned his patience. If he wanted to win the respect of the talyan, he couldn't keep backing down. Plus, he was more than ninety percent certain she wouldn't hit an injured man.

"I think you were possessed less than a year ago," he said. "I think I have almost three thousand years of written histories at my fingertips and another couple thousand of oral tradition on my tongue. So hand-to-hand, you might win, but in a debate I will wipe you out."

With a quirk of her lips, all signs of her demon vanished.

"Well, hopefully the next feralis is willing to argue the finer points of possession with you. I'll just tell you, this alleged rogue female isn't a science experiment."

"Of course not." A proper science experiment would be easier, tidier, and already under lock and key in the lab. He tried a little wheedling. "Don't you want to know how the *symballein* bond works between you and your mate?" Women—even demonically possessed women—always liked to talk about their relationships.

She snorted. "That's not going to show up on any spectral analysis." But her expression softened.

He wondered if he could achieve the same tempering response if he asked Ferris Archer, Sera's other half, about the bond. He rather thought his odds of not getting hit would drop well below the halfway point.

But since Sera seemed to have mellowed, he might have a chance. "I want to go with the talyan tonight when you look for Alyce."

"Liam will let you know."

That wasn't a yes. But it wasn't a no either. "I'll be much improved by a nap. See you tonight."

She inclined her head, again neither yes nor no. He supposed ambivalence was as much a symptom of teshuva possession as violet-shot eyes. "Sleep well," she said.

He'd sleep like the dead. Or someone who'd narrowly avoided death. He nodded back and slipped into his room.

Sera had left a pill bottle of analgesics by his bedside, and he dry-swallowed a light fistful. It was not the recommended dosage, but the FDA had never anticipated off label use as anti–demon spit painkiller.

He kicked off his filthy jeans and eased out of his shirt. He noted the bloodstains from his draining wound, and suddenly he had a better understanding of the league's rather shocking clothing allowance. Standing in his boxers, he wrapped his shoulder in gauze, then crawled into bed with a groan. The sagging middle where the springs had sprung sucked him down.

But sleep circled in the same way his inbound flight had gone endlessly round O'Hare, so he grabbed his specs and pulled one of his favorite books into his lap. His father hadn't been thrilled to part with the illuminated texts, but Sid had convinced him the opportunity to study female talyan with original manuscripts in hand superseded jurisdictional pettiness.

He donned archival gloves in deference to the old man and the old paper and hoped if he fell asleep he wouldn't drool on the pages.

From somewhere on the street outside, a truck honked, but through the gray concrete walls, the cacophony of the industrial district was more distant than a dream, as if the real world weren't allowed to intrude on this demonic sanctuary.

His churning thoughts slowed. No wonder the talyan clung so tightly to their monastic seclusion. Personality studies indicated that disconnection from close human relationships made a person more vulnerable to demonic possession, so statistically more talyan would display antisocial behaviors. But the real reprieve wasn't the teshuva's escape from hell; it was the talya's freedom from the tyranny of meddlesome life.

With league training and Bookkeeper tricks, the talyan stiff-armed death *and* life for the sake of their mission.

No wonder no right-thinking, right-souled woman would have them.

He and the talyan had more in common than he'd appreciated.

Eventually, his eyelids drooped. Through the haze of his eyelashes, the intricately drawn illustrations danced with strange wildlife, a tangle of angels and demons without clear distinction. That was probably true for most people—at least for those who'd avoided possession by some force more definitively aligned.

He blamed his gritty eyes for making him blink dumbly when he looked up and saw the visitation, as if one of the ethereal figures from the primeval text had stepped off the page, a fever dream come to life. He fumbled his drooping specs higher. "Alyce?"

She ghosted across the room, her bare feet silent on the linoleum despite the slight hitch in her gait. Through the dark curtain of her tangled hair, her pale eyes glittered, amethyst over ice. "Shh. I've come to free you."

A *ping* raced through his body, from the sudden acceleration of his heartbeat to his extremities, like a warning signal. "Free me?" He pushed the book aside, careful not to wrinkle the pages. "Did Liam let you in?"

"There was a devil-man at the gate." She fisted her hands in her skirt. The grandmotherly housedress lacked the ichor stains of her last ensemble, but the powder blue polyester was worn to near transparency in places. And now—this wasn't a good sign—there were fingerprints of blood in the folds. "I did not stop to ask his name, but I saw the devil in his eyes."

The *ping* went round his innards a few more times, gaining particle-accelerator speeds. Had she killed Liam or one of the other talyan? That would put a wrinkle in his reintroduction strategy. "They are possessed," he admitted, "but not by devils—or not evil devils, anyway. Their teshuva—the demons inside them—are like yours."

"Evil," she whispered, "Like me."

"Repentant," he corrected. "Fighting for the light now."

"There is no light for me."

"Not before, maybe. But now that you're here, everything is different."

She pressed her bloody palms together and raised her hands until her fingertips brushed under her chin. Despite the prayerful pose, her gaze speared him without mercy. "Is this where I die?"

He recoiled. "God, no!"

"Won't you banish the devil from me?"

"I can't."

Her hands fell back to her sides, and she averted her face. The *reven* around her neck guttered with a few violet lights, then faded to black, as if her teshuva hadn't the strength to maintain its outrage.

But she had incapacitated at least one of the talya to get this far. What *was* she?

Slowly, keeping his eye on her, he climbed out of the bed. His navy boxers weren't suitable for an audience with the Queen, but he wasn't indecent.

Alyce stood back, showing no signs of bolting. Instead, her gaze flicked back to him, touching on the gauze at his shoulder, the bruise on his forehead, and various contusions in between. "Were you badly hurt?"

He gave a one-sided shrug, sparing his wounded shoulder. "They were able to patch me up here, so it can't have been too bad. It would have been awkward at the hospital to explain the bite pattern."

"Don't. They won't believe you."

His fingers itched for a pen and paper. "You've tried? When?"

"I don't quite remember." Her wintery gaze darkened. "It did not end well."

That reminded him about the talya at the gate. "We need to go pick up the pieces of the welcoming party you left in the dust."

"He was rude."

"That happens with talyan. But you still shouldn't break them."

She nodded. "I did not understand they were yours."

He halted in the middle of grabbing his jeans. The Chicago talyan? His? Hardly. He was a loaner, not a keeper;

they'd made that clear. But he didn't want them either. He wanted London. Hopefully not until well in the future, when his father retired to putter around his garden.

Alyce was watching his face, her expression mirroring the furrow of his brows. "I've saddened you. But I had to come to you, and he was in the way."

He smoothed a hand down his face, erasing the quick, helpless calculations of his father's chances of surviving till spring, much less retirement. "You didn't make me sad. In fact, I can't possibly explain how happy I am to have you here. There's so much we can learn together."

He stepped into his jeans, wishing she weren't watching quite so closely, but intrigued by her empathic responses. How could a talya—endlessly driven by the teshuva to the farthest reaches of violence and destruction—keep any semblance of softer emotion and not go mad? Had the *symballein* link evolved precisely to provide an outlet for the emotions? For the madness?

What a spectacular find. Or, more to the point, how spectacular that she'd found him.

He had a half second to wonder how exactly she'd found him, when she reached out and flattened her palm over his belly, just above the unbuttoned fly of his jeans.

Chapter 5

Alyce held her hand against Sid's warm skin, though he sucked in a harsh breath to pull away.

She had never touched a man of her own will. She knew she should not touch him now. But now was all she had. *He* was all she had.

The textures of him tingled in her fingertips: the smooth planes of his flanks where hard sheets of muscle wrapped around into his rippled abdomen; the thin line of hair that connected the shadowed indent of his navel to the darker mysteries behind the button of his pants. . . .

"You are real." The icy places between her bones softened in relief, and she swayed closer. She had not imagined him. He was wounded, but alive. Here, now. And oh-so warm. "Not one of my delusions." She canted her head to gaze up into his eyes—eyes the same dusty brown as the leather of the book laid on his bed. "You won't disappear?"

He had to let out the breath he'd held to answer. "I am real. As real as you."

Slowly, as if she might run—or attack—he lifted her palm from his belly. He laced his fingers through hers and raised her hand to his chest. Against her knuckles, his heart pounded. The reverberations echoed through her veins.

"As real as you," he said. "See?"

She nodded in time to their linked pulse.

She might have stood there as day turned back to night, entranced by his touch, but he untangled their fingers. "Can we go find the other talyan? Don't be afraid. They won't hurt you."

The loss of his touch stung like ichor burns, and she tensed again. "They'll want to."

"They're just nervous."

"Of me?"

His lips quirked, and suddenly she wished she'd touched him there instead, to feel that soft curve. "You are very scary."

She lowered her head, letting her hair fall over her eyes.

"Alyce, I was teasing." He hesitated. "Well, exaggerating. Or maybe . . . Never mind."

That was the problem. She rarely minded. His mind, though, whirred with every word he said, taking him farther away from her.

Her chest tightened with dread. So long alone and adrift . . . She couldn't lose him, not when she'd just found him. But Thorne had tried to warn her. Even the devil knew she wasn't suited for proper company, despite the unstained frock. How sad that all those times she had fought him, when she'd clung to the ongoing battle as a reason to exist, she'd also been pitifully thankful that he had not feared her, that he didn't think her a worse monster than himself. Damned with faint praise by a man possessed. She took a sidling step away.

Sidney followed. "Alyce. Look at me."

She did. Or she looked at his mouth again. Words came from him so fast and furious, faster and more furious than the devil's. Yet she very much liked his mouth.

When she focused on his intent brown eyes, a hint of heat uncurled through the fog that had been her only companion, and she grasped at it like a lifeline.

What did Thorne know anyway, him and his devil's whispers? Well, he had mentioned that one thing, that thing old as evil. That required no words at all. And as the wanting burned away the confusion, she'd never felt more human, more alive.

Maybe the devil had one good idea.

She rolled up to the balls of her feet and pressed her lips to Sidney's.

So soft—his lips were every bit as soft as she'd remembered from that first fleeting kiss. And wonderfully warm, they curved around hers, like a secret smile she could feel but not see—a smile only for her. She supposed she could get used to being teased.

"My Sidney," she whispered against his mouth. Or she meant to. What came out of her was a moan, even softer than his lips.

She reached up to sink her fingers into his hair. The russet locks were just long enough to tickle the backs of her hands and send delightful shivers through her. Then she remembered the rest of his hair, the light sift of curls on his chest, and tighter lower down, and she wondered where else that might tickle her, so she let her fingers trip over his breastbone and down his belly. Ah, rougher than the silk of his hair, but every bit as pleasing to her touch.

His fingers wrapped around her upper arms. Good, or she might have fallen as her knees weakened. Mouth to mouth, their breath swirled and merged, a close, sultry mingling that promised deeper intimacy if they just—

He pulled away, and their lips parted. "Wait." He locked

his elbows and his grip on her arms kept her from step-ping back into his embrace. "Alyce, wait." His grasp wasn't really strong enough to stop her—and shook slightly besides—but she waited because he'd asked. "What are we doing?"

"I know the answer to this one," she said quickly.

His laugh was no more steady than his grasp. "How did you stay so innocent with a demon inside you?"

She froze. "I am not innocent." The eerie shiver in her voice made her wince. She didn't want to display more of her oddity to him, but neither did she want him to believe something of her that wasn't true. "You said we would learn together. You will not hurt me with your trials. And even if you do, I will heal."

His fingers tightened reflexively, then slipped slowly down to rest just above her elbows. "Hurt you with my . . . Alyce. I swear I won't let that happen. Not to you."

He closed his eyes, as if reaching inside himself—for pa-tience, maybe, or tolerance, or another reason to push her away. Whatever he was looking for in there wasn't about her, because she was out here.

She rolled her shoulders against his hold, and his eyes popped open. Through the dark depths, his willpower glinted at her, just as a fire-blackened iron, nicked by some harsh blow, revealed bare metal.

Whatever forces had shaped him were more merciless than mere demons.

Since he still held her at arm's length, she raised her hands to grasp his forearms, pressing the pulse points of their wrists together. She scolded herself for taking advan-tage of him. It had been so long since anyone had spoken kindly to her, she had been selfishly basking in his atten-tion. It was past time she gave some back. "Who was hurt, Sidney, that makes you afraid you will break me?"

His heartbeat raced against hers. "No one's going to get hurt. Everything will be okay. We are both here for a reason, you and I, and figuring it out is the only trial we'll be undergoing."

"Maybe we are here for this. To kiss."

He did kiss her again, on the forehead this time. It was sweet, but not as sweet as on the mouth.

Oh, she had never had such a wicked thought. This strange rush through her veins that blushed over her skin—it must be the demon that possessed her.

For once, she was rather glad of the devil inside.

She tilted her face up to him, wishing she were taller. She could take him down, as she'd done the devil-man at the gate, but she'd never pitted herself against an opponent she wasn't trying to incapacitate. Perhaps now was not the time to practice. But maybe soon . . .

He gave another low laugh, somewhere between shaky and husky. "Stop looking at me that way."

"I am scary," she reminded him.

He stared down at her, then gave his spectacles a nudge higher on his nose. The reflected light disguised his eyes. "Right then. Let's go see who else we can trick or treat."

He donned his shirt, and she helped ease the long sleeve over his wounded arm. Though the blue-and-white-striped cotton was finely woven, it was not as soft as his lips. She restrained a sigh to see that lovely warm skin hidden away.

"It will be okay," he told her.

His anxious tone told her he was trying to reassure himself as much as her. "I won't hurt your friends again," she said. "I surprised the one because he was tired and distracted, and when I stepped in front of him, he dropped his cigarette down his shirtfront." Otherwise, he would have been able to kill her with one blow—maybe two if she'd ducked. The lethal energy in him was much stronger than anything she could summon. "If they want to destroy me, I cannot stop them."

Leaving off buttoning his shirt, Sidney pulled her into his embrace, though she felt him cringe at raising his wounded arm. "*I* will stop them."

She nestled into his side and took the opportunity to slip her hand across his bare chest. Her hectic pulse settled into time with his. "I trust you."

His breath hitched under her palm. "You're going to kill me first, Alyce."

She tilted her face up to his. He did look flushed. "Fever," she guessed. "The devils are rotten with pestilence. I did not get to you soon enough."

"You're here now. Just stay close." When she tucked herself tighter against his side, he chuckled. "Maybe leave us room enough to walk."

She settled for holding his hand as they walked out into the hall. With only one hand free, he couldn't finish buttoning his shirt, and the intermittent glimpses of his skin soothed her. Walking these halls was better with him. The intense echoes of conflicting power that had nearly frozen her when she snuck into the building were muted when she stood with him, as if when they were together she could rise above her fear, control it.

She thought maybe she could kill these devil-men if she had to, for Sidney.

"You said you trusted me," he said.

She realized the low sound vibrating in her throat wasn't pleasure this time, but a growl. She put her hand over the demon's mark around her neck. "I do."

"Show me where you left the talya."

She picked her way through the building, avoiding the pools of power behind closed doors where she knew the devil-men were waiting. Sidney had said he would teach her the differences in the etheric flows so she wouldn't be confused as she had been before, thinking the restless forces crowding the alley during the attack had been anything besides the vicious horde. She would keep her mouth shut and not make any more mistakes as she had again today.

At the back door, she gestured. "I left him outside."

A surge of nerves made her bite her lip. Had she destroyed one of Sidney's friends? It had been so long since she *hadn't* destroyed those she encountered. It was the only thing she remembered how to do.

Sidney pushed up the big rolling door. A wave of cold air and vicious curse words accompanied the movement.

"Jesus fuck," shouted the man. He lay just outside the door, one leg twisted at an unnatural angle. The blood trail on the gray concrete steps behind him showed where he'd pulled himself along despite the gash on his close-shaved skull. "Westerbrook, get away from that crazy bitch!"

Sidney squeezed her hand. "You didn't kill him. Good girl." He released her and went down the steps, hands spread low out front and his voice soothing, as one would approach a wounded animal. "Ecco, relax. She's talya, new to the league."

That silenced the curses. "Another one? We missed a teshuva coming through the Veil?"

Sidney shook his head. "She's been rogue, unnoticed."

"Then she could be djinni."

From his tone, Alyce guessed that meant something worse than the beating she'd given him.

But Sidney just shook his head again. "She's one of ours. Yours."

"Mine," she whispered under her breath.

The man—Ecco—jerked toward her. Of course the devil-man could hear her. The devil was always listening.

She moved forward to the edge of the steps and looked down at him. "I thought you had stolen Sidney away; that you were keeping him prisoner in this fortress."

He scowled. "Was that an apology for throwing me into the Dumpster?"

She tilted her head in consideration.

"It was an explanation," Sidney interrupted, his tone brusque with a hint of warning.

Ecco grumbled but didn't press the issue. "Get me up. Now that I know we haven't been infiltrated by a djinni psycho bitch, I can go bleed in peace. Since she's just a rogue psycho bitch."

Sidney crossed his arms. "Don't be rude. That was what got you here in the first place."

"I wasn't rude. I said I liked her dress."

Sidney glanced at Alcye inquiringly.

She folded her hands in front of her. "His tone was insincere. And then I saw the devil in his eyes."

"Baby blue gunnysack dresses with no bra underneath always bring out the devil in me." Ecco ignored Sidney's hand and pulled himself upright to one foot. He balanced gracefully despite the twist to his other leg. "I guess meeting an unbonded possessed female made me forget myself."

He stood two steps down from them, and still he was nearly a head taller than Sidney—almost twice that to her. She took a step away from the glitter in his eyes. Not the demon. Something darker.

Sidney stood back from the byplay with a bland expression. But behind the shield of his glasses, his eyes narrowed, and his hands, tucked tight against his ribs under his crossed arms, were fists.

Which signs should she believe? She angled toward him hesitantly. "Sidney?"

"I want you to meet Liam and Sera and the other talyan."

Still his body sent her conflicting messages, and his words of welcome didn't match his flat tone. The discord jangled her nerves. "No. I want to leave."

"You can't go," Ecco said, as if she hadn't just broken his leg. "You belong with us now."

That decided her.

She took Sidney's hand and pulled him behind her as she jumped down from the concrete platform, avoiding the devil-man dominating the steps.

Sidney gave a surprised yelp, but she steadied him. Before he recovered his balance, she tugged him toward the fence's gate. When she'd come for him, she'd squeezed past the chain that padlocked the parking lot fence. Sidney's shoulders were too broad to fit through the gap, so she ripped the chain loose with a squeal and spark of metal.

"Alyce," he gasped.

"Damn it, Westerbrook," Ecco hollered. "Dereliction of duty, man."

"Oh, now they care about my duty," Sidney muttered.

But he did not pull his hand away, and so Alyce did not stop. His willingness eased the tension in her chest, because she would not have left without him. And she had to get away from the low thrum of devil energy. It made her want things—bad things; things she daren't want.

A tiny twist, deeper in her chest, around her heart, made her wonder if Sidney would be the one to pay for her fear and flight.

No, he had promised to explain, and then the fear would go. But she could not listen with the devils whispering around them.

The October air swirled as she hurried Sidney down the street. Large rumbling carriages—trucks, she reminded herself—blasted past them on obscure errands. There was so much scurrying around her. The sounds and the stenches ached in her head. Sometimes she understood why the devils wanted to bring everything to a halt.

In still, cold silence, she might finally remember.

"Alyce," Sidney said. "Wait just a moment."

She paused as he pulled back. She hadn't realized how far they'd come from the devil building. Her only thought had been to get away. Sidney's lips were compressed, the soft curves tightened with pain.

Remorse plucked at her. "Your wounds."

"I can't feel them through the cold."

"Cold?" She had forgotten to feel that too.

He fumbled with the buttons of his shirt and hissed under his breath.

Gently, she bumped aside his fingers. She hadn't noticed the bite in the air, but his skin burned through her like ice. "Let me."

She did up the buttons, but the thin fabric offered little protection, just as she'd done little to protect him from the devil-men. She'd let her fear pull him away; at least she could make him warm.

She wrapped her arms around him.

With her nose against the upper undone button, she sighed. Unlike the trucks and ferales and dank holes where she usually slept, he smelled good, like soap and clean water and some deeper scent—male and good. She breathed again. "I am sorry for running away."

His heart thudded under her ear. "At least you let me come along this time."

"I didn't want them to hold us."

"You seem okay with me holding you."

She glanced up at him.

He was watching her, but with none of that conflicting distance and tightness that had confused her earlier. His focus was only on her. And his mouth was soft again.

She could keep him to herself. She'd never had anything, but he was here, in her hands. The whispering little voice that moved through her usually suggested she destroy things. She liked this idea much better.

Possessed, she might be, but now she possessed him.

"I have a place," she said. "A place we can get warm." If she could just remember where she'd put it.

He nodded. "Take me there."

Yes, she wanted that very much.

Bookkeepers traditionally stayed out of fieldwork. A Bookkeeper couldn't hope to survive demonic fieldwork since that entailed mostly killing fields.

Bookkeeper traditions survived for centuries because good practice kept good practitioners alive. Not indefinitely, of course—they weren't talyan, after all—but it kept them alive long enough to pass along the traditions and lessons.

The importance of institutional survival had been battered into Sid's brain. But when Alyce had grabbed his hand on the warehouse steps, he'd tossed aside everything he'd been taught—all that generations of Bookkeepers had collected—to put his empty hand in hers.

Impulsive? Not at all. It was an opportunity for in-depth study that could upend everything those previous Bookkeepers had held infallible.

Now he wondered if he'd been a tad hasty.

"Not much farther," she said.

He was numb all the way through, which was better than feeling the pain. Thank God he'd put on his loafers before he left his room with her, but he hadn't bothered with socks, and now he couldn't feel his toes.

A few lost toes were a small price to pay for the inner workings of a rogue female talya. He just wished the inner workings were less outdoors in Chicago in October.

When he'd suggested grabbing a cab, she'd just looked through him. "How will I know where we are going?"

He didn't have his wallet anyway.

The city blocks stretched endlessly between traffic lights, and the relentless flow of traffic seemed at the same time more menacing and more remote when he realized he had once again foolishly left the security of the warehouse with nothing—no money, no cell phone, no one who knew where he was, nothing to protect himself.

Except Alyce, of course.

Though she might be most dangerous of all.

She gave a little cry. "There. I remembered."

He followed her gaze. "The art museum?"

"Almost."

She dragged him onward.

But she didn't take him up the elevated walkway that

led from the autumn-browned expanse of Millennium Park to the Art Institute of Chicago. Instead, she flanked the sprawling Beaux-Arts building and dragged him down to where the upper gallery spanned a set of railroad tracks.

They had to climb over the low concrete railing and jump down to the roof of a parked truck. His shoulder screamed at the abuse. But when he stumbled, Alyce caught him.

"So cold," she murmured. "Just another moment."

She led him along the tracks, past the unmarked doors at the base of the museum buildings. Light leaked under both ends of the suspended gallery above them, but they were blocked from casual view.

At a panel in the wall, just another slab of gray, she slammed her fist against the metal. The panel popped free, revealing a square of darkness.

Sid restrained a sigh. What was wrong with the nice museum café upstairs?

"It's a good place," Alyce said, as if she'd heard him. "The devils never come here."

He lingered outside the hole. "They don't like the art."

"What I can see through the new windows *is* very odd."

He stifled a laugh. He'd read about the museum's expansion. "So you don't like modern art?"

She faced him. "I am old."

His amusement faded. "Art, old or new, has a nullifying effect on the tenebrae. Given the choice, the horde avoids humanity's heartfelt attempt to make sense of its place in the cosmos."

"Is that what art does?"

"And the good stuff looks nice above a couch." He peered into the dark. "I don't suppose you have a couch in there."

"I have candles."

"Sounds great." He climbed through the open hatchway, and she pulled the panel into place behind them.

It wasn't as bad as her last bolt-hole. Once she lit the

candles with a half-used book of matches, the empty nook looked downright ... empty. But it was dry, and a boiler vent protruding from one wall shared its heat. Dry, warm, and tenebrae-free was good.

She stood at his side, her gaze darting from him to the stark walls and back again, fingers laced tight in front of her. "I kept food here, but it has been a while. And I just drink from the fountain across the street. I could bring you some. ..." Fingers still interlaced, she opened her palms into a shallow cup. Her eyes, when she looked up at him, were clouded.

He put his hand over hers, filling the cup. "I'm fine." He folded his legs under him and gently tugged her down to his side. "I just want to rest a moment."

She collapsed in slow degrees to rest on one hip, and the granny dress gulped her in its wrinkles.

Sid didn't blame Ecco for the crude, backward compliment about the housedress. For everything it lacked—style, shape, thread count—it only emphasized Alyce's delicate features. In the flicker of the candle, the washed-out blue polyester highlighted the color of her eyes, like the shadows in an iceberg. The hem covered her down to her bare toes, and Sid steeled himself against the urge to tuck the edges more tightly around her, maybe gallantly remove his shirt to drape around her thin shoulders.

But stripping again would hurt so much, he'd look more pitiful than gallant. And anyway, a scholar should probably avoid taking his clothes off around his test subject. Nakedness led to feeling, and feeling led diametrically away from thinking, and thinking was all a Bookkeeper had.

It was ironic that even though he'd lost the two most important women in his life because of Bookkeeping, this third had come *to* him for the same reason.

Alyce looked back into his eyes until he realized the silence had lengthened unnecessarily. He'd never encoun-

tered a talya with such stillness. Even the restless demonic
energies that a human sensed only through a primitive, tin-
gling awareness of lurking danger were banked in her, as if
the teshuva slept. Would her underachiever teshuva explain the limp he'd first noticed in the alley?

"Alyce, how did you stay alive?"

"The fountain," she reminded him. "It's very close. And
I found a carton of bruised apples once."

"I don't mean food and drink." Although that had obviously been in short enough supply. "Did you have others
with you before? Others like you? Who taught you how to
overcome the tenebrae? Who . . ." He trailed off as she
shook her head. "No one?"

"Not until you."

"How long?"

The slow shake of her head ceased, and her gaze went
through him. "Long."

The depth of wistfulness in the one word made his chest
ache as if he'd held his breath. "I wish your introduction to
the league had been . . ."

One corner of her mouth tilted just a bit. "Less bloody?"

"Well, with the talyan, that's not so much an issue."

"Tell me about them. About me." She leaned toward
him, so that the point of her shoulder pressed into his arm.
Though his stitches were on his other side, the trusting contact was almost sharper than a feralis fang. Had he botched
her reunion? After what had happened to Ecco, would
Liam brand her an unrepentant rogue?

He laid out the story like the worst of the unvarnished
Old World fairy tales: the battle between good and evil; the
teshuva who had been on the wrong side of that battle and
repented; the djinn, who'd lost but not repented and not
given up either, whipping the lesser evils of the horde-
tenebrae into endless, subversive mayhem; the angels and
demons—repentant and malevolent—that continued the

fight, unacknowledged by humans, except for the few resonant souls who unwittingly brought the etheric forces into their lives that changed them forever.

Though the cold hadn't seemed to touch her, now Alyce shivered against him. "What did I do to deserve this?" She pressed her forehead against his shoulder, muffling her voice. "Why can't I remember?"

"It's not a question of guilt." If it had been, he couldn't believe she would ever have attracted a demon's attention. "It was your penance trigger; like fault lines that run all the way through your life. When the teshuva came into our realm, seeking its redemption, its unbound energy was the earthquake that cracked the contours of the soul that matched it: yours."

She canted her head to gaze up at him through the tangle of her hair. "So I haven't really been alone?"

Had he ever heard colder comfort? "I suppose not." Though his wound panged in protest, he couldn't stop himself from reaching over to tuck the unruly wave behind her ear. Somehow, one dark strand looped around his finger, once, twice, and again, in a silky bond.

Her lips parted. She didn't speak, but his attention fixed on the glimmer of candlelight on the secret inner curves of her mouth. That kiss she'd given him as he'd awakened in the darkness after the alley fight . . . He'd been too stunned to make sense of it then. And now he had too much sense to try again.

He had to pinch out this flicker between them now, while it was no more threatening than the candle. Except he couldn't seem to let her go.

"Alyce, I'm sorry no one was there for you."

"All along, I had the demon." She leaned into his touch, her cheek resting against his knuckles. His pulse heated and flickered like the flame, reminding him that every conflagration started with a spark. "And now I have you."

Her artless trusting kicked up his heartbeat another

notch, in alarm this time. She ranked him alongside the te-shuva in influences on her life? "Now you have the Chicago league of talyan too," he reminded her.

"They'd still have me? After what I did?"

"There's a strong possibility they'll like you more than ever." He gave her hair a gentle, teasing tug, then forced himself to release her. The lock stayed coiled in a loose ring the diameter of his finger.

He needed to focus, and now he was thinking of jewelry. "When female talyan began reappearing, they brought with them talismans from their demons. The talismans serve as a failsafe, a kill-switch for etheric powers. Did your teshuva give you something? A ring or a bracelet or a . . ." She sat straighter and was shaking her head, but he continued. "Or a tiara? Nothing?"

She spread one hand to indicate the empty hole around them. "I have nothing."

Well really, how many places could she have dropped it—whatever it was—in this city? Chicago was only a bit more than two hundred square miles. Unless, of course, she didn't have a talisman because her teshuva was too weak to need one, or because she was rogue, or because . . .

"Sidney?" She nudged his knee, and he wondered how long he'd been thinking. "I can't go back there. Not yet. All of them together make me feel . . ."

Her pupils dilated, like a sudden spill of blackest ink, and in the depths, violet flared.

His heart missed a beat in limbic panic, but he didn't flinch. "I suspect, since you went through possession without a veteran talya to guide your way, your teshuva settled unbalanced in your soul. It chafes like an ill-fitting shoe." He smiled at her reassuringly. "Maybe that's why you don't have the talisman. Maybe that's why you don't like shoes."

"I like shoes," she said. "But they are hard to steal. Unless I kill someone on the street and take what I want."

Only half hearing her, musing to himself, he continued.

"The unbalanced teshuva would also explain your memory loss and your rather disturbed . . ." He stifled the rest of the analysis. How inappropriate to share his conjecture with the subject herself—and about as flattering as that house-dress.

Then his mind caught up with his ears. "Talyan destroy the horde-tenebrae. You mustn't kill people." Belatedly, he considered she'd been living with teshuva violence and without talya or Bookkeeper guidance. He found it hard to believe she'd have gone so far astray. But then, most people didn't believe in demons either.

"I have heard many mustn'ts." Her tone dropped an octave.

He frowned. "Killing people is one of the really, really don'ts. Especially not for shoes."

"But for evil, yes?"

"Well . . ." He might be a Bookkeeper, steeped in the lore and modus operandi, but this was out of his league. Maybe it was out of every league, which was why Liam Niall's Irish skin had gotten even paler at the mention of a rogue.

She nestled closer to him. "Which evils deserve destruction?"

It was like cuddling a pipe bomb, all thin, hard lines and precarious menace.

If he was going to contain the danger, he'd have to be as steady and dispassionate as any bomb tech. It would be hard to unravel the more-sensed-than-seen snarl of live wires with sweaty, shaking hands. Not just his studies were at stake but Alyce's survival.

The first time he'd been seduced by shadowy secrets, he'd been a heedless child and lost his mother. By the second time, with Maureen, he'd learned better, and he'd lost only his heart.

This time, at least, he had nothing left to lose.

Alyce angled her cheek against his shoulder to look up at him, her gaze fixed on his as if he'd spoken every word aloud. Too bad the Bookkeepers a hundred years ago who invented the energy sinks to dampen talyan etheric emanations hadn't created a portable version as protective against emotions as a bomb tech's Kevlar was against shrapnel.

He tried to plaster over his grim thoughts with a quick answer to her question about evils. "Stick with ending the nasties that don't look human. That's the malice and salambes—the smoky incorporeal ones—and the ferales like the big corpse-husk ones you pulled off me. Sound good?"

She nodded. "There are as many of those as there are mustn'ts and don'ts. I can never get to the bottom."

"But now you'll have help from the other talyan."

"And you." The fall of her dark lashes softened her gaze.

He stifled a twinge of unease. Certainly Kevlar would hold up against eyelashes. "Of course. Me. While you need it."

"Need you."

"Right." He cleared his throat. "Would you like to meet just one or two of them? They'll keep their teshuva latent and not overwhelm you."

"If you like."

No other Bookkeeper would believe in a talya this submissive, a teshuva subdued to the point of somnolence—at least when she wasn't sleepwalk-slaughtering. His unease welled higher. What if she really wasn't talya? What if her demon wasn't repentant?

"Alyce, why did you save me last night?"

She peaked her brows and gave him a disbelieving look, as if he were being unnecessarily stupid. "The devils . . . The ferales would have killed you. It is what they do. I destroyed them. That is what I do."

Did she have an instinct for good? Or merely for innate carnage? Could he unravel the two impulses and find what she was at her core without a slackening of the strict nonintervention policies of a good Bookkeeper? He'd have to; only a highly trained scholar could aspire to such heights of philosophical indulgence and metaphysical parsing.

And there were no repentant Bookkeepers.

He shook his head. "Whatever the reason, I am ecstatic you found me, Alyce."

"My demon—my teshuva—found you last night," she corrected. "It showed me the signs and told me something was different, something . . ."

"That it was finally ready to be part of the league?" He gave her an indulgent chuckle and pushed carefully to his feet. He held his good hand down to her. "Better late than never."

"I think . . . I saw . . ." Her shoulders tensed with frustration over whatever she was trying to say, then sagged. "It wasn't just my demon. It was more than that."

"There is much more," he said. "But you don't have to worry about it all at once. Let's go meet your teshuva's distant cousins, and they'll show you where to start."

He thought she would try to argue again, but she only sighed and put her hand in his. "Where to start worrying?"

"Leave that part up to me. That is what Bookkeepers do."

He should actually do more of that—worrying— especially about the easy, instinctive way she fit against him when she stood up, as if that part of him had been missing all along.

That part was *supposed* to be missing. He'd excised it very carefully from his life, as any good revisionist historian cut apart the past and rearranged it, cleaner, simpler, and with fewer innocent victims.

"You know," he said. "I really am happy you can nip off heads when necessary." She would never fall victim to impossibilities. She *was* an impossibility.

She might be nestled under his arm at the moment, with her shy smile, ferocity leashed and surprisingly soft, but she was utterly out of his reach, just as she should be.

Turning her over to the talyan was a necessary step so he could step away. To observe, analyze, and bear witness, a Bookkeeper needed distance. And if he feared the distance might tear something fragile—not in Alyce, but in him— well, as he'd told her, better now than later.

She was immortal; she'd survive. Ultimately, she didn't need him any more than Maureen had—or maybe a little more, for the moment, for what he could teach her. But that would fade, as he would. At least Alyce would still be there, fighting for the light. He'd take consolation in that, since he'd never have it for himself.

CHAPTER 6

Alyce followed her Sidney to another phone box at a busy little building. She tucked herself behind him to avoid the rush of cars in and out of the white-lined parking lot, but she couldn't escape the stink of burned coffee and the sweet-tart perfume of the garish candy wrappers swirling in the lee of the brick wall.

She winced at the strain in his voice while he spoke. "No, Dad, really, you don't need to send money. Everything's under control here. . . . Yes, I'll be careful." They waited while the call was patched through to the devil-men from whom she'd freed him.

For him, she would step back into that hell.

"Liam," Sidney said. "You found Ecco?"

Coming through the phone box, the brusque voice hit her ears clearly. "Hard to sleep through his swearing."

"Maybe you could send someone else to meet us then."

"Us?"

Sidney smiled at her reassuringly. "Alyce is with me."

"And you're still in one piece?"

Sidney's smile faltered. "As good as before." He rattled off their location.

The other man grunted. "I'll come."

The flat tone raised Alyce's hackles, and the remnants of Sidney's smile vanished. "Send Sera."

"You think she won't judge as impartially as I would?"

Sidney ran his hand down the back of his neck, and Alyce wondered if his hackles were up too. "We don't need a judge. And if we did, I'm impartial. Sera has been your Bookkeeper until now, and I value her insights. More important, she has tight control over her teshuva."

"Archer will insist on being with her."

"Not as jury and executioner."

There was no answer for a moment, just a muffled discussion even Alyce's sharp ears couldn't decipher. "They're on their way."

Sidney slammed the phone onto its hanger, the hand on the back of his neck clenched tight until his fingers bleached his skin. "Damn him."

Alyce touched his arm. "Never say that."

After a moment, he turned to her. "You're right. It's not my place."

"But, if you say he is evil, I can kill him."

"Alyce!"

"I was teasing," she said solemnly.

As they waited, the October clouds thickened until the sky, the concrete, and the steel buildings were all one shade. A few errant raindrops spattered the sidewalk and the pigeons pecking nearby.

"Their wings are brighter than the sky," Alyce said. "Maybe that is how they can fly."

"That and lift, thrust, angle of attack, aerodynamics—"

She moved her forefinger from his sleeve to his lower lip, and he stopped talking. "Do not be nervous."

"You think I'm nervous?"

"Your heart races. You avoid my eyes. You talk too fast." Yet she rather liked the velvety rub of his lip against her fingertip.

"You already said I talk too much."

"To hide. I hide in silence."

He took her hand and squeezed it. "Sometimes you make sense."

"Is that good?"

"It's good if Liam thinks you're lucid instead of a loose cannon."

"We're not on a ship."

He sighed. "So much for making sense."

She gave him an admonishing look. "Loose cannons are bad on a ship in battle. They roll over sailors and knock holes in bulkheads. But I think on land, a loose cannon would be more useful than a cannon that couldn't move."

He pursed his lips, and she wished her finger were still there—or her lips, against his. "Maybe you're right. But do you mind if I do the explaining to Sera and Archer?"

"You have the words," she agreed.

He eyed her, a furrow between his brows, as if she were one of those old books in his room where the ink had faded and run into strange new shapes.

She waited. This was how his books must feel, glad for his hands upon their pages, willingly giving themselves up to his serious brown regard with a soft, rustling sigh. No one else had cared to open them. They could only trust his focus would yield some satisfaction.

The thought of satisfaction—his and hers—finally made her shift, and he blinked. "I don't think anyone has shut me up as often as you do."

They stood in silence until a white car with large rust spots pulled up to the curb. A blond woman in a cherry red coat rolled down the passenger side window. "Hey, guys. Liam said you might want to get some lunch."

Her voice was pitched to friendly, and her slender arm hung out the window with relaxed carelessness. Nothing about her said devil.

When Sidney opened the back door and gestured Alyce inside, she found the devil—black-haired and stern-faced, his dark brown eyes hard as frozen earth—waiting in the driver seat.

She started to back out, but Sidney bumped her hip from behind. "Who's nervous now?"

The woman in the passenger seat punched the devil-man's shoulder, hard enough for the thud to reverberate through the worn fabric under Alyce's fist. "Quit it, Ferris. You're scaring her."

He flinched. "I'm just sitting here."

"You're glowering all over the place. It gets in the upholstery."

"Sera, she almost ripped Ecco's leg off."

"And you haven't been tempted more than once?"

The man—Alyce thought the surname Archer fit his sharp eyes better than the purr of Ferris—pinned her with a purple-tinged glare for a moment. Then he grinned. The humor warmed his whole face like spring. "Good point. C'mon in."

Alyce stayed with her haunches pressed back against Sidney. She could still kick him out of the way. But she had told him she trusted him. She couldn't run forever.

Even though running, kicking, and not trusting had kept her alive this long.

Sidney flattened his hand over her spine in a soothing caress and ducked in beside her. His big body crowded her across the seat. "Let's go. I'm starving."

He pulled the door shut behind him, and Alyce's ears rang from the compression. The space was so small, she had nowhere to go. Sidney reached for a strap on the other wall, and now he was pulling it toward her, reminding her of the men in the hospital who had bound her to the bed and wheeled her down the halls. Now the carriage was moving, moving, toward what . . .

"Alyce? Alyce, what's wrong?"

She half crawled into his lap to avoid the gray snake of the strap. Her breath hitched and caught, then raced away without her. "Don't. Do not tie me."

"It's just a seat belt," Sidney said.

"Westerbrook," Sera said with unruffled calm, "she's immortal. I think we can skip the seat belt, hmm?"

He opened his mouth as if he might object; then he let go of the strap. It recoiled with a hiss. "Right."

The vibrations of the car racked her. No, she was shivering.

Sidney settled his arm across her shoulders. "You don't even notice the cold."

"I'm not cold." And still she shivered.

Sera exchanged glances with the devil-man beside her; then she smiled at Alyce. "It's a little crazy, isn't it?"

"I was never crazy." Her voice shattered across three octaves, and the lowest rocked the carriage until the metal around them squealed.

Archer clamped both hands on the wheel in front of him. "Now who's scaring her?"

Sidney tucked her closer under his arm. "Everybody be quiet for a second."

The motion of the car still rattled her teeth, but the weight of Sidney's arm seemed to press the fear out of her. Finally the car caught up with her runaway breath, and she let out a tired sigh.

Sidney stroked her hair. "Okay now?"

"Tell me again—what is 'okay'?"

"Less loose cannon."

She nodded against his shoulder. It was his bandaged arm, but he didn't seem to notice.

From that shelter, she was able to look up at Archer and Sera. "Sidney said you are possessed by devils."

Sera slanted a look at Sidney, then nodded. "We call them teshuva."

"Sidney has given them so many names: malice, ferales, salambes, djinn."

"Those are different," Sera said. "You're like us."

Could she ever be as poised as the woman in front of her? Alyce shook her head.

"There's so much we want to tell you, and even more we want to ask you," Sera continued. "That's why I said it's ... overwhelming."

"Crazy," Alyce whispered.

"Just because we don't understand something right away does not mean it's a danger," Sidney said. His tone was instructive, as if he stood at a lectern, but his narrowed gaze on Archer held more meaning than his words.

Archer stared back at her in the small mirror above his head. "Although what we don't know can kill us before we figure it out."

Alyce met his eyes. "Sidney says I mustn't kill anyone."

"Well, isn't that thoughtful of him."

Sera elbowed Archer. "We promised them lunch. It's not far to Therese's."

Sidney stiffened. "The diner at the pier? I don't think that's a good idea."

"Just because we don't understand doesn't mean danger." The pitch of Archer's voice was mocking.

"I am hungry," Alyce offered. "I haven't been to the pier since the fair."

Sera gave her an encouraging look. "The art fair this summer? It was fun, wasn't it? Lots of fried food and not too many tenebrae to fry in return."

Alyce shook her head. "They called it the World Fair."

Sidney's arm over her shoulder twitched. "The World Fair? That was ... a while ago."

"That was 1933," Archer said. "Great Depression years. Lots of tenebrae."

Alyce straightened. "You were there?"

His eyes crinkled at the corners when he looked back at her. "Sorry—I must've missed you in the million-people crowd."

"I am shorter than you."

"I guess that's why we're feeding you."

Sidney's fingers twitched, tugging at her hair. "But . . . 1933?" His voice rose. "Alyce, how long have you been possessed?"

Alyce hunched under his agitated intensity, and Sera tsked. "Westerbrook, it's never gentlemanly to ask a lady her age." Her tone was teasing, but her half-shuttered gaze wasn't.

Alyce closed her eyes. All the conflicting signals buffeted her. Why couldn't they say and look and act just one way? Why did Sidney soothe her with his hands and chide her with his words? She already knew his mouth could be put to better use.

Fortunately, they were quiet again except for the rumble of the metal cage on wheels. She didn't open her eyes until the light dimmed as they pulled into a building full of neatly aligned cars. When Sidney opened his door, she scrambled over his lap to get out.

Archer was already there, his hand braced on the door frame. His black trench coat fell around him like threatening wings, ready to flare.

She followed the shimmer of violet that chased around the dark lines on his hand. Devil-man.

"You wouldn't leave before lunch, would you?" His voice dropped. "In the teshuva's quest to atone for their sins, I think they become overzealous in their privation. But we are still human, if not *only* human. We deserve some pleasures."

She tilted her head. "Even damned?"

"Especially damned." He opened Sera's door, and the mark across his knuckles flared as he held out his hand to her. She slid her palm across his and pulled herself into his embrace. Her long brilliant red coat flamed against the dark background of Archer.

Alyce watched from the corner of her eye. The aura that pulsed around them, invisible if she faced them straight on, deepened and darkened, shot through with lightning. Like a storm cloud just for them. Its energy tempted her closer and warded her off. *Not for you,* it whispered, *but somewhere . . . someone . . .*

"Alyce?" Sidney stepped out of the car, breaking her trance. "Come on. They'll catch up."

Archer snorted, and the two fell into step behind. "You know where you're going, Westerbrook? Liam told London about our secret diner, but you haven't actually seen it yet."

"I heard enough," Sidney growled.

Alyce tagged alongside, but a thread of unease tightened around her. There was more to this lunch than any of them was saying. "I know a place where the old women save bread for the ducks. There would be plenty for all of us."

Sera's mouth drew down. "What you do for this city, Alyce, deserves more than stale bread crumbs."

When they passed between the cars into a hallway of shops, Sera walked beside Alyce. "So, do you usually run away from the devils?"

Alyce looked at her.

Sera grinned. "The purple in your eyes says no." Her smile flattened with gravity. "Then don't run from us. Not anymore."

"You are all so loud," Alyce said. "So big. So bright to my eyes and impatient. Like the city."

Sera paused beside a recessed foyer that displayed windows brilliant with colored glass. The lettering on the doorway beyond said MUSEUM. "We're like the glass. Sharp and cutting when we're in pieces, but together we make something breathtaking."

Archer walked to the next door and yanked it open. "If by breathtaking you mean we stop things from ever breathing again, then yeah."

Sera stalked up to him. "Ooh, badass."

"I just prefer dark sunglasses, not rose-colored ones."

"But your eyes are so pretty in purple." She stood on tiptoes to kiss him. He tipped her chin up higher to deepen the kiss, and the ring on his finger matched the pendant around her neck, both opalescent stones shining.

Sidney watched with his arms crossed over his chest, one eyebrow cocked. "The mated talya bond in action."

Archer lifted his head. "That is not for you to know. Be grateful we're showing you the verge. It'll blow your dissertation—and your mind."

More new words rolled around like careless cannonballs until Alyce thought she might be crushed. "I thought we were getting food."

"The verge is dessert." Archer ushered Sera past, then Alyce, but let the door swing shut toward Sidney.

Sidney stiff-armed through with a glower.

The tang of peppers swirled past Alyce, and her stomach growled. She passed Archer, who was talking to the dark-skinned woman behind the counter where silvery tureens brimmed with stews and vegetables.

Sidney slid a tray in front of her. "What do you want?"

"Everything."

Sera laughed. "Say what you will, the girl knows her mind."

Sidney ignored her. "Let's start with something basic." He nodded at the woman behind the counter. "Just the rice and beans. I'll have the curry. Extra spicy, please."

Archer bumped Sidney's tray with another. "Make it two, Therese."

"Tough guys," Sera said under her breath. "I'll have the rice and beans too, and kanyah for after."

Alyce curled her lips in and hoped she wasn't drooling as Therese passed the bowls plus a teapot over the counter.

Sidney leaned closer. "Do you remember your last meal? Maybe before you were possessed?"

"Sid," Sera snapped. "Really, the only thing worse than asking about a woman's age is quizzing her about her diet. If you ask her weight, I'm going to deck you."

"I can estimate her weight." Sidney straightened his eyeglasses. "It's the rest I want to know."

Alyce missed the warmth of him, lingering at her shoulder. "I want to know too, but . . ." She shook her head, not sure if she wanted to jar the memories loose or warn him away.

Sera herded them toward the far corner with a view to the kitchen. "This is the talya table. You can tell by the extra jars of pepper flakes."

Archer squeezed into the booth beside Sera, but Sidney put his tray down and pulled an extra chair to the end of the table. Alyce clenched her empty hands. Maybe he'd seen her salivating and didn't want to sit next to her.

But he pushed a bowl her way along with a cup of yellow-green tea, and she decided to forgive him for the moment. The scents wafted up, complicated in a good way, as words could never be. She closed her eyes and inhaled.

When she opened her eyes, her spoon clattered against the bare bottom of the bowl and the other three were staring at her. Sidney pushed his plate toward her. "I can't finish."

He hadn't even started. Sera and Archer sat with spoons poised and still sparkling clean.

Alyce took a slower bite, savoring. "Thank you, Sidney. Sera, may I have the peppers, please?"

Archer snorted. "Yeah, she's talya."

Sera grinned at her. "Serves that teshuva right if you burn it out of you. It should have fed you better."

Sidney leaned back in his chair, arms crossed, subtly distancing himself. No, not so subtly, Alyce thought. Maybe she shouldn't have asked for the peppers, but the spreading warmth felt nice. And he had chosen to sit over there, away from her.

Sidney tapped the hinge of his eyeglasses, as if ticking off possibilities in his head. "How much of the memory loss might be long-term metabolic shock, not just faulty demonic integration?"

Sera passed pieces of kanyah around the table. "The teshuva provides perpetual physical maintenance, but some of the fine points get lost. Like daily sixty-thousand-mile overhauls without the detailing." She leaned against Archer. "And some of those details are really important."

Archer wrapped his arm over her shoulder. "Don't need a memory to massacre tenebrae. And after a while—never mind how long a while is—maybe you don't want to remember."

Alyce met his hooded gaze, the sugared peanut treat sticky in her fist. "I try to remember, when Sidney asks."

"Yes," Archer said softly. "Let's go downstairs and see what else gets shaken loose."

Sidney stayed firmly in his seat, blocking the way. "I don't like this."

"You haven't even seen it yet," Archer said. "As a Bookkeeper, don't you think you should not like something only with full knowledge of what you're not liking?"

Sidney's jaw clenched, and Alyce wondered what words he was holding back. He never seemed to bother holding back words, so they must have been very bad.

"I want to see," she told him. "If it can help me remember, if it can help you, I won't be afraid."

Archer's low laugh raised her hackles. "No reason to stop now."

Chapter 7

Sid had worked with enough ancient papyrus scrolls to know when something was crumbling out of his grasp. The harder he clutched, the quicker this meeting was coming apart.

He flanked Alyce as Sera led the way to the back of the diner where Therese gave them a distracted wave. Archer shouldered aside a full shelf of canned goods, easily balancing the heavy load to let Sera push back a plywood panel. She dropped out of sight, and Alyce reached out for the edges of the dark opening.

"Wait," Sid said. When she perked up, clearly hopeful that he would think better of this, he nudged past her. "Let me go first."

Could the talyan have found a more rickety descent? An old extension ladder was propped haphazardly on a painter's scaffold forty feet above the ground, and an even older ladder spattered with paint spanned the lower distance. The wooden frame stuck a purely spiteful splinter in his palm as he clutched the rails.

When he got to the dirt floor—half silty mud, as if a flood had passed through a tomb—he forgot the petty pain as he followed a thick tangle of power cables to a row of glaring klieg lights. The aluminum hoods were focused with unblinking intensity on a . . . What?

In the middle of the otherwise empty chamber lumped a meter-high hillock of bleached bone and twisted glass. If he squinted, he could decipher the outline of the detonated soul bomb Sera had described in a few terse paragraphs in the league archives. The glass orbs embedded in the freak-ish sculpture had contained the energy of damned souls like spiritual shrapnel. When the bomb had gone off, it had left a crater, not only in the floor, but through the Veil be-tween the realms and right into hell.

Mostly, though, the verge looked like an unwanted ex-hibit shoveled straight out the door of the Art Institute's newest wing; abstract post-futuristic surrealism at its ugli-est and most nonsensical.

Sid pushed his spectacles higher and tilted his head.

Nope. Still ugly.

Alyce dropped to the ground beside him with a splat. Conscious of her limping steps in the uncertain footing, he half turned to steady her.

From the corner of his eye, the hellhole gaped like a screaming mouth, aimed right at them.

"Holy shit!" He jumped toward the ladder, one hand on the highest rung he could reach.

Alyce, however, took a halting step forward.

Sera moved to join her. Archer leapt down from the scaffold above, his leather trench coat flapping. Sid flinched as the other man's boots barely missed his head. When he straightened and faced the verge, its glassy fangs seemed to have lengthened while he wasn't watching, each point glis-tening with a drop of black poison.

Alyce whispered, "It's hungry too."

In the hollow emptiness of the crypt, she sounded like a

ghost. Sid could have done without the rapt expression on all three talya faces. What did they see? When he stared straight at the portal, the verge was a pile of trash. But in his peripheral vision . . .

It wanted them. It wanted to suck their souls and hawk up their empty corpses like sunflower seed shells.

"What have you Chicago talyan done?" His voice broke across the words.

"Relax, Bookkeeper," Archer said. "It's dormant. Mostly. We think."

Sid made a strangled sound. "Tell that to the people of Pompeii."

Sera gestured at a row of milk crates at the base of the kliegs. "Pompeii didn't have those." The crates supported a small tower of instruments, only three-quarters of which Sid recognized. "Our last dear, departed Bookie was a megalomaniacal madman—aren't they all?—but he knew his way around a soldering iron."

Jolted out of his shock by professional jealousy, Sid edged around the gaping maw to study the machines. The boom in cheap consumer electronics had been a source of much glee for the engineering branch among Bookkeepers, though he had always kept more to the theoretical side of the equations. "It's just a resonance sensor with a remote alarm—admittedly, that is fascinating—routed through a . . . oh." He resettled his specs as he straightened. "Is that an etheric sequencer? With an inversion module?"

"Geek alert," Archer muttered.

Sera nodded. "A demonic ant trap."

Sid leaned closer and almost jumped out of his skin when Alyce murmured at his elbow, "What is that inside?"

"There's nothing. . . ." A flicker inside the beaker, like a half-invisible moth, shut him up.

"A soul fragment," Sera explained. "Thanks to Corvus, there are still bits wafting around the city. No tenebrae could resist such an easy snack."

"A baited ant trap," Sid said.

Alyce traced her finger over the gold-rimmed glass. "Poor soul."

Archer toed the stack of perforated paper neatly stacking itself beside a printer that ticked every few seconds. "Nothing has eaten it, which means nothing's coming over the verge."

Sid locked his knees to keep from stepping back. "When you told London you had opened a doorway to hell, we thought you meant . . ."

Archer gave him a moment, then crossed his arms. "We didn't stutter."

"We didn't imagine you meant this." Sid flung one hand out toward the gaping maw.

Sera narrowed her eyes. "You thought *we'd* imagined it?"

"Talyan have no imagination," Sid admitted. "But you are known to be . . . predisposed to postapocalyptic ideation. There were suggestions of group psychosis."

Sera's scowl deepened. "London thought we'd been taken over by evil?"

"If a demon can decide to repent, what's to stop it from unrepenting?"

"So they sent you?" Archer's harsh bark of laughter lacked amusement.

Sid stiffened. "I volunteered."

Alyce smoothed his sleeve as if patting down his hackles. "I could look inside. I would fit."

All three of them swung on her with a chorus in one breath. "No!"

Sid caught her hand, unwilling to let one word, no matter how vehemently uttered, enforce the command. "No, Alyce. If the door to hell is closed — at least for the moment — we are not peeping behind it just to see what jumps out at us."

Climbing out of the hole was worse than going down.

Chills spidered up Sid's spine until his shoulder went numb from the tension, as if the hole breathed death and damnation at their retreating backs.

Alyce stood in the doorway at the top, looking down, until he bumped her out of the way. "Did you see the way it sparkled?"

"I'm not like you." But he had seen enough that a full fortnight of Guinness wouldn't erase the image: female talyan, hell portals, imprisoned souls. Had good begun drifting back toward evil? Was one small rogue just the latest symptom of a fatal breakdown?

There'd been nothing like this in the multimillennia worth of archives he'd spent years of his life memorizing. And what could one human Bookkeeper do about it?

Archer secured the door while Therese watched them with steady dark eyes.

"Do you know what's down there?" Sid asked the diner owner.

"A bad thing."

"And it doesn't frighten you to be right on top of it?"

No purple lights moved in her gaze, but she felt a resolve more human and somehow more unnerving. "I have been closer to bad things. At least this time, someone cares." She handed a bag of kanyah to Alyce. "For you, little one."

Alyce clutched the wax paper baggie of golf ball–sized treats to her chest and murmured her thanks.

Sid—stomach churning with what he'd seen—dropped to the rear as their quartet left the diner and returned past the stained-glass museum toward the parking garage. Ahead of him, Alyce dug into the bag of kanyah. How could she eat after staring down hell's gullet?

Stupid question. She'd hovered almost a hundred years— if her comment about the World's Fair was to be believed— with her and her demon on the edge of starvation. His gaze lingered on her petite form an arm's length ahead of him. His two hands outstretched would easily span her hips, and her waist nipped in smaller yet. He should run back to the diner and get another to-go bag so he could feed her bite by bite....

Damn it, his brain was still rattling around like half a pair of dice. She'd survived without him bringing her sticky sweets.

He slowed, letting her pull away so that he wasn't tempted to more accurately measure her dimensions.

As if she felt him retreat, she glanced over her shoulder. For a heartbeat, she met his gaze; then she held out one of the mottled white and brown desserts, and he wondered what hunger had been in his eyes.

He shook his head and dropped his glance, focusing on her bare feet. Her demon seemed as incapable of providing for her as he was. She was still looking back at him, and her sideways step emphasized her awkward gait.

He seized on the puzzle gratefully. "Alyce, did you injure yourself again?"

Sera shortened her stride to Alyce's. "Again? What happened?"

Sid gestured at her left knee. "Alyce was limping when she fought the ferales in the alley, but the teshuva should have repaired any damage by now." The teshuva mended constantly on the cellular level, though it offered no pain relief.

Alyce shrugged. "It's always there."

Archer palmed open the double doors out to the garage. The stark black *reven* flowing over his knuckles flared violet. "The demon is supposed to reset the body to pristine factory defaults when it takes possession." His words bounced hollowly off the concrete pillars around them. "That's part of the deal."

Sera angled toward Sid. "You must have a theory."

Reminding them a rogue was, by definition, out of sync with her demon seemed unnecessary. "Research on talyan therapeutic interventions is scarce," he said. "We do know that which does not immediately decapitate, eviscerate, or exsanguinate a talya just makes him crankier, but by the time Bookkeepers see you after a tenebrae encounter, you're healed."

"Or dead and gone," Archer finished with a scowl. "No middle ground. So why is she stuck with the hurt?"

Sid shrugged his still-aching feralis-bitten shoulder as they reached the league car. "X-rays don't image ether-transmuted flesh, but I'll find the reason."

Alyce had tugged open the rear car door. Now she paused, and the frame creaked under her clenched fingers. "No hospital."

"Never," Sera soothed her. "But Nanette could help. She has a healing touch, and she knows what we are. This time of day, she'll be at the church."

Sid considered as he slid into the backseat beside Alyce. Sera's archive notes had bullet pointed Nanette as a friend of the league. Since she was possessed by an angelic force, would her goodwill extend to a rogue who walked with one foot in the darkness? Indecision whipsawed him as if the feralis had him in its grasp again.

No, this was worse than feralis fangs. Of course he was vulnerable to death, but to indecision?

Steeped in Bookkeeper lore, he hadn't seen that the mysteries had left myriad hairline cracks, until Maureen had shouted at him, right before she walked away for the last time. "Your crackpot ideas won't ever mean anything in the real world."

His Bookkeeper heritage had been secret, of course—she'd only supposed he had the most doddering odd thesis adviser—which made her accusation undeserved, yet still so true. He would have always been a closed book to her. It was amazing that his mother had stayed with his father long enough to bear children.

She would have lived if she hadn't. And he should have known he could never waver after the price had been paid.

"Your thoughts are louder than Archer's key," Alyce murmured.

He averted his face with a frown. "I don't know what you—"

Archer started the car with a grinding rattle as the worn gears inside the wretched vehicle slipped and finally caught.

Sid pulled his seat belt into place with one swipe and winced as the strap slapped his bandaged shoulder. "I'm not that rusty. Yet." He raised his voice, not that the talyan in the front seat needed it. "A second opinion sounds good. Call Nanette."

Alyce watched him a moment, then pulled her belt across her lap. She sat back, her finger resting on the escape button.

If only he'd left himself such an easy out. But a Bookkeeper was in for life.

And—unlike a talya—for death.

When they parked in front of the squat concrete building, Alyce stiffened, her heart beating a painful double tempo. "It looks like a hospital," she whispered.

Sidney took her hand and tugged her gently from her seat. "It's a church. See the pretty doors?"

Stained glass spread across both double doors in a golden sunburst on a cobalt field. Pretty, yes. She tucked herself against him as he followed Archer and Sera toward the church.

Alyce glanced back. Their mottled car waited alone at the curb, though traffic flowed ceaselessly past on the freeway just beyond a chain-link fence. Over the monotone rumble and the thick stink of exhaust, her senses were half-deadened. She hunched her shoulders, but Sidney was pulling her onward between the doors.

"See?" He squeezed her hand. "It's okay."

"It is okay." As she passed by, she trailed her free fingers along the cool lead seams of the glass. "I can break through those if we need to."

His reassuring smile stiffened at the corners. "You won't need to."

She looked down at the mosaic tile set in the doorway. BE WELCOME was spelled out in the same cheery blues and golds as the stained-glass doors, but she was not well at all.

Sera glided through the open, quiet vestibule with the ease of familiarity, calling out, "Hey, Nanette!" Her voice echoed from the bigger, unlit room visible ahead of them through another set of open double doors, flanked by decorative flags in the shapes of sunflowers and empty except for row upon row of stacking chairs.

A small, redheaded woman with milkmaid hips and creamy pale skin to match stepped out of the doorway down the side hall. She smiled a welcome, but she clasped and unclasped her hands in an unsteady rhythm over the pink heart embroidered on the front of her denim jumper. "Hi, hi. Just so you know—"

A man with eyes more gold than the stained-glass sun rounded the corner of the doorway behind her. Though the corridor was dark, the light through the open door made his white shirt glow. "Just so you know, I'm here too."

Archer and Sera stopped abruptly. Alyce grasped Sidney's hand to keep him from walking into their stiffened spines. The surge of clashing ethers hinted she might be dragging Sidney out through that glass, after all.

The man fixed her with that gilded glare. "What aberration have you brought to this house?"

The chill that lurked in the spaces between her bones leached through her. He wasn't talking to her; he was talking *about* her.

Between one heartbeat and the next, her muscles seized

as if her teshuva had taken her whole body in its hand, ready to drag her away.

"Mr. Fane!" Nanette's voice was an earnest tremor. "Cyril, please. You said you'd wait to see what they wanted."

"Maybe I meant lie in wait."

"Here I thought angels couldn't lie," Archer drawled.

"And I thought the talyan were repentant, but you're harboring a . . ." Fane's squint was as curious as Sidney's but edged with aversion.

Alyce fought the unbearable urge to flee and tugged sharply at Sidney's sleeve. He winced, but they had more problems than his bitten shoulder. "They are possessed," she warned.

"Not demonically," he said in a low voice. "Nanette is angel-touched, and Fane is a warden with the higher angelic spheres."

"That is why they are very not okay," she whispered back fiercely. "They might . . . They might . . ." She caught her breath on a helpless sound of uncertainty as she tried to explain. She had to go; she had to run . . . but only a dark void spread where her reason should have been.

Sidney pushed his spectacles higher, as if he could see what had stolen her words. "Might what? Don't be afraid."

Fane narrowed his golden eyes, which didn't lessen the lethal light. "She should be afraid. The sphericanum has overlooked the league's insurrection, but embracing this little imp is the breaking point."

He stepped fully into the hallway, revealing the sword in his hand. Though the blade was no longer than his forearm and softly pitted on the edges, the etched sigils traced on the metal wavered as if through intense heat.

Without a twitch of her long red coat, a knife—straight and deadly—suddenly glinted in Sera's hand. Archer bothered with no such subtlety. From beneath one blinding sweep of black leather, his battle-axe unfolded in a heavy fan of shining blades, each snick of spreading metal more decisive than the last.

He took a stance half a stride ahead of his mate. "Is the sphericanum up for waging a three-way war, Fane? If not, piss on that flaming sword of yours."

Sidney squinted. "That's a warden's hallowed relic? I thought it would be . . . brighter."

"Oh, it's burning," Alyce murmured. Her gaze felt melted to the sword, and she couldn't look away. Each flicker sent a wave of weakness through her knees, like a fever making her sway, though her pulse raced fast enough to leave without her.

Nanette stepped to one side, patting the air as if trying to extinguish something on fire—tempers, at least, if not the sword. "Everyone, please, calm down. We're all friends here."

Sidney stepped between Alyce and the sword. "Actually, Nanette, only you are listed as friend in the archives." He jerked his chin at Fane. "You have a question mark by your name."

Fane wrinkled his lip. "A question mark? I'm hurt."

Sera lifted one shoulder as she made her knife disappear into her sleeve. "Not a big black question mark. A penciled one."

"Allies at least," Nanette said hurriedly.

Fane's sneer twisted his face into harsh, uneven lines. "Allies wouldn't break the concord that has held us to our vows for aeons—"

"Well, you can't execute them here tonight," Nanette interrupted. "My husband will be here to let the chorus in for practice in less than an hour." She flattened her palms, hand over hand over the pink heart, her gaze on Sera beseeching. "Mr. Fane came after I talked to you. I didn't know—"

"I came when I heard you all were coming." Fane kept his sword at a threatening angle toward the talyan.

Archer mirrored his menace with axe poised perpendicularly to the sword. "The sphericanum bugs phones?"

"'Bug' is such a lower-realm word." After another moment, the point of Fane's sword dipped aside. "But I've heard the chorus. God knows they need the practice."

With a negligent flick of his wrist, as if he'd intended to get around to it eventually and had just been distracted, Archer collapsed the fanned blades of his axe.

Nanette stepped forward, her gaze on Alyce as soft as spring grass. "You aren't like the other talyan."

"My demon is faint," Alyce said. Not so faint that it didn't compel her to take a wary step back, careless of the hitch in her gait that had brought them here. The golden glare of the angelic energy blinded her and lengthened the shadows behind it. Anything could be hiding there. The ever-watchful devil danced along her nerves, with all the grace she lacked, and a protest burst from her. "They're coming."

Sidney's hand closed on her shoulder and made her realize how hard she was shaking. "Just Nanette. She needs to get close enough for a quick look."

A haze of gold threaded between Nanette's fingers like a cat's cradle. "Weaker than my angel even. Blocked somehow."

"Blocked?" Sidney frowned.

"It's not a technical term," Nanette murmured. "It's about feeling."

Sidney crossed his arms, his jaw set off kilter. "I can't fix her with a feeling."

Archer rumbled something low under his breath that made Sera utter a laugh, even lower and more breathy.

The private pleasure in the sound tore through Alyce. She'd rather face all the sharpened weapons in the room at once, but even as the demon urged her away, she raised her gaze to Sidney's. He watched her over the upper rims of his spectacles, looking every bit as desperate to leave.

And as dreadfully bound.

"You don't understand," she whispered.

"I want to—" Whatever else he'd been about to say shattered in a spray of breaking glass.

Alyce whirled toward the front doors. The teshuva jerked up her arm in front of her face to catch the brunt of stinging shards, borne farther than any blow should have propelled them.

The belling wave of demonic energy—so strong the blue and gold slivers hung suspended in the clotted air—almost buckled her knees.

Fighting the teshuva's hold, she spun back to Sidney. "Run!"

But the seven devil-men who strode through the splintered doors had other ideas.

Sid grabbed for Alyce, but her sleeve slipped through his fingers. Running *into* the fray. Bloody hell, he'd already done this once.

Trapped in the gravitational pull of her slight form, he took a step after her, but Archer's big body knocked him sideways. Sera, a stride behind, jolted him the other way. He stumbled and fell to one knee. Fane at least had the decency to vault over him.

Nanette hauled him upright, wrenching his shoulder, and he bit back another curse. "We have to get out of here."

"Not this time." He raced past her to the fire extinguisher halfway down the hall. He'd noticed it hanging next to Fane's head in case somebody needed to knock the smug angelic warden unconscious.

His shoulder protested more sharply when he ripped the red canister from its mooring. He didn't have time to read whether it was a Class A or C extinguisher. It certainly wasn't Class D for demons, but at least it could be used at a distance. He wasn't stupid enough to think he'd be much help in close quarters, except maybe as a distraction.

As quick as he'd been, the talyan and warden were

quicker. When he returned to the foyer, Archer, Sera, and Fane bumped elbows in a barricade of bristling fury and swinging steel against the invaders.

But beyond them, the djinn-men were a wall of unrelieved gloom.

Viewed straight on, they looked—except for their medieval array of swords, staves, and one sickle—like common thugs in dark jeans and black hoodies. But when Sid glanced around wildly for Alyce, twists of poison-yellow fog smeared the edges of his vision.

She charged past with one of the decorative flags wielded like a spear in her hands; a flimsy fiberglass spear trailing a vinyl sunflower.

The intruder with the long-handled sickle grinned when she barreled toward him. He spread his arms wide, free hand tilted palm up in a ya-kidding-me gesture.

He coughed out a laugh like a lungful of unfiltered cigarette smoke. "You're making this too easy, *heshuka*."

Sid didn't bother wondering what the djinn-man meant. He yanked the pin on top of the extinguisher and clamped down on the trigger until metal grated on metal.

The cylinder kicked hard in his grip. He aimed the cloud of white powder high for the djinn-man's malicious grin, thinking he'd at least trigger a blink. Instead, the powder hit the leading edge of the djinni's powerful aura—and clung like a smothering blanket.

The djinn-man shouted and swung his sickle through the fog, but the floating particles closed seamlessly behind the blade.

Alyce ducked the blind swing and darted in low. She thrust her flag spear upward with both hands. The djinn-man screamed, and his demon's etheric energy stained the cloud with sparks of yellow lighting. The *reven* around Alyce's neck shimmered violet as if in answer, and she jammed the spear deeper until scarlet streamed through the white fog.

Sid eyed the amplitude differences between the djinni's lightning and the teshuva's twinkle. Alyce's demon just didn't have the power to match, overcome, and absorb the other demon, so she wouldn't be able to kill the djinn-man. She'd at best made him unholy pissed.

The last spray of powder cleared the nozzle, and the extinguisher sputtered out in his hands. The sickle came swinging down through the thinning fog, on a collision course with Alyce's exposed spine.

Sid leapt forward, choking on the hanging particles. "Sera! Archer!" He thrust the empty cylinder ahead of him.

The sickle clanged into the metal and sliced halfway through. As the remaining gas in the extinguisher whistled out, the djinn-man loomed from the cloud, his eyes flaming yellow. Alyce's spear had pierced below his rib cage and emerged in a wreck behind his collarbone. His hiss of rage was even more demonic with the bloody spittle that dribbled from the corner of his mouth.

He hauled on the sickle, but the blade was trapped by the jagged gash in the canister. Sid clutched the extinguisher, muscles locked against the djinn-man's strength.

"Out of the way!" Fane lunged toward them. With his sword arced high over his head, his white shirt drew taut, revealing spatters of crimson and no corresponding holes.

The djinn-man keened, an inhuman sound, and the yellow afterimage of his djinni hovered in a funnel around him as if seeking to escape. In the demon's distraction, his wounds pulsed fresh blood.

Sid heaved the fire extinguisher, so hard the stitches in his shoulder popped audibly. But the djinn-man staggered, and Sid tackled Alyce, both of them falling to their knees just as Fane's sword swooped by them.

The blow missed them all by a hand span.

And still the djinn-man shrieked across multiple octaves. He staggered back, reaching not for the spear through his torso nor to ward off Fane's second X-marks-the-spot swing. Instead, the djinn-man raked his fingers through the fleeing miasma of his demon.

He'd have had more luck catching smog out of a tailpipe. The djinni tore itself free from the man. For a heartbeat, the two were superimposed.

Fane thrust once more, and this time the blow pierced both demon and man.

Another screech, unfettered by the human throat, ripped through the church. Alyce cried out and tucked against Sid's chest as the shock wave of ether blasted past them. He held her tight, wishing he could make himself bigger by force of will to cover every millimeter of her. Whatever force destroyed the djinni, he couldn't risk letting the backlash touch her.

The intruder, human again without his demon, sagged on the point of Fane's sword. The faintest line scored the warden's forehead between his eyes as he yanked his weapon free.

Sid pulled himself to his feet, hauling Alyce behind him, to finally do as Nanette had suggested and get the hell away.

The djinn-men had obviously come to the same conclusion. Two lay incapacitated on the floor at Archer's feet, and Fane's hallowed sword swept hungrily through them in twinned screams. But the other four pounded toward the door.

The one in the rear paused to slam the butt of his trident against the mosaic in the doorway. The blue and gold tiles fountained around him.

"Next time," he shouted.

He and his brethren vanished, leaving the low sun to shine through the broken door across the devastation.

Archer pursued but skidded to a halt amidst scattered glass and tiles, his cursing drowned out by the squeal of tires. "Next time?" He whirled his bloody-edged axe at the nearest innocent wall, but he hauled up short when Sera snapped his name.

Nanette crept from the hallway where she'd taken shelter. "Mr. Fane? Cyril? Are you hurt?"

From his hunched stance over his sword, Fane straightened abruptly. "They didn't touch me." His glance at the talyan was scathing. "You demon-ridden are fine, of course."

Sid touched Alyce's trembling shoulder and clenched his jaw to keep from reminding the warden that beneath their demonic overlays, the talyan were as fragile as any of them. "What the hell was that about?"

Sera toed the withering corpse nearest her. Without djinni energy to hold the years since possession at bay, time was rapidly reducing flesh to bone and bone to brittle shards. The bloodstains had already turned to dust. "They've never come at us before."

Sickle-man's body caved in with a soft, stinking sigh. Fane's lip curled in disgust. "Have you forgotten Corvus Valerius already?"

"He was alone," Sid pointed out. "And two thousand years of possession had made him insane. This"—he spread his fingers at the corpses—"was calculated."

Archer bumped the axe restlessly against his shoulder as he returned to their little circle. "Not so special. We've seen feralis packs ever since that damn Bookie weakened the Veil and brought through the demon that possessed Sera."

Sera rolled her eyes at Sid. "I tell you, chick talyan and nosy Bookkeepers really put a hitch in the league get-along."

Archer tangled his fingers in the chain around her neck and reeled her closer. The stone in his ring reflected the same coruscating whorls as the pendant at the end of the chain. "You know I'd go through hell for you, love. Because I *have* gone through hell for you." As if having her close made the axe redundant, he collapsed the sheaved blades and tucked the weapon into the fold of his coat. "The horde gathering is old news. Corvus even kept his own collections of lesser tenebrae."

"We're not talking about the lesser demons," Nanette pointed out. "Corvus, by himself, opened a doorway into hell. Imagine all of them against us. That hasn't happened since the First Battle."

Out on the freeway, an ambulance wailed, on its way to or from a siren-worthy accident. Though its haste implied there was still hope for someone, somewhere, by the time the sound reached them, the timbre had shifted, like waves through distorted glass, with overtones of malignancy.

Alyce whispered, "What was the First Battle?"

"When the traitors were tossed out of the divine realm," Fane said. "When hell was born."

"Oh. That's bad."

Talyan and angel-touched looked at her disbelievingly. She ducked a little farther behind Sid.

He gave a decisive nod. "It *is* bad. By definition, the djinn don't gather for good."

"It's been to our advantage that evil hasn't played nice with others," Fane said. "Even other evils. If that's changing . . ."

"That's bad," Nanette and Alyce chorused.

"As bad as the stench in here," Fane agreed. "How convenient I have body bags in my van."

"Certain advantages to owning a disaster restoration business," Archer muttered.

As they headed down the hall toward the back exit, Sera peered into the darkened rooms. "What could they have wanted?" She cast an apologetic glance at Nanette. "There's just not much here except you. And an intermittent healing touch isn't much use to a demon-possessed immortal."

Archer snorted. "Maybe they wanted a flaming sword of their very own."

At the back door, Fane held up one hand, stopping them all in their tracks. "Speaking of swords. Just in case . . ."

Sid tightened his fists as Archer, Sera, and Fane all drew steel. Why hadn't he grabbed the djinn-man's sickle? Other than because he'd be worse than useless with it, of course.

Nanette fished in the front pocket of her jumper. "Daniel makes me lock up when I'm here alone. Here's the key—"

Archer booted the door hard enough to bash anyone on the other side, and the three armed warriors fanned out. Alyce crept after them, and Sid paced right beside her.

The parking lot spread in front of them, cold and gray in the building's shadow. A white van stenciled LAST CALL CLEANING was pulled up near the door. Just beyond was a green sedan in the only other occupied space.

The driver side door was open, and a man's knees stuck from the car, his dress shoes flat on the ground, as if he'd started to get out and then sat back again. A dozen sunflowers lay scattered across the pavement, bright yellow petals half-submerged in a spreading pool of blood.

Nanette screamed and bolted through the door. Alyce grabbed the denim straps of her jumper. The devil inside her did not rouse, silent in the face of the inevitable, and she grappled with the other woman's distraught strength.

Nanette twisted against Alyce's hold. "Daniel! No!"

"Sidney, help me," Alyce gasped.

Together, they held Nanette back while the other two talyan and Fane ran for the car. All three halted short of the vehicle, faces set in identical stark lines, and Alyce's heart withered.

Her fingers slipped loose. Sidney held on for another moment until he met her gaze. She gave him a small shake of her head.

Nanette wrenched away from them and dashed to the car. Fane caught her before she slipped in the blood. Her cry wavered and cracked as she reached out to the figure slumped down across the seat.

Alyce turned her face away, concentrating on Archer's slow prowl around the parking lot. His fixed glare promised annihilation. Would she ever have that kind of power?

She waited until he ended his loop beside Sidney. "No chance?"

The big talya shook his head. "Across the throat, deep. No sound, no struggle, no chance."

Sidney jerked his chin at the van. "They slashed the tires too, marauding through, and he was just one more thing in the way."

"We killed them too easily," Archer snarled.

"It was not that easy," Alyce reminded him. "And there will be more."

Sidney pulled off his spectacles and pinched the bridge of his nose. "If only we'd heard something."

"We were too busy sparring with Fane." The axe handle creaked under Archer's violet-knuckled grip.

Even without a devil's hearing, the warden, pacing toward them, must have heard the bitter accusation, but Fane didn't protest.

"We have to call the police," he said. "Daniel's death can't go unreported, but we have all the evidence we need of a robbery gone wrong."

"Except they didn't take anything," Sidney murmured. "Just a life."

Fane glanced back at Nanette, tucked under Sera's arm. "I forbid her from seeing you, but she said the league could be our salvation." His lips curled in a sneer. "She couldn't have been more wrong. Get out, and take the bones with you."

"Don't leave her alone," Alyce said softly. "There is more than one kind of verge."

Fane gave her a vicious look that set her back a step. "If only you demons had stayed on your side of it."

Sidney tensed, but Alyce clenched the back of his shirt. "No more fighting."

Sera paused beside them, her hazel eyes bleak.

Nanette listed against her, as pale as if her blood had drained with her husband's. "I've healed dozens in this place, but I didn't even know he was out here, dying." Her voice wavered. "You would have known, you talyan. Your souls are bound." She raised her red-rimmed gaze to Alyce. "I didn't even have a chance to help you."

Fane pulled her away from Sera. "Save your healing for yourself, ward."

Nanette shook her head. "That's not how it works." She looked down at her hands, half spread and empty in front of her, as if she didn't know what to do with them. No golden light spiraled between her fingers now.

Sidney retrieved a thick black plastic bag from Fane's van, and the four talyan ghosted past the church office where the warden was saying into the phone, "Yes, I'm sure he's dead. Now send a fucking patrol car."

Alyce tried to focus on their gruesome task, but Nanette's quiet sobs filtered through the unlit church like incense smoke.

Archer, the dead djinn-men's weapons propped over his shoulder, herded them up the instant the last bone was bagged. "Out. Now. I hear a siren."

Sera drove. She pulled over to avoid a black and white car flashing its malice-red lights, hastening back the way they had come. Alyce looked down at the plastic bag and the shining blades jumbled behind Sidney's legs. She pulled her feet up onto the seat and snugged the hem of her frock around her cold toes.

She traced the hard, squared edges of the buckle that held her strapped to the seat. Under her finger, the invisible internal mechanisms latched together, holding fast. Fane had looked at her as if she were the opposite: ragged edged, dangerous, and ready to fly apart.

And they were right.

Had been right. But now she had seen the place where evil came. She had stood with the other talyan against that evil.

This was why she was still here—to see that nothing set

foot over the verge ever again. Or if it did, that it didn't get far enough to hurt anyone. All the frantic screaming through the years would finally make sense.

She half listened while Archer made a phone call, wrapping up the conversation with, "No question, this is bad."

After, Sidney quizzed Sera about the verge. She explained how a terrible lone djinn-man had used the power of imprisoned souls to rip his own hell-bound spirit from the Veil, tearing a pathway to the tenebraeternum realm of demons.

"Possession has always been a trade-off for demons," Sidney mused. "A demon matched to a vulnerable human soul is free of the tenebraeternum, but some of its powers are muted by human flesh."

Sera tilted her head thoughtfully. "The verge pinpoints a pure demonic source. If the djinn-men start working together against us, they could have the power to reenact the First Battle."

"And make it the Last Battle." Archer's voice dropped to a dire octave.

Alyce shivered at the faint echo of his teshuva. "That would be very bad."

"I would say unimaginably catastrophic," Sidney said, "but very bad will do."

She bumped her knees together restlessly. The whys and hows and how-bads did not matter. She knew what had to happen next. "Take me to your league."

Sidney crossed one arm over his chest and propped his chin on his other fist. "After what just happened, Liam is going to have a lot to deal with. Maybe now isn't the best time for the league to meet you."

"Westerbrook," Sera said with asperity, "the talyan are immortal, but they know better than most that death is always waiting. They're not going to want to wait to meet her."

"Maybe Ecco would disagree," Alyce said.

Sera pursed her lips. "Hard to tell with him sometimes."

"I will say I'm sorry," Alyce promised. "I do not want to be alone anymore." She put her hand over her throat, trying to keep her voice steady. "I don't want to be djinni."

"Oh, hon." Keeping one hand on the wheel, Sera reached back over the seat.

To take Sera's hand, Alyce loosed her death grip on the release button at her side. What a pleasure it was to touch and not draw ichor in black gouts. She smiled at the other woman.

Sidney slouched, and the contents of the bag at his feet clacked with his restive movement. "I don't know."

"It's not up to you," Archer said. "Just take notes."

From the hard clench of Sidney's jaw, Alyce feared he'd launch himself over the seat to get at the talya male. Sera clicked her tongue and faced forward.

When they reached the warehouse neighborhood, the afternoon light was failing, and shadows spread from the alleys as if they'd just been biding their time. Alyce peered up at the five-story warehouse where she'd found Sidney. It sat curb to curb, alone on its block. Its black panes of unlit glass reflected the end of the day without revealing its own secrets.

"At-One headquarters," Sera said. "Stronghold of the Chicago league. Alyce, you'll be our fourth female. At this rate, we'll have a volleyball team by next summer." She shuttled her gaze to Sidney. "You can be Bookkeeper and scorekeeper."

She drove around to the back of the building, pausing to let Archer hop out to open the gate. As they pulled through, the steel wire rattled closed behind them with the same ominous finality as the bones.

Sidney got out and held the car door open for her. "Alyce, if you're not ready . . ."

"I'm finally ready." The heavy metal trash box where

she'd tossed Ecco sat askew. As she shoved it back into place, it screeched across the concrete and loose gravel.

No one commented about the blood on the steps.

As if they crossed some invisible boundary, she felt the prickle of the devil forces down her spine. Welcoming. Terrifying. And she was one of them.

Archer leaned down to put his hand on the rolling door. "Ready?"

She shifted from foot to foot, wishing they'd stop asking, and glanced back at Sidney who pushed his spectacles higher. A closed book would tell her more with its cover. Didn't he want her here?

Too late. Archer yanked up, and the metal slats rolled back with a hollow roar. A scent, bright and sharp as lightning, spilled out over them.

Inside, the talyan waited.

Sidney stepped forward, his body half in front of hers. "Alyce, this is Liam Niall. He leads the Chicago talyan."

Liam Niall was dark-haired like Archer. When he inclined his head, the shaggy locks revealed the black devil mark at his temple.

Sidney continued. "And Jilly, his mate."

Alyce looked away from the Asian woman, only a little taller than herself. "His mate?"

A third taller woman swept back the wild tangle of her sandy hair. "Bookkeeper's got it wrong; he's her mate." She put her hand on her outthrust hip.

The one-armed man Alyce recognized from her first encounter with Sidney hooked the woman's elbow. "They are each other's."

"Nim and Jonah," Sidney said. Together, the two were magnificent, all tawny beauty and dangerous eyes. "Alyce, Nim was possessed just this August."

"Thank God I'm not the new girl anymore," Nim said.

"God did not do this to me," Alyce said.

Nim nudged her mate in the ribs. "I think she's one of yours, lover."

Jonah's smile matched the simple curve of his hook. "Alyce, if ever there was a place for God's grace, it is here."

She shook her head. "My place is slaying devils."

Nim smiled with all shiny teeth. "Yeah, she's one of us."

Sidney jostled Alyce's hand, recapturing her attention. "Archer and Sera, Liam and Jilly, and Jonah and Nim are *symballein*. That means the unique signatures of their perpetual idiopathic forces—their souls—are so closely aligned that they are essentially two halves of a whole."

"Which means he can keep up when I dance," Nim said.

"Means he's strong enough to stand up to me," Jilly said, straightening her spine until her spiky hair barely reached Liam's shoulder. He grinned down at her.

"He loves me," Sera murmured. The ring on Archer's finger winked as he wrapped his arm around her.

Alyce tried to breathe around the knot in her throat. They had found each other despite the shadows that lurked in their eyes and despite the devils that lurked under their skin.

Sidney turned her to face the rest of the room.

It was a roomful of talya males, all of them adorned in black, with big hands and piercing eyes. All without smiles. All without mates.

"This is Haji, the league's tracker, and Baird. Over there is Lev, and beside him Luka. Then Pitch, Amiri, and Gavril. Gavril has bare-handed techniques you might appreciate, Alyce. Against the far wall . . ."

The names blurred in her head into a fog of glimmering eyes shot through with violet sparks. Around them, the air twisted with the edgy power of their teshuva.

"I came here to kill devils," she blurted. "Nothing else."

"Don't worry about the killing." Ecco limped to the front of the line. "That's a given."

Sidney took another step forward until his broad shoulders were silhouetted against Ecco's dark bulk. "Ecco, Alyce was worried she had hurt you."

"She did." Ecco glared behind him when somebody snickered.

Alyce took a breath and edged up beside Sidney. "I am relieved it was not lasting harm."

The hulking talya's gaze lightened with the gleam of the devil as he turned back to her. "It might still be."

This conversation was fraught with undercurrents that plucked at the hairs of her nape. Her throat burned at the line of her collar where the black wheal of the devil warned her of danger.

As if she needed any warning.

Sidney sighed. "And here I thought unrepentant demons were bad."

CHAPTER 8

Sid sat in the folding chair beside Liam's desk, the thick legal pad in his lap bent nearly double under his fist. It was just as well Bookkeepers were taught to avoid exposing off-the-shelf electronics to amped-up talyan; otherwise he'd have cracked in half a thousand pounds' worth of fancy tablet PC.

"Pick a crisis, any crisis." Liam hunched over his desk, his thumb and first two fingers in a stiff tripod over the *reven* at his temple. "If the city's djinn-men are amassing somewhere, presumably they'll have to come up with a secret handshake before they call to order and come to massacre us in revenge. So I'll deal with Alyce first, since she's closest to burning a hole through my league."

The cardboard under Sid's fist collapsed. "She's not—"

"She needs to be bonded, now, if not sooner," Liam said over his objection. "Did you smell the ozone in that room? Or maybe that was brimstone, and they've forgotten they're supposed to fight for good."

Pacing behind him, Jilly scoffed. "That was testosterone."

"Worse than brimstone." Archer tossed a glance at Sid from his careless lean in the far corner. "This is a dangerous experiment you've begun. We balance on the edge between good and evil, and little Alyce is not a steadying influence."

Sid stared back at him without flinching. "All eight stone of her will drag us to our doom, undoubtedly."

"She got you out of your tweeds. That must be halfway to doom for a Bookkeeper." Archer's gaze weighed heavier than Alyce soaking wet. "Speaking of which, you might want to check that wound. You're leaking."

Reflexively, Sid touched his shoulder. The gauze pad was still in place, but it squished wetly under his fingers, and a fresh bloom of crimson brightened the oxidized stains on the front of his shirt.

A reminder that tweed *was* better; it was more absorbent, and the patterns hid all sorts of transgressions.

Sera perched on the edge of the guest chair across from Liam. She'd tried to call Fane, with no answer, and she'd twisted her tension into the cherry red coat over her lap. "Alyce might not make our lives easier, but possession isn't a choice. Not a conscious one, anyway. We can't blame Westerbrook for her sudden appearance."

Sid gave her a flat look. Was that supposed to be a vote of confidence? As if he *might* have summoned a teshuva if he'd gotten around to it?

Yet Bookie had done exactly that, and Sera's possession was the result. Sid tossed the crumpled legal pad onto Liam's desk. He wasn't a fucking stenographer.

He was supposed to be, of course. But never had the Bookkeepers' untouchable tenets of detached observation grated so close to the bone. The creed had nearly destroyed him—twice. This time he wasn't the one at risk; yet his heart beat harder with the urgency of his fear. "Alyce isn't a project or a problem or a possessed paramour."

The first two weren't entirely true—a smirching of Bookkeeper integrity—and the last . . . The last pierced him like a sharpened pencil lead.

All other extant female talyan were bound in *symballein* pairs, but Alyce had survived this long alone. She was special; he already knew that; so maybe she didn't need a talya mate matched to her soul. Almost every male talyan ran solo, and other than being brutal, raging, pitiless bastards, they seemed fine with their solitude.

Caught on the point of the thought, he was forced to observe how unworthy and wrong it was. Alyce had been alone long enough. Just because he wanted . . .

Hell, he'd watched without a word as Maureen walked away, taking with her his last link to a world where monsters were mere abstractions. But she'd deserved a man devoted to her, who hadn't already promised himself elsewhere, and her life had been at stake, if not her eternal soul. Hadn't that lesson taught him anything about keeping his wants out of his work, out of his life?

He focused with more effort than should have been needed, suddenly glad Jonah had volunteered to give Alyce a tour of the sanctuary. She would have read the riot of emotions on his face and known him for a crueler bastard than any talya.

He settled on simple fact: "This shouldn't be a problem. The leagues have always had to integrate raw recruits."

"Not erratic rogues," Liam countered. "Not females coming out of nowhere. And never so many so often." He leaned back to stare up at Jilly looming over him. "Sorry, Chan, but you almost broke me."

She pressed a smacking kiss to his forehead. "I love you too."

He straightened to look at Sid. "Integration is grueling, which you Bookkeepers don't appreciate, because you're around for only one or two virgin possessions a decade."

"Because we die of old age. How lazy." Sid refused to

think of his father back in London. He didn't need to consult the catalog of what serving as Bookkeeper for a talyan league took from someone.

"Holding the demon in balance is hard," the league leader said, "but holding the league together against these upheavals is worse."

Jilly brushed her hand down the side of his face where his *reven* flared. "We're here. I'm here."

Liam captured her fingers. "Which is why *I* am still here." He averted his gaze from Sid. "You know about rogues."

Sid nodded slowly at the nonquestion. "I've read about long-possessed talyan who lost equilibrium with their te-shuva. And newly possessed who never found it."

"Have you seen it happen?"

Sid noticed Sera and Jilly were watching the talya men with his same reluctant fascination. "I've read about it," he repeated.

"Not the same." Archer slouched against the wall, but the stark lines of his face gave lie to his relaxed stance. "They turn against everything, with no distinction between human or tenebrae, possessed or pure-souled, good or evil. Just . . . carnage."

"That is not Alyce," Sid said.

Liam lifted one eyebrow. "She ripped apart two ferales, spitted a djinn-man, and almost kicked your head off."

Sid resisted the urge to touch his forehead. He'd forgotten about the bruise when she pushed him away from the attack in the alley. "My head is hard enough to take it."

"And she Dumpstered Ecco," Liam continued.

"Archer thought that was funny." Sid wished he didn't sound quite so much like a schoolboy sharing excuses.

Liam glanced at Archer reproachfully.

Archer shrugged. "It was funny."

"How much more must this league take?" Liam pushed back in his chair, hands spread wide across his desk as if he had to hold it in place. "Last year, we lost good fighters—

good men, emphasis on good—against Corvus Valerius. Our three female talyan bring their own powerful energy, but as someone standing on a nuclear bomb might tell you, power is a frightening thing."

Jilly patted his cheek. "Gee, thanks."

Liam kissed her knuckles. "I have to wonder—is Alyce the stray neutron that starts the fatal chain reaction?"

The silence dug deep in a way only four demon-possessed warriors contemplating fatalities could dig.

Sid's hackles ruffled between unease and anger. The agitation propelled him to his feet. "If she's going to explode, I'd better get a front row seat so I can take good notes."

He stalked out of the room, wondering what whispers he'd hear following him if he had demon-amplified hearing.

Damn, but since when were the Chicago talyan sticklers for propriety? London had been thinking they were all practically rogue themselves. Couldn't they see her for the unique opportunity she was?

The warehouse echoed his footsteps back at him. The talyan had the quiet tread of most predators, but the halls were unnaturally still even for them. Where had everyone gone? Run off to hide from the freakish newcomer? Poor Alyce.

He poked his head into a few empty rooms, until a muted hooting drew him up the back stairs. The warehouse—once an architectural salvage business, a mundane front and money-laundering operation for the league until it became one of their last resources thanks to the embezzling Bookie— still kept an upper floor of antiques and junk. He hurried his steps. Maybe being surrounded by the old pieces, assisted by a few pertinent queries, would loosen Alyce's memory.

He took the last stairs two at a time and popped through the open door.

Just as an airborne red-and-cream-striped Louis XVI chair rocketed toward his head.

He ducked, and the chair exploded against the wall behind him in a stinging shower of splinters and horsehair stuffing. "Bloody hell!"

"Sidney?"

He straightened as Alyce materialized from between the shadowy towers of old furniture. "My God, Alyce, what's happened? Where's Jonah? Where's Nim?"

She hefted a counterpart to the destroyed chair in one hand, as if the carved oak weighed nothing. "Nim is hiding. Jonah went downstairs to find a hand."

"A what?"

Another missile blasted toward them. Was that a vase? Oh God, was it a Ming?

"Sidney, get down." Alyce swung the chair, and the vase—please let it be a reproduction—vaporized on impact in a cloud of white and blue dust.

While Liam and the others had distracted him, the rest of the talyan were trying to kill her!

At the far end of the darkened aisle, an ominous hulking form passed, clearly planning to sneak up behind them.

Sid bolted across the open foyer toward Alyce and grabbed her arm. "Come on—we have to get out of here."

"We just started."

"And I'm trying to stop them from ending it."

She frowned at him, her feet planted against his tug. "But I am winning."

"Only because you're still standing."

"I don't have to knock them down. I get points if I hit them and they can't hit me."

"Hit you? Why—?"

The whistle of another incoming vase silenced him.

Well, it was not so much the vase as the impact of Alyce's arm around his middle as she jerked him out of the way. The vase shattered out on the stairs.

He clamped one hand to his specs as she dragged him toward a sheltering maze of armoires. "I don't think this is a good game for you," she said.

"A game?" His yelp of outrage turned into a real shout as he tripped over the remains of a midcentury end table missing one of its legs. Probably used in a giggle-inducing round of stake-a-Bookkeeper. "Who's out there?"

"All of them." Alyce peered around the corner of one of the ceiling-high industrial shelves that held a tangle of chandeliers. Miles of chains and wires and hundreds of lampshades littered the shelves. "Except Jonah. He said he's not a lefty."

"Who's on your team?"

She grabbed a 1970s-era fixture and began unscrewing the globe. The frosted glass reflected the twinkling *reven* around her neck. "Now? You are."

His pulse beat heavy in his ears, drowning out anyone who might be sneaking up on them. Had she misread their murderous intent? Or was it really a game? If so, it was a fucking murderous game.

Although maybe not to an immortal hunter.

He had grown up knowing the world teemed with monsters his schoolmates forgot about once they left their picture books behind. And yet he'd never felt so alone.

Alyce watched him a moment, then held out the glass ball. "Aim for where they will be, not where they are. They are faster than the devils on the street."

The glass slipped against his damp palm. "How do I know where they *will* be?"

"They'll be coming for me."

"Alyce," he hissed.

But she had already slipped from behind the cover of the shelves.

There wasn't much floor space where she stepped out, just a haphazard jumble of tables, some of them stacked on top of each other, some of them turned top to top so the legs stuck up in a veritable woodland of potential impalements. Alyce slipped between them, her powder blue dress a ghostly blur in the darkness.

A darker form detached itself from the shadows beyond the chairs, on the other side of an upended Provençal-style butcher block kitchen table. Unless she could bend her vision around right angles, no way would Alyce see the talya from her position before he sneaked close enough to tag her.

Maybe that would end this insane game.

Or was it more than a game? A twisted talya courtship ritual, perhaps? A primitive proving of strength, speed, and fearlessness.

What a fascinating thought.

And even as his brain was polishing its spectacles and harrumphing thoughtfully, his arm drew back, muscles tensed until the feralis wound screamed. Knowing he was going to be housemates with American males, he'd watched a recording of baseball highlights on the transatlantic flight.

Those steroid-bulked athletes had nothing on his sudden fury.

Mated talya bond, indeed. Alyce was not a prize for the taking.

He hurled the lamp globe across the darkness.

Miraculously, the globe avoided every table leg and struck the skulking talya. The sound of breaking glass was loud in the stillness, and Alyce dropped to a crouch.

"You're out, Pitch," came a cry from above.

Barely visible in the red emergency exit lighting, Nim perched on the highest shelf, one hand braced on the heavy ceiling beam. She cut her stiff-held fingers across her throat.

On the ground, the male talya, Pitch, grumbled. "She didn't tag me out. Westerbrook did."

"How embarrassing," Nim said cheerfully. "Good thing he wasn't a salambe. Better luck next time, lover boy."

Alyce hurried back to him and held out another globe. "Good throw. Only seven left."

Sid clenched his teeth. How many had pitted themselves against her? The monsters.

But he refused to reach for the weapon. He wasn't part of this game. Neither, though, could he in good conscience let it continue. "Someone's going to get hurt."

Nim clambered halfway down the shelves, then jumped. She landed in a lithe crouch. "That was kind of the point."

"To hurt Alyce?"

"Stupid Bookkeeper. Of course not. To see who was willing to hurt for her."

"That's . . ." He groped for his suddenly missing words.

"Fucked up?" Nim supplied. "Hmm. It is, kind of." She ducked back into the shadows.

"Wait," Sid called to her. Pitch's glare prickled between his shoulder blades. He ignored the talya until he stalked off. "Alyce, we shouldn't—"

She brushed his arm. "This isn't like when we fought the djinn-man, you and I." Her earnest gaze met his, as hesitant as her fingers against his flesh. "This is for fun. No one gets hurt." A crash and a muffled shout from somewhere deeper among the salvaged remains made him realize the game had continued, with the male talyan eliminating one another. Alyce grinned at him. "At least not hurt for long."

Her sudden transformation from serious to prom-giddy made his breath catch. God, he'd forgotten she was still a young woman. Actually, she was not *just* a young woman, but in many of the ways that mattered, she'd been both cheated of and trapped by what she'd been at the moment of her possession. And yet she'd fought and killed some of the most formidable incarnations of evil walking their world. If the talyan needed to take the edge off the harsh realities of their existence with a fractionally less safe version of school yard dodgeball hide-and-seek, who was he to stop them?

Presupposing he *could* stop them.

He took Alyce's hand. "I'll try not to slow you down."

"I limp," she reminded him.

Whoever had triumphed in that other exchange would

be stalking them now, with the advantage of superior strength and quickness, sharper eyesight and hearing, and a demon's killer instincts.

They ducked into a row of shoulder-high racks strewn with odds and ends. Sid grabbed a fist-sized granite frog that would make a worthy missile and a . . . shite, the lawn gnome was plastic. But Alyce hadn't slowed, so he hastened after her.

There. At the end of the row was a bank of smudged windows, charcoal gray from the October sky beyond. A talya-sized figure in black flitted past. Alyce breathed out softly and cocked her arm, her glitter-painted Christmas wreath–cum–ninja shuriken throwing star at the ready.

Sid whispered her name—or didn't whisper, really, but more thought it and laid his tongue over the syllables, but she glanced toward him nonetheless. He tilted his head at the gnome in his hand and mimed lobbing it grenade-style into the next aisle, with a sweep of his other hand indicating the probable path of the investigating talya. She nodded and ghosted across the open aisle, staying in her row instead of crossing to the next row over with a shot at the talya.

She faded just a few steps into the shadows, lingering near the open aisle. Sid tossed the gnome over the top of the shelves, and the hollow plastic thunked noisily on the wooden floor.

Sure enough, the talya charged down his own row, parallel to Alyce. Without a glance at Sid, he crossed the aisle, fixated like a pouncing cat.

Maybe the talyan needed a movie night or two. Honestly, didn't everybody know that trick?

Alyce bounded out of her hiding spot and nailed the talya in the backside. The wreath burst apart in a shower of fake bay leaves and silver glitter.

"Baird, out," Nim called from another high perch. "Since when do you not watch your back, sparkle boy?"

"I was distracted, damn it." The talya brushed at the seat of his jeans and grimaced at the glitter on his palm. "Well, could've been noodle art."

Sid straightened, popping above the shelves where Baird could see him. "Yeah, that nickname would be worse."

The talya shot him the middle finger and a big grin full of white teeth. "Al dente, asshole."

From the corner of his eye, back the way they had come, Sid glimpsed a dark shape. Nim and Baird were trading another gleeful insult. Alyce stood halfway into the open aisle, her baby blue housedress much the worse for wear but still a pale gleaming target. She watched the byplay with her head cocked and that delighted little smile curving her lips.

Before he could call her name—whispered, shouted, or anything else—the bombardment was inbound.

As kitchen sinks went, it wasn't big—more prep-sink-sized. It was still going to hurt like a son of a bitch.

As heroic dives went, his was kind of prep-sized too. But he just needed to get between Alyce and whichever talya was sneaking up on her in the hopes of winning—or pinning—her heart.

He was still in midair when the sink smashed into his shoulder—the feralis-bitten one, of course.

Alyce spun toward him in a pale blue blur. Before his knee crashed into the floorboards, her arms were already reaching out to him, slowing his descent.

She saved his skull, but the point of his shoulder rebounded off the floor. The gray numbness was obliterated in a blinding white wave of pain like newsprint in a gasoline flame.

He cursed, not quite as loud as Alyce with her double-octave growl of outrage.

"What the hell, Pitch," Nim snapped as she jumped down to the floor. "You're out of the Alyce game."

"I wasn't aiming at her."

Sid righted himself, his good hand braced on the floor. Always nice to know he'd thrown himself into the line of fire for nothing.

Baird shook his head. "Westerbrook isn't a valid target."

"Not anymore," Pitch said. "C'mon—I didn't use the claw-foot tub."

Pushing Alyce's hand away, Sid drew himself to his feet. He refused to steady himself on the nearest shelf, and for a wonder his spectacles had stayed on. "That's it. This game is over."

Jonah hurried down the aisle toward them. A multi-pronged hook was attached to his stump in place of his right hand. "Why's everybody standing around? She didn't get everybody out already, did she?" He looked at Nim. "Do I owe you that fifty bucks?"

Nim shook her head. "Westerbrook called a halt. I think we shocked him with our childish behavior."

Jonah turned a glower on Sid. "We're not allowed a little fun?" Nim wrapped her fingers around his forearm, just above the cuff where the hook connected, becoming part of him. In the shadows of forgotten furniture, a half-dozen massive shapes converged, talya blackness broken only by heat-lightning flares of violet. They were the remaining hopeful suitors.

Alyce gripped a Christmas icicle ornament like a knife in her hand.

Sid returned Jonah's glower. "I guess my dictionary shows a different definition of fun. Bowling, for example."

"Well, you're playing in our world now," someone said.

Sid didn't bother identifying the speaker, though he thought it was Lev, the lanky redheaded talya—or maybe Amiri, the tall Maori. Didn't matter. They obviously all felt the same way.

And they were right. The only reason he'd stopped that sink from hitting Alyce was because it had been aimed at him. He'd just been in the way. He wasn't a talya contender any more than he was still suitable for . . . anything besides what he was, a bloody borrowed Bookkeeper.

He held himself as if someone had duct-taped his spine to a curtain rod, but it felt more like glass. "Sorry to spoil your fun. But I came up here to get Alyce. I want a baseline reading on her metaphysiology before you break her."

Nim gave him a steady stare. "She's strong." Her words sounded like a warning, one he wouldn't honor with a response.

He took the icicle from Alyce's hand and lobbed it to Jonah. Nim caught it. "It's getting dark out. You can go entertain yourself with the horde."

Alyce gave him a reproving look. "That is not a game."

The other talyan didn't chime in to agree, but the combined weight of their stares as the violet lights guttered out chipped at the stiffness of his stance. As twisted as his life had been, at least he *had* a life. The talyan had an eternity of death and destruction for the good of a people who would never know it. And he, who did know better, was flipping them shit.

He nodded once. "Of course, Alyce. And you'll be out with them just as soon as I clear you for service."

"We do want what is best for her, Bookkeeper," Jonah said softly. "Honing ourselves in the fight against evil is all we have." He reached for Nim with the hand he had left. "Well, that and each other."

It was such a simple touch; yet Sid's face heated at the contact. The other talyan melted away, as if they too were disturbed by the flare of energy. Sid's Bookkeeper brain wished he'd had them both rigged to an etheric resonance sequencer to capture that moment—maybe next time.

Without another word—really, what could he say?—he led Alyce out of the antiques graveyard, down five flights of stairs to the basement. His steps clanked wearily on the metal grate of the stairs. Alyce with her bare feet might as well have been a ghost.

"Thank you for trying to protect me," she said softly.

"You didn't need it." A flush of embarrassment heated his skin. Although considering the state of his shoulder, maybe that was just trickling blood.

"If I had, though, you were right there. Just as you were right there when the devil-man tried to stab me. Without you, I would be dead."

The memory of Nanette's scream echoed in his head, and he swayed a little. He paused with one hand on the rail.

Alyce flitted around to the step below him, peering up worriedly. "You are hurt."

"Not as bad as some others." He went around her and took a step down, but he stopped again when she touched his shoulder from behind.

The tentative contact should have been too light to register through the bone-deep ache, but his skin shivered at her nearness. He tightened every muscle, ignoring the way the ache intensified, to prevent himself from turning to face her.

"You aren't talya," she said. "You don't have to pretend. Not with me, not when they aren't around."

Her statement—not talya—shouldn't have stung. It was only the truth. But how could he explain to her that meant he had to pretend even harder? He didn't have the advantages of immortality or running rogue to cushion the blows.

That would explain his weakness when he just closed his eyes while she slipped her hands around his neck to undo the top buttons of his shirt.

From her perch on the step behind him, she slipped the oxford down from his shoulder. "Oh, Sidney. Why didn't you say anything?"

He bit down on a curse when she eased back the gauze pad. At least the fresh blood kept it from sticking. "Which time?"

"I should not have played that stupid game."

At the remorse in her voice, he couldn't stop himself

from turning to her. He pulled the shirt back into place, hiding the evidence of his human frailty. Except the gory stain still gave him away. "You were having fun. I was the one out of place." •

She shook her head, hard enough to make the dark locks of her hair dance around her face. "We were a good team."

He took the bandage from her. "Nanette might not agree."

She stilled. "Could we have saved him?"

"If we'd known the djinn-men were casing the joint, maybe. If we'd known Daniel was outside. If we knew where every act of evil was about to happen . . ." He couldn't muster a shrug. "Bookkeepers try to keep track of everything, but we're not that good."

"Not good then," she echoed. "But repentant."

"That is the theory." Leaving the open buttons of his shirt flapping, he continued their descent.

Familiarizing himself with the lab had been his first task when he'd arrived in Chicago. All leagues had the same basics, but each Bookkeeper customized to local needs. And a certain amount of intradisciplinary egotism meant that sometimes the sharing of ideas, techniques, and hardware improvements between Bookkeepers was not as robust as might otherwise have been ideal for the salvation of humanity.

But then, the battle between good and evil had been going on a very long time. No one had quite understood the need for a more concerted effort.

As interim Bookkeeper, Sera had kept sketchy notes of the changes the Chicago league had experienced. But she had been playing catch-up with the history and traditions even a novice Bookkeeper would have known.

Plus, her handwriting was terrible. Obviously she had her background in the medical fields. And now they'd been tossed the wrinkle of more overt djinn activity.

Point being, he had plenty to keep him busy; he could have waited to bring Alyce down here. He didn't have the lab organized to his specifications. He couldn't even log in to the league network since Archer had hacked the computers to trace Bookie's embezzling.

But he couldn't leave Alyce to the untender mercies of her would-be lovers.

Not yet. She didn't know herself. How could she be expected to choose among them?

"You are angry," she said.

He hadn't flipped on the lights. He composed his features before he did, then tossed the bloody gauze in the trash. "I'm not angry."

"Your teeth are grinding."

He pushed aside a stack of file folders on an exam table. "I'm tired, and my shoulder feels worse than when the feralis was chewing on it."

"Which is why you have dark circles under your eyes and you are holding your elbow close to your side. But you grind your teeth because you are—"

"Fine. I'm angry. Jonah should have known better than to put you in danger." No, he still wasn't being truthful. "*I* should have known better than to leave you with them."

"They wouldn't hurt me. They want me here."

"Well, I want you too. And I found you first." He patted the exam table. "Now, hop up."

Her gaze cooled with guarded distance. "You won't strap me down?"

What had happened with the doctors she'd gone to? Scratch that. He could guess what they'd thought. "No straps. Look, there's blood on your dress. Is it theirs or yours?"

"I think it's yours." She crossed to him and inched her hip up onto the table. "Why do you want me?"

"We need to know more about the female talyan. We need to find out what sparked your reappearance. We need to know what you know."

"I don't know anything," she said.

"Then we'll find out together." He walked to the other side of the table, and she owled her neck to follow his progress. "Just let me . . ." The streak of red across the back of her dress made his teeth grind harder. In the darkness upstairs, he hadn't noticed, but under the lab fluorescents, her skin gleamed white through the slashed fabric and smudges. "See, I was afraid of this."

She craned her neck a little farther. "I can't see. What makes you afraid?"

"That your talya friends play too rough. I thought no one tagged you." Had one of the males staked a *symballein* claim? Liam would be pleased.

Meanwhile, Sid held his breath, waiting for her answer, and each nanosecond stretched into eternity.

But she shook her head. "I jumped from one of the shelves, but my knee twisted. I fell into a piano. Nim said it wouldn't hold a tune anyway. To make it fair, she said I should stay on the ground because the men are too big to hide."

"Oh, and we'd want to be fair." In his relief—though he had no cause to be relieved—he couldn't keep the snide note from his voice.

"Not to the tenebrae," Alyce said. "But to one another."

How quickly she'd become one of them. Sid pushed down a twang of jealousy more sour than any old piano. "The wire cut right through you."

"It is nothing."

"Let's make sure of that." He pulled a crash cart closer to the table, found scissors, and carefully cut down the back of the housedress.

Alyce clutched the front to her chest and stared over her shoulder at him, eyes ringed in white.

He kept his focus on her back and made a scholarly sound of concern. "Yes, just as I feared. It looks like you hit high C."

After a heartbeat, her lips quirked. "I can't sing."

He lifted his gaze. "Really? I would never have guessed. You have a lovely voice."

"No . . ." Her eyes clouded. "I remember. He said I mustn't sing."

"Who said that?"

"My master. I remember."

Sid looked at her naked back, striped bloody where the wire had cut her. What had triggered the memory? "Why do you call him 'master'?"

"That is what he was. I remember his face. But I . . ."

Sid summoned up his American history. He knew Archer had been possessed during the Civil War, but white slavery hadn't been part of that conflict. Domestic servants from that period might have used the same word, though. He'd have to ask the talya male.

He poured hydrogen peroxide onto a square of gauze and wiped at the bloody streaks. Underneath, he found only diagonal red lines in her skin from lower lumbar to midthoracic, already closed. It was like a rejection of his touch, and a reminder that she was, as Nim had warned, talya strong.

But the wounds obviously went deeper than the teshuva could heal.

Though he dried her skin with a fresh pad, she shivered. "Never mind," he said gently as he came back around the table to face her. "It's not that important."

"It was my life, and it's gone."

"I'm here to help you find a new life."

She said nothing as he turned away to jot notes on his clipboard. Rates of wound repair were well documented in Bookkeeper archives, but not for female talyan. It wasn't significant enough for master-level work, but maybe if he took an apprentice . . . Except he wouldn't be here that long.

The scratch of his pen stilled. For a moment there, he'd forgotten this wasn't really his place. When he took over

London, some other Bookkeeper would have tea with Liam, spar with Archer, and continue unraveling the many secrets of the Chicago league—secrets including Alyce.

The pen made a dark blot on the paper as the felt tip bled out his hesitation. The stark proof of his conflicted desires shocked him. He'd given up everything to become London's Bookkeeper after his father; to want something else would make a mockery of those sacrifices. His only goal here was to unravel some puzzle from the Chicago league interesting enough to satisfy the Bookkeeper council of his qualifications. Quickly he finished his scrawl.

Besides, if he finished deciphering Alyce, the next Bookkeeper would have no reason to obsess over her. She'd be just another talya—female, true, and of a rarer vintage than the ones that had come along so far, and no doubt mysterious enough to keep a scholar intrigued for all the decades of his life—but still just another talya.

In fact, he'd put a reference in her chart to just leave her the hell alone. He shoved the clipboard away. His thumb skidded across the page and left a black smear that obliterated his words.

He wrestled down his unwarranted temper and turned to Alyce. The red scores on her back were little more than white lines now. "It might not be all-powerful, but your teshuva knits you right up, just as it should. Which makes me wonder about your knee." He circled around to face her and held his hands over her leg. "May I?"

She nodded, and he folded back the hem of her frock to midthigh. He cupped her right heel in his palm, his other hand behind her knee where he'd noticed the shortening of her stride. Her skin was silky under his touch, even the bony points of her knee and ankle softened by smooth, soft flesh. And she'd knocked him flat in the alley with one blow of that dainty foot—amazing, really.

He found himself lingering over the curves and hastened to explain. "Considering you run around the city barefoot, you have hardly any protective callusing. One downside of the demon's fine detailing work."

He straightened her knee by slow degrees. She sucked in a breath before he'd reached full extension.

He'd felt no distortion of the joint under his fingers, no faint grate of broken bones, no pop of misplaced ligaments. "Where does it hurt?"

"Inside," she said.

He held back an impatient sigh. Bookkeeper training required a certain forbearing temperament, but Alyce was a particularly opaque text. "How long . . ." He reframed the question. "Have you always had the limp?"

Although insignificant reminders of past damage remained even post-possession, the teshuva's virgin ascension should have zeroed out the structural imperfections of her body, like the ultimate drill sergeant perfecting a lone soldier for solitary combat.

She looked up at him, pale blue eyes half-lidded. "I remember. . . ."

He was focused on her, eye to eye, so he saw the moment it happened.

In his apprentice Bookkeeper classes, they'd studied other megavertebrate predators. Anyone working with immortal demon-possessed warriors whose sole mission was to destroy all forms of evil was well advised to learn the finer points of selective eye contact, noninvasive body language, and self-defensive tongue biting.

One of the first warning signs they'd learned was the "death eye."

"You'll recognize it right away," their instructor had said. "It's like looking into the eyes of death."

They'd all snickered at the time.

Sid wasn't laughing now.

Their instructor had explained how mammalian eyeballs were constantly in motion. The involuntary microsaccades supposedly allowed the eyes to refresh and correct their focus. The movements were tiny enough to evade casual observation, but nevertheless caused an imperceptible blurring of the eyes.

But in a moment of intense concentration, the muscles locked. With the tremors halted, the eyes became perfectly, lucidly clear. In a wolf or tiger or other predator, that sudden clarity signaled an imminent attack.

"Like looking down into a deep, dark well," the instructor had said. "At the bottom is the soul. And in the case of the talya—a demon."

Sidney's heart stopped too. He saw Alyce's demon, all right.

And he saw the ravenous verge didn't know the first thing about hunger.

CHAPTER 9

"I remember . . . ," Alyce said. But the memory suddenly blurred in a haze of other images—ferales in pieces; red-eyed malice and salambes shrieking as they fled.

Sidney blanched, and she bit her lip. Disappointing him hurt worse than the scratches on her back. She wanted to tell him, she did, but the memory was smeared away, as if the touch of the cold cloth had sopped it up with her blood.

She lowered her gaze miserably. "I would tell you, but it's all gone." Her voice sounded so plaintive, she didn't even believe herself.

"I'm sure *you* would tell."

She contemplated the odd emphasis he'd placed on the word while he busied himself with his papers again.

He wrote with authority, his strokes as smooth and steady as his hands on her skin. She clutched the front of the torn dress under her chin, and the quickening pulse in her throat banged against her knuckles.

When she'd kissed him before, in his room, he had told her to wait.

She had waited. She had *been* waiting a very long time, though she couldn't say how long exactly. And from what she'd seen in the demon-pierced eyes of the talya males, immortality did not make waiting any easier.

And if she followed that thought, as Sidney would do, she came to the question: What was she waiting for?

Before she could answer, Sidney was back at her side. "I want to get a closer look at your *reven*." When she gave him a quizzical look, he added, "The demon's mark around your neck."

The throb of tension that had seized her twisted from anticipation to something darker. "I do not like it. It's ugly."

"I need to register you in the league archives, and the *reven* can tell us the class and potency of your teshuva, even if we can't get a detailed history." He touched her hands and gave a downward nudge.

Her muscles vacillated between resistance and surrender. She didn't want him to see that part of her—or at least not *just* that part of her.

He rested his hand on her clutched fists, his palm so wide it nearly covered both of hers, but he didn't push again. "The *reven* isn't ugly, Alyce. It's uniquely you."

Unlike her grip, his eyes did not waver. She let him uncover her neck. His gaze, tracing down her skin, made her shiver again.

Her cheeks heated, and her heart pounded in wild beats. "It is the mark of the devil."

"Yes, I said that already." His tone was absentminded.

The acceptance in his imperturbable words loosened her desperate clutch on her dress while he went to a shelf of books and pulled out a particularly thick tome. He flipped through its pages as he returned to her side. "Look—here is our visual dictionary of *reven*."

The big book thudded on the table next to her. "So many."

"Yet so much we still don't know." He ran his finger down one page and flipped to the next and then the next to continue his perusal.

He had big hands, strong hands. She sighed. Big hands for big books—she wasn't big.

As if he'd heard the thought, he stopped to display the penned illustrations. The page looked as if someone had taken an entire goose and dipped it upside down in ink and dashed it across the paper.

"These are depictions of the *reven* of some of the strongest talyan ever to fight." He traced one complex swirl. "The depth and intricacy of the mark echoes the power of the teshuva."

She lifted her chin. "Mine is nothing like that."

He flipped a few more pages, then more and more until the lines petered out. These *reven* were as much like the first as a cup of tap water resembled Lake Michigan wind-whipped to viciousness on a stormy day. "More like this," he agreed.

"Does possession by a weak demon mean I am less damned?" She couldn't keep the bitterness from her voice because, at least to this question, she already knew the answer.

Sidney gave her a chiding look. "Your teshuva may not have the same destructive capabilities as some of its brethren, but the strength of its repentance is no less."

"Will that save me?"

"Save what? Your soul or your life?" He hurried on, as if he didn't want to hear which she meant. "As Nanette noticed, the emanations of a weaker teshuva get disrupted—tangled—in competing energy. When it can't hold its coherence against another signal, it will be altered and lost."

"You think that is what happened to me? I've been lost because my devil isn't strong enough to save me?"

Sidney backed away—giving himself room to think, she

decided—and leaned against the counter across from the exam table. "I think your teshuva is trying very hard to save you. To save you from things you don't want to remember."

She froze. He stiffened too.

Maybe he hadn't been giving himself room to think, but room to escape.

"I do want to remember." She made sure each word came out distinct from the others, lest there be misunderstanding.

"I don't think the teshuva believes you."

"And do you not believe me?"

He marshaled his words with the same care the illustrators of the book had used when laying out their *reven* drawings, in tidy blocks, no matter how messy the depiction within. "I know part of you wants to remember. But which part is you, which part is the demon, which part is the other parts of you?"

"I am not so complicated," she protested.

"We all are. Even me. Part of me wants . . ." He shook his head. "But that doesn't matter."

What did he want? The urge to know prickled through her. This must be how he felt about his many books—to open them up and to know them.

She stared at the capable width of his hands as he thumbed farther through the book. Toward the end, intricate and simple *reven* shared the pages, compared and contrasted.

His finger landed on one. "Ah, you don't have to worry about what your demon wants. But everything else will worry. You have a dread demon."

She tilted her head and squinted at the design, but it seemed too fanciful to match hers.

"Don't believe me?" He repeated her words with a little smile and took another step closer to her, one forefinger on the book, the other at her neckline. Since she was sitting up on the table, her face was even with his and he had to reach up to touch her. "It starts boldest here." His finger was warm at the crook of her neck and shoulder. "Maybe not so dark on you as in the book, but close enough. A sudden burst of energy, like a startled heartbeat." He traced her *reven* forward. "And here it stutters, like a frantic pulse."

Oh, what was her pulse doing? As if he controlled it with his words, her blood throbbed.

His voice lowered—and the throbbing in her body spread lower too—as his finger dipped into the hollow of her throat. "And here it pools and flares. . . ."

"Like what?" she whispered.

"Like . . ."

But words seemed to fail him, so she canted forward and pressed her lips to his.

His touch had not soothed her hurts; instead he had kindled a fever.

And it was good; deliriously good.

The torn gown she'd been holding slipped from her fingers as she reached for him, to bring him closer. He made a noise. Was that supposed to be a protest? She measured the width of his unhurt shoulder with eager pets of her hand, and then he was between her knees, the rough denim of his pants rubbing her bare inner thighs.

She rubbed back, and that was better than good.

"Alyce," he gasped against her mouth.

She threaded her fingers through his hair, because that sounded very much like the start of a protest.

And with his mouth open on that gasp, the wet heat of his tongue and lips was hers.

He groaned, and, like the pictures in his book of each devil matched to its sin, his hand moved to echo hers. With his fingers at the back of her head, he tilted her, just so, and she said, "Oh," to show him she understood and because she could not stop herself.

His tongue played over her lips and the front line of her teeth before dipping deeper. It roused the fever in her until she thought she would die with wanting what he was holding back.

She wrapped her heels behind his thighs and drew him closer. No holding back. She would not forget *this*.

He stumbled into her, one hand braced behind her to steady himself, the other steadied against her—against her naked breast.

He recoiled, hand flinching back as if he'd been burned. And perhaps he had been, given that she felt so hot. "Alyce."

She cursed the weak demon that apparently couldn't tempt him. "Are you afraid of my dread demon?"

"Afraid for you, more like." He grabbed at the crumpled folds of fabric in her lap and tugged the dress upward to cover her.

She refused to hold it in place. He'd been the one to cut it in back, after all. "That makes no sense."

"It would if you knew what you were doing to me."

"You can't hurt me. Nothing leaves a mark. Other than the demon," she added reluctantly. "And that's almost nothing; you said it yourself."

"There are different kinds of hurt. And I didn't say it was nothing." Still holding her dress in place with one hand, he twisted himself loose from her knees and slipped around behind her. He grabbed a tool from the cart and pinched it over the split edges of fabric. With four angry clips, he closed the tear.

"Those staples will hold until we find you something else to wear. Something without blood. Something with underthings."

She narrowed her eyes at his vehemence. "You thought I was in trouble upstairs, and you came to save me even though you could have been hurt."

"You aren't in trouble. You *are* trouble." He turned away from her, raking his fingers through his hair in distress.

When she had done it, she'd left the thick russet locks in

disarray. But his hands smoothed away the evidence of her touch.

Very little in the world showed evidence of her passage. That thought had never bothered her before—or even occurred to her before. She had drifted through the streets in shadows, as unknown and unknowing as the tenebrae.

Now she wanted someone—needed *him*—to acknowledge her existence.

So she slipped off the table, slipped out of her dress— the staples would *not* hold against her—and slipped up behind him in one stealthy flow.

He must have sensed he was being stalked, because he whirled around to face her. But it was too late, and he could catch her only as she moved right into him.

One arm went around his waist to keep him from escaping. One hand went behind his head to bring his kiss down to her. One hand . . . Oh, that was his hand anchoring beneath her bottom to drag her up against his chest.

"Damn it, Alyce." For once, the curse didn't hurt. His growl sent shivers through her as no tenebrae scream ever had.

With Sidney's arms tight around her, for once damnation and the devil seemed very far away.

Whatever slow instruction he might have given her before in the mating of tongues, he apparently expected her to have mastered by now. He bent her back, his mouth fierce and hot.

He didn't fear her. He wasn't running away.

She strained to bring herself closer to him, for even the scant space for their gasping breath was a separation she wouldn't allow. Not even room for thought, much less words.

His big hands framed the width of her ribs, his thumbs pushing up her breasts as he kissed the edge of her jaw, the column of her throat, the point of her collarbone.

The fever raced ahead of his mouth, centering deep in her core, as if lighting the way for his exploration.

She pushed down on his shoulders to urge him lower in case he couldn't follow the signs.

One moment they were chasing desire . . . and the next, cold distance separated them.

Sidney let out a surprised shout as he flew through the air. His arms windmilled, and his flailing legs knocked over the table with a ringing crash. He slammed into the wall. His shirt had slipped awry, and his wounded shoulder left a smear of blood.

Alyce whirled to face the attack.

CHAPTER 10

Sid's skull rang, and the flush of conflicting biochemicals in his bloodstream—lust, shock, pain—left him breathless.

Had he frightened her? Or her demon?

He patted around him until he found his spectacles. With one hinge bent, they sat seriously askew when he propped them on the end of his nose. He barely had time to focus before a black bulk filled his field of vision. Strong fingers wrapped around his throat and helped him to his feet, then lifted him another meter higher than that.

Gagging, he wrapped his hands around the thick wrist and found himself staring into Liam's ferocious purple glare.

"Bookkeeper, your studies go too far."

Despite the murderous intent in the league leader's eyes, Sid directed his attention beyond the talya male. "Alyce, no."

Liam glanced over his shoulder, then returned his gaze to Sid with one lifted eyebrow. "I take it the tonsil exam was mutual."

"Let him go." Alyce poised herself on the balls of her bare feet. It was the rest of her bare self that sent an agonized rush through Sid—that, and the sheen of the ridiculously tiny scalpel in her fist.

The little blade had served well enough to open her torn dress, and she looked fully ready to fillet Liam the same way.

Liam lowered Sid until his toes brushed the floor but did not release him. "Alyce, are you unhurt? Nim said the game upstairs got ... heated. I'm not sure she realized how heated."

Sid made another gagging noise.

Liam set him down flat-footed and stepped aside. "My mistake."

Alyce did not lower the scalpel. "Go away."

Sid bent to brace himself with one hand on his knee and rubbed the back of his head where he'd connected with the wall. "Alyce, please put the knife down. It was a mistake."

Her eyes had flickered violet as she faced Liam. Now she glanced at him, and the icy stillness of the pale blue told him his words had struck her. "A mistake?"

"I didn't mean ..." He hadn't meant the kiss, but now that he thought about it ...

His hesitation made her recoil. Her narrow bared shoulders folded inward to hide the *reven* around her neck.

God, she was so small. The lithe tension of her muscles as she'd strained against him moments ago had made him forget that. She had made him forget pretty much everything, obviously. But under the unforgiving fluorescent lights, without even the dubious protection of her torn housedress and with Liam's dark bulk for contrast, she looked unbearably breakable. No wonder the demon was so zealous in its protection of her.

Dread was worse than fear. Dread encompassed all that hadn't happened but might.

For the first time, Sid felt true affinity for a demon. The

teshuva was trying harder than he was to keep Alyce in one piece. And he was ashamed he was not living up to the moral expectations of an entity that had once stormed the gates of heaven.

He held back a groan as he straightened. He was getting roundly pummeled by all sorts of demons. And he deserved it.

He extended his flattened palm. "Give me the knife, please."

For the space of a blink, he stared into her frozen eyes and saw the demon looking back almost as if it were contemplating stabbing him—for what sin, he wasn't sure.

Alyce handed him the scalpel.

She handed it to him nicely—not as the demon would have, through the center of his palm, if not his heart—and still the breath whooshed out of him.

Despite what he had done to her—well, he hadn't done that much, but despite what he'd *wanted* to do—still she trusted him. The obligation weighed heavily on his shoulders, which were almost twice as wide as hers.

"I'm sorry," he said. To her. To Liam. To the raging erection trapped behind his fly. "It won't happen again."

Liam grunted. "If one of the other talyan had found you manhandling her like that, there'd be hell to pay. And hell does not come cheap around here."

Sid wished the other man hadn't said come.

Alyce made a low noise deep in her throat. The growl wasn't anywhere near as sexy as the moan, but his pulse still ratcheted up in a crazily eager response that ranked danger at the top of some heretofore unimagined list of things that apparently turned him on.

Or maybe it was just because *she* made the noise.

Damn.

She glowered at Liam. "I have lived without you for ... for a long time. I do not need another master."

"The league has archaic traditions," Sid reassured her, "but nothing that barbaric."

Except for the *symballein* bond, of course, uniting male and female talyan through unpredictable and uncontrollable forces they hadn't yet identified. If the link wasn't voluntarily chosen, was that so different from slavery?

But he wasn't here to judge—merely to study. If only he could keep his hands off his primary source.

He bent down in front of Alyce and grabbed the torn housedress, now with a few more holes where the surgical staples had ripped out. His head swam as he stood again, and it was everything he could do not to brace himself—against her.

He took a steadying breath. Even that was fraught with the scent of her—no perfume or lotion or bath wash, but just the simple fragrance of her skin. He wrapped the threadbare dress around her without his fingers roaming a millimeter from their careful course.

She looked up at him—Alyce did, not the demon—and he knew the quelling aspect of Liam's presence had only the faintest power.

Liam crossed his arms in a disapproving stance, gripping his biceps as if he were still imagining Sid's neck. "The storage room down the hall has extra clothing. Get some. Then feed the girl. I've seen more meat on a malice." He spun on his heel and went to the lab door. He looked back. "Move it."

The league leader obviously had more faith than Sid did in a bit of a reality check to break the spell between them. But moving away from her was the first step.

Covering her up was a good second step. Liam left them at the storeroom with a long, significant look at Sid. "I want you up in the kitchen in five minutes."

Alyce didn't watch him leave. She stood passively in the doorway while Sid rummaged across the shelves.

"What size are you?" He waited a moment. "Never mind. Small. Oh good, one of the other women must have insisted on more sizes or we'd never find anything to fit you. Here you go. A couple of each. Not much selection for color, but no holes."

He turned to her, the folds of black fabric wrinkling in his arms as he clutched the clothing to his chest—as if that was what he wanted to hold.

She stared up at him through her lashes. In another woman, the effect might have been flirtatious. On her, the look was more arctic wolf behind a low, dark thicket.

He swallowed. "What I did was inappropriate. I know you aren't ready for . . . for anything like that."

"I have been alone longer than I have been possessed."

The flat chill of her tone belied the churning depths of emotion underneath, in the same way as the frozen scrim of a winter-bound river hid the dangerous undertow. And still, everything in him wanted to step out onto the ice, to reach out a rescuing hand.

But he was a scholar, not a hero—not even a damned hero.

"You aren't alone anymore," he said. "You have the entire league."

She turned away, the white line of her spine like an accusation glaring through the tatters of her dress.

He took her upstairs and found her an empty room down a long hall with other talyan on both sides. The demon-possessed usually kept solitary, secret retreats elsewhere, he knew, like Alyce's bolt-holes, although undoubtedly nicer. But every league maintained a place for them to come together. Private and taciturn they might be, and still they needed one another. Alyce would come to appreciate the companionship they offered.

More than companionship—the thought tightened every muscle in him until the ache in his bashed head and bitten shoulder made him think he was falling into pieces.

He'd already witnessed the first stages of a talya courtship. He'd personally felt the temptation of demonic power. From now on, he'd have to keep his mechanical pencil and clipboard as sword and shield against his unacceptable attraction.

Alyce was not his. She belonged to the league, to the unwitting city, and to the fight. He had his own fight ahead of him if he was going to finally win London's approval. He just had to keep his eye on the prize.

But it was a nearly unwinnable battle with his wayward gaze to lead her to the bathroom, turn on the shower, place the clean clothes on the sink, and back away without looking for another glimpse of her pale skin.

"I'll wait for you in the kitchen," he said.

And he fled, because flight had always been the underappreciated younger brother of fight.

Liam waited in the kitchen, as promised—threatened, really.

The league leader, one hip perched near the humming microwave, eyed him. "Where's Alyce?"

"In the shower, hopefully."

"You aren't sure?"

Sid scraped a hand through his hair. "I'm not stupid."

"And staying to make sure would have been stupid." Liam nodded. "Throughout mythology, demon-touched women have been portrayed as overwhelmingly alluring. And that was just when the portrayals were merely in words or pictures. In the flesh . . ." He whistled under his breath.

A flare of anger made Sid's hands clench. "Well, the flesh will be properly covered now, in your commando fatigues."

Commando. That made him remember there had been no underthings in the pile he left for Alyce. And that reminded him he wasn't going to think of it anymore. The angry heat converted in a flash to something far less manageable.

Liam watched him with too-knowing eyes. "We might

not know how the *symballein* bond works, but I can tell you from experience that it makes a hash of good intentions."

Sid thrust his hands into his front pockets, to hide the white knuckles and release some of the pressure of denim on his prick. "You think the *symballein* link is somehow keyed to me, even though I'm not possessed?"

"Good God, no." Liam straightened. "You can't have Alyce."

"Obviously not," he said, even though the devil's advocate in him asked, *Why not?* And another part—the part that wasn't an advocate and was just a devil—whispered, *Fuck you.*

But Liam seemed satisfied with the words said aloud. "Good you agree. Because I don't think I could keep murderous talya hands off you. So make sure you keep Alyce's hands off you too."

Nim barged into the room, Jonah moseying behind her. "Was Alyce hurt? She didn't seem to have any problems with her right hook."

Sid tried not to squirm. "She's fine."

Jonah squinted. "You checked her over thoroughly?"

Liam's cough was disguised by the *ding* of the microwave.

Sid wished he could blame the fire in his face on the rush of steam when the league leader popped the oven door. "I found the minor wounds she received as part of your game," he said, drawing out the word with doubtful scorn, "already healed upon examination. I'll write up a full report in the archives later tonight."

Nim leaned against her mate with a relieved sigh. "I'm glad we didn't scare her."

"You should be more relieved her dread demon didn't take exception to your game."

Jonah lifted an eyebrow. "What would the teshuva have

done? Its etheric signature is so faint, we never even realized she walked the city with us."

"An orca's dorsal fin doesn't leave much of a wake either," Sid pointed out. He left the rest of that image to percolate in their minds. "There's more going on under there than we can guess."

"And let me guess," Liam drawled. "You're the man to get under there and figure it out."

Sid avoided the league leader's menacing stare. "I promised her answers if she came here."

"Just answers," Liam said, much more softly. Brows furrowed in identical lines, Nim and Jonah clearly sensed the unsubtle undercurrents.

"Those answers will make me London's Bookkeeper," Sid countered, trying to mask his defensiveness with a touch of offense. "I'll be out of here soon enough."

Nim stepped away from Jonah. "Hey, Alyce. Come on in."

The heat lingering in Sid's face drained. Shite. What had Alyce heard?

Her expression gave no indication as she slipped between the talyan in the doorway, silent even in the too-big boots. Though he'd picked the smallest available sizes, the black T-shirt and cargo pants ballooned around her and made her skin paler by comparison. She'd braided her wet hair and wound the long plait in a crown on her head to expose her simple *reven* like a grim choker.

"Oh, sweetie," Nim said. "What the hell? Those clothes are awful."

"Sidney gave them to me," Alyce said.

He winced. He had an inkling she might have heard his thoughtless retort to Liam's needling. Damn it, he hadn't meant to make her feel abandoned. He'd brought her to the league specifically to *give* her a place to belong. But that was all he could give her, as Liam—and Bookkeeper doctrine—made so painfully clear.

Nim clicked her tongue. "A man might think going out to conquer evil necessitates wash-and-wear. But we know better." She held out her hand to Liam with a wiggle of her fingers. "I'll need the At-One platinum, please."

"Don't do it," Jonah warned.

With a sigh, Liam pulled out his wallet. "Get her what she needs."

Sid straightened. "I can—"

Liam's gaze snapped to him, a flicker of violet lighting the *reven* at his temple. "You declared her fit and fine. We'll take care of her from here, Bookkeeper."

Sid didn't budge. "Fine, yes, but not fight-ready."

Nim sniffed. "Who said fighting? We're going shopping. And don't worry; all the good sales are over."

"We're doomed," Jonah muttered.

Nim kissed him. "But we'll look damn fine. Ready, Alyce?"

Sid tried to catch Alyce's glance, but she never looked his way.

And once again, a Bookkeeper gave his best to the league and was left with nothing.

Chapter 11

Alyce felt the traces of him all around her—the weight of his gaze between her shoulder blades, the heat of his fingers still burning her breast, the taste of him—as she dogged Nim's footsteps out of the kitchen.

He was leaving—not now, but when she had given him what he wanted. And what he wanted was not her kiss—he hadn't wanted that, apparently—but her memories exposed, her expected place in the league filled.

Teasing her, a memory flickered, no more than a voice, hazy with the distance of time. *This one will do.* It was the master who had chosen her. Mingled hopelessness and dread had twisted in her stomach then, and she had to swallow back a foul taste like ashes.

She touched her neck, and under her fingertips, the *reven* pulsed. Had the devil loosened its iron grip on her recollections? Was it reminding her not to trust the men in her life? How cruel. But then, it was a demon.

Nim led her out to the cars, aligned under the lone lamp that buzzed and flickered over their heads.

Nim didn't strap herself in, so neither did Alyce, and they left the lot in a rattle of gravel.

The other woman did not speak for a time, and the grip of tension across Alyce's shoulders eased. She concentrated on the flow of the city outside her window. So quickly it passed, too fast to grasp more than a sensation.

Rather like her last . . . how many years? "How old do you think I am?"

Nim divided her attention between Alyce and the road. "You were maybe early twenties, I'd guess, when the te-shuva got ahold of you. Hopefully you were at least twenty-one and had your first legal drink before the demon started metabolizing all the alcohol so you couldn't catch a decent buzz. But how long ago that was . . ." She tilted her head. "I don't know. I'd take a wild guess if I could, because unlike everybody else, I don't mind being wrong. But I haven't ever seen anything like you."

Alyce slumped in her seat.

Nim patted her knee. "No worries. We'll get you up to speed."

"That is what Sidney said. But he is leaving."

Nim's expression hovered somewhere between sympathy and dismissal. "It's not you. He never meant to stay. He's made us his pet project so he can prove how awesome he is." Both emotions seemed to deepen, drawing her features into inhumanly remote realms when she looked at Alyce again. "We won't leave. Not ever. We might be heinously butchered by tenebrae, but now that we've found you, we won't leave you."

"It was Sidney who found me," Alyce said wistfully.

"Sweetie, if you're looking for an arrogant bastard with commitment issues, we've got way more where that one came from. You'll get the chance to meet on more intimate terms when you aren't throwing furniture at them. Thanks for winning mc fifty bucks, by the way. I made Jonah pay up since you would've cleaned their clocks. With grandfather clocks."

Alyce let Nim go on, extolling the virtues of the various talya males, but once she'd said "intimate," Alyce's thoughts circled back to how Sidney's arms had wrapped so perfectly around her.

"I have not had strong drink," Alyce interrupted over Nim's description of one talya's mastery of the cut-down crossbow in urban warfare. "I have never chosen a man either."

Nim huffed out a laugh. "Well then, you're out on the town with the right girl. As for the right man . . . Let's see what we can do."

Unlike Sidney, who seemed to need to wander all over Chicago to find phone boxes, Nim carried a little phone of her own. She parked the car and called Jonah. "I'm not going to make it back in time to go hunting with you tonight. We're on a different mission here. Take somebody to cover your ass—somebody big, like Ecco—and meet us at the Coil afterward."

The small phone made eavesdropping harder, but Alyce smiled at the long-suffering sigh that gusted through the device.

"I love you too." Nim made a kissing noise and folded the phone with a snap before turning to Alyce. "We have our own hunting. This, sweetie, is a mall."

Once through the wide circling doors that snatched people in and spit them out, saturated in strange and overpowering smells, Nim said, "First stop, shoes. Sadly, your shoes should be practical, as I've rediscovered more times than I care to admit. But then, I think, we can be forgiven a ridiculous plunge into Forever 21."

The shoes they found were, as promised, flat, hard treaded, lace-up, and sturdy, though Nim sighed louder than Jonah had over a pair of spiky red heels with only the thinnest of straps holding sole to foot.

"But it's almost winter," Alyce said.

"And wouldn't they look stunning in the snow?"

"They'd look cold."

Nim gave her a sour look. "You're worse than Jilly. Enjoy your combat boots."

She took her revenge at their next stop as she hustled Alyce into a curtained room. "You stay here. Take off those black horrors and I'll bring you something more appropriate."

"Practical for chasing devils, like the shoes?"

Nim shushed her. "You said you wanted a man."

Alyce craned her neck to see around the other woman. "The talyan will be coming here?"

"Not likely. This is truly their version of hell. Now stay."

Alyce obediently slipped out of the clothes Sidney had left for her—left behind, just as he'd left her. A flicker of anger canceled out the touch of breeze on her naked skin, and the hard stomp of her new shoes felt good as she paced the tiny room.

She was nothing but a curiosity to him, a puzzle to unfold.

When Nim brought back the clothes she'd chosen, Alyce knew she could show Sidney that she had nothing to hide.

Really, *this* was evil's secret hideout?

Thorne leaned against a scrawny maple tree that had sucked all the sustenance it could from its narrow island of soil at the edge of the huge parking lot. Sprawled in the middle of the cracked pavement was the Bowl Me Over.

The retro neon sign—not neo-retro, but dating back to Thorne's own childhood—over the entry was half dismantled, but the streetlights beamed their ugly illumination, dull white as a dead man's eyes. With a prick of his djinni, Thorne read the sheet of paper taped to the double front door.

UNDER CONSTRUCTION FOR PRIVATE BOWLING LEGION

"I suppose you couldn't say league," he muttered.

He'd wrung the location of the ahāzum gathering out of Carlo before tossing him off the boat. He might have suspected Carlo was trying to make him look foolish, bringing him to such an inauspicious place where the impatient city pressed close on all sides, but the djinn-man had been too wrecked to lie.

The cars parked near the entrance didn't lie either, all late-model conspicuous consumption and shining waxy under the lights.

DJIN I. DEEPBLU C. IMEVL.

Thorne shook his head. "Vanity, thy name is legion."

The doors were locked when he tried them. He had an invitation of sorts. He could just knock.

He had a djinni. He could just tear the doors down.

Well, shit. He had brought his lock picks since Carlo had reminded him of the good old days. So he let himself in with only a quiet *snick* of yielding tumblers.

Thanks to the djinni, he might walk on wind chimes and make no noise. But he didn't forget that those who gathered within were possessed too.

The foyer was darker than the parking lot, and every bit as ugly with the cheap pine-coffin wall paneling. The djinn didn't need lights, of course, but most of the possessed clung to the delusions of their humanity. They liked to hide their darkness in the light.

So Thorne followed the faint glow of yellow deeper into the building.

Ahead of him, the unlit lanes stretched away from the empty chairs and the snack bar that even hours after closing still stank of nacho cheese.

Nacho cheese and sulfur.

At the far end of the lanes, only partially visible between

the pinsetters, the djinn-men of Chicago had gathered under the bare bulbs of the bowling alley's back room.

Thorne settled himself cross-legged on a scorer's table to listen.

"... not enough of us yet," Carlo was saying to the dozen others. "Magdalena is disappointed."

Thorne wondered if the queen bitch had taken out her disappointment on her lapdog. If so, she'd been discerning in her punishment, since Carlo had been freed of the and-iron wrapped around his heart. He paced briskly in front of the gathered men, and his djinni's energy simmered around his slick gray suit like a kettle on high; the old mobster was clearly enjoying the return to organized crime.

Not everyone seemed so enthused. "I came tonight because you made promises, Carlo. I don't give a shit about Magdalena's disappointment."

Thorne peered through the pinsetter, silently cheering the sentiment. Fuck Magdalena. He didn't recognize the other djinn-man—he would've remembered so many platinum chains reflecting off diamond-studded teeth—but that wasn't surprising. He knew Carlo well enough to relish stabbing him only because the wise guy had explained to a bewildered, raw djinn-man on a now-distant night why an entire bottle of Thunderbird no longer worked its obliterating magic. Of course, Carlo hadn't shared until said-empty bottle had been smashed apart and pressed to his throat.

Thorne had to wonder what advantages Carlo had so freely promised on Magdalena's behalf. And why hadn't Carlo offered *him* those advantages? Thorne shifted in irritation. Just as well he'd learned to take what he wanted without asking.

Carlo strutted in a tight circle, the yellow light from the bare bulb greasing his hair like margarine. "Out of us all, only Magdalena has had the nerve to call the ahāzum, to continue what Corvus Valerius began."

The doubting spokesman tapped his chin, jangling the

platinum chains over his tight-fitted T-shirt. "Blackbird began by—let's see—losing his head, then his soul and his demon, and then—oh yeah—the last shreds of his miserable life. What could possibly be the next step?"

"Ending the secrecy."

Djinni energy flared with an acrid stink. The pinball machines on the other side of the snack bar briefly pinged and strobed, a disturbingly cheerful soundtrack. Thorne closed his eyes while he curbed the demon, knowing his own sockets would be beaming night prowler zeal.

"That's psycho," said Chains.

"If Corvus had torn the Veil between the demon and human realms wide open, that would be psycho," Carlo said. "Magdalena will reveal what we are: all-powerful, invincible, gods in our own right. And goddess. We'd run this city."

Gods of Chicago? Thorne restrained a snort. But who wouldn't want to be called a god? Certainly the gathering of djinn-men in a defunct bowling alley were now muttering with eager tones.

He peered at them again. Seen through the mechanical struts and flywheels of the pinsetters, their bodies were a Cubist portrait of disjointed evil. But their isolationism was coming to an end, apparently. Maybe they'd forgotten in this sudden mania that most of them had renounced their pantheistic histories long ago. There could be only one great spirit.

He could guess who would claim that place. And Magdalena would never be satisfied with a mere city.

"Corvus wanted to pit hell against heaven, not to rule," Chains argued. "He believed if the djinn and angels fought without intermediaries—without us—he would be free. I am not interested in being free to die, spitted on an angel's sword."

"What makes you think the sphericanum will act?" Carlo held his hands together in a prayerlike pose—a little something he'd picked up from Magdalena, no doubt.

"Things ain't never been worse for them. A lone djinn-man nearly brought down the Veil. And the sphericanum has done"—he spread his hands—"nothing."

"The league—"

"The talyan barely stopped the rift from widening, and they left a doorway standing open in its place, if we dare go through." Carlo shrugged. "Well, Magdalena dares."

Chains scoffed hard enough to bounce the platinum on his chest. "Dares what? Collect minions like salt and pepper shakers?"

"She attacked a talya patrol at a sphericanum church."

At the surge of ether this time, the bank of video games burst, glass faces cracking down the middle with the violent electrical storm. The vintage Ms. Pac-Man at the end finished the meltdown with a dirgelike woo-woo-woo.

Carlo nodded in satisfaction at the undeniable response. "She's found a way into the sphericanum wiretaps, and she heard the talyan and a couple goldies were meeting. She sent me to put the fear of God into them." He laughed at his joke.

Another djinn-man, standing back out of the reach of the lightbulbs, hissed out a laugh of his own. "And I hear your test run got an F for fucked. Four out of seven departed djinni is not a passing grade."

"We had orders not to kill the talyan," Carlo explained with a scowl. "The league has a rogue female, and Magdalena wants her for us."

The demon beat in Thorne's blood like a war drum, deafening him. Magdalena had gone after Alyce? What interest could that evil old monster have in the faint sparkler that was Alyce?

Never mind that he should be asking himself the same question; he should have bent that andiron right through Carlo's heart.

Carlo continued. "Taking out a warden's hallowed sword

is a trick. We'll be ready for the sphericanum next time. As for the league ... Magdalena has plans for them."

"And for us, presumably." Chains bared his diamond-bright teeth. "Why isn't she here to speak for herself?"

Carlo tipped his hands up, in a what-can-you-do motion. "She called the ahāzum. The rest will follow, and with the angels cowering behind their gates while our traitor talya brothers put out fires, there will be no one to stop our ascent."

No one?

Thorne took one silent step. Then every muscle in his body seized, locking him in place.

What was he thinking? There were too many of them standing under the bare bulb. Though they would not all side with Carlo, some would be swayed by the promises of godhood. His demon had obviously done the math and decided not to engage. Thorne let out a slow breath until his muscles were his own again.

The djinni might want to fall in line, but what Magdalena wanted, she could not have—not when he had wanted it first.

As silently as he had come, Thorne departed. At the front door, he ripped down the sign, shredded it between his fingers, and plastered it up again with scraps of the tape.

C UN T BOWLING FOR LEGION PRIVATES DE STRUC ION

Damn, not quite enough letters. He jabbed his fingertip with the lock pick until the corrosive ichor bubbled up in his skin. The glass smoked as he stenciled the second *t* in "destruction." While he thought about adding punctuation, the djinni healed the wound, so he left the rest of the paper pieces to scatter on the wind.

Sid paced the halls at the warehouse as the night ticked onward. Each step jolted his shoulder under the fresh dressing, but when he tried to lie down, his senses strained to capture any hint of Nim returning, or the talyan who had gone out on their eternal nightly mission.

Nothing.

Somewhere out there, the league was lessening the city's burden of darkness, and yet he felt the gloom settling on him. Guilt. Frustration. Anger. Even the lab with all its ledgers and machines and secrets to be revealed held no distractions for him tonight. Mending his specs had taken only a moment with a loop of duct tape, since of course the prime physical specimens of talyahood had no need of spectacle repair kits.

Finally, the lights of returning cars beamed through the foyer windows, casting a grand labyrinth of shadows amidst the columns and crossbraces. Sid hurried out to the loading dock, but only a handful of men entered.

His heart almost stopped. "What happened? Where is everyone? Was there a battle?"

The first two talyan swept past him, unheeding.

He stepped directly into Gavril's path. The talya stopped to scowl at him. "There's always a battle. Or we wouldn't have to go out."

"Did everyone . . . ?" Sid couldn't even force the words past his teeth.

"Die?" The talya male grinned, but with an edge that gave his Slavic features a brutal air. "Not tonight. So they went to the Coil to celebrate not dying. That, and to hang with the rogue."

Sid stiffened. He'd read about the Mortal Coil in Sera's notes on the league's assets—and enemies. The owner of the night club didn't fall into either category yet. "They took Alyce there? They might as well have taken her out against the tenebrae."

"I think they might still do that," Gavril said.

Sid swore.

Gavril cocked his head. "Why the nerves, Bookkeeper? If you want to know what makes a talya tick, you have to see her in action. And judging from the etheric blowback on the hunt, I'm guessing somebody is going to get a lot of action tonight."

Frustration melted into fury, dissolving through Sid in a rush. "Then why aren't you there, queuing up for your chance at her?"

Gavril stared past him, his gaze unfocused. "Risk the *symballein* bond? Do I look stupid as well as damned? The only thing worse than eternity alone would be eternity trapped with someone. I have enough forces sharing pieces of my skin." The talya glided away.

Sid looked out the open bay door and hurried for the street.

He had his wallet this time, and the cab driver was quick when he saw the gratuity. They pulled up in front of the Coil before Sid had gotten any further on his plan.

He couldn't stop her; he couldn't save her; he had perhaps ruined his chance to study her after his badly timed comment earlier. And still, here he was.

Despite the late hour—or early hour, depending on the reference point—a line of club-goers straggled out on the wrong side of the velvet rope. A talya-sized man shone his flashlight on IDs and waved away Sidney's credit card.

"Cash only," he said. "Next."

Sid shifted so the couple behind him couldn't shoulder past. "I just need to check on someone."

"I'm sure she's moved on without you," the bouncer said disinterestedly.

"Alyce is still here?"

The bouncer elbowed Sid to one side. "Man, I don't even know who Alyce is. But if she's here without you, obviously she's moved on, wouldn't you say?"

Bloody fascinating—a sidewalk psychologist. "I'm with Liam Niall's crew."

That got a laugh. "When I asked if he was hiring, he told me all his positions are full. I know he didn't make an exception for you."

Sid wondered if adding the ache of his grinding teeth to his shoulder, his head, and his professional ego was going to be the end of him.

"Westerbrook, what are you doing here?" Archer stepped out through the club doors, Sera on his arm.

Sid had never been glad to see the broody talya before. "I came to check on Alyce. You didn't leave her in there alone, did you?"

"Just her and a dozen new best dancing buds." Sera poked Archer. "I should have made you work harder for me."

"I don't dance," he said.

"You love to dance."

"That lie will earn you an extra aeon in purgatory."

Sid thought his enamel must be worn to bare nerves. "Could I interrupt this regularly scheduled pair bonding long enough to borrow a few greenbacks?"

Archer peered at him. "Attitude will get you nowhere."

"Not true," Sera said. "Attitude gets you everywhere." She pulled out her wallet.

Archer lowered his voice as the bouncer dealt with another few people. "It'll get him ass-whipped by that bunch inside."

"Westerbrook can handle himself. Right, Sid?" She held the fanned bills just out of his reach.

"It's never the Bookkeeper who needs the lecture." Sid plucked the money out of her fingers with more force than necessary.

She blinked, as if his vehemence surprised her. "Stay away from the mixed drinks. Bella swaps labels and still waters 'em down. Actually, don't drink anything you don't open yourself. And have fun."

Archer steered her to the street. "Just stay out of the way."

Inside the club, Sid found he couldn't stay out of anyone's way. The interior was darker than a nightclub needed to be, as if the inevitable black lights and half-burned-out rope lights would reveal too much. Between the murk and the crowd, he bumped into a dozen people—none of them talyan, apparently, since his head was still attached to his shoulders. He fought his way to the bar with no sign of Alyce or the others.

He stood at the sticky Formica, aggravation surging through him.

A barmaid circled her wet bleach rag past his fisted hands. "What can I get you?"

"Nothing at the moment, thanks." He added in a mumble, "Unless you can tell me what the hell I'm doing here."

The barmaid's cat's eye glasses glinted in the neon of the liquor logos. "You must be looking for Liam's crew."

He'd intended the question more figuratively, but he'd take whatever answers he could get. "Actually, I am."

She grinned, the flash of her white teeth deepening the feline resemblance. "I'd recognize that special brand of darkness anywhere."

She tilted her face upward. Behind her glasses, the lights shone across her eyes in a clouded blur of cataracts. "They're in the loft."

Sid followed her blind gaze up to the second story. If the main floor was unnecessarily gloomy, the upstairs was just black. Without her direction, he would never have noticed the balcony level. Of course, the talyan would prefer such a place.

"Stairs are over there," she said. "Tell the bouncer Bella said it's okay."

Sid frowned. "'Okay'? That's your security password?"

"Nobody misuses it twice." She smiled, and again he was reminded of a cat—the kind that might hide the limp bodies of pet hamsters in his shoes.

He thanked her and slid a tip across the bar, thinking one of the other barmen would retrieve it. But she took the bill with one hand, her other hand busy below the level of the bar. Before he could turn away, she pushed a tumbler across to him. The drink gleamed an unnatural yellow under the neon.

"On the house," she said.

An impatient patron inserted himself between Sid and the bar, and he stepped away.

A short, dark corridor led to the stairs. Sid repeated the barmaid's terse approval, and the bouncer—twin to the thick-necked bruiser on the street—stepped aside.

Did the hamster walk into the cat's mouth with this same sense of inevitability?

He took a sip of the liquid fortitude and almost missed a step. Some heinous concoction of cheap burning whiskey and fruity syrup supernovaed through his sinuses. It was not at all weak as Sera had warned.

He downed half of it before he reached the upper landing.

The loft wasn't as noisy as below, nor as dark as it had looked from the bar. Stubs of votive candles burned in a dozen chipped tumblers—Sid ran his fingertip around the rim of his glass—giving just enough light to define the corners of the low tables surrounded by even lower couches of indeterminate color. The atmosphere was set for self-indulgence and sprawling ennui, but the talyan couldn't play that hipster role if their souls depended on it.

Instead, they stood in concentric rings, the veritable wall of broad male backs to Sid, enclosing the Liam-Jilly and Jonah-Nim pairs, and, at the center, Alyce, looking over the balcony.

Despite his position on the very outside, Sid thought he'd never seen a lonelier figure than the wisp of a girl, her hand gripping the rail as if she might throw herself over.

When Nim had snatched Alyce away for a shopping spree, Sid had known he'd find her either barricaded in the grim shades of talya destruction or—worse yet—tricked out like Nim in some cleavage-enhancing, cock-teasing latex extravaganza.

Which made him blink even harder at the vision in white before him.

The simple fall of the skirt only emphasized her slender lines. Her hair, coiled in the braided crown on her head, revealed the column of her throat, and the demure round collar cupped ghostly hands around her *reven* that shimmered violet with her disquiet.

All she needed was some of the blinking neon from below announcing SACRIFICIAL VIRGIN HERE.

And the talyan were gathered like hungry dragons.

He should add footnotes to known tribal matrimonial customs. He should run home and grab a recorder to compare the etheric flares captured during street battles to the fierce energies he sensed swirling around them now. He should . . .

He tossed back the rest of his drink and set the glass down gently on one of the empty tables. He meant to set it down gently, anyway. Somehow the glass cracked. Now he knew where all the broken candleholders came from.

Despite the stern clack, only Alyce turned. Against the white dress and her white skin, her icy eyes burned with a pale blue fire.

Her expression didn't soften, still as cold and remote as the moon since she'd heard him choose London over her, and he realized he'd wanted her to be happy to see him. He wanted her smile to invite him through the ring of prowling talyan to her side.

Several millennia of Bookkeeper doctrine stood in direct opposition to his wants, though he couldn't quote the exact passages right at this moment, but what did they know? He was just one man, and she, despite her demonic burden, was still a woman, the woman he couldn't get out of his otherwise ruthlessly disciplined mind. Despite all the unspecified fears, really, how could this shimmering awareness between them destabilize the world?

Even as his head spun from the alcohol in his empty belly, his determined footsteps carried him through the first ring of talya males. Tonight, he was through taking notes.

CHAPTER 12

A tremor swept down Alyce's spine, riding an anonymous surge of keen expectation.

She had never been around so many overwrought people. When the lights above the dance floor swept the crowd, the garish illumination captured fleeting moments of expressions. A blue frozen laugh. A red openmouthed shout. A yellow head thrown back in abandon. The unfettered passions sent another wave of shivers through her bones, as if trying to vibrate her into ill-considered action.

The talyan wanted her. Nim had promised they would not attack, though the marks of their demons glittered brighter than the club lights. Jilly had also promised to put her heavy boot through their backsides if they touched Alyce without her permission.

Alyce wondered what the fierce little woman would do to Sidney.

Then, as if conjured by her thought, he emerged from the stairwell.

To her devil-riddled eyes, he stood out against the shadows like one of the candles in the cracked glass. His light gleamed through his flaws until her eyes watered from looking at him.

There was more light to him than shadow, which was more than she could say for herself. No wonder he wouldn't stay.

She let the tears blind her, so she didn't have to see him watching her from a distance that was impossible even for a powerful demon to cross and utterly hopeless for her. She would do anything to stave off the dreadful moment when he would walk up to her and say good-bye.

Through the haze of weakling tears she glimpsed the starry night of red watching eyes.

Ah, *that* was who was so excited about her misery.

Without raising her head or drawing attention, she murmured to Nim, who stood closest, "Do you see them? We're surrounded."

"Can't miss 'em. Tall, dark-souled, and disgustingly handsome. You'd think in a few thousand years between them of walking this earth, they could come up with one pickup line."

"I meant the devils."

"Yeah, all that teshuva tweaking makes the *reven* light up like a pinball game." Nim scowled. "Sorry I made you the shiny silver ball."

"The dress is very pretty." Alyce brushed her palms down her thighs. Around her, the net of etheric energy pinged on her skin as it tightened another notch. "I'm talking about the tenebrae."

"What? Where?" Nim whirled, her hand at the small of her back. She kept a blade there, Alyce had noticed. The grim-faced man at the door to the club hadn't noticed, despite his air of officiousness, because he'd been too busy looking at Nim's long, bare legs.

But the concealed knife would do no good against these devils.

"Up," Alyce said. "No, don't look. You'll bring them upon us."

"We can take them."

"You are stronger," Alyce agreed, "but the panic downstairs would be . . . messy."

Nim nodded. "The horde-tenebrae always like the juicy tang of panic." She leaned toward Jonah and spoke into his ear.

He stiffened but didn't look up. "Let's take it outside."

As if someone had thrown a match on the line of black powder connecting them, the demon marks on all the talyan flared violet at once.

Tucked like black mold into the nooks and crannies in the ceiling girders, the malice shrieked and were echoed in a deeper register by the larger salambes. The cry reverberated in the big gray boxes that boomed music below. The song cut out and projected the horde's voice in a vicious roar. People on the dance floor dropped to their knees, hands clamped over their ears.

Alyce winced. "We have to get out. Maybe the devils will follow us."

"They will if I tell them to," Nim said. She threaded her fingers through Jonah's.

To Alyce's astonishment, the talya tucked her into the crook of his arm and kissed her. It was a scandalizing kiss, her breasts tight against his chest, his hook gleaming low against the yielding curve of her spine. The backlash went through the teshuva and tenebrae alike in a shuddering wave.

Alyce was already heading for the stairs, shoving between the frozen talyan.

Sidney stepped in front of her. "What—?"

She grabbed his hand and yanked him along.

Her passage broke apart the stillness, and they fell into line behind her and Sidney. Liam was right at their heels. "Thank all the saints you were paying attention."

"There are no saints here." She hunched her shoulders against the gathering storm cloud of devils overhead.

"Through the back, to the alley," Jonah said. "Nim will lure the malice with us."

In a wave of blackness all their own, the talyan swept through the stunned crowd. Someone was tugging at wires around the big music boxes, muttering, "Damn speakers."

Yes, Alyce thought, all the talking had almost damned them. She didn't want to hear any more from Liam and the others about all she would be with them—or worse, hear the words they didn't say; the look, lonely and hungry, that was only in their eyes.

She'd show them what she did with lonely and hungry.

They burst out the back door into the empty alley. The windowless walls of the buildings rose up four stories on both sides, a canyon of chipped brick and rusting steel. From the vents and grates in the upper floor of the club and from over the roofline poured the greasy smoke of the devils.

"Time to rumble," Jilly muttered.

As if in answer, the music inside the hall kicked on again, the deep notes throbbing through the walls.

Sidney tugged at Alyce's hand. "What's happening?"

She pointed. "You can't see them."

He frowned. "Just . . . shadows?"

"Horde." Nim's voice was almost a croon. "Come to Mama."

They came in a stinking rush of broken rotting eggs, as if night's darkness sped down the wall, obliterating every detail.

Alyce had never fought with others before, and she tried to watch with her new understanding, the new words Sidney had given her, though her muscles cramped with the urge to flee. If this many of the devils had come for her alone . . .

But the talyan stepped forward in a wall of male flesh,

the two talya women nearly lost between the broad shoulders. A furious sweep of etheric energy belled out ahead of them. The devils that hit the teshuva power boiled into foul steam.

"Bloody hell. I should have had another drink." Sidney rubbed his eyes and squinted, as if trying to separate what his eyes saw—or didn't see, or half saw—and his mind knew. "This isn't how it's supposed to go, is it? Why are there so many?"

"Nim and her demon call them to slaughter," Jonah said. "Makes hunting far more efficient lately."

But Nim shook her head. "I can't take the credit. These were already gathering, even before I called. Alyce saw them first."

Half of Liam's attention stayed on the talyan slowly shredding the tenebrae. "What did they want? You?"

"Not me," Alyce said. "They wanted the wanting."

Liam pointed at Sidney. "You. Care to decode?"

Alyce pulled her hand free of Sidney's when his gaze settled on her with as much curiosity as he'd had when he'd studied the horde above them.

He didn't seem to notice her withdrawal as he considered their little grouping. "The league is usually so careful about damping its energy. All the desires and fears and furies. The emotions that power all of us are amplified by the teshuva, which give the talyan more strengths—and more vulnerabilities."

She didn't need more vulnerabilities. It was bad enough to be alone, afraid, confused. But she did know one thing, and she'd wanted to show them.

She stepped outside the protective circle of talyan.

Sidney's surprised call didn't stop her; nor did the other talyan. The bright flare of their eyes followed her.

The ferocity of their teshuva had thinned the devils, but the dozens that remained were whipped to a rage. Singly, they might feed on despair or frustration and be content to spread their malaise like a creeping sickness.

En masse, they wanted to devour her.

So she let them.

Sidney shouted again, more vehemently this time. From the surge through the talya energy, she knew they had rallied to hold him back.

Really, they should get a little farther back.

The devils surrounded her, their nasty mouths latched on the flesh exposed by her pretty new dress. They fed her their horrors. No, not theirs. She hadn't recognized that until now, when Sidney had made her face her flickering memory. These were her own half-known horrors, sucked from her and regurgitated, more vile than before.

Their whispers leached through her veins. *Master. Madness. Hang the witch.*

The *reven* around her neck tightened as the teshuva finally roused. She had thought maybe she had to hurt for it to hunt. But now she understood; it was too weak to waste itself on the chase. She was staked out as victim while it waited to take its unwitting prey from behind.

Now that her eyes were opened, the experience was rather more gruesome. But she stood, swaying, hands in fists.

The malice exulted in her fading strength as they consumed the last of her sickened outrage and the pain of their violation and delighted in the more delicate flavors of deepest despair. A larger salambe loomed closer, not so patiently waiting its turn.

She tasted the first stirrings of dread—her own dread, tainted as grave dirt. In another heartbeat, death would come.

Not for her. Her demon longed for the horde in its embrace.

"Alyce!"

Sidney's shout, rough and frantic, rang from the bricks and forced her eyes open.

Liam grappled with Sidney, who struggled against the talya's hold. Sidney swung his fist with more vehemence than aim.

And knocked the bigger man to the pavement in a tangle of his canvas duster.

A shock rippled all the way around the talya circle. Even Jilly stood a stunned moment before rushing to her mate.

As if the demon-possessed warrior had been nothing more than an inconveniently closed door he had to get through, Sidney bolted beyond the shielding energy of the roused teshuva.

"No," Alyce whispered. Scarcely past her lips, her plea withered in the miasma of the chortling malice, wound tight round her throat.

Sidney's gaze fastened on her.

At the same moment she realized she'd gone too far. In her silly hurt at Sidney's rejection and the conceit of flaunting her demon, she'd brought too many malice to her to feast. Fortified by her torment, they would flay Sidney for dessert.

Because of her.

Malice sheathed her bare arms in a crawling shawl of shadows, but with every last thread of her token power, she lifted her still-bare hand, fingers spread in a white star to ward him off.

But Sidney ignored her warning and laced his fingers through hers.

She couldn't feel his touch. The negative energy of the malice was extinguishing her, moment by moment, as it overwhelmed her demon.

"Don't do this alone." His voice through the distortions of the malice surrounding her sounded so far away.

But he was going back to London, she wanted to remind him. She would be alone again.

Sidney's steely gaze reflected the violet of a dozen rampant teshuva. But though his lucky shot had flattened Liam, he couldn't loosen her from the miring weight of malice. The irresistible compulsion that had drawn her to find him in the alley just one night ago wasn't strong enough. She wasn't strong enough.

So he drew himself to her.

No! She wanted to scream her denial to save him from the demons swarming around them. But she was weak, so weak in the presence of such potent temptation, and when he bowed his head to kiss her, she lifted her mouth to his.

That she felt—a fleeting touch of heat and swirling light and life.

Then the teshuva burned through her in a sudden rush, scouring away all thought and any emotion, save one impulse that was hers and hers alone: *This.*

The salambes fled, and the malice might have screamed—half-formed mouths dripping with her anguish—if they'd pulled away faster. But the etheric power exploded them like swollen ticks.

The talyan swore and ducked, their violet-glowing eyes wise to the spatter. Only Liam's hand between Sidney's shoulder blades as the talya finally reached them spared his human flesh a bad ichor burn.

The brick walls glowed sickly with devil sign, and a querulous thin cry drifted up as the scattered shreds of ether drifted down.

Alyce rocked back onto her heavy boot heels, their sturdy weight holding her upright.

"Steady," Sidney cautioned. But his voice shook. "Are you okay?"

She considered. "Nim said I would need practical shoes."

Then even the boots weren't enough support, and she crumpled into his arms.

*   *   *

Sid cradled Alyce in his lap as the car bumped over the railroad tracks around the warehouse. "What the fuck?" he mumbled. "What the fuck?"

"Stop saying that," Jilly growled from the front seat.

"Why? It's true."

"Just because she uses a slightly different technique—"

"Her teshuva could have been overwhelmed—she could have been killed!—while we watched."

Liam rubbed his jaw gingerly where Sid had punched him, though the teshuva had already erased the bruise. "Isn't that what Bookkeepers do? Watch?"

Sid shot him a furious glare. "You had a shitty Bookkeeper before. Get over it."

"Bookie would have seen us all killed, and happily, to capture a demon's power for himself. That's shitty all right."

"That wasn't me." Bloody hell, he couldn't even begin to explain how that wasn't him, how he'd never wanted to step outside the Bookkeeper boundaries. In fact, he'd done everything in his life to stay properly within bounds. How his father would shake his head at the irony.

Alyce stirred in his arms. Her soft moan ruffled the shirt against his chest and vaporized any pretense that he was at all detached.

"Alyce?" He brushed aside the dark locks of hair that had loosened from her braid.

Jilly peered over the seat. "Is she awake?"

Sid looked down into Alyce's wide eyes and tucked her closer to his chest. For once, he didn't want to talk, and Alyce seemed willing to rest in his arms. He'd wait to yell at her. "Just get us home."

When they pulled into the warehouse lot, he hefted her into his arms and carried her inside, past the line of silent talyan.

Gavril took a half step out of the line. "Is she—?"

Sid passed him without a word.

Liam paused to say something to the men, but Jilly followed him to the room he'd given Alyce earlier, Nim behind her with shopping bags slung from her elbows.

Jilly pushed open the door and flicked on the light, then whisked around Sid to turn down the covers. "Put her down; then you can go and we'll—"

"Forget it."

He laid his too-small burden on the bed and faced the other women.

Hands propped on her curvy hips, Jilly stared back, her expression the opposite of flirty. "You have no idea what you are doing."

"I have lots of ideas. I'm a Bookkeeper."

She scoffed. "But you don't have *the* idea. The one you need most. The one where you realize you're totally wrong."

He gritted his teeth. "If I'm wrong, then I'll come up with a new idea. It's the scientific method."

Nim echoed Jilly's snort and tossed the shopping bags next to the bed. "With arrogance like that, I can't believe you're not talya."

"And I can't believe you two are still here."

They stared at him another moment.

"You're going to hurt her," Jilly said.

"And you almost killed her."

Guilt flickered over the other woman's face, and Nim ducked her head. "I can't believe that's how she's fought the tenebrae all this time. To give herself over to them . . ." She shuddered. "I'd do anything to stop them from touching me."

Jilly touched her shoulder. "Now that we know what she's been through, we can show her another way."

"Not tonight you can't." Sid walked toward them, using the momentum of his body and their remorse to force them out.

Nim made one last about-face at the door, forehead crinkling with concern. "It's not right, your staying with her."

He braced his hand in the doorway, in case she thought

she was coming back in. "This, from an ex-stripper? Jonah's missionary days coming back to haunt you?"

She narrowed her eyes at him. Jilly tugged at Nim's arm, still managing to shoot Sid a bossy look. "You'll call for us, right away, if—"

He shut the door in their faces.

Oh, he knew they could kick the door back in his teeth— even Nim in her high heels—but he was counting on their shock at Alyce's performance to hold them at bay. It would never occur to a talya to become the quarry.

They couldn't understand. Hell, he couldn't either, but understanding was his task, in the same way theirs was to risk themselves. Alyce just had a more dreadful way than most.

"That demon of yours cuts both ways, doesn't it?" He turned back to the bed.

She lay curled on her side, hands fisted under her chin. "I heal fast."

"Good thing." He sat at the foot of the bed. There was plenty of room with her knees bent to her chest, even with the big black boots taking up an inordinate amount of space. "Is this sort of collapse normal for you after a fight?"

"I don't know. I've never tried it against so many before."

He closed his eyes, glad for the sake of his suddenly wobbling knees that he was sitting down. "You terrify me."

"I thought it was only dread."

"Only." When he opened his eyes again, he realized that even with perfectly functional legs, he wouldn't just walk away from her. "Let's get these lovely new boots off you."

"Do you like them?"

"They are very . . . steel-toed."

"Nim says either the heel or the toe should be a weapon, and I couldn't stand up in the shoes she liked best."

The image of slender Alyce in white stilettos rocketed from his brain stem to his occipital lobe, burning a permanent pathway in his brain as it flashed like lightning in front of his eyes. It made him think sitting on her bed wasn't his best idea ever.

"Right. Shoes off. Sheets up. Sleep." He could work the steps and still make his escape.

When he tugged at her laces, she sat up. "I can do it."

He caught her hands and turned them palm up. The crescent punctures of her nails had healed into the faintest of moons, but the bloody streaks remained. "You get your boots off. I'll get a washcloth."

In the bathroom, he found her blue granny dress neatly folded, bloody smears right side up. She'd kept the rag, as if she might need it later. How could he reassure her that this was her new home when he had already revealed how quickly he intended to leave?

He stared at himself in the mirror as he ran the water to warm it.

What did he want? How could he even ask that when he'd chosen to give up everything for London?

He gripped the edge of the sink.

The double thuds of her boots hitting the floor made him straighten, and he wrung out the washcloth.

God, he was in a peculiar mood tonight. He'd barely seen a thing with his limited human vision, but that moment in the alley had opened his eyes.

He returned to Alyce's bedside. She sat with her knees still pulled up to her chest, feet tucked under her hem. She held out her hands, palms down, so he perched beside her and tucked her hands between the damp folds of the cloth.

"It was interesting," he said. "What you did out there, by yourself."

"I wasn't by myself." She regarded him steadily. "You came. And you shouldn't have."

Her words were true enough, which didn't lessen their sting. "Yes, well, you did all the hard stuff, such as turning the malice into etheric dust motes."

She stared down at their joined hands. "Not much, is it, compared to what Sera and Jilly and Nim can do?"

"They're different from you, as they are different from one another. That's part of their strength." He'd meant the words as consolation, but now that he said them, he wondered at their deeper meaning. Together, the first three talya women formed an unusually effective hunting team. Was that demonic evolution? Or was there a more organized hand at work?

"You think even more than you talk," Alyce said.

He realized he'd been silent a long moment and chuckled. "A hazard of the job. Not so hazardous as yours, of course." He swiped the cloth across her hands.

She showed him the immaculate flesh. "Okay?"

He nodded and tossed the cloth on the bedside table. He started to rise, but she took his hand.

He hovered awkwardly, one foot on the floor, one knee still bent on the mattress.

Her eyes glimmered. Not violet, not tears. He couldn't quite identify . . .

"Stay," she whispered.

Ah. Right. "Alyce, I know you heard when I mentioned London—"

"I'm not asking forever. Stay now. Stay the night."

"Alyce . . ."

"There's not much night left. I know dawn is coming."

That should be a good thing. The return of light meant the tenebrae slunk away; it meant they'd survived another fight. And yet her voice trembled with wistfulness.

He supposed days and nights hadn't meant much to her, lost with her demon.

It wasn't pity that moved him, but awe at her fragile strength, that she could fall before the tenebrae and yet stand again. He knew he'd never have such endless resilience.

In his own inconsequential human way, he'd tried to be strong, when his mother had walked away from the cold and silent house where Bookkeeper secrets had gathered in a smothering dust. But as his girlfriend had discovered, the words with which he'd tried to fill the silence were hollow. And she too had left. Then the metaphorical distance between them that she always complained about had become an existent and enduring entity.

Maybe becoming the London league Bookkeeper wasn't the be-all, end-all aspiration he'd proclaimed. Maybe it was just an end. But it was a place he knew and understood, and there he wouldn't hurt anything—anyone—who didn't deserve it.

He pulled free from Alyce's grasp, and her shoulders drooped.

He curled his fingers behind her neck, half expecting her *reven* to shock him as her gaze flashed up to his.

"You've bewitched me," he murmured. "It's the only explanation."

Her eyes widened. "Witch?"

"I should know better than this." He drew his other knee up onto the bed, and she dipped toward his greater weight. "I do know better."

"We can only know so much," she said. "Even you."

"Are you teasing me?"

"No. Maybe. Stop talking." She lifted her face, an invitation. "Stop thinking."

And he took the invitation—and took her. He kissed her until her lips reddened, and an answering flush rose in her pale cheeks. He buried his fingers in her hair, combing out the last of the valiantly clinging braid. She moaned against his lips, and the civilized part of him said, *Wait*, while the rest of him—a burgeoning part, in more than one sense—urged him onward.

The rush of it terrified him.

Was he no better than the tenebrae? Taking what she offered so fearlessly, with a not-so-secret darkness in his heart?

He groaned her name again, more helpless than she had ever been. Bewitched. Bedeviled. Be damned.

For once, he understood the talya thrill to freefall.

She pulled herself up to her knees, hands framing his face to slide his specs away. They clattered somewhere in the shadows. Well, he had plenty of duct tape.

She matched him, tongue to tongue, lips, teeth, and she laughed against his mouth, a breathless sound of delight that made him feel like a talya-sized hero, swelling his heart, his head, and less noble parts of him. He swept his hands down her arms, left bare by the white dress. Crystal white in October; what had Nim been thinking?

Alyce rocked into him, bumping his hands aside. She'd tugged the dress out from under her knees, and before he could speak, she'd yanked it over her head.

No sacrificial virgin had underthings like this.

He offered half a thought of apology toward Nim's obvious shopping prowess, and then all thought evaporated.

White silk and lace. Barely enough to fill a shot glass. As a man with a scientific bent, he should have been thinking in terms of milliliters, but since his brain had gone missing . . . Yeah, a shot glass was more up his alley right now.

His hands hovered just beyond the curves of her breasts, hesitant to land on that purity.

Alyce took a deep breath, and his burst out of him as the cool silk filled his palms.

She tipped her head back, and the sweet thrust of her breasts stroked up to his fingertips. Raw lust closed his grip, gentled only by the tremor in his muscles. The instinct to overwhelm her shook him to the core.

He was not that man.

His body listened only to the tactile scuff of lace against the pads of his fingers. The sensation abraded the wisps of his restraint.

In one caress, he pushed the straps down her shoulders

and unhooked the back, freeing her. She had such pale skin. Had it ever seen sunlight?

Never mind the hot eye of the sun; had any gaze at all but his rested here?

Mine. The impulse was so archaic, so primitive, he blushed at it. Not Homo sapiens at all, but Neanderthal. Where was his fucking club?

Her hands went to his fly, and he groaned.

Right.

She freed his heavy flesh as smoothly as he'd stripped her. He hissed out another breath when she grazed his hip bones as she peeled down the waistband of his jeans. They moved together, and her quick fingers undid the buttons of his shirt.

Pressed skin to hot skin, he closed his eyes, trying to steady himself.

But with eyes closed, his other senses only expanded. Hearing her gasp as she rubbed against his chest, he inhaled the heat and fragrance of her breath. His taut muscles raged against the confines of his will. Each rock of their knees on the mattress threatened to overturn him, demanding he take her down.

Not a man, not even a primordial hunter, but a beast.

The howl of recognition in him tore through the last of his self-possession.

He yanked out of his shirt—a button popped at the wrist—and he tipped her to her back.

She stared up, eyes bright and bold, as she kicked off the white panties.

"God, you're beautiful," he whispered.

"And naked," she said.

As if he might have missed it. "Do tell."

She smiled and opened her arms.

The smile, simple and welcoming, ripped through him. "You want this?"

"No more words. You need this too."

He did. As he'd never wanted anything so much. Not even the Bookkeeper's archive key.

He couldn't speak that, and apparently he wasn't thinking again either, because somehow she had rolled him, and now she hovered over him, the last of his discarded clothing dropping from her hand.

"Now I'm naked," he pointed out.

"You don't have to tell me."

Her lips descended, moonset slow in the darkness, inevitable. Her kiss touched down, and, hidden below the horizon of their coupled mouths, the arc of her tongue stroked his. Like some ancient mythology, her shadowed mysteries drew him deeper.

In the yielding of her body, he found himself above her again, the edges of his vision narrowing so only she remained, pale skin on white sheets, her dark hair spread like an inverse halo—a damned angel.

A shudder racked him, and he lowered his head, capturing her lips. She burned, coming back to life.

"So cold you are," she whispered. "Come into me."

No art. No poetry. If he'd ever known words, he forgot them, and between one heartbeat and the next, he was inside her.

Her wet heat gripped the length of him with unspeakable pleasure. The stroke as she drew away wrenched a groan from him, then redoubled when she impaled herself again, then again, and again in sweet torture.

The force of his desire rose, topped itself, reaching higher, a wave ripping itself apart in a frenzy of chaotic energy. He would die here, blown apart like the tenebrae.

Best give her what he could before he went.

His mouth on her breast made her arch, driving her deeper on his cock. He almost lost it then, but some niggling sense of male pride held him together. He slipped his hand between them and found the heated center of her passion. She bucked, fingers biting into his shoulders until he winced. He'd have bruises in the morning.

But she'd have at least this memory, damn it.

He forgot mind, body, and soul while he feasted on her. Each moan, each tremor, pushed him closer to the edge. But he wouldn't fall, not without her.

"Alyce," he said, "take me. Take it all."

Her half-lidded eyes flew open, her gaze fixed on his. "Sidney . . ." And then the ripple that started inside her expanded outward, through her limbs, through him. She made a noise, halfway between a scream and the throaty laugh she'd given him earlier, and buried herself in his arms.

The riotous waves that had nearly overcome him washed through her, echoing back to him in concentric rings down his aching flesh.

He came in a violent rush that unlocked his elbows and dropped him like a stone onto her. Fortunately, she was immortal.

Gradually, his breath returned, though his brain was slower to catch up, still fried and off-line. He kissed the racing pulse under her jaw. Her *reven* twitched when she swallowed.

"Oh, Sidney," she whispered. "I had no idea."

"I'm the idea man," he agreed. He thought he kept most of the gloating out of his tone. Whoever had come before him obviously hadn't made an impression. Except the need to stake his claim wasn't dissipating.

"I didn't know." Her voice wavered. "When you said I should take all of you . . ."

"I was overcome too. Really." He pushed up onto one elbow. "Okay?"

She considered for a moment. "Very okay. And you?"

He laughed.

She didn't. "I thought you might hate it."

He brushed the tangled strands of her hair aside, his chest aching a little with tenderness, as if her grip had reached inside him and bruised his heart. "What would I possibly hate about the feel of you coming apart in my arms?"

She blushed. "I meant the demon."

"That's as much a part of you as your lovely eyes."

"I didn't mean my demon."

His fingers slipped down to rest against her *reven*. "What?"

"Your demon."

"My—?"

He started to pull away from her as she touched his shoulder. When had the bandage come off? That feralis bite could have gotten blood everywhere. . . .

Except the ragged wounds were gone, just a faint white jigsaw shape, crystal clear in his spectacle-free, flawless vision.

He scrambled back to his haunches. The chill that swept down his spine had nothing to do with his naked exposure.

She sat up. "All those demon lights, all that ether . . . More than just the malice came down on us tonight. I didn't understand what it was—it didn't make sense—but there must have been another demon among them. Yours." She reached out, and the tips of her fingers just brushed the black curving lines that curled down from his breast to the front point of his pelvis bone. "You are possessed."

CHAPTER 13

When Sidney recoiled from her touch, Alyce said, "I thought you knew. I thought that was why you stayed with me tonight."

"Knew?" His voice broke. "I didn't have the faintest fucking clue."

"But you punched Liam. And you came to me through the malice." And then he had whispered, so sweetly, *Take me*, taking and giving in one blissful communion.

In that instant—body, heart, and soul aligned—the haze that had been her only companion for so long had lifted. In the clarity, staring into the depths of his brown eyes was like finally finding the earth beneath her feet, and she'd felt there was a place for her.

That he flinched from her now ate like venom through her veins and blackened her heart.

"I didn't know what I was doing." Louder and harsher his words came, as if he could raise a jagged wall to defend against the truth—against her. Those bristling defenses scraped her raw.

"Not so clear when it's you, is it?" Bitterness leached the last of their shared warmth from her limbs, and she drew her knees up tight. "The circling teshuva must have been why the tenebrae came down on us at the club, following you."

"But . . . it's impossible. How did no one within the league notice an unbound teshuva?"

She hunched her shoulders. "I noticed. That is what drew me to the alley with the ferales. And you."

"Then why didn't you tell me?"

The tight anguish in his voice, sharpened to a point with accusation, stabbed her. "I didn't know what it was. It was just another thing I didn't understand. And you seemed to know everything already."

His breath burst out on a curse and a discordant laugh mixed together. He staggered off the bed, and his heels slammed hard on the floor. "You are wrong. I'm not like you."

She rocked forward to kneel on top of the covers. "The shine in your eyes says otherwise."

His hands hovered over the *reven* with the same horrified hesitation as a gutshot man staring down at his death. "This can't be happening."

She braced herself on the tousled sheets, a twinge of provocation stiffening her shoulders. "You tried to tell me it wasn't so bad that I was possessed. Did you lie then?"

Again he swung his head up to her, the focus of his ire. "You didn't have a choice."

"You didn't either."

"You didn't have a choice *anymore*," he clarified. "It was already done."

She bit her lip. "Do you mean you could have fought it off, as we fight the tenebrae? That *I* could have fought it?"

He flattened his palm over his hip, fingers digging into the coiling lines of the demon's mark. "Of all people, I should have been able to say no. Who else but a Bookkeeper ... But I was never supposed to be a Bookkeeper anyway."

She shook her head. "Why—?"

"A Bookkeeper can't be talya. We stand outside your world and our own."

"That sounds awful."

"That's how we stay objective." He paced at the bottom of the bed, three short steps and back again. The vicious whirl at each turn made her stomach clench. "It's all I had."

Now you have me. The words rose on her tongue. But for once, she did not speak her mind plainly because she knew his response would shatter her.

He was teaching her, more than he knew.

He snatched his jeans from the floor. Even in his eagerness to dress, his hands avoided the *reven*, as if it might spread like wet ink. "I have to go."

"Where?"

He slipped into his shirt and yanked the front panels tight around his body. He swooped down and rose again, clutching his eyeglasses. "Don't ... Please don't mention this to anyone."

"You think the talyan won't notice another demon?"

"I'll explain the teshuva. But"—he gestured vaguely as he jammed the unneeded spectacles on the bridge of his nose—"the rest of this."

The bed—and her, naked in it.

She refused to reach for the covering sheet. "And what would I say?"

The heat in his face reminded her of the desire that had warmed them both, but he was already sliding away.

He fumbled for the door handle, his demon-perfected vision skewed by the corrective lenses, but he didn't remove the spectacles and he didn't look back. The latch clicking closed was louder than the footsteps carrying him away.

She pursed her lips and slouched back on the pillows.

She should let him go. He was shocked, hurting, blaming her. She should keep her mouth closed and wait for him to come around again.

Waiting she knew. Untold years had passed her as she waited in her haze.

Without another thought, she rose and went to the bath to clean herself. What a delight it was to have warm water at her fingertips.

The white dress was spattered with dried blood and ichor from the tussle behind the Coil, so she dug through the shopping bags next to the bed. She found the spray bottle of liquid that Nim had promised, no matter how bad the fight, would remove all stains. Too bad it only worked on the external signs.

Alyce pulled on another new dress, also white. "White for innocence," Nim had said while they shopped. "What talya could resist?" The ribbed fabric clung to her body, but it went down to her knees so she didn't bother with the underclothes. She left her boots behind too. Sidney would not go far.

She didn't know much, but she was coming to know him.

The warehouse halls stretched silent around her. Nim had explained the concept of energy sinks that dampened the teshuvas' emanations when they gathered together. Still, the faint signatures swirled in Alyce's awareness. One thread—brighter to her senses than the others—tugged her downward, down the stairs to the basement lab.

Of course, he'd have to know for certain.

He slumped on a stool beside the table where he'd kissed her. She touched her lips. If she tried that again, would she rouse him from his doldrums?

No, he was holding fast to his old ways. She couldn't take that from him as cruelly as her past had been taken from her.

She crept around him and pulled up another stool, out of temptation's reach. She sat and waited. Waiting was easier next to him.

Still, it was a long time before he spoke. "It's true."

She didn't answer since she couldn't disagree.

"I was going to run a spectral analysis, do a deep retinal scan—the teshuva presence warps certain structures of the sclera, you know."

"I did not know."

He tightened his fist in his lap. "Well, it does. But it's quicker to just shove a scalpel through your hand and see if it heals."

That explained the little knife on the table beside him, next to the abandoned eyeglasses. A smear of crimson discolored the white paper sheet smoothed over the surface. "Still hurts, though," she noted.

"Like hell."

She offered him a tentative smile that faded when he didn't reflect it.

"I can't be possessed, Alyce."

She cocked her head. "You just said—"

"Certainly not by a middling-ranked crave demon." His fist pressed into his flank over his hidden *reven*. "My whole life, I wanted one thing—*one* thing: to be a Bookkeeper."

"My whole life, I only wanted . . ."

His gaze sharpened, and she realized the Bookkeeper hadn't gone far. "Did you remember something?"

"Nothing." She lifted her bare feet onto the stool to hug her knees. "I remember there was nothing I dared to want."

"Nothing at all?"

"And that's what I got. Nothingness." How peculiar, then, that she had wanted nothing and her teshuva had led her to the crave demon that wanted Sidney. And yet he didn't want her.

He shook his head. "It's not nothing. There's a whole world below the one where most people live their entire, oblivious lives. It's beyond fascinating."

She blinked. "Fascinating?"

"Good. Evil. The battle that started it all. The fight that

never ends. And I just wanted to be part of it. But the Bookkeeper post passes from father to eldest son. I could have gone my entire, oblivious life without knowing what my father and brother were, without knowing what they knew."

"Why would they keep that from you? Even as a child you must have had this curiosity."

He gave a short, wry laugh. "Oh, I was suited to it. But the rules were set in stone. Quite literally."

"But they changed the rules for you."

"Hardly. My brother told me everything so I wouldn't tattle on him." He leaned back against the table with a sigh. "I was seven. He was thirteen. Most Bookkeepers ensure they have only one son. From the first, I was a mistake."

Alyce tightened her lips. "I heard your father's voice over the phone. He loves you."

"And I worshipped him. Which is why it hurt to watch him and Wes disappear together for hours into their workshop. So when Wes told me to come with him one night, of course I went."

"He told you all their secrets."

"He snuck me through the back door of a liquor store, shoved a flask of whiskey down the front of my pants, and told me to run." Sidney clenched his hand in his lap. The place where he'd stabbed himself as a test had faded to almost nothing.

She studied the gesture. "And your clever escape marked you of interest to a devil who would one day—tonight—recruit your prowess in the fight against evil."

He snorted. "The clerk caught on instantly. Wes vanished. I panicked and fell down in the parking lot. The glass sliced my femoral artery." He flattened his palm over his hip bone, fingers resting where a bottle would have nestled. The blood spatter echoed the swirls she had seen of his hidden *reven*, as if the old wound had bled through the years. "But I suppose that *was* my penance trigger. That instant marked a change of course that set me on the path to where I am now. Didn't appreciate it at the time since I was bleeding out in the parking lot."

"One way to get your father's attention," she said. "He must have been furious with your brother."

"He never found out. Wes told me if I shut up, he'd show me the workshop. He had a novice Bookkeeper key by then. After I recovered, Dad gave me a whipping and an excruciatingly boring lecture on alcoholism. But I kept my word, and Wes kept his."

"Was it worth the whipping?"

He spread his hands, taking in the lab, and for a moment the drab white walls and sterile technology glowed with his reflected enthusiasm. "It was everything I dreamed. The best fairy tale with all the monsters come to life. And it was my secret." He lowered his hands. "Except it wasn't really mine. It was my brother's."

"Still, your father must have been pleased with your dedication." She wished she'd known that boy. The strong, blunt shapes of the man he would become must have been present in the child who had known his own mind so young.

Sidney shook his head. "No one found out, not for a long time. When I was twelve, I wrote the papers Wes needed to make journeyman. He was eighteen then, and trying to balance university—regular classes, with girls and everything—with his Bookkeeper duties. He liked the real world better. The journeyman work was hard, and I wanted to turn in his application research with something that would really make the Bookkeeper masters sit up and take notice."

"That would make your father notice you."

His lips curled without humor. "You know me better than I knew myself."

"You were so young." Now she wished she'd known that boy so she could wrap her arms around him, to meet his gaze and reassure him someone, sometime, would see him for himself.

"Which is why I completely buggered the attempt to sneak into a feralis den and collect tissue samples."

She straightened so abruptly, her chair rocked. "Why would you think—?"

"I wasn't thinking." He stared down as if the square floor tiles held an answer. "I crawled out my bedroom window in the wee hours of the morning. I planned to rifle the den—Dad had maps of nesting sites all around London—before the feralis returned and be home for breakfast with none the wiser."

She slipped off the chair and crept up next to him. She boosted herself onto the counter but didn't touch him. She just leaned a little closer to share her presence. "What happened?"

"If I'd not always had my nose buried in a book, I would have noticed how my mum kept watch. Her husband and her eldest were always gone about their own business; she wasn't going to lose another child to strange activities she wasn't allowed to share. Maybe after the liquor store, she suspected I'd do any stupid thing to get Dad's attention."

"She followed you."

He jerked his head once in a nod. "And while she lectured me on my various sins—sneaking about, stealing pin money for bus fare, breaking a mother's heart—the feralis returned."

"Oh no." Unable to stop herself, she leaned her forehead against his shoulder—his feralis-bitten, teshuva-healed shoulder.

"I'd studied these things and knew what they were. Even then, I couldn't believe it—not the awful reality of it."

He closed his eyes and touched the center of his forehead, as if he could push the memories down again. Her demon had tried to do that for her. But it was too late—then and now.

He continued. "I don't know what she saw. My father never told her anything about demons. She thought he worked for a covert government agency with some code of secrecy. Whenever she got down about it, he'd joke that if he told her what he wanted for supper, he'd have to kill her. That always made her laugh."

He took a deep breath that bumped his arm into hers. "It was just one feralis. Husk composition, mostly gull and crab. Stank worse than the Thames low tide. When the barnacle's feeding fans started to eat her, she screamed at me to run."

"I hope you did."

"I'd brought forceps to collect the samples, so I stabbed those into the barnacles. They snapped shut. Almost bit my fingers off. One slap of the wing knocked me senseless. At least I didn't have to watch her die." Though Alyce couldn't see his face, half-obscured by his hand against his head, she felt the shudder rip through him, telegraphed to her through the press of his arm where he hadn't pulled away. "I woke up in league headquarters. Until then, I'd only read references to it in Dad's notes, and I would've done anything to see it. But not like that."

"A talya saved you?" Had his teshuva summoned one of its brethren to save him, just as she had been drawn to the alley? Was it even back then watching over him, a fallen guardian angel? She didn't think Sidney would appreciate the possibility, not now.

"Everyone said it was dumb luck they found me." He finally lowered his hand and rubbed at the bloody streaks across his knuckles—all the evidence that remained of where he'd cut himself. He obviously was unconvinced what sort of luck it had been. "There wasn't enough of Mum to bury, and the league couldn't allow a human investigation. So Dad put it around that she'd gotten tired of his long hours and left him. The ladies she talked to over the fence had heard her complain often enough about Dad, so they believed it."

He grimaced. "She was snipped out of our lives so neatly,

as if she'd never been. And I realized Dad had married her for exactly those reasons. I wondered if I went through his notes, would I find a checklist: acquire long-suffering wife; spawn future Bookkeeper; preserve world in formaldehyde and three-ring binders. . . ."

Alyce folded her hand over his to still the obsessive chafing. "You remember her, though."

He pushed to his feet. "Not that it mattered." He tossed the soiled scalpel in the sink and washed his hands. "My brother took it hardest. He left his Bookkeeper key behind and just . . . left." He rested his dripping hands on the edge of the sink. "Dad was devastated. I went after Wes, of course, to pick up the pieces as I always did. He told me there were no more pieces. I had them all."

"Is knowledge like that? Only one person may possess it?"

"Knowledge, no. Secrets, maybe." Back at the exam table, he yanked the paper sheet loose from the end and unspooled a fresh length across the surface. He crumpled the old piece. "I was young, but I was ready to take his place. I knew everything he should have known. The senior Bookkeepers came down hard on my father for missing our trickery. But Dad was popular with the other masters, and by then his cancer had been diagnosed, which made the question of succession more problematic."

"But you're here now. They must believe in your work."

He put the scalpel in a small oven and set a timer. The stink of heated steel drifted through the lab as he purged the knife, burning away the last traces of proof of his possession.

Other than the demon now lodged in his soul.

When he faced her again, his hands hung empty at his sides. "They expect me to fail. They said making sense of the upheaval here this last year is impossible. They think there's nothing to be done except what we've always done."

"That is not enough," she said.

"I might have agreed, especially after what happened at the church. But I have failed, exactly as they predicted." His smile cracked hard and unamused. "Well, not *exactly* as they predicted."

He walked toward the bank of gently humming machines she had no names for and stood facing their blank displays. He tilted his head wearily to one side, as if he too were trying to make sense of the dials and triggers. "What am I supposed to do now?"

The undertone of desperate dismay triggered the devil in her. It uncoiled with a familiar, threatening chill that might have frightened her once, as she lost control of herself. But Sidney had noted that its dread cut both ways. Did the control work both ways too? Who was the master in her soul?

The chill seemed to lift a bit, and between its loosening mists, she caught a glimpse of what she'd been.

"I didn't know either," she said softly. "When I was possessed, I thought the world had come to an end."

Sidney's shoulders stiffened, and he turned to face her. "I didn't say *the* world was ending. Just *my* world."

"What other world did I know?" She curled in tighter on herself, as if she could squeeze out memories. "I wasn't smart like Sera or strong like Jilly or sensual like Nim. I was small—only a servant." The teshuva's haze hovered around her vision like a stubborn fog bank. Very deliberately, she said, "I remember . . ." And an edge of the fog peeled up. "I remember my master spoke of devils. He reveled in them as a goodwife delights in her hens' many eggs. In his speaking, he summoned them." She took a breath, and when she exhaled, the teshuva's protective mist dissolved. "His words conjured fear and brought the demon that came for me." She looked up, refusing to hide her face. "If I had remembered before, I would have recognized yours. I could have told you."

Sidney gripped the counter behind him. "I know you couldn't have stopped it. No one could."

"But before you said—"

"Wishful thinking. Possession occurs when the demon resonates with the weakness in your soul. The weakness doesn't vanish just because we know it's there."

She couldn't hold herself any tighter. "Then we had no choice. Despite what Nim likes to say."

He came slowly across the room, and she wondered what force drove him. His teshuva? Her self-pitying words? He stopped just out of reach.

"I have to talk to Liam. He's going to be furious. And then I have to call my father. Will you go back to your room now?"

"I could go with you." The suggestion sounded small, squeezed past her constricted throat.

He shook his head. "I know the dangers of an unsettled possession. I'll be fine."

That wasn't why she had offered. But her throat closed the rest of the way, and there was nothing left to say.

CHAPTER 14

"Is it Friday yet?" Liam spiked his fingers through his hair again, though the morning wind chuffing across the warehouse roof kept trying to flatten it. "This week has sucked."

As reactions to Sid's revelation went, it could have gone worse.

Clouds were massing higher, but at the horizon, the pale blue sky was quartz sharp—the same shade as Alyce's eyes, bright with desire.

The view kept blurring as Sid struggled to focus around the corrective lenses of his spectacles. Finally, he tucked them into his breast pocket. "You think your week's been bad?"

The league leader scowled. "I'd finally gotten the crew hammered into some shape that wasn't slicing at itself as often as the enemy. Then you showed up and threw everything out of whack. And then Alyce. And now you again."

"So sorry." Sid pushed a hefty dose of sarcasm through the word.

"Sorry is right. Sorry excuse for a . . ." Liam bit back the rest.

"No worries, old boy. I already said it myself. Shitty Bookkeeper. Worse talya. What was the teshuva thinking?"

Liam waved one hand. "None of the league—Bookkeeper or talya—has ever pretended to have a clue what the demons think."

Sid wondered if that was supposed to be some sort of apology. "On the plus side, you don't have to convince me I'm possessed."

"True. And that part is always so awkward and circular— 'yes, demons exist; no, you're not crazy; yes, demons exist'— like some damn square dance." Liam straightened abruptly. "Fuck. I know who your partner was, don't I?"

Despite the chill in the wind, Sid's face heated. "I hope you'll be discreet with your hypothesis," he said stiffly.

"Only thing worse would be if you'd slept with Sera or Nim."

"Not worried about Jilly?"

"She'd kill you before I could." Liam groaned. "Why couldn't you have balanced the teshuva's virgin ascension the old-fashioned way? With a nice round of fisticuffs? Any of us would've been happy to oblige. But I suppose you found your own virgin ascension."

Though Liam's tone was more cynical than crude, Sid's gut tightened as if someone had punched him. The shock radiated up from the newly etched *reven* on his belly and stole his breath.

And his common sense apparently, since he suddenly found himself toe-to-toe with the rangy league leader.

Toe-to-toe did not mean nose-to-nose, unfortunately. He canted his head to pin the taller man with a hard stare. "I'll ask you not to say such things about her."

Liam did not move a muscle, and still his presence seemed to double. The demon's mark at his temple flared violet.

Sid had always considered himself a pro at conflict avoidance. After all, as a mere child, he'd weaseled his way into a quasi-military/religious underground organization that had taught paranoia to the Templars. Everything he'd achieved had come from books and brains and that early bit of black-mail.

Brawn had never been his MO. The demon was defi-nitely a bad influence, because even once he thought it through, he didn't back down.

Liam gave him a slow blink. "I am not going to fight with you now, talya. You are already good and possessed."

Sid tried to roll his weight from the balls of his feet to his heels, a nonconfrontational, purely conversational stance. The effort had him swaying from side to side. His muscles were not his own anymore—not entirely.

"Knock it off, teshuva," he hissed. "I don't want to fight with you too."

Liam's lips quirked. "Just give in to it."

"It wants to punch you."

"Oh. Then I hope you win this fight."

"I want to punch you too."

"Goodness. How did we not notice you were talya mate-rial?" Liam tilted his head, letting his direct gaze slide off Sid's. "Probably all the tweed distracted us."

Between the note of almost fond amusement and the re-direction of the challenging stare, the tension across the back of Sid's neck eased. He angled his body toward the open sky. "I don't plan to start giving in to any random impulses, mine or the teshuva's."

"Other than the one earlier tonight." Liam lifted one eyebrow. "You need to understand the well-being of my talyan is vital to the city. And to me."

"Alyce is . . ." Various words jumbled through Sid's head and then sank beneath a layer of pure primitive sensation—possessiveness. He couldn't hold back the announcement any more than he could stop his body's immediate heated reaction to the thought of her. "Alyce is mine."

Liam sighed. "Yes. I got that. And you are hers." He propped his big fists on his hips. "And both of you are mine. I will not have a pair of interlocked rogues running wild in my city. God knows what chaos you'd unleash."

Sid clenched the front of his shirt where he'd done up the buttons unevenly. His wrist pressed against his hip bone, and even through the fabric, he swore he felt the spark of the *reven* flaring in time with his radial pulse. "Worse than what you had before we showed up here?"

"Smart-ass." Liam rubbed his forehead. "It has been a long night. It's going to be a longer day. We'll present you as a *symballein* pair to the rest of the league first thing tomorrow. Maybe I'll have Jilly make cookies for the occasion."

Sid stiffened. "I can't stay here. I have to go back to London. My father and the league there are expecting me."

"Expecting this?"

Sid bristled. "Of course not. I have to talk to him. To them. I'll make them understand."

"And Alyce?"

"She will come with me." He'd have to explain to her too. Never mind that he'd done a terrible job of explaining anything so far.

"You think the Old World is ready for a feral waif and a possessed archivist?"

Sid's muscles tightened again at the doubt in Liam's tone, but this time he welcomed the teshuva's forceful poise. Being on the wrong side of one war had obviously given it the ability to take a few hits and come back swinging.

But he thought of Alyce's way, and for once he kept his mouth shut.

Leaving the league leader to watch the sun clear the rooftops, Sid returned to his room—his own room, not Alyce's. He couldn't face her quite yet. And he still had to call his father.

He dialed on the antique rotary behemoth scented

faintly of cigarette smoke—undoubtedly a rescue from the salvaged junk upstairs. The apprentice Bookkeeper who served his father picked up on the first ring. "At-One London."

"Hullo, Hugh. Is Dad back from lunch?"

"He sent me out for tea on my own today."

Even through the long-distance line he heard unsaid words, like the bitterness of cheap tea leaves. Or was that the work of the teshuva, picking up clues so subtle he'd missed them before? "Hugh? What's wrong?"

"I think he throws away the biscuits I bring. He's getting so thin."

"He has stage four cancer." Sid almost bit his tongue. That was definitely the demon, blunt and cruel.

"So you should be here," Hugh snapped back, no devil but honesty in his tone.

Sid took the hit. Let the teshuva heal that pain. "Which is why I need to talk to him."

Without responding, Hugh transferred his call. His father's phone rang several times before it clicked over. "Son?"

Sid closed his eyes. How could a mere voice—far away and softer than it should be—hurt him? "Dad, how's it going?"

"Inevitably forward, with moments of relativity."

"You've been reading Stephen Hawking again, haven't you?"

"Needed something to tide me over. Hugh won't share his manga since I made notes in the margins."

"We all have our limits," Sid said. "Speaking of lines in the sand, or concrete, as the case may be ..."

"Chicago has always been a contrary league," his father mused. "And since their last Bookkeeper was unreliable, I don't doubt they'd give you trouble."

"Actually, Liam Niall wants me to join them."

"As their Bookkeeper? It's not London, but—"

Sid winced at how badly he was mangling this. "As talya."

Silence.

Even the teshuva couldn't pick up a sound. "Dad?"

"What happened?"

"I wish I knew." He thought of the blank pages in the Bookkeeper archive tally, and his fingers itched for a pen. "I *really* wish I knew."

"Sidney . . . Son, this is . . . I don't know what to say."

Considering all the words tumbling through his brain, none of them in coherent order, Sid could relate. "Not much *to* say. Which is possibly why the talyan don't tell us anything."

"You sacrificed your soul to get an inside angle?"

Sid tried to deflect the defensive flare at the accusation. "Bookkeepers make sacrifices all the time. Say good-bye to blissful ignorance, a nine-to-five job, any meaningful family dinner conversation. . . ."

"Sidney, this is not a time to joke. The other European masters will never accept a talya in the Bookkeeper ranks."

"Why not? Who better to understand?"

"But the danger—"

"Somewhat offset by immortality." Sid tried to keep his tone teasing.

But his father was having none of it. "The danger isn't to your life and soul—at least, not *just* that—but your impartiality."

Sid sat heavily on the corner of the small desk. "What's the point of impartiality? It's not as if we're going to root for the other side."

"The teshuva *were* the other side." Through the phone, the creak of a chair conjured up the image in Sid's head of his father leaning back at his big polished desk, quite unlike the dinged hutch tucked away in this empty room in a salvage warehouse. "The teshuva were part of the army that sought to vanquish light and order and life. That they repented is marvelous. Without them making amends to scour the earth of the remnants of that dark army, we'd be even deeper in shite."

Sid choked back a laugh. "Is that the approved Book-keeper term?"

His father wouldn't be distracted. "The angelic- and djinn-possessed exist in complete opposition; yet neither have their own version of Bookkeepers. Why not? Because they are sure of their actions. Right or wrong, dark or light, they strive forward. The teshuva, though, they can never again be certain they are on the path. And so they have us. Their conscience. Without our unblinking, dispassionate witness, they may again stray."

Sid remembered sneaking the Bookkeeper key from beneath his brother's pillow and creeping down to the workshop in the dead of night. He had never been dispassionate about what he'd learned. "Doesn't there come a time when one's deeds outweigh one's failures?"

"For all their good intentions now, the teshuva cannot be trusted. They broke their faith once."

As Sid himself had, came the unspoken corollary. A stillness, chill as death, sank into his bones. It was not just the condemnation he heard in his father's words, but the demon, accepting its punishment.

He'd wanted into this league, to know its secrets, come hell or high water. He'd have to watch out for floods since he'd already conjured hell. Maybe the weakness of wanting that characterized the crave demon had made *it* vulnerable to *him*.

"Dad, do you think I betrayed you?"

In the second period of silence, the hiss of distance and the rush of blood through his ears seemed muted, as if the demon had pulled deep inside him and didn't want to hear the answer.

"It's not about me anymore, Sidney. My time here is past. Whatever I say, the other masters will weigh this with your unorthodox entry into the training and ..."

"And think I am a rogue Bookkeeper. I've read the suggestions for dealing with a rogue talya. What is the protocol among Bookkeepers?" He couldn't keep the remoteness out of his voice.

"You know perfectly well there is no protocol since this has never happened before."

Not really the answer he wanted to hear. He might risk facing the council of masters himself, but he wouldn't put Alyce in front of them. They *did* have rules about her kind.

All the years of studies that had spread so steadily under his feet crumbled around the edges. He'd always lived between two worlds—the Bookkeepers who hadn't wanted him and the humans who would never have believed him. Now he stretched into a third dimension with the talyan.

Of course, the real world *was* three dimensional.

"Dad, I'm sorry this is coming as such a shock. It's been . . . unsettling for me too." He was relieved that mastery of the understatement came as industry-standard with Bookkeeper training. "When I get home—"

"Don't come to London, Sidney."

Short words delivered like crossbow arrows.

Sid gripped the edge of the table. "What?"

"There's nothing left for you here."

"You're there."

"Not for long." A hesitation, and Sid braced himself for another volley. "Wesley is back."

Sid closed his eyes. "And I can only say again, 'What?' "

"Right after you left. We had tea together today. We talked a long time. It was good."

Hugh would be overjoyed the old man was eating. "I wish I could have joined you while he is in town."

"He's coming back. To the league. For good."

"Had I even left Heathrow yet?"

"Sidney," his father chided.

"I don't care about winning the council's favor, Dad. I want to be there for you."

"You were. All the years when your brother was gone, you were here."

And now that the prodigal son—the one who hadn't killed his mother—had returned, what use for the place-holder? Sidney remembered the steel cold against his cheek as he'd pressed his ear to the closed and locked workshop door, straining to hear the voices of his father and brother.

The possessed tended to lack close connections in the world; such isolation widened the flaws in their souls that made them vulnerable to demonic possession. He'd never considered himself one of those people, but apparently the teshuva had known better.

He didn't remember what he said after that, but he didn't think it was horrible or even particularly strained. His father asked him to call back soon; he promised—and the promise bounced around the hollow of his chest—then he hung up.

It was all very civilized, really, considering.

He threw the phone.

Whipping the cord behind, it bounced off the wall with a crash and a startled *bing* from its chimes. It left a satisfying dent in the plaster, and he was viciously glad he hadn't been calling on a cheap plastic cell.

Without warning, his door opened. Alyce slipped inside.

He looked away. "I told you to go to your room."

"But I belong where you are."

"I know this is hard for you to understand, because you don't remember how much time has passed since your possession. But this is a new era. Women don't belong to anyone anymore."

She tipped her head, studying him.

The fury in him that had launched the phone surged, like an electrical current seeking ground. "I am not your master, Alyce."

"I know. My master was a bad man. The memories are

coming back to me, in flashes. The teshuva doesn't hold me so hard when I think of you holding me."

His anger dissipated, leaving him flat. "The talyan cling to their solitary ways. I never thought the teshuva might want something else."

"I don't know if I want to remember more."

"So, did you come here to break up with me?"

She tilted her head another degree, toward the debris on the floor. "You've been breaking things without me."

It was hard to tease her when they barely shared the same language. He crossed the room to the broken phone and gathered the pieces. Without the churning anger to justify his behavior, he felt stupid to have ruined the old thing. "I just called my father."

She obviously realized she didn't need to ask how the revelation had gone. "No man would want this for his son."

"Liam didn't take it much better, and he needs all the talyan he can lay his hands on." He dumped the phone in the trash before he pulled the broken spectacles from his breast pocket.

The sticky duct tape snagged on his fingertips; then the specs clattered to the bottom of the dustbin.

She laced her fingers in front of her. "I want you to stay here."

He straightened slowly. How did she speak her mind like that, without fear? He'd abandoned her, rather rudely despite his understandable shock, after sharing . . . Well, according to what he knew of the *symballein* bond, they'd swapped more than body fluids; they might've exchanged shards of their souls.

He couldn't blame her if she ripped out his heart and took back whatever pieces were rightfully hers.

He sat on the edge of the bed. "Come here."

She didn't hesitate, but instead just settled beside him, close enough that her fitted skirt lapped his jeans.

Not even skin-to-skin, and still his body prickled with

awareness. Whatever beating his emotions had taken, the energy between them flowed unabated.

"I think in some ways you have the advantage on me," he said. "Everything I've read about and analyzed and debated doesn't mean much compared to what you simply know."

She shook her head. "I don't understand anything."

"Maybe not understand, but you've survived more than most on instinct alone."

"You told me you would help me, and you brought me here. I want to do what I can to help you." She gazed at him, her icy eyes an eerie mix of danger and innocent clarity. He wondered if the Arctic explorers of yore had felt the same tremor of excitement, stepping out onto the shifting floes in hope of enlightenment.

Of course, a lot of them had wandered off, starved, and frozen to death, their north-pointing compasses gone haywire as they lost the difference between the direction they'd always thought was right and what they discovered was true.

He'd never been a huge fan of analogies.

But it was daytime in the city, and only late October, which didn't get *that* cold, even in Chicago. So he nodded. "Take me out, Alyce. Show me your world."

They hopped a cab into the heart of downtown, and Sid was grateful for Alyce's silence. She probably was afraid if she opened her mouth, he'd start talking again. Didn't gag orders come standard issue with being talyan? Instead, he purged those old memories in the same way the demon erased scars.

Now they rolled around the place like unsettled marbles, dangerous underfoot. If Alyce had no one to hear her, no wonder her teshuva took her memories away. He was already sick of hearing himself, and he'd been possessed only a few hours.

The cab dropped them off on Wacker, next to the river. While he paid the driver, Alyce crossed the wide sidewalk and leaned on the concrete balustrade that overlooked the water, the gray towers looming beyond her in a hard straight frame around her gentle curves. He stuffed his hands in his pockets and observed her.

He'd gotten his first pair of spectacles when he was five. His astonishment when he'd realized that trees even at a distance had individual leaves had made his father chuckle. That same jolt of discovery went through him now as his demon-sharpened gaze lingered on the white arch of her cheekbone and the dark silky waves of her hair against the rough black wool of the coat he'd found for her.

She glanced over her shoulder and saw him watching. A hint of rose warmed her cheeks. "I thought you must be empty."

He thought of his father and Wes taking tea. "I'm not really in the mood for brunch."

"Not you. The demon. It sustains itself on tenebrae. I didn't understand any of it, but even in the beginning, when we fought the devils, I felt it feed."

He wrinkled his nose. "Brunch sounds better."

"The talyan hunt at night, but the devils—your tenebrae—are less guarded during the day," she told him. "That's when I fight them."

"The teshuva, like all demons, are stronger when our human sides are disadvantaged; in darkness, under stress, whatever. The league prefers to fight at night to hide any leftovers."

He joined her at the rail, and she pointed. "Look— there's a likely spot for malice."

Across the river, a broad walkway seemed to float just above the waterline. Benches and lampposts decorated the riverwalk, but now, under the menacing clouds, the concrete path was empty. "What am I looking at?"

"The ichor around that doorway."

The feeble October sun hardly bothered to cast shadows through the vellum of clouds, and still it washed out the elusive demon sign. Her senses must be finely honed to pick up any etheric disturbance. "I see a closed maintenance access."

The building at street level, above the riverside path, was under construction. Judging from the tattered vinyl sign flapping from the security fence, work had been under way for some time. Probably the weak economy hadn't helped the speed of renovations. One more winter of Chicago winds and there'd be nothing left of the sign.

"Closed, but not sealed," she said. "A dark place for the malice during the day, and they can sneak out with the night to find their brunch."

"Their preferred meal being us humans."

"Not us, not anymore."

The reminder set him back a mental step, and he followed a stride behind her as she crossed the bridge and took the stairs down to the riverwalk. How quickly he forgot he wasn't entirely human anymore. No wonder years had passed for her without note.

The riveted metal door spanned wider than his extended arms and must have once accepted deliveries at water level when the river had been more a path of commerce. Now, tufts of brown moss sprouted from the crack between door and frame.

Sid frowned. "So, how do we do this? We could find a way in from above since there's no real security. I didn't see a camera or—"

Alyce kicked the corner of the door—once, twice. The metal buckled with each blow. "Or we could just go this way." She grabbed the corner and peeled upward.

He winced at the squeal of stressed steel and glanced back toward the sidewalk where they'd looked down at the door. The cars whizzing by on Wacker seemed oblivious. "That is more straightforward."

She slipped out of her coat and folded it into a tidy triangle, which she left on the nearest bench. "But we could talk about it some more."

"Certainly not."

She eased past the bent metal.

How loudly would the other talyan laugh if he suggested they attempt to leave the city in better shape behind them? But as they stepped out of the light into the glimmer of red malice glares, he remembered "better" had different meanings.

"There are more here than there were in the alley," he murmured. "And that time, they almost sucked you dry."

"Good thing you are with me this time."

"But I don't know what I'm doing."

"Neither did I."

"But you do now, yes?"

She crept farther into the darkness, luminescent in her white dress, with the malevolent stars twinkling above her.

His vision shivered and refocused, and he realized the teshuva—quiescent in the sunlight—was rousing.

Rousing and hungry.

The damp stink of old brick couldn't hide the fouler stench of rotten eggs. "I smell birnenston," he whispered. "This is a feralis lair."

"Was," Alyce said. "Only old bones now."

She stopped in the center of the chamber. The space stretched to all sides, far enough and dark enough that his teshuva didn't even bother enhancing the view. His skin prickled. When he'd said he wanted to know the talya secrets, he'd thought that would involve more knowledge, more light, less . . . Yeah, that was dread.

Alyce raised her hands, and the malice freaked.

Sid might have indulged in some shrieking of his own, but the malice didn't leave an opening on any frequency. They scattered, the gleam of their eyeballs leaving crimson contrails through the gloom.

Those closest to Alyce spiraled down toward her out-stretched fingers. But before the oily specters reached her, they thinned to nothingness as her demon overwhelmed the lesser energies. Only their cries lingered.

That left about three-quarters of the horde heading straight for the open door—the open door behind him.

Alyce spun toward him, the dissipating ether a graceful streamer behind her. "Stop them, Sidney."

He held out his hands as she had.

Instead of thinning, the malice hit him like an avalanche of half-frozen, rancid marmalade. Sticky and bitter, it grated his skin with broken ice crystals.

He might have screamed then.

His teshuva flailed in the tenebrae chill, and his muscles locked seizure-stiff. With each pull of the malice mouths, he tasted the sour corrosion of their evil.

No, not theirs. His.

How deeply had he hid his exhilaration when Wes's departure cleared the way into his father's heart? How far down had he buried the guilt over his mother's death? Not so deep or so far that the malice didn't find it and dredge it up like a putrid hairball.

No wonder a demon from hell had found a place for itself in the cracks of his soul.

He sank to his knees.

"No, Sidney." Alyce knelt beside him. The white folds of her skirt washed into his narrowing vision. "Don't let them so close. Hold them back."

The malice or the memories? Now he understood how she'd survived tenebrae predation. The teshuva hadn't let her remember how she deserved this pain and horror and sickness.

He would like to forget too. But that wasn't his way. He'd never forgotten his feelings; he had just bottled the wretched things and observed from a careful distance, as he would any dangerous energy. Such was the Bookkeeper way.

He wanted to pull away from her—or maybe from himself—but she reached through the malice barricade to take his hands. Her pupils contracted to pinpricks as the teshuva's violet swelled. Though he outweighed her by a few stone, she wrapped her arms around him and dragged him up with her, breaking through the tenebrae crust. "Be with me, Sidney."

He could watch. He could contemplate. And he could die.

He'd been trained to be dispassionate, but the crave demon wanted. It wanted more. It wanted her.

It seemed ill-advised, thoughtless, and rash to do anything but run, so he kissed her.

He tightened his grip, and her heat sizzled through the deep freeze in his veins. The demon within him reveled in the sparks that raced through his veins, centered in the *reven* that pulsed oh-so close to parts of him that wanted to be even closer to her.

Mouth and breath and racing heartbeats matched one to the other.

Whatever flaws the demon had found in his soul seemed irrelevant when he was with her. Whatever was broken, missing, or ugly in him no longer mattered.

When he raised his head, the malice were gone, and only the faintest smear of ichor gloaming lit the basement. "What just happened?"

"A kiss," she said.

She meant it as an explanation, not a request, but with no horde to fight, the demon seemed to sink away, replete, and his purely male impulses rose, not at all satisfied, so he kissed her again. When he finally reined himself in to draw back, he thought his heart had thundered off without him, leaving him breathless and light.

She blinked, her pale blue eyes shining under half-lowered lashes. "I meant, the kiss is what happened."

"I know what you meant." His husky growl surprised

him, and he cleared his throat. "Was that the talya version of a first date?"

"And the teshuva version of a betrothal feast."

He held himself unmoving. "Betrothal. The teshuva move fast."

"Keeps us from being gutted by ferales. We should try those next."

"Whoa." Despite the inadvertent flinch from the word "betrothal," he tightened his grasp on her. "I'm not up to the same speed as you."

She didn't look contrite. "Hurry."

"For a girl as old as you are, you are very impatient. I want to look around."

"There's nothing else here. Except the two of us." She narrowed her eyes a bit more with a flirty fluttering. "Is that what you mean?"

Despite all that had just happened, his body roused to her innocent guile. Apparently, the only energy to recover more speedily than a well-fed teshuva was unfulfilled male lust.

It was impossible to focus with her icy eyes burning through him. He took her by the shoulders and turned her to face toward the walls. "There's something about this place. Your teshuva sees the little things mine doesn't. What do you see here?"

She nestled back into his hands, but her tone was serious as she pointed. "The bricks are burned, there and there. Ichor scorched, deep. See? From the destruction of tenebrae stronger than malice."

"Like ferales and salambes." He followed behind her to peer at the wall where the mortar seemed to melt and sag. "This was the site of a talya battle?"

"There are many such places in the city. You won't find markers, though—no one to know who fought; none to say who survived and who didn't."

"That would have been my job." Sid straightened and dropped his hands from her shoulders. The loss prickled, but was it the loss of her trusting warmth or the hard work he'd thrown away? "As Bookkeeper, I would have kept those records."

She went to the doorway and stood framed in the wan sunlight. She looked back at him; her gaze and the sky, melded together as one hue, dazzled him a moment. "We will have to remember ourselves."

On the way out, he paused to bend the door back into some semblance of fitting.

Watching his own hands mold steel, he couldn't hold back a stunned laugh. "Incredible."

But then he held Alyce's coat while she slipped her slender arms through the sleeves. He trembled a little when he turned the collar up to protect her against the wind, and her dark locks tickled his knuckles. With each moment going forward, he would have to balance between teshuva violence and human shock, between every day and eternity.

He shook his head and took a few steps away.

Abruptly, he turned and looked up in a burst of realization. "Wait. Now I know this place." He tapped the back of his skull as if he could knock the reference loose. "It was in Sera's skimpy notes about the last year. This was where Corvus Valerius brought her to try to tear into the tenebraeternum."

"There was another verge here?"

"No, this first attempt was a failure. They ended up destroying the building but not Blackbird. The verge at the pier . . . I think that's the beginning of something worse." Sudden energy—his, not the teshuva's—revved through him. "There's still so much we don't know, and now . . ."

"Now you are even more a part of it," she said.

God, she saw right through him. And what did it say about him when the feral waif with no memory of her past tried to reassure him that he still had a place in the fight?

He tried to summon another smile. "Me and my demon, we're there."

If only because they had nowhere else to go.

* * *

Alyce tried to shelter in the lee of Sidney's broad shoulders as they followed the riverwalk toward the lake, but the chill wind sneaked around him to nip at her ears. Still, the little whistle of it was louder than her companion.

His uncharacteristic silence worried her. But she knew one way—well, another way besides kissing—to distract him. "When did the world stop believing in demons?"

Sidney drifted to a halt near the decorative grillwork rail, the focus of his brown eyes going vague.

Ah, it was the look of a scholar confronting an interesting question. She paused beside him and tucked her nose down into the collar of the black coat he'd wrapped around her earlier.

"Some people still believe in demons," he said. "Many more people would say they believe in evil, even if they don't think much about what that means." He leaned his forearms on the railing to stare out, as if the history were written in the gray chop of the water. "Paine's *Age of Reason* in the 1790s let the masses question the mythologies they had taken for granted, including the existence of the devil. Maybe go farther back, to the First Great Awakening of the 1730s, when religion became a personal encounter with God, not an externally imposed experience engineered by intellectual and spiritual superiors. Before that, some of the more unfortunate elements of the Reformation still cropped up: persecuting heretics, burning witches, and believing in demons."

He took a breath to continue, then let it out again. "More words, right? But you did ask." His wryly amused expression faded. "Alyce?"

Despite the shelter of her coat, she shivered uncontrollably. "What did you say?"

"Which part?" He turned toward her to rub her arms, but the friction of the wool felt far away. "Are you all right? You asked when the world stopped believing in demons."

"And witches."

"In this country, I think the last witch hunts petered out beginning of the eighteenth century. The point where doubts crept in was probably the Salem trials in— Alyce!"

Without her conscious thought, she was running.

The demon whipped her like cat-o'-nine-tails against the backs of her legs, driving her onward with the uncontainable urge to escape.

She forgot Sidney was possessed too.

She'd gone a half-dozen strides before he tackled her from behind. They went down in a tangle of flapping coats.

She fought him. "Get away. Get away."

"Alyce, I'm not leaving you like this."

"We have to get away!"

"From what?" He hauled her upright, his head swinging side to side as he tried to track the threat.

Her breath heaved. "I don't know. My devil says get away."

"My teshuva says I'm going to have bruises from that kick, but nothing worse."

She strained against his hold. "There is worse. There was worse."

Sidney led her to the closest bench and pressed her down. He held her there when the teshuva tried to straighten her legs again, despite the suddenly fierce ache in her knee. "Why doesn't your demon want you to think about the Salem witch trials?"

"It was me," she whispered. The cold of the bench, the water, the sky, sank into her bones and out through her skin on the other side, as if she didn't exist in between. "I killed my master. I was the witch."

CHAPTER 15

It all flooded back to her in a cold rush, as if the demon had spewed back the memories it had hidden, and she clung to Sidney's hand lest the deluge wash her away. "Every night that summer, the master of the house came to my room and whipped me. He wanted me to confess."

"To being a witch?"

"To admit I was tempting him. He said he wanted me to stop."

Sidney's fingers tightened on hers. "Why did he keep coming to your room—at night—if he didn't want to be tempted?"

"I asked that too. Then he used his fists."

"So the teshuva killed him."

She pulled free of Sidney's gentle grasp and ducked her forehead to her knees, fingertips pressed to her temples. In her head, the gray tide seemed to roll closer, a threat and an escape. "No." She wasn't sure if she spoke to Sidney or to the teshuva. She did not want the pardon of willful blindness from either of them. "This was before the demon. I killed him."

She raised her head, refusing to hide. She might be afraid to confront the memory of what she'd done, and the demon had granted her reprieve for a long time, but the dread—the not knowing—was worse.

Sidney raised his hand to cup her chin, his thumb soothing her cheekbone to brush away the bruises that had long ago faded.

It was as if she were one of those oversized tomes in his lab, strapped to hold the weight of musty pages together, the constraints loosened at his touch. The memories fell out in a flurry, so she could pick up each one, dust it off, and remember.

"I was a servant in his house. After my father died and we lost the farm, I needed to take a position. I had nine years on my contract, and I'd served seven. Seven years seemed like such a long time, but . . ."

"But not compared to more than three hundred years in service to the teshuva." His hand slipped to her shoulder, and he pulled her close under his arm.

She curled up against him, his presence more of a shield than even the thick wool of the coat. "Three hundred years? Has it been that long?"

"I suppose you haven't been reading the papers."

She rested her head on his shoulder and closed her eyes. "It's so clear now. Not the three hundred years, but before. As though no time has passed."

His storytelling voice rumbled through her. "As far as the teshuva is concerned, that's no time at all. When it possessed you, it couldn't find the balance it needed to keep you—"

"Sane?"

He squeezed her. "Coherent. Those centuries must have passed for you as they would for an unbound demon, just drifting. I wonder how you got from the East Coast to Chicago."

"Drifting. Before I met you, I avoided any talya; when I saw their eyes, I knew I was too weak. But I remember pieces. Mostly pieces of the tenebrae." She pressed her hands over her closed lids, as if one more layer of flesh could block out the visions. "There was a hospital that locked me up. And there was a church. I went to a church once and asked the man there to chase the devil from me. Or kill me. He might have been the janitor." She forced herself to put her hands in her lap and look at him. "Not enough to fill three hundred years, is it?"

"And do you remember when the demon came to you? Your teshuva buried it for a long time."

She was silent a moment, feeling the ebb of the demon daze. But had she really struggled clear, like climbing a mountaintop to rise above the clouds, or was this an outbound tide that would sweep in again? "Why is it letting go now?"

"Because you're strong enough now to balance it, strong enough to remember."

She didn't feel particularly strong. Only Sidney's arm around her shoulders held her upright. "Maybe because you're here, to hear and explain."

Though he didn't move, his body stiffened almost imperceptibly, and she wriggled out from under his arm, from under his weighted stare. "Or maybe not." She paced toward the rail. "Even if I remember, I don't have to think about it. That's what you do."

"I know exactly the second the teshuva took me," he said, as if she hadn't just refused to share. "When we stood in the alley last night and the malice swarmed you, I knew I couldn't stand there and watch."

Away from the curve of his arm, the wind off the river snapped at her, and she shivered. "So I am the reason you are possessed."

"That isn't what I meant. I want you to know I wouldn't just stand and watch, and talk, and study. I want you to believe I'm not here for the footnotes alone." He didn't reach out to her again, but his gaze was steady.

She stared down at where she'd twisted her knuckles white and tried to match his detached tone. "A devil had come and was loose among us. One of the slave women who belonged to the farmer down the lane, she knew. She had the sight, but no one believed her."

"No one but you."

"Not even me. But—but when the master said I was tempting him, I knew what would happen. *That* I could see as clearly as the old woman saw the devil circling. We'd already heard the fates of the evil women of Salem."

"Was there no one you could go to for protection?"

"Everyone had gone crazy. They saw witches in the women and devils in the dogs and evil in every shadow."

Reluctantly, he nodded. "The lesser tenebrae are drawn to the etheric energy of an unbound demon."

"And the demon was there for me." She took a breath. "I didn't know that, but I knew my master's frustration would boil over into accusations. I did tell then."

"Considering the time period, it must have been hard for a servant to report her employer's misbehavior."

She shot him a disbelieving look. "Hard? Impossible. I didn't tell them the truth. Not the whole truth. I went to our neighbor, whose cow had broken into my master's fields and later died. I said my master poisoned the cow."

She wrapped her arms tight around herself, scant replacement for his warm bulk. "I said I'd been whipped to stop me from speaking. After the magistrate saw the wounds on my back, they took me away. The neighbor accused my master of witchcraft. They hanged him. And he wasn't the only one."

Sidney sat back on the bench as if she had pushed him. "You?"

"No. I . . . watched. I only watched." She clutched the tightly buttoned neck of her coat until she couldn't swallow past the knot of her fingers. "Once I tried to scream. I think that was the moment the demon came to me."

Sidney rubbed his eyes. "I don't remember all the specifics of the Salem witch trials."

"I do," she whispered. "The pointing fingers. The black cloaks of the magistrates. The dead."

"I've read how symptoms mistaken for deviltry—convulsions, hallucinations, that sort of thing—might have been caused by ergot poisoning in the rye crop."

"That and the wandering demon." She wouldn't accept his false consolation. "The demon that wanted me. And my words added to the dread."

"You were as much a victim as any."

"But my words started the deaths, and I didn't die."

"I think you've found there is worse." He leaned forward, elbows on knees as he stared at the river. "The teshuva resonated with the flaw in your soul, but it came to you where you had no chance of becoming what it needed. Worse, its presence brought the tenebrae, which only deepened the burden of its debt to the light. Maybe it thought—as nearly as we can imagine it thinks—that it was doing the right thing to make you forget for so long."

She scowled. "Or maybe it was easier for the devil to have a servant who didn't ask awkward questions."

"I like questions."

The blunt statement eased her grip around her neck. "You aren't afraid when I ask."

He shook his head. "Too stupid to be afraid."

"Too curious."

"Same thing, maybe." His eyes reflected the gloomy water. "I've been told not to go back to London. The place I thought I had is gone. And I can't even feel bad about it because it means Wes is home, with Dad, where he should have been all this time."

"Can you talk yourself into believing that?"

His sideways glance struck hers. "Eventually." His lips quirked. "If I talk long enough."

She stood, wavering just a bit, as if she'd suddenly found Nim's sky-high heels strapped to her feet. She wasn't any taller, but her perspective had changed, and the demon shifted in her. Was it accommodating the changes, or just uneasy?

Sidney was at her elbow in a heartbeat, though he kept his hands to himself. "Okay?"

"It all looks different. How many times have I walked here and not remembered?"

"We'll find the answers, somewhere."

"There's one place we know to look. And I *am* hungry." She steadied herself without reaching for him, but it was good to know he was there. "How about some diner food?"

Alyce pushed back from the table, her hand over her belly. "How did I forget to eat all this time?"

"I don't know," Sidney said. "I guess the teshuva was eating for two."

Therese bustled up with another plate. "You haven't tried the piri-piri."

Alyce groaned. "I don't think I could— Oh, it has hot peppers?"

Therese beamed. "Is there anything you're afraid to try?"

"Not a damn thing," Sidney drawled.

A smile eased the thoughtful crease permanently etched between his brows. To have his focus firmly on her warmed her more than the spicy food. As a servant, she had been invisible. She had preferred to be invisible, since the alternatives were worse. The weight of his gaze, though, made her feel not pinned but wanted.

Good intentions did matter. She told herself the prickling in her eyes was only the heat of the peppers.

She was happy. She shouldn't even think it, for the suspicion that feeling happy practically begged evil forces to snatch it away. Although her suspicion was entirely warranted, considering what she knew of evil forces. But maybe she had to be fair, since those evil forces had brought her to Sidney.

And speaking of evil forces . . . "You want to look at the verge again, don't you?" She pushed her plate away, the peppers suddenly roiling in her belly.

He nodded. "I didn't have the eyes to truly see it before. I'm curious."

In the storeroom, he uncovered the doorway. He started his descent while she tugged the door back into place.

At the bottom, the glaring lights beamed on the verge and the recording machines whirred gently. Sidney picked his way across the patchwork of raised pavers that kept them out of the ooze and went to read their cryptic messages. She circled the mutant feralis husk and leaned in to watch the sluggishly churning other-realm energies.

It still looked like a mouth to her. The ether inside it roiled like an incessantly licking tongue. Whether it had something to say or was just a hungry maw, she couldn't tell.

Sidney's muttering distracted her, while the nearness of hell quelled her demon—and maybe she'd been a little too happy or she might have realized they weren't alone.

When she straightened away from the verge, a forearm closed tight over her throat.

CHAPTER 16

The leather-clad arm cut off her shout of warning as effectively as the overpowering wave of a superior demon disrupted her teshuva. She remembered this terrible feeling of helplessness. The crippling etheric blow had been the same the last time she'd tangled with Thorne.

"Miss Alyce, what are you doing down this rabbit hole?" His whisper in her ear was pitched so low she almost missed it.

Across the verge, Sidney was unfolding an accordion of paper that one of the machines had been spewing in a tidy stack beside it. "Interesting," he said. "There was a spike just before we—"

He whirled around. "Alyce?"

The harsh lights left the periphery in darkness, but his gaze locked on hers for a heartbeat before shifting upward, to the devil-man who held her. "Let her go."

"That's the first thing you want to say? Not 'Who are you?' Or maybe 'What do you want?'"

Sidney let the paper drift to the damp ground. "I don't give a fuck who you are or what you want. You're holding Alyce."

"Ah." Thorne's breath held a note of amusement—and a darker thread Alyce couldn't pin down. "You must be Sidney, the *symballein* bastard. Well, I know you won't be able to form a coherent sentence while she's in my arms."

With a hand between her shoulder blades, Thorne shoved her away. She stumbled to her knees, and the soggy ground oozed between her fingers.

Her teshuva flared and guttered, beaten back by the other demon. She stayed in a hunched crouch. "What do you want, Thorne?"

Sidney moved toward her. "Alyce, you know him?"

Thorne reached for the small of his back. From beneath the trailing edge of his black leather jacket he pulled a gun. "Just stay right there, Anglo. I've heard what you *symballein* pairs can do together."

Sidney took another step around the verge toward her. "She asked you a question. What do you want?"

Thorne cocked the gun and aimed it at Sidney. "Didn't I tell you to stay right there?"

Sidney slid another half step her way. "You did, but I've been told I'm a better talker than listener."

Thorne shifted the small black mouth of the gun toward Alyce and pulled the trigger.

She flinched from the boom, reverberating in the closed space, and braced for blood. Instead, mud splashed her from where the bullet struck a few feet from her.

Sidney froze. "She's immortal." Despite the bravado implied in his words, his voice shook.

"And I aimed to miss. I am an excellent shot with a large-bore weapon. By that, I mean both my gun and my demon. As for my personal endowments . . ." Thorne shrugged. "Not relevant. Unless we're interested in finding out how enduring is the *symballein* connection."

"Forever." This time, Sidney's voice rang in the hollow room.

Thorne's teeth flashed in the bright lights. "Not quite so long if I put a bullet through her heart and my djinni prevents her teshuva from plugging the hole."

Sidney straightened. "Djinni?"

Thorne's gaze slid to Alyce. "You didn't tell him you had a djinni ex-boyfriend? Ah, you wound me."

"I have wounded him," Alyce told Sidney. "Or tried to, but he resisted."

Thorne laughed. "You've offered me plenty over the years, but never a blow I couldn't take."

"The talyan killed Corvus Valerius," Sidney pointed out in his official lecturing tone, but his expression was as dark and hard as the gun. "Before lunch, we stopped to pay our respects at the demolition site where Blackbird lost what was left of his soul."

Thorne's smile vanished. "I'm nothing like him. I've never fought the league. Only Alyce, and she always starts it."

Alyce rolled her gaze apologetically toward Sidney. "I didn't know the teshuva don't attack the djinn."

"Because you lose." Thorne twitched the gun restively when Sidney drew a breath. "I know, I know. Except against Corvus."

Sidney let out the breath. "If you aren't here to fight us, then what are you doing *here*?"

Thorne shrugged. "I heard about this flaw in the Veil, and I wanted to see it. I like oddities. A quirk of mine for which you should be grateful, since it's why I didn't kill your addled Alyce long ago." He peered at her. "And since she's here, I think I'll take her back now."

After a frozen heartbeat, Sidney said quietly, "If you truly think you can take her, then we *are* going to fight."

"Oddities are collectible," Thorne said. "Some of those collectors are big and bad—worse than me."

"I am not an oddity." Alyce straightened from her

crouch. The paver in her hands slurped from the mud. "And I am never going to be yours." She flung the rough-edged square at Thorne.

He fired off another shot, and a corner of the airborne paver shattered.

But the bulk of concrete hit his hand. The gun spun off into the darkness to land with a splash somewhere in the shadows.

The downside of being a clever male was talking oneself to death—or if not to death, to distraction.

But Thorne's djinni wasn't distracted anymore. It came roaring to the fore in a psychic blast. Had it been acid, it would have stripped flesh from bone.

The etheric blow tumbled her backward across the mucky floor. Two of the big lights exploded. Confused she might be, and mostly blinded, but even as she fell, she angled toward Sidney.

She crashed through some piece of machinery. A metal edge ripped up her thigh, and she choked on a mouthful of mud when she caught her breath at the pain. But her flailing arm slapped into solid flesh where Sidney had been knocked down too.

He pulled her under him, covering her against the cyclone of muck and shredding paper. "That might have been a little crazy."

"We can't take him as we did the malice. Not even with two of us," Alyce said.

Sidney growled under his breath but said only, "I have another idea." He reached out to one of the upended machines. Despite the stinging whirlwind of filth, his fingers danced without hesitation across the surface. The little row of lights that strobed left to right suddenly reversed.

"Thorne wants to start a collection? This usually collects stray ether to gauge demonic presence," he said. "Get ready to run."

"What is it going to—?" The lights flickered faster, and the machine whined a high-pitched warning. "Oh."

"Sera's notes said Corvus made a hole in the floor. That's our way out."

The last light shattered, leaving them in darkness, except for a vicious yellow glow: Thorne's djinni.

Alyce clamped her hand over the gash in her leg as they scrambled across the slanting floor. With the teshuva dormant, the blood seeping through her fingers didn't slow. As if to make up for the wound, the hitch in her step had all but vanished.

Ah, the power of dread. Water rose around their ankles. "There's no hole."

"This water came from somewhere," Sidney said. "But where—?"

The collector he had toyed with detonated. Amorphous scraps of ether streamed out, corkscrewing through the air. Too much chaotic energy for her teshuva. Her vision went utterly black.

From Thorne's wordless cry of rage, she guessed the same had happened to the djinn-man.

Sidney dragged her onward, and, in one more step, they found the hole.

Even the most dedicated Bookkeeper couldn't bulk up enough to challenge a talya for a Mr. Fighting Evil in the Universe belt. Possession added a finishing cut impossible to achieve by bench presses alone. But since a stereotypical bookworm physique wouldn't have helped his status, Sid had conscientiously penciled workouts into his schedule.

If he'd known those boring laps in the pool would come to this, he'd have put in a few more hours—in indelible ink.

Fortunately, the teshuva downed his breath and added an etheric boost to each stroke as it fled the djinni's overwhelming waves. Slight Alyce was a deadweight in the water, dragging at his shoulder as he hauled her behind him.

The pier was wide. He'd have to swim deep and long to get them out from under it. There was no way to avoid popping up where they might be seen. That worry didn't even make his top-ten list.

There it was—the jade glow of sunlight through water. He aimed for it, each kick and each reach of his arm a flare of agony as his muscles burned beyond the teshuva's ability to repair the cellular damage.

He burst to the surface. The air stabbed into his collapsed lungs like shards of glass. Delicious.

He keeled over to his back and hauled Alyce up against his chest. Strands of her wet hair streaked oil-dark across her face, her skin as gray as the sky.

"Lazy girl," he gasped. "Breathe."

They'd emerged on the parking lot side of the structure, and no one lingered near the edge to throw them one of the rescue rings. But there was no Thorne either.

Was the djinn-man coming after them? Or would he climb the ladder into the diner and go after Therese?

Fear dripped down Sid's throat like sour lake water, and he shoved the thought away with his first sidestroke toward the pier. There was no reason for Thorne to attack the woman. He might do a bit of terrorizing as he went through, but why would he bother with worse?

Oh, because he was *evil*.

After only a few strokes, Alyce regained consciousness in a thrashing of limbs. She knocked away Sid's grasp—and promptly sank.

He dove after her and dragged her up, both of them sputtering.

She slapped at the water as if she could claw her way to the top. He maneuvered behind her to slip his arm around her chest again. "Relax," he shouted, though it sounded ridiculous when bellowed into her ear. But it would be too damn embarrassing to drown this close to shore.

He pinned his chin into the crook of her neck where the flesh around her *reven* had gone transparent with the unrestrained energy of her demon.

"We're safe," he said, then added, in all truthfulness, "At the moment. Unless you push us under again."

Her legs kicked a few more times. "I didn't drown. I *am* a witch."

She wasn't naturally buoyant, but he was able to hold them steady as he treaded water. She stayed limp as he hauled them to the steel wall rising up from the water. There was no ladder, just rusted metal. With nothing to give him leverage, he couldn't boost her up.

She launched herself off his body and slammed her fist into the steel. Then she sank again.

He dragged her up. "What the hell?"

"Make another."

She hadn't hit square, but he clung to the dent as he punched another hole. He hung on while she crawled up him to make another handhold in the impromptu ladder. Three more and they climbed out.

They stood dripping on the empty sidewalk, Sid half bent over with his hands braced on his knees.

"Do we have to tear apart the city while we save it?" he muttered. He pushed himself straight. "We have to make sure Therese is all right. And call Liam, but I'm sure my cell didn't survive that dunk."

They cut through the small outdoor amusement park in the middle of the pier rather than going through the interior halls. No sense raising eyebrows at their sodden state or, worse yet, getting trapped by Thorne and raising hell.

Alyce hurried beside him as they passed between the Ferris wheel and the towering window-and-steel wall of the Crystal Gardens building. "Thorne wouldn't hurt Therese, would he?"

"He's possessed by a very nonrepentant demon. He tried to shoot you, remember? And then steal you."

"I think he still resents the time I tried to sink his boat."

"He has a boat?" The information diverted the sick

churn in Sid's gut at the promised kidnapping. "Did you see it when we walked through earlier?"

She shook her head. "I would have said something."

"You two seem on close terms." He winced at the note of accusation in his voice as the ugly mix of jealousy and anger curdled in him like crypt mud. So much for being diverted.

She glanced at him sidelong. "We have been close. That is how he has shed more of my blood than any dozen lesser tenebrae."

"He said he had taken other things from you."

"A few good blows, yes, and insults when I had the breath."

"Did he take your teshuva's talisman?"

She hesitated, her bottom lip curling between her teeth. "I don't know."

"Think, Alyce. Corvus tried to take Nim's, to turn her powers against us. Did Thorne want the same when you fought?"

"I—I can't remember."

He grabbed her arms and faced her straight on. "This isn't the time to retreat into your old trance."

She jerked out of his hold. "It isn't my memory. I'm remembering more of my time before the demon, but once it came to me, it blocked so much. Whatever happened during my possession, that memory still belongs to the teshuva."

Sid speared his fingers through his hair. "This is bad."

She wrapped her arms around herself, where his hands had been, and water sluiced from her no-longer-white dress. "Why are you angry with me? I *tried* to kill him, but he has always been stronger than I am."

Stronger than Sid too. The sensation of the demon quailing in him had been worse than food poisoning, a queasy mix of achy, shivering sick weakness, where the best idea had been to curl up and die.

He'd lost his mother and Maureen to the demons. He couldn't lose Alyce too. That threat poisoned his soul.

When they rounded the farside of the pier, the exterior door of the diner stood propped open with a whiteboard A-frame sign advertising the lunch special.

They peered cautiously through the door, and Therese smiled with a touch of confusion. "Back for another course? I thought you were downstairs."

Sid edged inside. "No one else came out?"

She stiffened. "A few glasses broke, all of a sudden, for no reason. If someone came through from the back, I might have missed them while I swept. Was someone else down there?"

What was he supposed to say? Sera's notes listed Therese as friend with the only entry being *She has seen evil*. That wasn't a security clearance, as far as a Bookkeeper was concerned.

Not that he was a Bookkeeper anymore.

"Please call Liam for us," he told her. "Tell him we encountered . . . a difficulty. We'll take another look."

Therese didn't ask more. "Thankfully the lunch rush is over."

They went straight through to the storeroom, moved the shelf, and peered down.

"Dark," Alyce said.

"Because we busted out all the lights."

"Yes. Also, the verge is breathing out the dark."

He recoiled a little. "How do you know?"

She held out her bare arm and ran one fingertip over the pale upright hairs. "I feel it."

"A dunking in Lake Michigan in October might leave you a bit chilled too."

"I don't feel the cold. They burned witches."

Why was she drifting back toward spacey Alyce? The stabilizing influence of the league should have been helping by now. He clamped his hand over her forearm. "You weren't drowned. Or burned. Or hanged." Despite the mark the demon had chosen to leave on her neck. "You weren't a witch."

She rolled her arm under his hand and matched his grip, pulse to pulse. Her stare was icy. "Maybe not then. Let's go."

They descended the ladder—Alyce hopping down each rung on one leg as if her knee bothered her—but the crypt was empty. Sid's demon, on high alert, cast every corner of the chamber in an eerie demon glow.

No lurking djinn-man. If there had been, the teshuva no doubt would have been hightailing for its hiding place behind his solar plexus.

"Thorne must've dived out too." Sid's fists tightened at the thought of the djinn-man sharking through the water behind them. "Or maybe he broke the glasses to sneak past Therese."

"Or he went out the other way." Alyce pointed at the verge. "Through there."

Sid stared at the turbulent doorway into hell. The demonic entity within him didn't retreat, but the triplicate thud of his heartbeat rattled his chest. "That possibility scares me even more than the ones that had already occurred to me."

They climbed back to the storeroom, and Alyce limped across the tile floor into the kitchen area while Sid pushed the shelves into place.

He followed her, frowning at her halting progress. "Our teshuva came back online as soon as we got beyond Thorne's reach; yours should've healed the worst of that wound."

She twitched aside the hem of her bedraggled dress and twisted to look down at the back of her thigh. "It's still bleeding."

The intake of breath at the sight of her white skin stuck in his throat. He couldn't even blame the demon for that inappropriate lustful reaction. Here she was, soaked and hurt, and his thoughts immediately went to removing the remainder of her clothes.

"Let me see." He turned her away from him beneath the bright kitchen light. "Bend over the counter there." He'd never found it so hard to concentrate. His hands actually shook as he lifted her skirt.

The sight of her thigh, streaked with blood and livid with internal bruising—human fragile—doused him like cold lake water. "I don't understand. Did Thorne land a shot with some antidemon bullet?"

When he probed the surrounding tissue gently, she tightened her grip on the edge of the stainless steel. "I fell into one of the machines downstairs."

"There shouldn't have been anything hazardous to the teshuva, nothing to interfere with its energy after we got away from Thorne's djinni." He frowned. "But something is preventing the wound from closing."

She flinched away from his fingers. "It didn't hurt when Thorne was chasing us. I ran without limping."

"Other things to worry about." Then he thought about what she'd said and followed the tight clench of her hamstring higher up her leg. "When Thorne was after us, our teshuva were out of commission. Something your humanity handles better than the demon?" The muscle was so contorted, no wonder she limped. He'd felt the old scarring during her physical at the lab—and when they'd gotten physical later—but that didn't explain the flare-up now, unless during the attack something old had been uncovered. Nothing like new wounds to refresh old pain. But why would the djinni attack exacerbate an injury when her clashes with other tenebrae had resulted in talya-standard healing?

Down the curve of her thigh, where the tendons narrowed toward the back of her knee, the jagged tear thinned, but his fingers brushed a hard knot too hard even for teshuva-strengthened musculature.

Her eyes widened when he plucked a paring knife from the magnetized rack above the cutting board.

"It won't hurt much more," he promised. "But something got you, and it needs to come out."

Alyce's gaze locked on him. He slid the knife between the edges of the wound, and her eyes flared brighter violet. "It wasn't the djinni." Her voice broke into the lower demonic register. "It was the angel."

"What—?" Sid hesitated when the knife tip scraped against another metal. "Don't move."

As if the contact had completed a circuit in her, the memory poured out. "I was in the hay field. Only winter stubble was left, but we needed broom straw." She touched her forehead to the counter, muffling her words. "I saw them fighting. Angel and djinni. Light and dark."

"You witnessed an etheric battle? Anyone with skewed vision—children, artists, schizophrenics—might see demons or angels, which is why they're supposed to be more circumspect."

"I shouldn't have been there. I was young, and it was near dark and so cold, but it was better there. . . ." She lifted her head with a hiss when he prodded deeper. "Better alone in the dark than in the house with my father's body. We were waiting for the burial, waiting as long as we dared because we knew that as soon as he was in the ground, we'd be chased from the farm to pay his debts."

Though the narrow blade did little extra damage, he tightened his jaw against the horror of cutting into her. He felt as monstrous as those who had carved apart her childhood, scavenging for any treasure. "Who won, angel or djinni?"

"I don't know. They screamed as they fought, and the frozen ground boiled into steam that blinded me. I ran, but too slow. There was a burst of light—angel gold or djinni yellow; I don't remember—they were too much alike. I fell."

"Something hit you. And it's still here." Sweat stung the corner of his eye. All his previous surgeries had been on lifeless feralis husks, not soft, shuddering flesh. "That battle you witnessed was your penance trigger, one end of the fault line that ended with your possession."

"By the time I staggered back to the house, the mourners had come and gone, only muddy footprints left behind. No one noticed I'd been missing."

Sid gave the knife a tiny twist. On a spurt of blood, the embedded object surfaced in a gleam of glassy gold.

"I guess the djinni won that battle." He grabbed a towel from a clean stack near the dishwasher and pressed it against her knee. When he pulled back, the wound was already closing, and the shard was nestled in the middle of the bloody cloth. To his demon's mesmerized vision, the shrapnel—just a bit shorter and narrower than his finger— flickered like the last flame of a dying campfire. "No wonder your teshuva's been on the blink; this fragment came from an angel's sword."

Chapter 17

Alyce was relieved she'd left her wool coat hanging on the back of a chair when she'd gone down into the verge crypt with Sidney. At least she had something to hide her drenched, stained clothes. Across the empty diner, he revealed the sword shard wrapped in the bloody towel to Liam, Archer, and a half-dozen other muttering talyan.

She sat with Nim and Sera. Jilly had stayed at the warehouse to mastermind the night's hunt. Apparently, the league had chosen new prey.

Or maybe it had been the other way around. She rubbed the back of her thigh. The knot that had been there so long—longer even than her possession—had flattened. She knew when she looked again, it would be gone, just as the limp and other wounds had disappeared. Dared she hope the scar tissue that had tangled her mind would vanish too?

"I ruined another pretty dress," she told Nim.

The talya woman shrugged. "I'll introduce you to the miracle of bleach in the delicate cycle. And credit cards."

Alyce let out a relieved sigh. "The league has strange machines for everything."

"Nothing strange enough to let us zip between realms on a whim," Sera said.

"Is that what happened to Thorne?" Nim sat back. "Corvus opened the verge, but he had no control over it. Jonah and I were with him in the no-man's-land at the end, and he and his djinni were as shit-themselves scared of falling into the tenebraeternum as we were. It might have been where they came from—where all demons come from—but it was no place they want to go back."

Sera drummed her fingers on the table. "So, what did Thorne want with the verge? You say he implied the djinn are talking behind our backs, and we already fought them once at the church. If they are gathering, by definition it can't be for anything good."

None of them had an answer, so they sat in silence.

Therese bustled up. "What can I get you?"

"Answers?" Nim suggested.

"Tea?" Therese countered.

Sera nodded. "And bring four cups."

Therese returned with a tray of unmatched china. She poured for all of them, stared at the fourth cup a moment, then sat. "Liam may close the diner. Because it is dangerous, he says." Her accusing gaze shuttled between Sera and Nim.

"Don't look at me," Nim said. "I eat danger for breakfast. But I think that's not what Liam wants you to serve."

Sera nodded. "When he suggested you move the diner here, he thought it would be a good opportunity."

"It has been," Therese said. "I would have lost everything when my last landlord sold out."

"By good opportunity," Sera clarified, "I think Liam meant unlikely to have strange men creeping around in the basement."

"There are many strange men creeping around the basement right now," Alyce pointed out.

Therese tipped her teacup toward Alyce in an approving salute. "Exactly. Is this danger confined to the basement?"

Sera opened her mouth, then closed it when Nim said, "Not really confined, no."

"Life is risk," Therese said. "That I know, even if I don't understand all you are doing."

"You should tell her," Alyce said. "No one wants to be kept in the dark." She contemplated that a moment. "If they have the choice."

Sera cleared her throat. Nim drank her tea.

So Alyce hunted for the words to explain to Therese. "A slave woman, Tituba, near my village outside Salem, was accused of witchcraft. She disappeared; probably she was killed. Could you run? If you had to?"

Therese shrugged. "It's never that easy, is it? The chains are not always so obvious."

"I still feel them too," Alyce said.

"Tituba," Nim said abruptly. "That's Nigerian for 'atone.'"

Sera stared at her. "Excuse me?"

Nim shifted in her chair. "Since Jonah spent so much time there, I've been reading about African demons." She quickly took another sip of tea.

Therese pushed her cup aside. "Demons?"

"That is what is in the basement," Alyce said. "That is what sits with you now. Lodged within our souls."

Sera and Nim groaned in tandem. "You make possession sound so . . . creepy," Nim complained.

Therese blinked at them. "You are possessed. By demons."

"Repentant demons," Sera said. "We're good guys."

Therese glanced toward the male talyan. "And them?"

"Bigger good guys," Nim said. "What's in your basement is . . . not good. And we wanted to keep it buried."

"But it is not your battle," Alyce said, "so you should be able to run away if you choose."

Therese stared at her cup. "I don't know what to say."

"Besides 'You all are stark raving mad'?" Nim nudged sugar packets across the table. "Here, these help."

"Demons," Therese mused. "That would explain things." She pulled her cup back to her and dumped in three sugars. "I won't run. And not because I am such a slave to my fear that I am too stupid to run."

"Then you're doing better than I did," Nim said.

Therese shook her head. "I think you are doing much good. How can I help?"

"You already do," Sera said. "By giving us a reminder why we're here."

"I left my home once. If nowhere in the city is safe, then I would rather do what I can."

Perhaps his demon had warned him of the talk behind his back, because Liam approached their table, hands on his hips. "Therese," he started.

She stood. "You can't close the diner. This is our place. All of yours. And mine. We will make our stand here."

He lifted an eyebrow at the talya women. "You sharing trade secrets?"

"No secrets," Alyce said.

"Not anymore anyway," Nim amended.

Before Liam could demand an explanation, Alyce stood and went to find Sidney. He must have explanations by the dozen by now.

He was helping Pitch push the shelf back into place. "And we need to finish draining the crypt before we can seal the hole in the floor. I wish a bolus of concrete could do the same to the verge."

Pitch grunted. "What's the demonic equivalent of concrete?"

He'd probably meant the question facetiously, but Sidney straightened, his eyes losing focus as he considered. "Demonic quick-set . . ."

Since he would stand there until an answer came to him,

Alyce moved in front of him. She couldn't help the jump of her pulse as his gaze locked on her.

"They found the gun in the muck," he said. "Also in the muck were all the printouts recorded during the fight. So we don't know if Thorne accessed the verge. We can just add that to the list of things we don't know, such as what he's doing next."

Alyce thought a moment. "We could go to his boat. That is his only home."

Pitch snorted. "You think he just tells everybody where it is?"

She nodded. "He has signs all along the river."

Pitch stared at her. "Why didn't you say so?"

"You didn't ask."

There was so much he wanted to ask her. Sid sat beside Alyce in the back of Liam's car as they cruised streets parallel to the river, looking for the signs Alyce had told them about.

"What kind of signs?" Pitch had demanded. "Signs like ichor smears? Like talya heads on pikes?"

"Like big pictures stuck on tall posts," she'd said.

"Billboards?" Sid straightened. "He's a djinn-man with billboards?"

Now Alyce leaned over his lap to point out the car window. "Over there. Across the bridge."

THE *RIVER PRINCESS* EVENING CRUISE. The words were left justified to make room for a woman with Caucasian coloring, a Native American costume, and breasts by a plastic surgeon with more silicone than ethics. Her high-heeled moccasins pierced the Web site address at the bottom of the sign.

"Rich men get on. Poor men get off," Alyce said.

"Riverboat gambling isn't allowed on the lake." Jilly, in the front passenger seat, poked at her phone. "Internet search says the *River Princess* has a few outstanding complaints—all from legitimate offshore casinos—but no associated investigations."

Liam grunted. "Thorne must know somebody—or he knows where some body is."

"The sailing schedule shows open boarding tonight," Jilly said. "Shall I make reservations?"

"We didn't have time for a company picnic this summer," Liam mused. "What with battling evil." His smile was sharper than the princess's heel. "And talyan do like to gamble."

Alyce shifted in her seat. "What do we want with him?"

"Whatever he wanted with the verge," Sid said. "He's the closest connection we have to the intentions of the djinn, and if they have plans for the verge . . ."

"He won't tell." Fretfully, she tugged at her seat belt. "Well, he might, just because he likes to show how clever he is. But he won't tell us anything useful if we all confront him."

Sid bristled. "Do not say you want to get on a boat with him alone. Whatever relationship you had with him was . . . was before, not after you threw a paver at his head."

"At his hand," she corrected. "Because he was trying to shoot me." She let the belt retract with a snap. "*That* is the kind of relationship we had."

Liam drummed his fingers on the seat back. "You have a better idea, Westerbrook?"

"If the *River Princess* is Thorne's base of operations, a quick, quiet recon might find something, anything, on this gathering of djinn." Sid scowled at Alyce. "Without unnecessary shooting." He smoothed the scowl when he glanced back at Liam. "After our run-in today, chances are Thorne won't be wasting his time on a pleasure cruise, so I'll have the place to myself."

"You?" Alyce's voice was small.

Sid didn't look at her. "I'm the obvious choice. Best qualified to judge any information Thorne left lying around. Least valuable if the mission goes awry."

"I don't rank my talyan for sacrifice," Liam said.

Jilly tapped her phone on the dash in counterpoint to Liam. "We could follow in Jonah's boat. The *Shades of Gray* is outfitted for running dark. If you get dumped overboard, we can recover you."

Sid tried for talya humor. "Alive or dead?"

"Yes," Jilly said.

"No," Alyce said.

"You'll go together," Liam said. When Sid drew a harsh breath, the league leader pinned him with a glare. "Just in case sacrifice seemed like an option."

Alyce nodded and settled back in her seat.

Sid wanted to scream his rejection.

When Liam had first contacted the London league, seeking older records than any kept in the New World, he'd danced around the information he wanted. Eventually, he asked what they had on long-extinct *symballein* pairings. Specifically, how long did the bond last?

Once the Bookkeeper masters had overcome their shock that the *symballein* bond existed, they'd laughed at the commitment phobia that reared in the face of eternity.

Now Sid understood. Liam hadn't feared the bond lasting forever; he wanted to make sure it did.

That was hard to do when half the bond was stretching toward suicidal curiosity.

For once, Sid didn't mean himself. But damn it, if he couldn't talk the Bookkeeper talk anymore, and he didn't walk the talya walk, what was left?

"Thorne has hinted, more than once, he wanted something from me," Alyce said quietly. "What if it was my teshuva's talisman? What if he took it? The thing that could make me a real talya."

Sid scowled. "You are possessed by a repentant demon. That makes you a real talya." If he said as much to himself, would that make it true?

"You know what I mean. I want it back from him." The

determination in her voice left no room for discussion. With the removal of the interfering angelic relic, the drifty Alyce was coming into focus—hard, sharp focus. "What time does the *River Princess* leave?"

"Not until nine," Jilly said. "Easier to slip out of sight, I suppose, and deal the cards in the dark."

"Then we have time," Sid said.

"For me to change clothes?" Alyce asked. "This dress would terrify even a djinni."

"For me to teach you to swim."

Back at the warehouse, Alyce was hustled away in the triad of women to find a swimsuit and something suitable for a night of breaking and entering. Sid went down to the labs.

For a long moment, he stood in the doorway of the darkened room, listening to the soft whir of the mainframe as it rolled over some problem in its mechanical guts. Such a comforting noise as it methodically and dispassionately— oh, and bloodlessly—worked its way to a solution.

This was where he'd belonged, just another methodical, dispassionate, and bloodless machine.

But in two days with the Chicago league, he'd thrown his methodology right out the window and gotten excessively bloody, and as for the passion . . .

Technically, these were not the answers he was seeking.

He finally flicked on the lights. While he'd driven around the river with Alyce, looking for billboards, Archer had returned to the warehouse earlier with Thorne's gun and the shard taken from Alyce's leg.

To Sid's human eye, the gun looked more dangerous: a cheap, ugly, short-barreled thug of a gun. But his gaze kept shifting to the shard, the teshuva's vision overlying his own like a jeweler's loupe.

The shard had been placed in an isolation cabinet. A pink sticky note on the front of the glass read *WTF?* in Sera's handwriting.

The revolver lay on the counter, cleaned of crypt mud, its hollow point rounds unloaded. The computer monitor behind it displayed nested tabs of what Archer had found through his wireless skullduggery. Sid pulled up a chair and minimized the windows as he read.

To his surprise, the gun did have a history. One of the first to bear a serial number after a 1968 law, it had passed through the hands of a gun dealer, Rose Red Pony. And Red Pony had her own history on the next screen. The FBI had opened a file on her after several arrests where she'd been agitating for violence during otherwise peaceful civil rights marches. Whether her motivation had been equality for all or better sales for herself, the conspiracy case against her had become irrelevant when the gun shop and the flop-house above—a known hangout for dissatisfied protesters—exploded. No one had survived.

Clicking on the page of known associates and presumed deceased, Sid scanned the list until his gaze locked on the name: *Thorne Halfmoon, suspected bomb maker, remains unverified.*

Dead? If only. Quickly cross-referencing the names with burial records, Sid found funeral matches for all but one. Of course not. Throne had descended not into a pauper's grave but into possession.

Archer had ended his search there, apparently satisfied to know their enemy's full name and probable possession date since the possessed rarely left deep footprints. This was one reason the demons chose them. Still curious, Sid followed the electronic trail down through the years.

While older records were only haphazardly being digitized by police departments, local governments, and libraries, Bookkeepers had learned to take advantage of industrious amateur genealogists. Their findings—from scans of yellowed family Bible birth ledgers to snapshots of weathered tombstones—often captured the ephemera that history forgot.

The possessed were just such ephemera, but Sid refused to feel pity, for himself or Thorne.

He scanned several active forums before he found a link to a Thorne Halfmoon. The genealogist was following a different family line but had posted a Polaroid of a half-dozen young men framed in the girders of a skyscraper, their hard hats tucked under their elbows. Sid didn't need to read the names typed neatly along the bottom of the screen; his gaze locked on the rawboned, buzz-cut youth standing a little apart from the rest. A shadow from the girder cut across his face, the set of his unsmiling mouth already as hard edged as the steel.

Sid pushed back in the chair, contemplating the black bore of the gun and the smaller hollow tips of the ammunition. The glimpse into Thorne's past was every bit as dark and empty: the makings of a djinn-man. Had the younger Thorne felt the forces of darkness gathering around him? As he stood on those suspended beams, had he sensed the cracks in his soul that made him vulnerable to the demon?

If he *had* known, what would he have done differently?

When Sid clicked the little *x* in the upper right-hand-corner of the photo, all that remained on the computer screen was the gray on black @1 logo and the ghostly reflection of his own face. The question reflected back at him too. Knowing what he did now—what he would have known before his possession if he'd stopped for half a second to really listen to Alyce's halting explanation of the etheric energy that had surrounded him—would *he* have done anything differently?

The casters of the chair creaked as he shifted, his mind whirling through the choice that had passed, untaken. No wonder Archer had stopped his search on Thorne. Train-wreck curiosity was too macabre; there was nothing left to examine, not even in the pieces of his own life.

Sid ran the gun through an etheric sequencer, hoping to identify the demonic signature that might pinpoint the class of djinni they were up against, and his lip curled in an involuntary sneer as he remembered Thorne's braggart comments about his shooting skills. The reaction was the teshuva's, of course, not his own, since firearms mastery was not something a Bookkeeper could claim.

Sid tamped down his impatience. A master Bookkeeper wouldn't try to hurry an investigation any more than he would pull an algae culture into bloom. A talya, however, was a master of forceful impatience.

He'd been left with the worst of both worlds; no power, no patience. If only he could weld those helplessly spinning wheels of himself into something useful again.

In the corner of his vision, the shard of the angel relic wavered in its burning-unconsumed eternity like a warning.

Or maybe, like an idea.

"Just give in to it, Alyce." He had to raise his voice a little. In the midst of family hour at the YMCA, the pool overflowed with children shrieking and adults looking the other way.

She sputtered. "If I give in, I go under."

"That's your dread talking."

"The demon doesn't talk."

He glanced around. No one was close except a trio of young girls, their beaded cornrows clacking as they whirled and splashed one another and screamed.

He turned to Alyce. "Just listen to me. Lie back on my hands."

She eyed him with clear misgiving, then sighed and eased herself horizontally.

He kept his palms flat under her shoulder blades. "Now relax, spread your arms out to your sides, and arch your back."

"My ears get wet."

"Water in your ears won't kill you. Not being able to

float might." There were so many other ways a talya could die, but she was probably better able to defend against those than he was.

She sighed again, more aggrieved, but did as he said.

He kept his gaze fixed on hers. But at the top of his peripheral vision, he couldn't help but notice the thrust of her breasts as she tried to comply with his directions. The white triangles of stretchy fabric reminded him too much of the clothes he'd removed from her the night before. He was suddenly very glad for the baggy fit of his trunks and the frenetic action in the pool that obscured any sight line beneath the waves.

Alyce peered up at him. "You aren't relaxed."

"We're about to trap ourselves on the boat of a former terrorist possessed by a demon who has already tried to kill us once, nosing around for secret dirt that will set us on a collision course with the worst monsters in the city. Why wouldn't I be relaxed?"

"At least you're standing up." She jutted her lower lip. "Why did you want to go to Thorne alone?"

"It would be safer."

Her eyes widened, stricken. "You thought you'd be safer without me?"

"I thought *you* would be safer."

She tilted her head back farther to lock gazes. "I was the youngest daughter of a poor farmer. I was a servant, a lunatic. Even the angel and demon who fought above me never gave me a thought."

The emotion in her eyes was deeper than any pool, at once buoying him up and stealing his breath with the threat of drowning.

"I thought about you." His voice sounded hoarse to his own ears. "See, when you get distracted, you float fine."

Once he called her attention to it, she tensed and started to sink. He levered her shoulders up and put her on her feet. They were near the shallower end, but she was not tall, so when she faced him, the waves lapped down her décolletage.

The trio of girls had moved closer, and their antics pushed Alyce toward him as the water surged over her shoulders.

He lifted her and turned to shield her against the splashing. Before he could put her down again, she circled her arms around his neck and levered herself higher on his body to fold her legs behind him. His pulse kicked up a few waves of its own.

"Once again, you are right." From her perch around his waist, she looked down, and her husky voice surged through him. "I am distracted, and look how I float."

Beads of water sparkled over her *reven* like crystals on a black velvet choker. If he leaned forward just a fraction, he could press his lips to the hollow of her throat. Except this was such the wrong time, no matter what the craving in him said.

Not that there had yet been a right time. He supposed immortality and the *symballein* bond would take care of that, unless they were viciously slaughtered later tonight.

"Alyce," he murmured, "does nothing frighten you?"

"Those children might still get water up my nose"—she tilted her head—"and finding this swimming suit was an unpleasant experience, bordering on terrible. The teshuva wanted to tear everything into tiny pieces. Tinier pieces."

He smiled. "And yet you overcame."

"I did. Do you like it?" She lifted herself higher out of the water, her legs tightening around him. He shifted his hands under her backside to hold her up. The soft curve of her bottom and the flex of muscle in her thighs made a slingshot of lust that catapulted rational thought into another time zone.

He caught his breath, gaze fixed not on the white bikini but on her darkening eyes. "I like it."

Her smile picked up where his had vanished. "Good. I cannot wait to hear what you think about the dress."

He wished he'd found something nicer for himself. Archer had said Thorne's illegal riverboat gambling operation catered to high rollers and that they should try to fit in.

They'd agreed Sid's posh accent would earn him a pass with an expensive collared shirt, rumpled just enough to imply a certain carelessness with his money. But later, when Alyce came down the steps of the YMCA in a white cocktail dress, one shoulder bared and a thin white scarf trailing around her throat, he wanted a tuxedo—and a limo, maybe with a hot tub, and an evening that didn't include unrelenting evil.

He gestured at her white ballet flats. "No boots?"

"My black ones clashed."

Since he couldn't drag his gaze off her, he supposed she knew what she was doing. Certainly Bookkeeper tradition didn't cover uniforms for possible suicide missions.

Maybe they knew basic talya black covered all occasions.

He held his arm out to her. "You look beautiful."

Beyond beautiful. In her pure white, her hair braided in a dark corona, she gleamed against the muddy fall hues of the city—fall, as he had fallen.

He gave himself a shake. Not fallen so much as pushed by the demon. The urges of the *symballein* bond just honed the edge of the stairs he was currently tumbling down.

When her fingers settled lightly on his sleeve, the touch vibrated through his bones, and he struggled to keep his voice even. "No coat?"

"I didn't want to ruin it."

She shivered, just an infinitesimal quiver, and he drew her under his arm. "I thought you said you didn't feel the cold."

"I don't. At least, I didn't."

"I think removing the angelic relic from your body is allowing the human and demon energies to finally come into balance, as they should have been all along. You'll probably notice more changes—hopefully all good—as the resonance aligns."

"Maybe." She gazed up at him. "Mostly I feel cold when I'm with you."

He frowned and started to pull away. "I'm sorry."

"No." She caught him before he'd gone far. "I feel warm and good *with* you. The sunshine is brighter. But I feel the cold too. I had forgotten, and now I remember."

The thought froze him for a moment, as if all the cold she'd forgotten had been pumped through his veins. That was a duty to the *symballein* bond he hadn't contemplated. The demon that fit itself to the flaws in a human soul offered immortality, strength, quickness, improved sensory acuity, and a remarkable affinity for anything sharp, pointy, heavy and/or plain old deadly. It didn't make the sunlit world shiny.

The only thing that could do that, if he remembered his popular rock'n'roll ballads correctly, was love.

Alyce loved him.

Of course, the *symballein* bond implied a certain intimate working relationship, what with balancing the broken shards of each other's souls—and having sex.

How had he forgotten the element of love?

As a secretly aspiring Bookkeeper, he'd memorized the periodic table of the elements before he'd had his first wet dream. Then he'd seen a video of the *Hindenburg*—watched in gut-curdling horror as fire ate the world's largest airship to a smoldering skeleton—and learned how there was so much more to that first innocuous element, hydrogen, than a single tidy square, even with the atomic number, could explain.

Looking into Alyce's eyes, he realized love was apparently like hydrogen.

The first element. Simple. All-encompassing. And violently, dangerously explosive.

What could he say? "I don't want you to be cold."

How inanely beside the point.

A yellow cab honked as it passed another car, and he eagerly stepped past her to raise his hand. "I'll ask the driver to turn up the heat," he promised her as the cab pulled to the curb.

"Don't bother." She slipped past him when he held open the back door and settled herself. She patted the seat beside her and cast him a look with violet flames smoldering under the ice. "I have you."

Suddenly, demonic possession, the rise of a djinn army, and gaping doorways into hell seemed the least of his worries.

CHAPTER 18

On the ride to the dock where the *River Princess* waited, Sidney was quiet, but Alyce didn't pester him. He was probably working out a way to get onto the boat, get all his answers, and get off without needing her questionable swimming skills.

Best to leave him to his thinking, because she wanted to keep the dress dry and silky smooth so he could tease it from her later.

She'd felt his interest while they floated in the pool. And then she'd *really* felt his interest when she'd wrapped herself around him. That had been inappropriate on her part, the sort of behavior her old master would have been entirely justified in calling temptation.

But the sight of his strong, nearly bare body had tempted her first, and his gentle hold on her shoulders had stripped whatever restraint she might have considered.

Another shiver went through her—memory of how gently he'd stripped her in bed—but she stopped herself from touching him and distracting him from his thoughts.

Time enough for that later.

The cab dropped them off amidst a flow of sleek and satisfied people reeking of alcohol. Soft music piped from the bars lining the river. Sidney steered through the crowd, polite, but clearing a way for her to the gangplank. Small tea lights lined the walkway out to the boat, and a yellow spotlight illuminated the name at the prow, but the rest of the boat was dark. The bowed and tinted windows reflected warped images of the activity onshore without a clue of what happened within.

A small group had just crossed into the boat as they made their way closer. Another man stood at the foot of the gangplank, thick arms crossed in plain disinvitation. As they approached, he stepped to block the path onto the boat.

Sidney waved one hand with a touch of exasperation. "Was I supposed to bring a bottle of champagne to crack over the bow?"

"That's only when launching a ship for the first time, sir," the man said.

"Well, it is my first time." Sidney laughed, a touch too loud. "That explains the wine I've had." He waggled his fingers at Alyce, so she sidled up under his arm. "Hey, luv, did you call ahead?"

She shrugged one shoulder. She made sure it was the bare shoulder. "I forgot."

"Of course you did, luv. Which is why I hold the money." Sidney pulled out his wallet and fanned out a handful of bills. "That should do it."

"Sir, I'm afraid we can't—"

"I'm always afraid too." Alyce lowered her tone into demonic range as her teshuva responded to the nebulous fears circling the man and twisted his worries back to him. "Thorne likes you that way."

While the man gaped at her, Sidney freed another few bills and stuffed them in the other man's shirt pocket.

"Nothing to worry about, right, old chap?" He patted the bulging shirt pocket hard enough to nudge the man aside. "I see they're casting off the lines. You should watch out."

He tugged her down the gangplank before the man could protest again.

"Won't he come after us?"

"To watch an annoyingly drunk Brit lose his money at the tables and his mind over a vision in white?" He smiled at her, a little crookedly.

She bit her lip. "Is it too late to think maybe this is one of the bad kinds of ideas?"

"Quick, quiet recon," he reminded her. "Thorne obviously has a very comfortable setup here. He won't sacrifice that for mere pesky talyan."

His logic made sense. She found that comforting, although it would have been more comforting if her teshuva hadn't felt so small in her, withdrawn to the very depths of her being, almost lost to her senses.

She felt alone. She felt . . . human.

They stepped onto the smooth, dark deck. Beside her, Sidney looked so at ease, the rich russet waves of his hair ruffled and his sleeves rolled back in defiance of the October chill. She slipped her hand into his.

He looked down at her with a faint smile. "Yet another strange date."

"I'd go anywhere with you."

His smile flickered out. "Well, let's at least go inside the cabin where you won't freeze."

She snuggled up against him as they walked. He'd remembered that she'd said she felt the cold, felt everything, when she was with him. The thought warmed her from the inside, even more than the heat of his body beside her.

Yet he felt stiff against her shoulder. Probably he was more worried than he wanted her to know. To reassure him, she gazed up at him, focusing all her belief in her eyes, and squeezed his hand.

His answering smile looked a little seasick.

Inside, subtle pools of lights flowed around high tables, gleaming on the mellow woods. A handful of women circled with trays of glasses as tall, thin, and white-gold as the servers themselves.

Sidney snagged a glass and held it out to Alyce. "Champagne?"

When she lifted the fizzing contents, she sneezed, and her demon uncoiled a notch. "To drink?"

"Remember when I explained to you about cocktail parties?"

"The men drink too much and the women wear pretty dresses." She smoothed her hand down her thigh. "But not much fun, you said."

"And that was before a demon-revved metabolism made it impossible to drink too much. Still, a glass or two will help us blend in."

"And if I break off the cup, the stem is long and sharp enough to be a weapon."

"That too." He stepped away. "It looks like there's more room belowdecks; that's where I'd keep the big games. And private rooms. Let's look around up top until we sail."

The upper level was smaller, with intimate low seating and even lower, more intimate music piping through the walls. Several couples already occupied the forward seats, so Sidney guided her to the back with a hand at the base of her spine.

Through the thin fabric of her dress, his hand warmed her. The silky stuff moved under his fingers so his palm shifted in slow circles over her spine. She wanted to dump the glass and return the caress, but that wasn't their mission.

So instead, she took a sip and sneezed again. The demon spiraled higher as the dark heat of Sidney's hand and the sparkling coolness of the champagne met deep in her belly in some sinful alchemy.

She liked it. It made her legs steadier while the boat, pulling away from the dock, rocked under her.

As they glided out to the lake, she drained the rest of the glass and set it aside, though close enough to grab if she did need a weapon. But now that her hands were free ...

She threaded her fingers through his and tugged him to the back of the room. The lights of the diminishing city glittered through the tinted windows, casting highlights in place of shadow. Still, she could not read his eyes.

But the champagne made that seem unnecessary. Her demon flickered unsteadily, and her senses shimmered like the city lights. She drew their clasped hands down the outsides of her thighs, framing their embrace.

"Kiss me," she whispered. "It will help us blend in."

He frowned. "I should have guessed your teshuva might not process alcohol as thoroughly as a stronger demon."

"I am okay." She was coming to like that word, almost as much as she liked champagne.

The boat tilted a little—or maybe that was just her—so she took the opportunity to pull herself closer to him. The silky scarf around her neck chafed at her sensitized skin, a reminder how there'd been almost nothing between them in the pool—and nothing at all between them in bed.

She tilted a bit more, angling against his chest, and gazed up at his mouth, so far away. If he was as tall as the other talyan, she wouldn't be even this close. Still, the unyielding stiffness of his spine held him apart, though the thud of his heart rocked the whole world.

Again, maybe that was just her.

"Kiss me," she urged, "so I don't forget."

"Alyce ..." Her name surfaced from someplace in him deeper and darker than the lake around them. He pulled her closer—not that there was much closer to be had. His fingers, still tangled through hers, pinned her hands at the small of her back.

When his lips swept hers in a hot wave, she moaned and

arched into him. The stiffness that had gone out of his spine reappeared elsewhere, and she reveled in the sweet heat that swelled through her in answer.

She would happily forget the world if she could stay in his arms forever. . . .

Abruptly, Sidney brought their hands together in front of them again, between their bellies, forcing them apart but putting them both within reach of some even more likable places. "Alyce, wait. I know the *symballein* bond has resulted in some metaphysiological connectivity that may inspire feelings in you of—"

"Feelings like making love?"

He swallowed, and he looked as if he might sneeze even though he hadn't had any champagne. "For example."

She nodded. "It is a nice feeling, isn't it? As though all is good with the world."

Despite the soft sway of the boat, unlike her own soft swaying, he went utterly still. "After everything . . . *with* everything, how can you say that?"

"Because I'm with you."

If she'd driven the words through his heart on the stiletto of a broken champagne glass, Sid would not have been more shocked.

Oh, he'd guessed—maybe even *said* to himself in the privacy of his own head—she was feeling something for him. But most people were too careful to expose themselves with such vulnerability, to say what they felt without a defense, without a fail-safe. The weakness of her demon and the loss of its talisman somewhere in the centuries had left her without those. Now the truth was clear; this was not a bonding he could observe safely from a distance—or even up close with asbestos gloves and a polycarbonate face shield. At the bright gleam in her eyes, his thoughts went instead to vastly more personal protection.

Was his heart trying to get away . . . or get to her?

Despite all his studies, he didn't have an answer, so he did what any good researcher would do.

He took a step back. Their linked hands stretched between them awkwardly.

"It's hard to say what we're feeling," he started.

Her steady gaze pinned him like a petrified insect to corkboard. Even though he was a scientist, those had always seemed sinister. "It's not. Don't use so many words."

"This isn't the time or place—"

"Does that matter?"

He didn't think he could brush her off with a relativistic joke about time/space and matter, about how if it mattered, matter would change the geometry of space/time and inevitably—gravitationally—draw them together. . . . Yeah, that was not the direction the conversation needed to go.

"A crisis relationship seems more intense because the situation escalates so quickly—"

"I've been waiting three hundred years."

"And emotions are under such pressure—"

"Because that never happens anywhere else."

He frowned. She didn't do sarcasm very well. "Do you want me to explain or not?"

"Not. You came to Chicago to delve into the *symballein* bond, but you won't even talk to me."

"I talk," he protested. "All the time, or so you've said."

"*At* me."

That wasn't true; he'd told her things he'd never said aloud to anyone. Over her one bare shoulder, the lights of the city blurred with distance and the dark glass—disappearing, like his escape options. "I came here to write a paper, not become the subject of one."

She released his hands, and the abruptness set him back a half stride. "Is that what I am to you? A question for you to study?"

"Of course not." This time his protest wavered. Because she had been that, in the beginning. "But I was taught all along, a Bookkeeper needs the detachment, the distance to see clearly." He tried to smile. "Even if he wears glasses."

She didn't reflect the smile, and her eyes were darker than the night behind her. "Then your father must be very proud of you."

A champagne glass stiletto twisting in his chest would be less painful. "I came to Chicago because my father has doubted me since I got engaged."

Her hands went to her throat but stopped short, tangling in the white scarf instead. "Engaged."

"To be married."

She took a long breath, but her question was short. "Why?"

"The usual reasons. Because I thought I loved her. Because I thought I knew better than my father, thought I could do what he hadn't done: be a good Bookkeeper and a good husband." He hesitated, then added, "Maybe that last part isn't quite a usual reason."

"What happened?"

"A year ago, Maureen and I had a fight about where I'd been all night. I was behind in my records because the horde had been unusually active. . . ." He frowned. "I wonder how that corresponds to Corvus's first attempt to rupture the Veil—" He cut himself off. "Anyway, I stormed out. I was on the street outside league headquarters when I stopped swearing long enough to realize she had followed me."

Alyce's voice drifted, thin as the scarf. "Like your mother."

"Nowhere near as bad. The feralis killed my mother. Maureen just asked me to choose."

"And you chose Bookkeeping."

"Dad couldn't give Mum what she needed. She followed us partway down the Bookkeeper path, and she died. I wasn't going to let that happen to Maureen." Again, he hesitated, longer this time, but the unsaid truth ate through his heart. How did Alyce do it? With a few words and her quiet stare, she dredged up secrets he'd buried even from himself. "Honestly, I wasn't going to let that happen to me again either."

"I understand."

"I saw the light on in Dad's office. It must have been painfully obvious what was going on. When Maureen left, I went up to see him. He told me I'd done the right thing, that he wished he'd left Mum before. . . ." He dragged one hand through his hair. "I am—was just a Bookkeeper. I don't have it in me to survive that again. Look, we can talk about this more—"

"But we don't need to," she said.

"—when we aren't facing our possible deaths."

She never even blinked. "Okay."

He hesitated. "Okay. Okay as in 'all is good with the world'?"

"It doesn't just mean that, though, does it? It also means you don't want to say anything else."

He studied her opaque gaze. If being with her was like heading into an Arctic adventure, he was definitely standing with a foot on two different ice floes. That couldn't end well.

To his vast relief, the other couples had risen and were heading toward the stairs, which would break up their little chat. "I think it's action time. We should get down there."

"Okay."

He ground his teeth. "That's why we're here. And don't say okay."

She didn't say anything.

They followed the other couples down and found most of the guests drifting toward the lower deck with soft murmurs and expectant laughter.

Could there be any fewer lights? Only the glow of rope lighting under the treads kept the stairs from being a death trap. Once he'd thought death trap, the hairs at Sid's nape prickled. As he'd told Alyce, he suspected Thorne wouldn't blow up his golden geese just to roast a couple talyan. Even djinn-men had expenses.

In the main room, the green felt tables glowed like emeralds under the pure lights, and the cards shone with the matte gleam of pearls as the dealers opened fresh decks and began to shuffle. The usual blackjack and poker tables were set around the larger roulette and baccarat areas. There was even a table set with a stark chessboard, though no one seemed to be interested.

The crowd seemed to know where they wanted to be, which edged Sid and Alyce to the outside of the milling group. They paused along one wall beside a large recessed fish tank. The tank housed only two gorgeous yellow fish. Just a few centimeters long, the fish patrolled the middle of the tank like soldiers on parade. Sid realized a thin sheet of glass separated them.

"Betta splendens," he said. "Siamese fighting fish. I wonder if Thorne bets on cocks and dogs too."

Alyce leaned closer, one finger hovering near the glass. "He would not hurt these. He is vain, and they are the same color as his eyes when his djinni ascends."

Sid scowled, but he had to admit, the fishes' flowing, rounded fins were unmarred and beautiful. He turned away. "What's at the back there?"

Alyce followed close behind him as he made his way across the room. "Are there basements in boats?"

"Probably not. But back rooms . . ." He pushed at the closed door, the same dark wood as the rest of the wall.

No one turned their way, but Alyce and he both flinched at the sudden belling wave of etheric energy.

"Waving the white flag, are you, Anglo?" The drawling voice held no amusement. "Surrender her, then, and maybe I'll let you go."

CHAPTER 19

In the presence of Thorne's djinni, Alyce felt her demon shiver, as if someone had shaken the champagne bubbles in her stomach and the deflating fizz had exited through her bones. But she stood straight against the internal quaking. Just because she felt the cold now didn't mean she had to respond. "Don't shoot."

Thorne lounged in his hard-backed chair. "Save it for someone who might listen."

"Just trying to save you the inconvenience, the blood, the screaming. . . ." Sidney tipped one hand palm up.

Thorne smirked and echoed the gesture: They were two friends sharing a wry amusement. "And I admit, I'm too curious to shoot you yet."

Alyce winced at the "yet."

"Plus . . . ," Sidney continued. He held out his other hand, and this one pointed a gun. "I'd have to shoot back."

"Sidney," Alyce whispered.

Thorne laughed. "That won't kill me."

"Not kill you, no, only incapacitate you with a hollow point bullet I've stuffed—like a very small lead and gold Christmas turkey—with shavings from an angelic sword." Sidney smiled back at the djinn-man. "Then I'll kill you."

Thorne's expression blanked. A thin ring of virulent yellow glowed around his pupils. "You didn't find that in your archives."

Sidney shrugged. "I found the sword fragment in Alyce, disrupting her demon. And I'm guessing—just guessing, mind, but I'm willing to explore opposing viewpoints if you're so inclined—it'll do the same to you."

Thorne sat up straighter in his chair. "A sphere relic in her? I wondered why . . ." His smile returned, but twisted. "I knew you were special, Alyce, with that glow around you. But you weren't my redemption; you were just fucked up. Two wrongs don't make a right, and two outcasts still can't find an in."

Alyce froze. His mouth was distorted in the lying smile, but the words between his lips were straight and true. "I found a place. You could too—"

"No." He surged to his feet. The force of his djinni heaved in answer, but it didn't break free as Sid lifted the gun. "I won't be part of the misguided, hopeless few again. Unlike most of my ancestors, I've lived long enough not to repeat my mistakes."

Sidney's gun never wavered. "You're not part of the gathering djinn?"

Thorne slowly sank to the chair again, not in defeat, but with infinite weariness, one elbow hooked over the back. With a flick of his fingers, he indicated the casino beyond. "Forget the ahāzum; I have all this. What more could a tribeless Indian want?"

Alyce stood against his glowering regard. "If you don't want more, give me back my teshuva's talisman."

Though he didn't move, Thorne's sprawling stance became more of a lie. "I needed nothing of yours, ever."

"Then give it back."

He sat straighter and rephrased, emphasizing the words. "I never stole from you."

Alyce considered his tone. He sounded bored, which worried her. Was he telling the truth this time?

Without the restraint the teshuva should have given her at possession, she would never have the confidence of the other talya women. She'd live out her immortal life with constant fear of drifting back to rogue. She tamped down the rapid thud of her heart, but it thumped back like a body that wouldn't stay buried. "The teshuva's memento was all I had."

Thorne shook his head. "You had only the rags on your back when they dumped you out of the asylum." He leaned forward again, his arm still hooked over the back of his chair as if he tried to hold himself back but couldn't. The yellow rings of his eyes expanded. "I saw you that first night, stinking of the hospital and stumbling from the benzos; do you remember? You attacked me."

She pursed her lips. "The teshuva must have been starving."

"I hit you hard enough to knock you out of your shoes—no loss—but you kept coming. You were fearless." His fingers splayed across his desk. "To the djinni, you shone like . . ." Abruptly, he pushed himself back. "Just as well I never found my inner light if it's so damn crippling. But that was the angel relic in you. It's gone now. It was never meant for either of us, and here you are, on the path laid out for you from the beginning."

The realization froze her. What other path had he yearned for? Whatever it had been, he was right; it was closed to them now.

If she hadn't been so still, she wouldn't have heard Sidney's infinitesimal sound of agreement. He refused to meet her gaze.

"But there is a new path," he said. "The doorway leading into the demon realm. Why were you there, Thorne?"

Thorne gave him a lazy smile. "You want answers? So do I. Let's bet on the flip of a coin."

"I'm not a gambling man," Sidney said.

Thorne scoffed. "Alyce would bet me."

"I'd fight you again."

"Alyce." The warning in Sidney's voice trembled through her.

She lifted her chin. "What do you want to know, Thorne?"

"The verge was Corvus's doing. Why?"

Sidney stared at the djinn-man a long moment, then shrugged. "Corvus's djinni wanted to unleash hell on Earth. Corvus wanted to be free. They both got what they wanted."

Thorne huffed out a laugh. "Idiot. He had money, power, and eternal life, and still he needed more. Why did—?"

"Our turn," Sidney interrupted. "If you have everything you need, what do you want with the verge?"

Thorne's lip curled. "Nothing. But the others do. And I wonder why."

Sidney stiffened. "Who are the others? *Where* are they?"

"Ah, my turn," Thorne said with singsong teasing. "Why is the league keeping the verge open?"

"Because nothing in our archives tells us how to stand on the edge of hell and ask it to go away." Sidney fixed the other man with an unwavering stare. "Do you know how to close it?"

"No, and even if I did, I wouldn't go up against the forces who want it."

"And who is that again?"

Thorne leaned back in his chair. "Maybe I will call this hand."

"We're not betting," Sidney reminded him. "We're trading."

"My people never got the best trades from your kind, especially when you have the gun. We're doing better with the betting."

"You can't change the rules."

"I'm the house."

Sidney's jaw worked on his irritation, chewing back words. And words were all they had against the djinn-man. They couldn't actually shoot him, not with the unwitting passengers aboard; they could only force him to hold his djinni at bay.

Words were such little things—well, not all of Sidney's were little—but Alyce had seen Thorne flinch from some of them more than at the threat of angelic bullets. "If you had my love, Thorne, would you turn from the dark?"

Despite the threat of the sphericanum bullets, demon energy swirled in terrible waves, prickling her skin.

Thorne sat utterly still. His face seemed carved from some otherworldly stone, harder, darker, colder. The stone split and his white-toothed laugh tore through the simmering ethers. "What a stupid question. Something old Corvus would have asked; he was likely senile even before his head was bashed in, you know." He placed his hands in front of him, half hiding his mouth with his steepled fingers. "I told you I have no interest in following his path, especially if it takes me to the verge of hell."

"Then stay away from his handiwork," Sidney said, "or you might suffer his fate."

Thorne stiffened. "We might have been able to trade, but you will not order me in my own territory."

"Friendly suggestion only," Sidney said. But Alyce heard the insincerity in his voice. Not that he tried particularly to hide it.

Thorne stood. "Unless you want to test that *symballein* bond, get out."

"We're in the middle of the lake."

"I guess that is the path you chose. You can't shoot me without a mess you don't want to clean up either."

He advanced on them, circling the desk, and the force of his reviving demon pressed them back. Behind them, a sliding glass door opened to a small deck, the overhang of the deck above leaving it deep in shadow.

A pitched fight didn't work for either of them, but a no-fuss drowning ... Left with no option, she and Sidney backed out the door.

She was glad for the floating lesson when she saw there was no rail around the deck but only black water a few feet down. She shivered.

Sidney must have seen. He turned back to Thorne. "We'll wait to return to the dock. Then we won't speak to you again."

Thorne's laugh was curt. "I notice you don't say you won't *bother* me again."

"Depends on your definition of 'bother.'"

"The definition where you decide I'm a threat and take me on as you did Corvus."

"He brought that on himself."

"And I told you I won't."

"We'll just have to trust you." Sidney's answer was a sneer.

"Get off my boat," Thorne snarled. The djinni added a rumbling roar to his timbre. "Now."

Alyce took Sidney's hand. He was more afraid for her than he was of Thorne, and that could make him do something bad. Fingers laced with his, she stepped over the side.

The tumble could have been more graceful. Her skirt went most of the way over her head, making it hard to relax and float. But Sidney untangled her as even the scant light-ing of the *River Princess* pulled away.

Thorne waited at the edge of the deck a moment, then disappeared inside. The slam and crack of the glass door echoed above the churn of the engines. With the disappear-ance of the djinni, the teshuva revved up. The urge to flail her way to shore kicked her heart over, but she resisted the panic and drifted in Sidney's arms.

"Well, he didn't throw us overboard," she said.

"You jumped. That's taking control of your destiny."

"You were going to shoot him, weren't you?"

"You attacked him often enough, you said, and he didn't seem to mind."

"I don't think he'd take a bullet from you. I was special, remember?"

"Yes, you are."

She wasn't sure what to make of his tone, so she just floated.

"Why the hell did you ask him that question?"

She stared up at the sky. It was gray, the low clouds blocking the delicate stars and reflecting the harsher lights of the city. It was almost as unknowable as the vast, dark depths beneath her where she'd never be able to stand on her own two feet. "It was an experiment."

"In making me crazy?"

"Thorne wanted me, wanted to love me. But still he said I could not turn him from his path. Which tells me, once again, I am too weak. Not my demon this time, but me."

"Alyce—"

"You didn't want me to kiss you."

"What?" His hands under her shoulders jerked.

She struggled not to stiffen and sink. "I said—"

"I heard you. I just don't think that's relevant at the moment."

"No, I suppose not. That is what I realized. You don't want to be bound to me. Like Thorne said, you had no choice."

"I'm here," he said, but his voice was defensive.

"You don't want to let me drown. I appreciate that."

"Alyce—"

But with the return of her demon, she felt a lucidity long lost returning too, as if the teshuva had a view of both the sky and the murk underneath and was willing now to share with her. "I've never been a burden before."

"You're not a burden. I can hold you up with one hand—"

"I've always toiled, on my parents' farm, for my master, with the demon. I won't be a burden to you."

"Alyce—," he said, trying again.

But she pulled out of his arms. She'd unwrapped the white scarf from her neck as they stood at the stern of the boat, and now she waved it over her head. She started to sink, but with one paddling hand, she kept herself upright and signaled with the scarf again.

Out of the darkness, a *halloo* echoed. A single thin light skipped across the waves and struck the white scarf like a blink of lightning.

"It's the *Shades of Gray*," Sidney said.

"They said they'd be behind us." Alyce lay on her back again, looking up, as Jonah's boat pulled closer.

Archer leaned over the railing, one hand outstretched with a large orange ring on a rope. "You said you'd be thrown overboard, Westerbrook. Must be nice always being right."

"Get Alyce."

"Done." Archer dropped the ring to her, and it landed with a splash. She grabbed at the float. Archer and Gavril hauled her up.

Gavril wrapped a towel around her shoulders. "Should we get Westerbrook too?"

She gave him a look, and he turned back to the side with Archer.

Another moment and they had hauled Sidney into the boat.

"Got 'em?" Jonah called from the wheel.

"All aboard," Gavril said.

Archer sat on the seat that lined the pointed prow. "Did we learn anything useful?"

Sidney toweled his hair, and, with a shake of his head, the brown waves fell into place. "That an assembly of djinn-men is called an ahāzum, and the ahāzum is interested in the verge. That Thorne isn't interested in either. And that he doesn't know what to do with any of it any more than we do."

"So, nothing much we didn't already guess."

"We learned that I was insane," Alyce said. Her hair dripped in lank strands over her bare shoulder.

Archer and Gavril suddenly appeared very interested in the pretty city lights.

Sidney cleared his throat. "Just because Thorne remembers you with the other deinstitutionalized patients doesn't mean—"

She whirled on him. "Nothing much we didn't already guess."

He gave her an admonishing look. "Don't. Whatever you were is not what you are."

"I guess you would know." The cruelty of the reminder struck her before the last words cleared her tongue. Did she taste a whiff of sulfur? She turned away, drawing the towel tight around her shoulders.

They stood with the width of the small boat between them, and she felt endless miles apart. Any hope of finding the teshuva's talisman withered to nothing. Thorne had known her longer than anyone else, and he had nothing to offer. When she hadn't known she was missing the talisman, it hadn't mattered, but now . . . No wonder Sidney didn't want to be bound to her.

Despite his kind words, since he'd found her, she hadn't changed at all. She was still damaged goods—out of control, untutored in the simplest aspects of the talya mission, and not even powerful.

She wasn't sure she liked this new clarity.

No, not true. The clarity made very clear to her that she didn't like it at all.

Archer was quizzing Sidney on the configuration of the *River Princess* and any details Sidney might have noticed. Sidney was scowling as he estimated the number of passengers, how much money might be changing hands, whether a swimming talya could sneak onto the back of the boat through Thorne's lower deck, and what sorts of explosives might best sink her.

Jonah turned the *Shades of Gray* toward the city, and the lights starred on the tears in the corners of her eyes. She ducked her head into the folds of the towel. She didn't like crying either.

What was she? Not just human; not true talya. The only one who might understand her suspension between worlds was . . . Sidney. And she did not want to speak to him of her failings. She might never speak to him again.

CHAPTER 20

At the warehouse, Sid returned the revolver and angel-point bullet to the lab. Alyce had not spoken to him the rest of the ride back to the marina where Jonah kept the *Shades of Gray*, nor had she thawed during the car ride to the warehouse.

He'd hurt her. But damn it, what was he supposed to have said? That he might have . . . feelings for her in return? All his life he had trained to be a Bookkeeper, and Bookkeepers didn't deal in feelings. Feelings were uncharted territory. He'd never found a single fucking chart on feelings anywhere in the London league offices—not once.

He threw himself into his computer chair, ignoring the squelch of his lake-soaked pants. Liam had asked for his notes on the relic shard and possible uses, not to mention jurisdictional issues with the sphericanum. His fingers rested on the keyboard without typing.

He was cold and cranky. He should go change before he caught a cold. Except being chilled didn't actually increase the chances of viral infection with the common cold. And possession eliminated any chance at all.

Besides, he was curious. . . .

A quick search of Chicago mental health facilities in the 1970s yielded the usual hits of haunted insane asylums. The eager ghost hunters were more right than anyone might guess about restless spirits roaming the abandoned hallways of the old institutions. The overcrowded, underfunded facilities would have attracted heavy infestations of tenebrae. When the patients were released on their own recognizance, with the theory that some combination of mainstreaming, community services, and warm fuzzies would fix their problems, they would each have taken their burden of misery-hungry malice. And no doubt more than one frail, terrified patient— thrown suddenly out into the world—had fallen prey to voracious ferales.

But where had Alyce come from? If Thorne remembered her from one of the waves of deinstitutionalizations from the 1970s, would she have left behind evidence—say, a teshuva's talisman—in her patient records?

It was a long shot.

An hour later, Sid admitted it wasn't just long; it was impossible. Too many years had passed. The records of most facilities were lost or destroyed. Many of the buildings had been razed for apartment buildings and shopping centers. He wondered how much etheric agony lingered in the dimensions around the old places. It would be interesting to chart the decay over decades.

Extended sitting and disappointment crimped his muscles. It would have been nice to have found something to break the ice with Alyce.

"Like what?" he grumbled to himself. "'I found your old yearbook. Here you are in a straitjacket.' Lovely."

He blanked his search from the computer. He had no more excuses. When had he ever less looked forward to talking?

An attacking horde would not go amiss right now.

"Westerbrook. You have a minute?" Archer stood in the doorway.

The talya male might be up for a fight. "What do you need?" Sid settled his hip on the edge of the counter. He wasn't Bookkeeper anymore, but this was still more his territory than Archer's.

The league leader prowled the edges of the room. "Where's Alyce?"

"I don't know." At Archer's sharp glance, Sid realized he shouldn't have admitted it. "She went to her room."

Archer grunted. "Or so you hope. I'll check on her—"

"I'll do it," Sid snapped. "Later. What do you want?"

"I need to know your intent."

"Well, I was thinking dry socks would be a start."

Archer crossed his arms over his chest. "Don't play stupid now. What is your intent toward Alyce? And the league?"

"What do you care?" Sid matched the cross-armed stance. "For centuries, each league has been self-sufficient, and each talya has been, for all intents and purposes, an independent contractor."

Archer's lips twisted. "Sure. We take care of our own health insurance and retirement."

"That's the way it has always been." Sid refused to squirm. He hadn't made the rules. He had just learned them.

"That's the way it was for me," Archer agreed. "Half the time I wouldn't even come back to the league headquarters after a night wrestling the horde. I'd just phone in my continued existence so Bookie could keep a plus sign by my name in the archives."

Sid knew the slim volume Archer meant. Bound in some delicate hide, the first pages were speckled with the spatter from quill pens. The chart was kept on computer now, and it had more rows and columns than Archer implied. But the first column was still a list of league talyan, and the very last column was indeed full of check marks and a final "check-out" date. "I'm sure all your Bookkeepers have been thrilled to make note of your survival."

Archer ignored the snide aside. "I was the first to find a talya mate. Having a place to return to means something now." He fixed his dark gaze on Sid. "That is not theoretical or subject to dissection. I will annihilate anyone who gets in the way."

"Then I don't see what this has to do with me."

Archer sighed with impatience. "If you don't, then you definitely didn't deserve to be our Bookkeeper."

"Fine, I get it." Sid tightened his grip across his chest. "But I don't have to like it."

"You have to love it. Love her."

Sid recoiled, cheeks flaring hot. "I can't believe you of all people just said that."

"I love Sera with everything I am. And what I am now is much more than what I was, before the demon, before her."

"If you sing, I will annihilate you."

Archer's smile turned a little vicious. "You should see the poetry." Then his smile vanished, leaving only the vicious. "If you can't love Alyce, leave her now. She'll forget you."

But she wouldn't. Sid felt that as sure as he felt the muscles of his arms bunch under his clenched fingers, rejecting Archer's blunt conditions. Maybe before she would have forgotten, but she had come too far to go back now.

Had he? And what did that mean?

He wanted to make a chart of his own—a nice flowchart, maybe, of how he'd gotten here and where "here" went next. But he feared he'd find only a thick gray haze shot through with violet sparks.

The despair had a dampening effect on any self-preservation instinct. He straightened, letting his arms fall loose at his sides as he met Archer's challenging glare. "It's between Alyce and me. The league can piss off."

For a slow heartbeat, he wondered if the other man would swing at him.

Then Archer nodded. A trace of respect showed in the faint quirk of his lips. "If you need advice on either aspect . . ."

"I don't."

Archer shrugged. "Take good notes. Maybe the next *symballein* pair won't have to struggle as much."

Sid waited until the other man had gone before he slouched onto his chair again, uncertain what he should do next. It was a little early to call his father, and anyway, did he really want to have a conversation about his love life with London—or God forbid, Wes—any more than he did with Archer?

His thoughts spun wearily, the cogs barely engaged, the teshuva seemingly uninterested in helping him.

Was this what being a master Bookkeeper would have been like? Facing overarching metaspiritual conundrums alone in his lab? Archer was right; he had always thought he'd be studying the puzzle from above, not lost himself in the maze. How did he figure out where to go from here?

He pushed to his feet, hard enough to shove the chair back into the wall. Whatever he might have been before, now he was just hiding down here. Maybe, as Bookkeeper, he would have been as his father had explained—a separate conscience, keeping watch, making suggestions, shaking his head with distant dispassion.

Too late now.

He walked through the quiet hallways, his teshuva stretched out ahead of him like a blind man's cane. Most of the talyan were out after tenebrae, seeking any clues they might find about the ahāzum. Only the few who'd manned the *Shades of Gray* were in the warehouse.

And Alyce.

He closed his eyes and let the demon guide him.

He found himself in the darkness of the top-floor storage. The last time he'd been standing in the doorway, only the intermittent bulbs and emergency exit lighting had given his human eyes hope to see. Now, the whole room was a wilderness of shadow and deeper shadow. The twisted shapes of old and broken salvage took on a strange if ominous beauty, like the modern art Alyce hadn't appreciated.

"Are you here?" he called softly.

No answer. That was all the answer he needed.

He pulled the door shut behind him with the rusty squeal. Good. She wouldn't be able to sneak away down the stairs. She'd have to beat him fairly.

He suspected she'd be delighted to beat him.

He moved swiftly past the table jungle and through the tangle of light fixtures. He slowed in the jumble of urns—how many concrete planters and long-dried water features did one salvage company need? Half the urns could have easily hidden a crouching Alyce.

He didn't bother looking inside them. She wouldn't be hiding.

He kept a wary eye on the high shelves and stacked pallets. Without Nim to set rules about fairness when playing with the big-boned boys, the lithe and light talya would take every advantage. What advantages did he have?

"Alyce, I came here to tell you something."

Silence met his salvo. But not a vast, empty silence as it would have been had he been alone. It was a close, something-watching-him-from-behind silence.

"I screwed up. But I understand now."

"Understand what?"

Just as he'd known: No woman would let a man claim understanding without demanding proof.

He turned toward the echo of her voice. Judging by the bounce and distortion of sound waves, his teshuva guessed she was somewhere in the rows of abandoned funerary art—as if the urns hadn't been pointless enough. Who bought a blank headstone secondhand? Worse yet, who bought a used one? At least there were no dead bodies up here in storage.

Yet.

He edged around a marble obelisk and came face-to-face with a one-winged angel. Its stance—off-balance and half-threatening, half-fearful with its face averted—made him think of Alyce. His heart stuttered painfully at the comparison even as he made sure to avoid where the second wing had been; only exposed rebar now, it could gut a man.

"I hurt you," he said. "You have a right to be angry."

Another moment of silence settled into the headstones, and then she said, "That's what you understand?" Her tone, chill as the granite slabs, reflected her lack of enthusiasm.

He frowned. That had been a sincere and thoughtful admission, validating her feelings.

The sneaking suspicion nipped at his heels that maybe a soul of pure, unadulterated emotion like Alyce didn't need his understanding or validation. She said what she felt and to hell with the consequences.

Even if hell *was* the consequence, because everything about her pushed him to a dangerous passion beyond his comprehension.

Her delicate etheric signature glimmered like a faint star in the darkness, almost lost in the glare of the city's rampant emotional energy, the close shine of the talyan, and the interfering haze of the tenebrae. But he knew where to look. With his demon ascendant, he triangulated, he plotted—and, okay, he guessed a little—then he gathered his legs under him and leapt to the top of a mausoleum at the edge of the piled stone.

How the freestanding burial chamber, easily seven feet square, had come to be in the attic, Sid couldn't guess, although he absently calculated the minimum weight of the intricately carved marble and estimated the load-bearing capacity of the floor joists. The mass was incrementally increased if he added the slight talya he found there.

Her cold fury added nothing to the floor's burden and everything to his own.

Alyce stood with her arms crossed, more the avenging angel than mournful. Her eyes and *reven* glittered with amethyst sparks. "What are you doing here?"

"Looking for you. I thought you were going to your room."

"Because you told me to?" She lifted her chin to a hostile tilt.

She'd seemed so willing to follow his suggestions before. But she was not a child or an invalid. The powers of observation he'd fancied so finely honed had failed him. He hadn't seen what he hadn't wanted to see. "I thought you'd want to go to bed."

"I thought you might too. And I wanted to be alone."

Ouch. So she considered him capable of blowing off the depths of her affections . . . and then coming to her bed anyway. If the mausoleum had been dropped on his head, he couldn't have felt any more crushed. "Alyce, I didn't mean to hurt you."

"It is what we do."

"To tenebrae, not to each other. You told me that once."

"The devil part of us hurts the tenebrae. The human part learned its lesson well."

As she'd learned her lessons from him. He'd been so determined to hold himself apart, detached, and now she stood in her no-longer-white dress, as cold and untouchable as any of the desolate statuary around them.

And he knew, with every neuron firing in his scientific brain, that it was for the best.

CHAPTER 21

Three hundred years of innocence, gone. Despite near slavery, despite demonic possession, she had been innocent. And in a handful of sunsets, this man had opened her eyes and unveiled her desire; he had taught her the meaning of sin.

But Sidney had left her there—alone.

Even the devil had not been so cruel.

Now he came to her, to *explain*. She could not believe now the things she had said and what she had revealed to him. She would have been smarter to have turned her back on a feralis. At least then the pain would have quickly ended.

But he was talking again.

"...the influence of the *symballein* bond," he was saying. "That's the reason you—we are infected with these epidemic emotions."

"Possessed and infected." She was careful to purge any of those epidemic emotions from her voice. "How inconvenient."

He peered at her, clearly uncertain of her mood, as well he should be. She drew herself in tight and hard, like slamming the empty mausoleum door closed on its hollow core. Nothing inside, not even death.

That she would reserve for the tenebrae. Shredding the darkness around her had kept her alive, if not exactly whole, and the league had a place for her in everlasting servitude. That could be her solace again.

"Thank you for the swimming lesson," she said.

He narrowed his eyes even more, maybe because this time he did hear her sincerity. "It was my pleasure."

Never again.

She straightened. "If only we had learned more."

He seemed eager to hear what he wanted to hear now. "Thorne gave us a few clues. So I wondered if you want to take a trip out to Holygrove Hospital."

"A hospital? Why?"

"It's not really a hospital anymore. It closed in the early 1970s. I'm wondering if you might recognize it."

"You think I was there."

"Maybe. Chicago had several asylums. Most are gone or changed, but Holygrove lingered in disrepair for a while and was finally abandoned."

A bolt of something tried to pierce the cold, hard exterior she'd drawn around herself. Not hope. She wouldn't allow that. Curiosity, she would call it. "You think my teshuva's talisman might be there."

"We shouldn't hope," he cautioned.

But she'd already told herself that. She would never be anything to him but a curiosity, and so that was all she could give back.

She jumped down from the mausoleum, surprised at how lightly she landed despite the heaviness in her body. "Where?"

"What better time to explore an abandoned insane asylum than right before Halloween?" Sidney muttered.

He'd spoken so quietly, even a teshuva should have missed it, but despite her best intentions, Alyce still found herself attuned to his every word.

Not that he ever said the words she wanted to hear.

A blustering and oddly warm wind had torn apart the earlier clouds. The black sky, with a few pinprick stars, glistened between the gray remnants. It was an apt comparison to her clarity, which had been returning ever since Sidney had removed the angelic relic.

With every passing moment, more pieces were revealed. There were just scraps from the years between her possession and Sidney's appearance, but those scraps, like fabric pieces, still held their pattern and color, if not their completeness. With enough pieces, she could cobble together a past.

She stared up at the center tower, the two halls flanking away on either side. "It seemed bigger when I was strapped in a wheelchair."

"Do you remember how long ago?"

She turned to look back at the apartment buildings that had crept up to the edges of the grounds. "These were empty fields when they brought me here. When I left, the streets made a grid on all sides."

Sidney shook his head. "Decades. How could they not notice that you didn't age?"

"I didn't change, but they did. Often. It was not a forgiving place." She frowned. "I probably didn't make that any easier."

From the scowl on his face, he didn't feel very forgiving either. "There would have been records of your admittance and your therapies—as uninformed as they would have been, considering."

"That didn't stop the straps."

His jaw clenched. "Then someone should have at least noticed that the straps didn't leave bruises for long. And then they should have wondered. . . ." After a moment, he shook his head. "Of course they didn't wonder, and even if they had, they wouldn't have come to the right conclusions. I'm being unfair."

She glowered. He could be fair to those long-gone torturers, but not to her. "I want to go inside."

"I don't know how stable it is."

"Why should *it* be stable?" She stalked past him.

The sloping manicured lawns that spread vaguely in her memory had been eaten away by the city until only an overgrown patch of weeds remained, like the shriveled legs of a dead spider. But the brick building still stood tall and officious, though all its windows gaped, broken. The darkness within lent the illusion that the night was a black sheet behind it, as if the building itself were a facade, only a single brick deep.

Maybe she could push it over with her hand.

She kept her fists tucked under her arms as she climbed the front steps. She'd kick down the door instead.

But the double doors hung slightly open, buckled on their hinges. In the foyer, age had warped the linoleum floors and softened the lintels over the doorways enough to sag, giving the corridors an off-kilter look. Despite her simmering anger, the moodiness chilled her. The drear emotions of the inhabitants had tainted the place down to the mortar.

She swallowed against the stink of mildew that coated the back of her throat and gazed out the door with a touch of longing. "Sometimes they took us on walks around the grounds."

"Why didn't you run? They couldn't have stopped you."

She turned her gaze on him, realized she still had the wistful longing on her face, and scowled instead. "Where would I run to? I already knew there was something I couldn't escape. I thought they would make me better." She stared down where her wrists crossed over her chest, fists under her arms. They'd bound her in the white jacket the same way, but he was right; the bruises around her wrists had never lasted. "For a time, the teshuva liked the easy hunting. There were always malice, grown fat and slow on the misery and desperation here. The way they screamed when I crept up behind them and the teshuva tore them apart . . ." She shuddered. "Nobody noticed those screams on top of all the others. Which made me even more certain I was mad."

"Some people suffering deep mental disturbances do actually see the tenebrae for what they are. Whether that's cause or effect of their troubles . . ." Sidney shrugged. "Like you, they wouldn't have the words to make anyone believe."

Now she had the words for what she was, what she'd seen. And yet she felt as trapped and lost as the years she'd spent behind these walls.

She spun away from him and headed down the hallway, avoiding the slick damp patches on the floor that made footing treacherous.

He hastened to catch up. "Where are we going?"

"I want to see more."

To her demon's vision, the tenebrae signs had paled to the faintest of ghosts, just a few ichor smears where a feralis had retreated to add a carcass to its husk. Without human habitation, there was nothing to entice the tenebrae in any number.

Only graffiti scrawls, tatters of windblown debris, and slivers of broken glass relieved the institutional monotony of the halls. She peered into the empty rooms, but other than a few bits of memory—as uninteresting as crumpled cigarette butts—nothing seemed worthwhile.

Until they got to the therapy room.

There was nothing much to distinguish it from the other rooms—except for the table, bolted to the floor.

She edged inside, shuffling her feet through a drift of old leaves.

Sidney paused in the doorway, his shoulders filling the space. "Alyce?"

"Here's where it went away, at least for a little while." She circled the table, trailing one fingertip over the heavy steel.

He followed her into the room. "What went away?"

"The devil." She stopped in the middle of the long edge of the table, opposite where he stood. Thick rivets marked where the straps had been, though only small rings of worn leather remained, pressed to the table. Four shallow depressions marred the squared edge.

She angled her wrist and covered the depressions with her fingers. They fit. Perfectly.

Sidney did the same on his side of the table. His larger hands eclipsed the embedded fingerprints. A soft sound she couldn't identify left his throat. "Electroconvulsive therapy worked against the teshuva?"

"Maybe for a day, I couldn't feel it. I couldn't see the malice. I still knew they were there, but I could pretend. Then night would fall."

He was silent a moment. "I don't think I've ever read anything about ECT and demonic emanations. But I suppose, in theory, two such intense bursts of energy, interacting or interfering . . ."

Anger pulsed in her, dimming her vision. "It wasn't theory for me."

He lowered his head. "I see why you'd want to forget."

Bitterness, like the sour stomach that had plagued her after the shocks, made her stare at him with more bile than she wanted to acknowledge. "You have no idea."

But when he raised his gaze, she was caught by an answering resentment. "You think I didn't wonder what life would be like, not having to know about the battles between good and evil?"

She stared at him uncertainly. "You wanted to know everything."

He gave a low, harsh laugh. "Doesn't that make me more of a certifiable lunatic than any patient who ever came through these doors?"

She shook her head. "Then why didn't *you* run?"

"What? Like my brother? It was too late for me, even before possession. If I'd left after I realized how much being part of the war would cost me, that would mean my mother died for nothing."

She bit her lip. Maybe Sidney couldn't love her, but that didn't mean he'd never loved at all. Of course, he would dedicate himself to the Bookkeeper world to pay for his mother's death. Only her own cravings—not demon-driven, just hers—had made her think she could win a place in his heart. "You're right."

He gave himself a shake. "I didn't mean to hijack your memories. This is your place. What are you thinking?"

In this place where she'd been crazy, he wondered what she *thought*? "I think this is a waste of time. If there was ever anything of mine here, it's long gone. Like everything else in my life. Whatever price I paid, I'm never getting it back."

He headed for the door. "Maybe there are records in the basement." But as he spoke, he was shaking his head. "Except that only works in the movies."

She straightened. "My past is gone. Whatever future I want, I will make for myself."

She laid her fingers over the old marks once more. Then she heaved backward and ripped the table from the floor. It snapped off its base with a metallic screech as the weld broke free. The slab flipped one end over the other into the wall, and the age-softened plaster crumbled away in rotten white chunks.

One of the rivets that had held the straps rebounded and rolled across the floor in an ever-decreasing circle near her foot. She stomped on it before it could complete its doomed spiral.

Sidney shifted. "Feel better now?"

She moved her foot and leaned down to retrieve the little metal ring. Instead of a flattened disk, it was gently rounded around the edges. Simple, weak, torn free—how appropriate. She slid it over her right-hand ring finger and held her hand out to admire the band.

When she closed her fist, the metal felt strangely warm, as if the horrendous stress that had broken the table had transferred to the small circle. Maybe it appreciated the return of fear and violence. Maybe it had waited just for her.

She'd always played the smaller role in her life: youngest daughter, lowest servant, helpless victim. Now she would be a partner in full—not to Sidney, who didn't want that, but to the league.

"Okay," she said. "I'm done."

Thorne woke slowly, his head pounding.

He smacked his lips, still half dreaming the sour tang of liquor and vomit. Damn, but he despised falling into the drunken Indian stereotype. He hadn't done that since . . . His breath hitched, not on stale alcohol but on the stench of rotten eggs.

He swung his legs off the side of the bed. When he tried to push himself upright, his knees buckled. He caught himself, barely, before his head smashed onto the floor. His fingers skidded across the wet floor.

What the . . . ?

His bedroom was toe-deep in water. And since he suddenly remembered his bedroom was a lower berth on the *River Princess*, not his childhood old singlewide on the rez, water wasn't good.

And he hadn't been drinking except for a single tumbler of scotch to calm himself after Alyce and her big brave Anglo had abandoned ship. He shook his head, and his braid slapped his cheek hard enough to rouse him to attention.

He tried to pull his legs under him again but succeeded

only in making a bilge water wave around his silk pajama bottoms. Where was his damn djinni?

His vision doubled, then redoubled again, until the walls of his berth seemed a million miles away. Had crazy Alyce slipped him a Wonderland pill to make him smaller?

A poison pill to shrink a demon . . . Birnenston.

He always kept the toxic leach of the djinni off his sheets. He was at least that civilized—or had been for a long time. He'd learned to keep himself chained.

Anger burned off some of the mental smog, and he gathered himself for another try at standing. He wasn't going to drown like a baby in an inch of water.

With one elbow hooked over the mattress, he managed to get to his knees. He shook his head again, and when his eyeballs stopped rolling around, he focused on the room.

Water was gurgling under the door, slow but steady. But that wasn't the worst.

The streaks of sulfur yellow climbing the walls were much, much worse.

He cursed. This wasn't some wicked wet dream of his demon. Someone had invaded the *River Princess* and infected her with birnenston.

The noxious by-product of tenebrae accumulated wherever too many of them gathered. In sufficient amounts—such as, oh, say the amount currently wallpapering his bedroom—it could spontaneously ignite. And the birnenston was toxic to any spectral thing, including the horde themselves. Even evil didn't want to sit in its own shit.

It was yet another good reason to have rejected Magdalena's idiot henchman and his invitation to tea and mayhem.

Except now he didn't have someone to pull him up. He was alone.

Thorne looked around at his slowly sinking ship. He'd told the talyan he'd rather be outcast than a pawn again. But there were other places on the chessboard.

Only two sides existed, though, and Alyce had already chosen.

He tsked at his muddled thinking. Hadn't he already told them they'd never had a choice?

And when he stopped tsking, he realized that the soft ticking continued. He hadn't heard that sound in forty some years.

Somebody hadn't trusted the birnenston to do its dirty work without a bit of incentive; there was a bomb aboard.

"Fuck," he said.

Burned, drowned, and blown to bits. That somebody wasn't giving him a lot of options.

Never mind waiting for his djinni to crawl up from his depths. His anger spiked to fury, and he jolted to his feet and toward the door. He missed the door and hit the wall with both palms outstretched. The birnenston ate into his hands, but he couldn't yank back without losing his balance. Better to lose some skin. That the djinni could replace.

How degrading. He worked his way down the wall to the door and jerked it open.

Water, almost knee-deep outside, swept in and knocked his feet out from under him. He went down with a curse and a gurgle.

At least the dousing thinned the birnenston smog in his head. He righted himself more quickly this time and waded back to the door.

The lower deck was awash. A few items drifted on the current pulsing in from his office as the *Princess* wallowed, sinking aft. A clear plastic baggie—knotted and half-full of water—bobbed past him, a piece of paper affixed to the knot.

That hadn't been onboard earlier.

If he could dismantle the timer . . .

But when he eased the bag from the water, instead of a nice brick of C4 explosives, two yellow shapes circled in front of his eyes.

His half-moon bettas . . . Trapped in the confined space, they'd been after each other, and their perfect half-circle fins were shredded.

Alive, read the note. *For now.*

Bag clutched in his hand, Thorne waded for the stairs. The farther from his room he went, the faster he moved. By the time he hit the main deck — the morning sun near blinding to the frantically ascending djinni — he was running.

He wished he hadn't been so paranoid as to remove the gangplank to the pier every night since Carlo's visit. It was going to be a long jump.

He launched himself across the empty space between boat and pier just as the *Princess* exploded. The pressure bashed his eardrums, and he flailed, like another armful of kindling thrown into the air.

He hit the pier and rolled. The rough concrete tore his bare shoulders as he curled around the baggie tucked to his chest. Around him, pieces of the *Princess* rained down, ignited at both ends and burning toward their centers with the ferocious, slow-consuming hunger of the birnenston. There'd be only black char when the fire went out, but it would take a preternaturally long time.

Someone was screaming, but it wasn't him.

The heat of the explosion scorched his back as he walked away. When he was done, he'd make sure there was *nothing* but black.

CHAPTER 22

"I swear it wasn't me," Archer repeated. "It was just an idea."

"It was a good one," Sid said. The other talyan, gathered in Liam's office, nodded.

Liam threw down the newspaper on his desk. The above-the-fold photo on the metro section featured the *River Princess*, listing hopelessly and engulfed in venomous yellow flames. The heat had blown out or melted the tinted windows, and a brilliant blue autumn sky puffed with white clouds shone through the holes. Sid might have blamed overly enthusiastic Photoshopping for the unnatural color and the downward sweep of the conflagration. Except he knew it wasn't so much unnatural as supernatural.

"A birnenston-fueled fire will make great footage for the evening news," he said. "She might still be burning."

"At least no one can get close enough to be infected." Liam turned to the laptop Archer had brought. "They're updating the story hourly and still haven't speculated on a cause."

"Speculation will get them nowhere this time," Sid assured him.

Liam let out a sound somewhere between a grumble and a sigh before pinning Archer with another annoyed look.

Archer raised one hand. "I swear."

"Hoarding that much birnenston isn't a talya trick anyway," Sid pointed out. "Whatever metaphysical quirk makes our demons repentant spares them that nastiness."

Liam rubbed his temple. "Why would one djinn-man poison another?"

Jilly bumped his hand aside and took over the massage. "Why does Ecco drink right out of the OJ cartons?"

"Because he's a rude beast," Sera said. "That's reason enough for a djinn-man to court the eternal enmity of another?"

Jilly shrugged. "They probably have their own ideas about what makes for courting, same as we do."

Sera shook her head. "I don't think destroying Thorne's home, key source of income, and the external manifestation of his persona in one fell swoop is a good way to make friends."

"But it doesn't give him a lot of choice about what he does next, does it?" Sid tapped his pen against the notepad on his lap. "If they wanted to drive him in a particular direction . . ."

"Like into a blind fury." Archer tweaked the computer out from under Liam's nose. "I'll keep an eye on the story. I'm curious if we might get a hint—maybe from the insurance claim—who might have benefited from covering for his illegal gambling operation."

Liam grunted. "Run it by Bella. She has a sense for shady business in this town."

Archer held his hand out to Sera. "We'll see what we have by tonight."

"The forecast calls for rain later," Sid said, "but the fire won't go out until the boat sinks and the birnenston dissipates. Then there won't be anything for the fire marshal to collect, much less analyze."

"Maybe we can make sure of that," Liam said. "I'll send Pitch to put a hole through the hull if necessary."

Archer lifted one brow. "You want to send him that close to a djinn-man. Sometimes I wonder. . . ."

"He's subtle," Liam said. "He won't leave a sign to follow."

"It won't matter," Alyce said. "Thorne will blame us."

Sid watched her twist the rivet on her finger and wondered if she could wind his nerves any tighter. "Why would he blame us? As I said, birnenston isn't a teshuva weapon."

She kept her gaze on the ring. "I didn't say he would think we did it. I said he'd blame us."

"Unreasonable," Sid objected.

Finally she slid him an arch glance. "You can tell him that."

"He'll have enough on his plate for today," Liam said. "What with avoiding the reporters and police."

Alyce shrugged. "But tonight . . ."

Liam stood, and the talyan followed suit. "Everybody, take a nice nap this afternoon."

They split up in the hallway, Archer and Sera to follow the cyber trail, Liam and Jilly to track down Pitch presumably, and Alyce . . .

"Wait up." Sid hurried after her while the others continued on their way. "Where are you going?"

"To my room, as Liam said."

Sid's hackles prickled. "Because he said." His tone fell flat.

She kept walking. "Because it made sense."

"Oh well, in *that* case . . ."

She stopped abruptly and faced him. "Am I not allowed to follow good sense when I hear it? Does that not fit your understanding of a rogue?"

He bristled back. "You've been displaying some of your previous aberrant ways since we got back from the hospital, and just now you seemed almost admiring of Thorne's reprehensible behavior."

Her eyes widened. "Admiring? I am dreading it."

"Well, your demon has a special affinity for dread, so that would explain—"

She stepped right up to his toes. "Explain what?"

"Why you like him."

"Like him? I've tried to kill him. More than once."

"And didn't succeed."

She gave him a disbelieving glare. "Because he is possessed by a powerful djinni, and I have the demonic equivalent of a windup toy."

"Or maybe because you didn't want him to die because he was there for you when no one else was." He watched her closely.

She stiffened and took a step back. "He came around occasionally to poke at me and watch me flail. Which, yes, now that I think of it, is really very reprehensible." She gave him a meaningful glare.

He tried to shut up. After all, why was he needling her? Because she knew Thorne best? That made her an asset, not an enemy. And yet he found himself circling her, looking for the weakness in her armor, for a way in.

She was weak, just as she claimed, but somehow she had closed herself against him. "You're changing," he said.

She narrowed her eyes. "That's a rogue for you. So erratic."

"Why are you wearing that rivet?"

"It fits."

"That's . . ."

"Unreasonable? Aberrant?"

He wouldn't apologize for the words. If she was backsliding, they needed to get her back on the talya path. "That's the sort of memory you don't need."

"What makes you think so?"

His jaw worked, but he couldn't spit out anything that didn't sound stupid.

The angry spark in her eyes eased just a bit, and she nodded. "You're learning."

"What the hell is that supposed to mean?"

"That you don't know everything."

"I know you've been quiet and withdrawn ever since you destroyed the therapy room and took that piece away with you."

She sighed. "You think the ring is making me withdrawn?"

"I think we pushed your rehabilitation too fast."

"Is that what you were doing in my bed?" She tilted her head. "Fixing me?"

"Not just you," he conceded. "My demon's first ascension—just as your teshuva has been unbalanced all these years—made me susceptible too."

"But you're over it now, and I'm still . . . aberrant."

A curse of frustration surged up in his throat, but that wouldn't very well prove his own balance. "I just meant you shouldn't dredge up memories that are going to set you back."

"Missing memories is what made me crazy," she said. "I thought you'd understand; the more I know, the less I fear." She held out her hand. The rivet was a dark stripe across her pale skin. "I lost the teshuva's talisman somewhere across the years. I was left adrift. This can be the symbol of us beginning anew."

His heart skittered. "Us . . ."

She curled her ringed hand into her chest, her gaze unwavering. "The demon and I. Who else?"

The violence with which she'd flipped the steel table was nowhere in evidence, yet he ached as if she'd thrown him across the room and knocked the breath from him. "Who else. Right."

She watched him a moment. "Did you need something from me?"

Answers churned through him, each less coherent than the last. How could he answer when he had barely formulated the questions? A good researcher didn't *want* any particular outcome. He didn't anticipate results. He observed what *was*.

And she had said she loved him.

He stared into her eyes. Not so clear and still as before; there were shadows and secrets shifting below the icy blue.

Did she love him now? Did he want her to? And when had he stopped knowing his own mind?

He shook his head. "I don't need anything else."

She turned on her heel and left him standing there.

Hard to believe, but the Bowl Me Over looked worse in the light of day.

Thorne supposed the same could be said of him. The birnenston explosion had left him shaking and sick as no fortified wine ever had. The scrawny maple tree at the edge of the parking lot was the only thing holding him upright.

When the silver limousine rolled into the lot, the reflected glare of sunlight stabbed his eyes. He sucked down a few quick breaths, trying to force his djinni higher. Instead, he gagged on the lingering taste of sulfur and crumpled to his knees. His palm skidded across the pavement. The cracked asphalt peeled up divots of skin before he caught himself.

The limo eased to a gentle stop just beyond his tight-clenched knuckles. The door, when it swung open, barely missed his bowed head.

Pride—or panic—coursed down his spine, urging him to straighten, but the sudden demonic presence was an unrelenting heavy hand on the back of his neck.

He kept his gaze fixed on the high heels that emerged, one, two, in front of his nose. The satiny pumps were the same color as night storm clouds over the city that swallowed all the multicolored light and reflected back only gray.

"What reverence you show me, Mr. Halfmoon, but please, get up." The feminine voice was as satin-smooth as the gray heels, though the sharp point was hidden—for the moment.

Thorne's stomach clenched, somewhere between a dry heave and a futile attempt to right himself. Only a hard grip on his biceps got him to his feet.

Still swaying, he stared into Carlo's squinting sneer. "I take it you gave Magdalena my message?"

The wise guy's lip curled up another mocking notch. "Was a shame that fireplace on your boat was so squeaky clean. Well, I guess you got one fire out of it anyway."

Thorne wrenched his arm from Carlo's grip, tearing the office drone dress shirt he'd taken from the dry cleaner to replace his birnenston-stained pajamas. He continued the quick upward thrust with a crack into the wise guy's septum.

Carlo howled and staggered back, clutching his face. Thorne steadied himself in the ratty sneakers that had been the only shoes at the dry cleaner—taken *off* the dry cleaner. That had been just a casual bit of obligatory violence, reviving his djinni not at all. Bloodying Carlo, though, felt good. The demon in Thorne finally settled into wary stillness.

This left him facing Magdalena, without the other djinn-man in the way.

The djinn-men, like most apex predators, were not overly numerous and stayed out of one another's territory whenever possible. In his decades possessed, he'd met fewer than a dozen of his brethren face-to-face. But even he knew of Magdalena.

Not that anyone knew much. She was as beautiful as they'd said, sloe-eyed and naturally red lipped, with rich dark hair and sun-kissed skin despite the lateness of the season. And now he knew the rumors of her powerful djinni were not exaggerated either.

"Carlo," she said, raising that satin voice to be heard over the wise guy's muffled cursing, "stay with the car, will you? Mr. Halfmoon, walk with me a moment."

Did he have a choice? His feet started moving without his conscious thought. Apparently not.

"'Walk with me,'" he growled. "You learned that line from your pet mobster."

She met his narrowed gaze directly and inclined her head, dark waves of her hair shifting around the shoulders of her slim dove-gray suit. All the drab tones should have sucked the life from her; instead, her coloring seemed even more alluring. "Carlo has been telling me about gathering like-minded souls, about creating a family, if you will."

"No doubt he has," Thorne said. "He likes to talk."

"And I am a good listener." She guided him out of the parking lot, following the chain-link fence. Though the slabs of sidewalk concrete had buckled in places, she glided forward as if those high heels never touched the ground. "So, Mr. Halfmoon, what do *you* want to tell me?"

His throat worked, choking on his djinni's wordless disturbance. What would it say if it had a tongue of its own? "I suppose 'Go to hell' won't help my cause."

Her laugh was like industrial smoke, darker and grittier than her smooth voice. "Some might say, by joining *my* cause, that's exactly where you'd be going."

Curiosity forced him to ask, "You'd say otherwise?"

"While I appreciated his verve, Corvus Valerius wanted to pit hell against heaven with this realm as the battlefield. But I've found war to be . . . intrusive. The tenebraeternum can stay locked tight. I just want to borrow a bit of it, as needed."

Already the force of her demon, even idle, horrified him. If she had access to the eternal well of evil . . . "Hell isn't a bank," he said.

She laughed again and leaned toward him to rest her hand on his arm where Carlo had torn the shirt. "More like a stock market. You ran a casino; you should understand. No one gets rich playing the bank."

Standing so close, her perfume teased him; something lush and exotic, but applied with a restrained hand so that even his djinni strained to capture the essence of the fragrance . . . and recoiled at the nearly imperceptible stink of cordite. Though her fingers were warm, almost uncomfortably so, his skin crawled at her touch. Before he could pull away, she released him. She turned to the chain-link fence and curled her fingers through the steel wire.

"No," she murmured. "I'm not trying to make this earth a living hell." Her gaze fixed on the scene on the other side of the fence. "It's already that. I just want it to be my hell."

Focused as he'd been on Magdalena, Thorne had dismissed the background shrieking as his freaked-out djinni. But the ruckus actually rose from the half-pint fiends confined behind the fence.

The daycare center playground was decorated with pumpkins and hay bales that the children tumbled over with raucous glee. Since most were in costume—and empty candy cellophanes gusted in the whirlwinds of their capering—he guessed they'd been celebrating the coming of Halloween.

He slanted a glance at Magdalena and swallowed hard at the dark void in her stare. "Thanks for the invitation, but I have my own hell."

She watched the children another long heartbeat, then trailed her fingers down the chain-link fence. Her white-tipped nails strummed the metal strands with a discordant rattle. When she finally turned to him and smiled, against her white teeth, her lips looked almost bloodred. "Of course you do. And you are alone there. Wouldn't you rather be with us? Isn't that why you came here today? Because you have nowhere else to go?"

Only because the djinni bastards had burned his *Princess*. Thorne made himself smirk, disguising the rage of his loss with a flippant one-shoulder shrug. "I'm here because I knew Carlo would come eventually. And I planned to kill him."

She turned back the way they had come and raised one hand in a negligent wave. "Ah, you are brothers under the skin, and brothers will fight."

"Are you giving me permission to skin Carlo?"

She gave him a reproving look as the limo sharked toward them on the wrong side of the street, wise guy at the wheel. "In the end, you are the same, and you will fight together."

On one hand, she was probably right. Now that he'd met her and felt the black-hole magnetism of her demon, he didn't think that Chains or any of the other skeptical djinn-men would hesitate to join her. The counterculture associates of his day had liked to proclaim "power corrupts," and if the opposite was true—that corruption was power—then Magdalena was absolutely powerful. What djinn-man could resist such magnificent malevolence?

He wavered a little in his stolen shoes. She never dropped her gaze, but the thick fringe of her lashes narrowed. She was calling on her djinni, not to bring him to his knees, but enough to weaken his resolve.

And if he didn't bend, she would break him.

His heartbeat hung suspended, as it had the moment all those years ago when he realized, with his fellow revolutionaries sleeping in the house above the basement lab, the timing device on the bomb was locked and counting down.

Alyce had always feared that the demon-ridden were monsters. With Magdalena, there was no need to question.

She was definitely a monster.

But he kept his voice as light and steady as the touch he'd used on unstable explosives. "With such excellent specimens as Carlo, I think you don't even need me."

"I want you all." Her dark eyes widened, and from the black depths peered the same hunger as when she'd looked at the children. It was not so different, really, from how those children must have looked at the Halloween candy that had once filled those empty wrappers now scuttling ahead of the wind.

The limo coasted to a stop beside them, and Carlo stepped out onto the curb to open the back door for Magdalena. "My lady, let's go. The fundraiser dinner starts in an hour." He squinted at Thorne, an evil look compounded by the smears of blood from his broken nose. "He ain't worth missing the hors d'oeuvres."

Thorne forgave the wise guy for all his bad manners if he'd just hustle his damn lady out of there. Nevertheless, no open bar tab, no number of courses to a meal, would fill the void in those bottomless eyes.

She slipped into the maroon leather interior, but Thorne's relief was short-lived as she rolled down the window. "I'll find you again," she promised.

And although he had nowhere else to go, nothing else to lose, he was suddenly afraid.

Nowhere to go and nothing to lose—was this how birdbrain Blackbird had raged as the pieces of him were chipped away?

Thorne crouched beside the white van's shining tires and tucked the equally black strands of his unbraided hair behind his ears. He sliced the lock pick across the pad of his thumb and grimaced at the stink, worse than the new rubber next to him. Blood, ichor, and birnenston welled up in threads of red, black, and yellow, festive as a coral snake and far more deadly.

With unhurried thoughtfulness, he painted his cheekbones. The toxic ooze ate into his flesh, and he tasted salt as the deep furrows siphoned his tears downward.

Corvus died to reach his vision; there must be another way.

The white clouds had thickened all day to an ashen gray, condensing toward black like his poor boat. They bellied down now to spit rain in his face, but nothing could extinguish the burning pain of the birnenston on his flesh.

The *Princess* was drowned. A cruel goddess was rising. And his innocent little Alyce . . . had never been his.

See, this was why a man was better off alone.

The talyan would come to curse the *symballein* lash, he had no doubt. But in the meantime, they'd triggered a torrent of changes that had yet to run its course. Who would be left standing and who would be swept away?

He'd bragged to Alyce, and to Carlo of the gaping chest hole, that he walked his own path. That was what he'd told himself while his grandmother dragged him down from the apartment roof one night short of his seven-night vigil. He would find his own way.

And look what a clusterfuck had ensued.

He'd been a slow student at the rez school, and worse when he'd been sent to his grandmother in the city. Maybe if his spirit guide had appeared. Maybe if the bomb hadn't gone off, or—better yet—if he'd never twisted the wires together. Maybe if the radiance he'd seen in Alyce had held out any chance for him . . . But no. He was what he was.

Possessed by evil. But he would not allow anyone else to lead him by the nose. It was time he mastered the darkness in him, by himself, since the light had never been burning for him.

That last encounter with Alyce had shamed him. Held at bay by an Anglo toting his own gun . . . He needed to get back his edge.

War paint complete, his djinni roused to a fury, he crept past the Last Call Cleaning van. SERVICES IN DECONTAMINATION AND STERILIZATION, promised the lettering on the vehicle.

They'd need those services after he was done.

"Idiot!" Nim bounced hard on the mats.

"Who?" Gavril straightened his black T-shirt. Throwing Nim over his shoulder had left a wrinkle. "You or me?"

"You! Okay, me. Just . . . ouch." She pulled herself to her feet with a grimace.

Alyce stepped forward. "I'll try now."

Nim limped off the mats to stand in the wan gray light filtering through the warehouse windows. Fretful rain spattered against the glass. "Did you see what I did wrong?"

"You let him catch you."

Nim snorted. "My mistake."

Gavril took a few circling steps to the side as Alyce walked into the empty corner amidst all the salvaged junk. He had bowed to Nim. He did not do the same to her, Alyce noticed.

She followed him along the circling path he'd set, their bare feet silent on the mats.

He studied her, eyes unreadable. "Jonah asked me to work with her, to streamline the reflexes her teshuva has given her. He worried—needlessly—that his missing hand makes him less of an instructor. He worried—rightly—that he would be too gentle with her."

Nim snorted again. "His mistake."

Gavril inclined his head, but his gaze did not leave Alyce. "You do not need such streamlining."

Nim put her hand on the lush swell of her hip. "Did you just call me fat?"

They both ignored her. Alyce shrugged. "We have been together a long time, my demon and I. But we are weaker than we should be because I do not know what to give it. I don't know how to be with it."

Gavril's gaze was still dark. "Your *symballein* mate should show you. He has no excuse not to."

"He has many excuses," Alyce said softly.

Nim sucked in a breath. "Maybe we shouldn't—"

Gavril held up one hand. "I have no intention of pursuing this opening." His smile at Alyce was cool and sharp. "No intention of pursuing you, other than here, around this attack."

"I don't intend to be caught. In either way."

"Then let us begin."

Gavril did not catch her long enough to throw her—although he laid hands on her twice and managed to trip her once—but the chase left her panting. In the end, she managed a leap that sucked the last of the energy from her legs. She planted both heels in Gavril's chest with a mighty kick that drove him back to the windows. His elbow cracked a pane, and if she'd gone for the follow-up, she might have shoved him through the glass to a debilitating, if not fatal, fall.

She hit the mat and rolled backward, coming to a stop in a low crouch, one hand steepled before her. The demon arched through her, straining toward the fight. In the bottom of her vision, the rivet ring glinted with a twinge of violet.

Gavril waited against the windows. "You might not know all the demon needs, but your instincts haven't failed you." He gave her the bow he'd withheld before, as smooth as the raindrops rolling down the glass behind him.

Lounging on her belly at the edge of the fight, propped on her elbows, Nim pouted. "How come I didn't get instincts?"

"You did," Gavril said. "You talk over them."

"True." She coiled her legs around to sit. "Enough ass-kicking for today?"

"Until tonight," Gavril said. "And then it will be for real."

Despite the saucy tilt of her head, Nim's eyes were serious as her gaze slid from Alyce to Gavril. "Speaking of talking . . . You won't mention any little *symballein* spats, right? Just between us girls?"

Gavril grimaced. "Any of the others could have chosen to be up here to enjoy your indiscretions. They are not brave enough. So they will get no advantage from me."

"Great." Nim bounded to her feet. "Let's have ice cream."

Alyce looked over with interest. "What is ice cream?"

Nim hooked her arm through Alyce's elbow. "Sweetie, let me show you heaven."

Gavril shook his head and stalked away.

Down the stairs to the main floor, Nim was silent. But when they got to the kitchen, she paused before reaching into the freezer. "It's not easy being *symballein*. I used to get stark naked in front of strangers, but nobody saw my soul."

She spooned out a bowl of ice cream for herself, then solemnly handed Alyce the carton and the ladle. "Go for it."

"I tried that. I said I loved him. He, the man of many words, said nothing."

Nim winced. "I meant go for the ice cream."

"Oh." Alyce stared down into the chunky chocolate depths. "I shouldn't have said anything."

"To me or dumbfuck? Sweetie, you can tell a girlfriend anything. A man, not so much." She shoved her spoon into the ice cream as if the frozen lump were a particularly unfeeling heart.

Alyce took a bite and waited while the confection melted across her tongue. The demon stretched one last time, tightening and relaxing every muscle in a long ripple; then it was quiet. "I frightened him. I saw it in his eyes."

"I'm sure you did. They are easily scared that way."

"Not Jonah," Alyce said. "Not Liam or Archer."

Nim laughed. "Not *now*. But before . . . As quick as they are to run *to* trouble, a talya male is twice as fast running *from* the *symballein* bond. Which is just silly, when the two are fairly synonymous."

"But what should I do?"

"What do you want?"

Alyce contemplated the chocolate on her spoon. The sweet darkness made her hungry for more. "I want him."

"Remember when I said it wasn't easy?"

Alyce inverted the spoon over her tongue and nodded.

"Well, you won't be, not anymore. Let him fight for it."

"Fight?" Alyce swallowed, and the sugared cream raced through her system. "But we were talking about love."

"The only thing *worth* fighting for," Nim said. "Are you strong enough?"

"My teshuva—"

"Not the demon. You."

Alyce hesitated. "I don't know."

"Fair enough. Maybe you don't really want him."

Denial reared up in an instant, the demon a heartbeat behind in solidarity. Alyce narrowed her eyes.

Nim smiled. "You're strong enough. But it could get ugly. If he resisted that white satin underwear . . ."

"He didn't."

"But he managed to break free of the lace." Nim tilted her head in thought. "Well, maybe *he* is stronger than I thought too. We'll have to enthrall him well."

"He likes puzzles. I'm too simple."

Nim snorted. "No woman is simple. He was just blinded by those pretentiously nerdy glasses. You'll show him. Tonight, when the league goes out. Come to my room at sundown. We'll see who's chasing whom."

Alyce bit her lip. "But what if—" A jagged bolt of energy not her own seared across her awareness.

She found herself on her knees, Nim beside her, hand on her shoulder. "Alyce? How hard did Gavril hit you?"

"Didn't you feel—?"

Nim stiffened. "Everybody's suddenly on attack. The warehouse sinks aren't dampening it all. Let's go."

The other woman really did think she'd be a help, Alyce marveled. And she would be, she swore to herself, if only she could stop clutching her temples.

The leashed uproar was worse in the foyer, etheric energy sparking like lightning in the cool, rain-scented air. The wall-to-wall black of the talyan split around one redheaded angelic-possessed.

"Nanette." Nim hurried forward to join Sera in the

seething morass of motionless talyan. How they managed to do both—seethe and be still ... Alyce crept up behind Ecco. His bulk seemed to absorb some of the furious energy.

"I'm fine, I'm fine," Nanette was saying. "Help Cyril."

The sphere warden lay sprawled on the floor, his face a disturbing shade somewhere between the concrete and the white of his pristine linen shirt—pristine except for the blooming crimson across his belly.

Sidney shouldered between the talyan. "Put pressure on that. Stop the bleeding. His angel isn't like the teshuva; it won't do the work for us."

"Typical angel," Ecco mumbled.

Alyce slipped out from behind him and went to Sidney's side. He had flipped up Fane's shirt, and she held back a gasp at the vivid, vicious wound surrounded by ichor scorch.

"What happened?" Nim had brought a towel to her workout. She tossed it to Sera, who made a thick pad and pressed it to the gaping red gash.

"A djinn-man," Nanette said. Her shoulders shook until Nim wrapped an arm around her. "I was closing the church when Cyril came, bleeding. He said he'd been attacked and told me to bring him here."

From the woman's blank stare, unmindful of the way her red hair dripped rain around her cheeks, Alyce knew she was picturing the moment again, probably superimposed over her husband's attack. Alyce wondered if she would ever go back to the church again.

Blood seeped through the towel between Sera's fingers. "We need to get him to the hospital. Now."

"No," Fane rasped. "They'll come for me there."

Sidney half rolled the warden to check his back for an exit wound. "The djinn-men?"

Fane hissed like a curse: "The sphericanum."

The talyan shot one another mystified glances.

"He lost his abrasax," Nanette said. When they only

shrugged, one after the other, she added, "His blesséd weapon."

Ecco's eyes bugged. "He *lost* it?"

"Didn't lose it," Fane growled. "Djinni fuck took it."

"That's why the sphericanum will" — Nanette swallowed hard — "not be forgiving."

Ecco scratched his close-shaved head with a sound like sandpaper. "Huh. I always thought the side of goodness and light automatically included forgiving. Like, 'If you order now . . .'"

Sidney interrupted. "If we're saving his life, we need to get him down to the lab. Ecco, help me carry him."

As they trooped downstairs, Sera sent various talyan peeling off on other errands: to inform Liam, to recon the church, to patrol the warehouse roof in case a maddened army of angelic-possessed came to reclaim their fallen.

"They won't care," Nanette murmured as they positioned Fane on the exam table. "No one from the spheres came to Daniel's funeral but Cyril."

Nim and Ecco herded her to one side of the lab while Sidney and Sera washed their hands and consulted over Fane's belly.

"Gut and bowel aren't involved," Sera said.

"This isn't a full ER suite." Sidney glanced over his shoulder, his brown eyes fierce as the seething talyan but in a different way, focused thought and brisk action welded together. "Alyce, my hands are clean. Can you push the crash cart over here? Thank you."

"People die in ER suites all the time," Sera countered.

"Hey," Fane said. "Patient right here, listening."

Alyce cleared her throat. "The bullets."

The two talyan and the warden stared at her.

"That's a little harsh even for us," Sera said.

But Sidney nodded. "Good idea, Alyce."

"Hey," Fane repeated, more weakly this time.

Alyce hurried across the lab to the glass-fronted cabinet

with the cryptic pink note stuck to the front. Inside lay the shard from her leg—chipped away and smaller now from Sidney's experiments—along with the bullets. How much would be enough?

"Nanette," she called gently.

The woman joined her and sucked in a breath. Her hands went to the glass as if she could reach through without obstruction. Golden light from her hands, the shard, and the fragments of the shard stuffed into the tips of the bullets pulsed in rhythm.

Alyce popped open the cabinet, and Nanette reached in with slow reverence to cradle the shard in her palm. Streamers of radiance spilled between her fingers like water or sand that never ran out.

"It's beautiful," Alyce said. "And deadly to us."

Nanette nodded. "And healing. With the right touch and a little luck. And help and time and—"

"Patient right here, dying," Fane said.

"Hush." Nanette faced the room. "As for the rest of you, I know this is rude—"

Fane plucked at the blood-soaked towel over his belly. "And hush wasn't?"

"But can we have privacy? The laying on of hands is a sacred moment."

"And we aren't sacred," Ecco finished. He stalked out the door without looking back.

Sera stuck her clean hands in her pockets. "Holler if you need anything."

"Oh, he might holler." Nanette flicked her fingers. The golden light spattered like raindrops. "But please don't mind him."

Fane tried to push himself up on his elbows. She nudged him back.

Sidney ushered Alyce and Sera through the door and pulled it shut behind him.

Sera leaned against the wall, her arms hanging limp at

her sides. "Should we be worried about leaving our precious league secrets in there with a couple of angels?"

Sidney shrugged. "Nanette seems sweet, and Fane is otherwise occupied. And I think the sphericanum has bigger concerns now."

"It's our fault," Alyce said.

Sera frowned. "What, that Fane can't fight?"

"That he had to fight Thorne."

Sidney echoed Sera's frown but more fiercely. "What makes you think it was Thorne?"

She folded her hands in front of her and waited.

He started to rake his fingers through his hair but stopped at the sight of the blood. "You would know."

Sera drummed the wall behind her, then pushed herself straight. "Okay, typical crappy talya luck says you're probably right, it's Thorne. But that doesn't make it our fault he attacked Fane."

"Specifically, my fault," Sidney said. "I gave him the idea an angelic sword would make a fine demonic weapon."

"I believe I was the inspiration," Alyce countered. "You just refined the concept."

"Damn it, enough." Sera pointed an admonishing finger at each of them in turn. "There's plenty of repenting to go around—just ask the teshuva."

Alyce shook her head. "Maybe we'll ask Thorne."

CHAPTER 23

"Run," Jonah whispered.

Sid glanced at the other man. "What?"

"They're after you."

Since the warehouse loading bay was full of talyan gathering for the night's hunt, it seemed unlikely the tenebrae or the sphericanum had invaded. Anyway, his teshuva was dormant. "Who's after me?"

"The girls. Alyce."

The teshuva didn't twitch, but other parts of Sid did. "What are you talking about?"

"I'm telling you. I recognize that look. It doesn't bode well."

In the room of large, black-clad males planning their routes through the city, it was hard for a moment to pick out the smaller women, especially since they seemed to be sneaking around the bigger bodies.

Sid shifted from one foot to the other. "Maybe they're after you."

"Nim already has me."

Was that a note of censure in the other man's voice? "Alyce knows she can come to me for anything."

Jonah lifted one eyebrow. "But she went to Nim instead. And she was upstairs sparring with Gavril earlier, before Fane and Nanette showed up."

Now Sid's teshuva did rouse, a slow coiling of possessiveness. It was so unlike him. He was not that sort of man. Of course, that was the point. It wasn't the man but the demon. He tried to tamp it down. "I think she's smart to take advantage of all the strengths and skills the league members can offer."

"Uh-huh." Jonah's doubt lengthened each syllable.

Sid gritted his teeth if only to keep the teshuva from letting out a roar.

She was decked out, from the dark braid of her hair to her big boots, in talya black, blending with the males, so he didn't see the problem until she stepped under one of the loading bay lights and the harsh fluorescent gleamed off the hard shine of leather.

Black leather.

There were legitimate reasons to use leather for work clothes. For example, quality leather gardening gloves, heavy boots, and cowboy chaps wore smoother, lasted longer, and protected better than lighter-weight materials.

There was no excuse for a strap-up leather bustier.

Jonah groaned. "Nim . . ."

The talya female minced over to him. The wild corona of her sandy hair was neatly bound in a ponytail, and her oversized black T-shirt was actually tucked in. "Yes, sir? Reporting for duty, sir."

"Troublemaker."

"What? I just—"

Whatever she *just* faded from Sid's hearing as Jonah hauled her away. Not that he was listening. He stalked toward Alyce.

As combat apparel, he supposed it made a certain sense. The bodice laced close around her body and left no loose folds of fabric to catch on feralis claws. The long sleeves, with the pointed cuffs covering the backs of her hands, fit her like a second skin, a skin that would hold up to ichor spatter better than her own, at least long enough to dispatch the tenebrae doing the spattering. And, of course, it was black.

On the taller, curvier Nim, the bustier would have bordered on indecent. On Alyce, the laces closed tight, eyelet to eyelet, without a suggestion of skin. This made him wonder what, if anything, she was wearing underneath.

A simple inhalation—he'd been doing it all his life—caught raggedly in his throat.

As if in echo, her breasts rose and fell on a breath. The bustier wasn't so meek and modest as to hide that. Her *reven* made a plain choker around her neck.

"I see you're ready to rumble." His voice sounded wrong, too deep, with a note of menace.

She turned her back to him and reached around her side. For a heartbeat, he thought she was going to flip him off. How quickly even a rogue absorbed talya arrogance.

But then she tugged at one of the filigreed and studded embellishments at her shoulder blade . . . and half withdrew a knife. The thin, silvery blade flexed against its hidden sheath, supple like a boning knife. Six of the embellishments, three on each side, descended along her sides, tucked into decorative chevron striping down the back of the bustier. The exposed, delicate hilts were perfectly sized for her small hand.

She glanced over her shoulder at him. "Clever, isn't it?"

"I never would have noticed the knives," he said with complete honesty.

"Nim said it's good for sneak attacks."

"I bet it is." He certainly felt sideswiped. From the unsubtle, longing glances from the other talyan, he wasn't the only one.

She bit at her lower lip, watching him. "Do you think Thorne will come after us tonight?"

"Who?" Sid shook himself. "Thorne. I think he's after something, and whatever he riles up probably falls within the league mission statement."

"And if it doesn't," Archer said as he came up, "we'll write ourselves a new mission statement."

"Signed in ichor," Sera added. The pendant around her neck twinkled violet like her eyes.

Sid stared at her. She was the closest thing to a Bookkeeper the Chicago league had had for close to a year. Her background was so similar to his—the education, the intellect, the curiosity. If she had been a firstborn male child of a Bookkeeper, the masters would have passed around cigars. But she was unapologetically, fully talya in that moment.

And when she curled her hand around Archer's elbow and slanted that violet-shot gaze up to him, she wasn't just talya but *symballein.*

Unrepentantly so.

Before Sid could consider the implications, Liam hopped up onto a chair to raise himself above the heads of the tall, muscular, well-armed crowd. "Listen up, talyan. Pitch lurked around the *River Princess* all day as she burned and never saw a sign of Thorne. We know he spent part of his evening gutting Fane. As for what he's been doing the rest of the time . . . Well, I can only think he's been brooding, and we all know what that does to us."

A ripple of amusement softened the crowd not at all.

"So stay sharp. Sharp as your favorite blades. Because whoever out there is willing to attack a djinn-man in his home, and whatever a djinn-man thinks is bad enough that he needs to arm himself with an angel's sword, is more than willing to obliterate us. Unless we get it first."

There was no cheer, but Sid's demon tightened into a ball of restless craving.

In pairs and triads, the talyan filed past Jilly and her map. In quiet times—a relative term, of late—they patrolled their favorite haunts independently, clearing the city of horde-tenebrae, one dark corner at a time. But with a djinn-man on the prowl, Liam had assigned teams across the city. They would be far enough apart to cover some ground, but close enough to come to each other's aid, should the need arise.

Assuming they had time to call out to one another.

Waiting for final orders, Sid edged into an unoccupied corner and flipped open his cell phone. His fingers hovered over the keypad a moment, then punched out a quick number and waited through a few rings that gave him too much time to think.

"At-One London." Despite the predawn hour on the other end, the answer was crisp and authoritative.

"Morning, Wes."

This pause was longer than the first; long enough that he almost hung up.

Finally, a groan sighed down the line. "Not yet it ain't." Wes's voice crackled with the sleepiness he'd held back before. "What the hell, Sid?"

"You'll have to be more specific, I'm afraid."

"Dad told me everything."

"I'm sure he summed it up nicely. But I have another note to add. We're going after a djinn-man who's shaping up to be orders of magnitude worse than Corvus Valerius. I e-mailed what we know so far, in case—"

"Don't say it."

"Saying we might be slaughtered doesn't make it more likely to happen."

"Not saying it means I don't have to think about it."

"You're going to be Bookkeeper of London, bro." Sid let out one notch on the rein of his demon to growl, "You'd better fucking think. Since you can't leave. Again."

That was the worst sort of scientist: letting the dread of

*what could b*e become the horror of *what was*, creating the outcomes he'd anticipated.

Even as he thought it, Sid winced at his hypocrisy. Hadn't he done exactly that with Alyce? After his mother, after Maureen, he'd feared he'd never be able to open his life to another.

And he'd made his fears come true.

It was too late to beat himself up, but no doubt there were entities aplenty standing in line to take care of the task.

"You're right," Wes said quietly. "I don't know what you're facing—hell, I still don't know all of what I'm facing—but I won't make you come back just to kick my ass." He hesitated. "Although I hope . . . I do hope you'll come back sometime."

"Maybe." Sid turned to face the loading bay, the talyan spread out before him like one of those monochrome black-on-black-on-black canvases he found so hard to appreciate as art. "My place is here. But I'm glad you're with Dad." The admission slipped from him as easily as the teshuva healed a hangnail. Because in the end—and this very well could be the end—it was true.

"He's in his office," Wes said. "Do you want to talk to him?"

It was Sid's turn to hesitate, the teshuva in him providing no protection from this. And maybe Wes understood, because the line clicked over without another word.

"Sidney?"

"I'm sorry, Dad." The apology cracked out of him.

"For what, exactly?" The hum of curiosity was as personal and familiar to Sid as his own handwriting. "Being possessed?"

"For that. For letting you down. For letting Mum—"

"No." Dispassionate though his father claimed to be, the sharp refusal halted all discussion. "The demons were none of your doing, not the tenebrae that killed your mother, not this teshuva now. And you never, never let me down."

Sid bowed his head into the cup of his hand, the phone cradled against his ear.

His father's voice softened. "From the moment your mother told me she was pregnant again, I knew you'd go your own way. You were quick and fearless and always knew your own mind. I would have been proud to call you London's Bookkeeper after me. But more than that, I am proud you are my son."

Sid closed his eyes tight. What he wouldn't give to have his father and Wes at his side, to talk over this attack, to talk about anything at all. . . . "Do you think you could keep the other masters from declaring me rogue if I came home for a visit?"

"Somehow I don't think they could stop you with a few words. So," his father continued, "about this girl. She's the one?"

Liam had pushed up the loading bay door, and the night air swirled through. Sid lifted his head to breathe in the fusion of wet concrete, chilled steel, and something else, some primeval incense of coming battle. "My demon says so."

"And you?"

Hadn't he seen Alyce as two entities in the beginning? Girl and demon in discordance had been vulnerable, the girl confused and the demon lashing out. But they'd come to a balance. Now he was the one stumbling.

Was it too late?

The talyan were filing out of the warehouse to the waiting fleet of cars, solemn in their black like a line of mourners headed to somebody's funeral. "I have to go, Dad, but . . . I'll call you later." Though he'd told Wes otherwise, he wished saying the words could make it so.

"I told you before to be careful—"

"Definitely too late for that," Sid muttered, but he pitched his voice only to the teshuva's range, so he heard his father's continuation.

"And you didn't listen. Perhaps you knew better than I all along. So be happy instead, Sidney."

The words, part command, part plea, jolted him, and he mumbled out his good-bye just as the dark-haired, bustier-clad source of his too-lateness—and his happiness—slipped past him.

Gavril crossed the loading bay on an intercept course that would have put him in line right behind Alyce. Sid snapped the cell close and quickened his step to edge out the other man.

Gavril raised one eyebrow but fell back a slot.

Sid's spine crackled with tension—not that he thought Gavril would attack from behind.

From the front maybe.

Why had Alyce gone to the other male? Of course, it was easy to answer, even for his Bookkeeper brain. Alyce didn't want his jealousy and selfishness. She wanted love.

After his father's questioning, frustration made his muscles clench, like the demon given no place to unleash. Great. The emotions he did have were nothing he could give her, and their dark churn confused whatever insight he might have found.

And he thought he could call himself a talya male? He just didn't have the height, the weight, or the guts for it.

At least he had the brooding thing down.

He was silent as he climbed behind Alyce into one of the waiting cars. Baird jangled his keys, and Amiri took the front seat. They flowed into the exodus.

After a few blocks, Amiri cleared his throat. "Isn't it nice it's not raining anymore?"

Oh God, they were going to talk about the weather?

Sid jittered the cell in his palm and slanted a glance at Alyce, keeping his gaze elevated from the hand span of white skin above the leather bodice. "You know how to use your phone?"

She nodded. "Nim showed me earlier."

No doubt Nim had done a thorough job while tarting her up. He stuffed the cell into his coat. "Do you have it with you?"

She gave him a level look. "I have pockets."

Where? He almost asked, but then he might reveal that he couldn't believe those fitted black leather trousers had room for pockets. But he'd also be revealing his disapproval because the trousers—another hand-me-down, obviously, tucked into the tops of her boots—weren't *that* snug. Just fitted enough to provide a stark outline for her slender hips, just tight enough to make him think about what was inside.

Okay, he had apparently mastered talya brooding and now lusting. And he had room for plenty more sins where those had come from since *he* wasn't wearing skintight leather.

"We're supposed to hunt the blocks south and east of Wacker, outside the park." Amiri glanced over the seat. "Boss-man said those are your stomping grounds, Alyce. Any thoughts on where to start?"

She blinked at him, surprise softening her mouth. "I'm not sure."

"Maybe the underground garage off Michigan Ave," Baird suggested. "It's dark and spooky, perfect for tenebrae."

Alyce shook her head. "We don't want a few malice. We want Thorne. And if I know him . . ." She slid a glance sideways, and Sid forced himself to unclench his fist. "He'll be mourning the *River Princess*, so he'll stay near the water, along the river or by the lake."

Baird clicked his tongue. "We'll cross the river at Dearborn and find a place to park. You two walk west along Wacker and double back at the Franklin Bridge. We'll go east and circle round on Lake Shore. Call if you see anything, and we'll come running."

"Likewise," Sid said curtly.

Finding a parking spot on a busy night downtown was enough to spawn a few negative-energy malice. Baird grumbled at a cute little family dawdling in the crosswalk with an infant in a stroller and a straggling toddler.

Amiri punched his shoulder. "They're why we're still here."

"And they'll never know it." Baird tightened his hands on the steering wheel. "They'd at least look up if I nudged them."

Amiri punched him harder.

Alyce sat forward in her seat. "Go around the block. I know a place where we can leave the car."

There was an open parking spot, but only because no one would be foolish enough to leave a car in the narrow, dark alley.

Amiri peered around. "Will it still be here when we get back?"

"Will it matter much if it's not?" Sid got out and shut the door—not hard, yet he still knocked off a few flakes of rust. "Trust me—no one wants this car."

"Jilly gets very sarcastic when we squander resources," Amiri said. "You've never had to listen to her 'kids in China would be happy' speech at her vegetarian dinners."

Alyce was already at the mouth of the alley, her slender black-clad frame outlined against the wet shine of the street and the headlights of passing traffic. "Speaking of dinner, I smell birnenston. Let's go."

They crossed the bridge according to their plan and separated. Sidney looked back over his shoulder at the other two men walking off. Alyce folded her arms across her stomach. Clearly he didn't want to be alone with her.

"Don't worry," she said. "If we run into anything, we can call them back."

"I doubt we'll need to. Chances are, we won't find Thorne first."

Oh well then, if statistically he wasn't worried about her weak teshuva leaving him with no one to defend his back . . . He just didn't want to be with *her*.

"I'll walk the north side of the river," she said. "If you walk the south side at the same time, we'll cover twice the ground."

"No. We stay together."

"The *symballein* bond?"

His jaw worked so hard, she thought he would chew through whatever held him back from speaking. She wished he would, so he would speak without thinking. Then she might hear what he felt instead of what he thought he should say.

He turned and walked away. "It's too cold to stand still. And we're supposed to be stalking something."

She lingered a half step behind. Another couple passed them, walking in the other direction, arms linked, and admiring the view of the river and the city and each other. She stifled her jealousy. Under different circumstances, she and Sidney might have been such a couple. Without the fate of good and evil, the *symballein* chains . . .

No, that was a delusion, and she was done with those. Under different, nondemonic circumstances, Sidney would be with someone named Maureen and she herself would be nothing—not even a memory.

"We're almost opposites, your demon and mine," he said abruptly.

The headlights from the passing cars cast hard shadows across the even harder lines of his mouth. She'd done that to him—she and the demon. Her fingers curled, as if she could recapture the softness of his lips.

"Mine to crave, and yours, craven, to fear." He stopped. "But you're never afraid. So actually, I'm wrong again."

"Sidney . . ."

"And I said I wanted to study the *symballein* bond." He shook his head. "A terrible Bookkeeper conceit, to think I could understand what it means to be that closely entwined with someone else."

She put her hand to her throat. If only the lack of emotion were infectious, like a birnenston that burned away every nerve ending so she'd never feeling anything again.

"I understand if you hate me now." His lips quirked without humor. "I can see very clearly how you would, because I hate myself."

"Don't. You didn't ask for my love." She was grateful the tight laces of the bustier kept her spine straight and her shoulders back. "I'm the one who didn't know how it works."

"How it works? Love doesn't have a methodology. Which is why Bookkeepers can't do love."

Apparently her emotions did still work—unfortunately—because the word felt as if all six delicate knives along her back had been driven into her heart at once. She dredged up a wan smile. "Maybe you should write a handbook for *symballein* pairs."

"At least the 'how-not-to.'" His hands twitched as if he'd been about to reach out to her, but he just made fists at his sides. "Alyce—"

His cell phone rang with the urgent call of a hoot owl.

She turned away, but he ignored the call. "Alyce, I would rather have died than hurt you."

Then her phone rang like a church bell. She answered.

"We found Thorne." Jonah's voice was curt, flat, and all the more terrifying because of it. "He's calling tenebrae through the verge. In the middle of a Halloween parade."

CHAPTER 24

As he and Alyce raced back to the car, Sid cursed himself with every bootfall.

He'd officially failed at everything he'd come to Chicago to do. Finish his Bookkeeper training? The teshuva had derailed him, and he'd become a novice talya. Analyze the consequences of the *symballein* attachment? Alyce had sent him one icy-eyed glance, and he'd lost all objectivity in the bond. Determine the nature of the tenebraternum verge?

Now Thorne had beaten him to the punch.

Punching something had never sounded so good.

Baird and Amiri were pounding back from the other direction. Baird slid across the hood in fine action-hero form and had the engine started before the rest of them had piled in. He sent the car squealing out of the alley in a bumper-thumping bottom-out that left sparks in their wake.

It was a quick ride down Wacker to the pier, faster still with Baird at the wheel. It would have been even quicker if not for the milling crowd meandering across the streets between the little fountain green space that marked the entrance to the pier and the parking area.

"You've got to be kidding," Baird growled as the traffic cop whistled at him and held out a hand to stop the car. A veritable herd of costumed children scampered in front of the car—half of them leaving, half just arriving—the princesses and miniature comic book characters in sugar-fueled accord with the little horned devils and rubber-faced monsters.

The marquee over the pier announced COSTUME PARADE AND TREASURE HUNT. PAINT A PUMPKIN!

"Oktoberfest," Baird said. "It's all craft beer and Halloween masks—perfect for talyan."

Alyce craned her neck to peer out the window. "With a midway carnival. Thorne likes games of chance."

"A djinn-man who plays ringtoss for a chance to win goldfish . . ." Sid shook his head.

"The place is crawling with people," Amiri said.

"I'm sure there will be enough pumpkins for everyone," Sid said. "Whether there will be a parking spot, however . . ."

Alyce's fingers dug into the back of the car seat. "If the tenebrae come forth, with all these children around . . . We can't let them see. They don't deserve to know evil." Her face was drawn, her gaze stark without a trace of bracing violet.

Sid eased her hand from the tears she was making in the cheap vinyl and laced his fingers through hers. "We won't let them see anything. The only nightmares they'll have tonight will be of high fructose corn syrup."

Her grasp tightened. "You can't say that, not for certain."

He looked at her without blinking. "I just did."

After a moment, her death grip eased, and she nodded.

Then she turned, opened the car door, and bailed out.

Sid choked on a curse and scrambled after her. "Baird, ditch the car and find us."

"Right behind you," Amiri said.

They raced for the diner at the end of the pier.

The amusement park was packed, with the Ferris wheel and the miniature golf course at full capacity, the carousel's calliope tune a cheerful counterpoint to the screams of the children on the Tilt-A-Whirl with their manufactured fear of being flung violently into space.

"This is bad," Amiri said as they dodged the crowds. "Really bad. Last time we knocked big holes in Navy Pier, there was no one here."

Sid glanced back over his shoulder at the six-story Crystal Gardens that glittered behind the park. The shine of the amusement park lights, distorted on the atrium windows, worried him. "If Thorne calls through the tenebraternum, the raw demonic emanations will subvert the glass and metal of the atrium: a larger version of Corvus's soul bomb. The verge could expand to several hundred times its current size."

Amiri took a stumbling step, and Alyce stared at Sid in horror.

"Maybe you could hold off on the good news until we're surrounded by pure evil," Amiri suggested.

Sid shrugged. "Consider it a motivational speech."

Amiri let out a bark of laughter. "You are finally talya."

Sid didn't slow, though the pronouncement rattled him.

He was talya. He had the demon to prove it. Now he just had to prove it to himself.

They skidded up outside the diner.

And halted, nonplussed. There was a line to get in.

A young man in a starched apron offered a tray of toothpicked meatballs. "Good evening, sirs and madam. A sample while you wait?"

"Thank you." Alyce plucked a toothpick from the tray. She rolled her eyes at Sid and Amiri when they stared at her. "For energy."

Sid backed away a few steps, pulling them with him.

"Would Jonah's team have gone in without us? Against Thorne and how many tenebrae?"

"Not enough to spill out," Alyce said reasonably. "Not enough to swamp our teshuva."

Right. He was letting his dread run amok. He peered at Alyce. Despite her weakness, despite centuries of not knowing what had happened to her, her fear had always been for others—horror at what had happened around her, fear for what she might do. It had never been fear for herself.

Even now, after learning of the endless mission they faced, she met the challenges without flinching. She did not question, did not dither, did not hesitate.

She was everything he was not.

He was suddenly fiercely glad he had turned her away. If she felt the momentary pain of rejection, that was nothing compared to an eternity of dreading her bond to a man who feared even love.

A sharp whistle from across the pier distracted him. Nim balanced on the far railing, one hand braced on the deco lamppost beside her. Alyce was already on her way, Amiri behind her.

Sid fell into place. He should have taken one of the waiter's toothpicks for a backup weapon. Thorne's Saturday Night Special hardly made a dent at the small of his back where he'd shoved it into the waistband of his jeans. Encased in the round's lead jacket, the splinter of the angelic relic wasn't even a blip on his teshuva's vigilant radar.

"Therese called," Nim said without waiting for their questions. "A man identifying himself as a sewer inspector came by the diner. Nobody remembers him leaving. You see where this is going."

"Thorne is down there," Alyce said.

"Right. You win an all-expenses-paid trip to the demon realm."

Beside Nim, Jonah shifted restlessly. "Pitch and Gavril are in the diner. They'll run interference if any ferales are drawn to the uproar. We can't hide a full-scale demonic invasion, but we might prevent a few human deaths." His expression was bleak.

"Where is everyone else?" Sid asked.

"En route. You four were closest."

"We can't wait," Alyce said. She glanced at Sid. "Thorne isn't like you. He isn't patient or thoughtful. He'll force the verge wider, whatever he has to do."

Nim shuddered. "What could he want from the tenebraeternum? There's only one thing there: a helluva lot more demons."

"That's what he wants," Alyce said. "More tenebrae."

Jonah paced a few steps. "Corvus was the worst the league ever encountered, and even he didn't try to amass a demon army from the other side."

Alyce said softly, "He's not the worst anymore."

As the others argued, Alyce shivered at the chill threads of the devils all around her: the muted background of the city's tenebrae; the sharper strands of the teshuva nearest her; and somewhere not too far, the harsh power of djinni.

But even awash in the competing demonic energies, she still felt the bite of the October wind. It was not a good feeling, and yet . . .

Despite Sidney's rejection, she hadn't faded back into the demon's hazy spell. Her teshuva had settled, finally, into its place in her soul, the rivet ring a reminder that she was strong enough to control her dread. She was still Alyce; she still remembered.

Damn him for ruining her.

Not for taking her to bed. She'd wanted that. Not even for giving her back the horrifying memories of her penance trigger and possession. No, she was ruined merely because she felt she was. Because she *felt* at all. Ruined, razed, left in rubble, her feelings lay like broken foundations around her, only shattered glass and sharp stone and fragments of what could have been.

Thorne must have felt the same, to see his boat burned and sunk, the enemy breaching his gate. No wonder he wanted to pull the cold and darkness around him.

She understood. But all she had was her meager power, that simplest of emotions—fear. She wasn't like Nim, Jilly, and Sera. Whatever power they drew from the *symballein* bond, she didn't have the strength to take for herself. She was alone again. At least she still had the comfort—cold and alien, but comfort nonetheless—of her demon.

It coiled within her, its agitation tightening her throat and choking back her tears.

"Thorne can't believe he'll just widen the verge," Nim said.

"He has Fane's sword," Jonah said. "No doubt he believes he can do quite a bit."

"He could set loose many souls," Alyce finished. "How many people are on the pier right now?"

They fell silent, and as if in answer, the voice of the crowd rolled over them.

Sidney shifted. "Alyce, you told me once you'd never seen Thorne hurt anyone."

She stared at him. "I told you once I loved you. My judgment is not to be trusted."

"So," Nim said into the awkward silence, "down we go."

"We could call in a bomb threat," Amiri said. "Put those traffic cops to good use clearing the pier. And we wouldn't even be lying."

"That might work." Sidney rubbed his chin with his Bookkeeper abstracted expression. Then abruptly he focused. "But you don't agree, do you, Alyce? I recognize that look."

She had a look? And how did he know what she was thinking almost before she did? "If you try to warn everyone, you'll panic them. I've seen frightened mobs. We'd bring the city's tenebrae down on our heads, never mind what's waiting on the other side of the verge."

Nim swore under her breath. "Then we just go in. With the lure power of my teshuva, I should be able to hold—"

Jonah wrapped his arm around her waist. The gleaming hook rested at her hip. "We should be able to hold."

"*We* should be able to hold any crossover demons in the basement until reinforcements arrive." Nim crossed her fingers.

Nobody called her on the wishful thinking.

The five of them eased past the line into the diner, amidst much grumbling. "Hey, no cutting," one man said.

"Maybe you want to take our place?" Amiri growled under his breath.

Inside, Jonah cornered Therese. "Can you get everyone out of here?"

She glanced dubiously around the full seats. "They won't be happy."

"We don't need the negative emotions," Alyce warned. "We should just go."

"Stop in the kitchen on your way," Therese urged. "I have knives. Good knives."

"Nothing to rival a sword, though," Sidney murmured.

As they descended the ladders, Alyce cast a wary eye over the space. Even with her teshuva at high alert, there seemed no end to the space. The walls were lost in shifting shadows with no apparent source, as if large, unseen forces moved between them and the light.

The verge was widening, with all of hell on the other side. And hell was hungry.

CHAPTER 25

The transmuted glass and bone husk that marked the verge was invisible in the mist. Sid wasn't sure whether it was worse to see the disturbing mouth of hell, or to know it had gaped wide enough that now he was looking past its tonsils.

His demon-altered vision skipped and pixilated, like a smudged DVD, as it tried to reconcile his human knowledge with what he was experiencing, collating the physical and metaphysical planes. But even as the Bookkeeper in him marveled, he knew he had nothing to compare.

Except maybe the nothingness that haunted Alyce's eyes.

She was right behind him on the ladder, her big black boots nearly on his fingers as she hastened downward. He wanted to shove her back up the ladder, out to safety.

But there was no safety out there, and besides, that wasn't what they were about.

He realized then that he'd never—not even when that long-ago bottle had broken in his waistband and the smell of blood and liquor had choked him—felt anything to compare to the dread that gripped him now.

Thorne was nowhere to be seen either. Damn, at least a flaming sword could have lit a few of the shadows.

When they got to the bottom, Amiri clutched his own short sword vertically in front of him, though there was scarcely room on its hilt for his nervous double-handed grip. "This isn't right. Where are we?"

"The Veil, the no-man's-land—the no-demon's-land—stuck between the realms," Nim said. "And now there's a gateway through the Veil. Why do you think we called it the verge?"

"Because it sounded cool." Amiri's voice cracked.

Jonah shot him a glance. "I know this isn't what you're used to. The male talyan have hunted strictly on our side of the Veil, picking off the horde dregs. Now you're seeing what's beyond. Ladies' night starts here."

Amiri shook his head, a little wildly. "The dregs have been plenty bad enough to keep us busy. And sometimes dead."

"Oh, you can die here too." Nim stood as close to Jonah as their drawn weapons would allow. The curves of their knives nearly matched—his large enough to qualify as a sword, hers smaller and balanced for throwing. "The rules are different here on the edge of hell, but that one stays the same."

Nim raised her hands, and Jonah hunched his shoulders as her knife waved near his ear. As she stretched herself to full height, the cuffs of her skinny-leg jeans lifted to reveal an anklet curved over the strap of her high heel shoe. The talisman glinted with violet highlights.

Alyce made a soft sound, and Sid angled himself between her and . . . and whatever might happen next. She twisted the asylum rivet around her finger as if the restless movement might rev her demon.

Maybe it would; what the hell did he know?

Nim's brows furrowed. "Who's out there?" she whispered. "You're hungry? Then come get us. You know you can't resist me."

Sid swallowed against the menace that deepened her voice. The shadows seemed to have no such concerns. The swirling gray mist tightened into double vortices, spiraling in toward Nim's outstretched hands.

Jonah stood behind her. His good arm wrapped low over her belly and anchored her to his chest. His sword arm—literally a sword in place of his missing hand— waited, cocked to eviscerate anything that came too close.

Not that even a wisp of mist could have worked its way between their bodies. Their perfect accord tugged at Sid, and he put his hand over his chest as the emptiness in him answered the damning lure.

He and Alyce had been given the chance to bond. But he'd been afraid. In his heart, he'd fancied himself some bold pursuer of knowledge. Instead, he'd run from the mystery.

And now it was that emptiness in his torso he felt watching the etheric dance of the *symballein* pair: his missing heart; the unfolding mystery that was Alyce.

The mist and shadows drew toward Nim like a magician slowly pulling away a diaphanous curtain.

In the amorphous realm of the Veil, the verge was a sculptured modern art shape that seemed to have expanded in all visible directions and taken on a disturbing new life. Among the layers of gray, Technicolor glimpses of the outside world surfaced in the glass orbs studding the bony feralis husk.

One aperture showed the Ferris wheel spinning with unnatural speed. The riders' faces distorted from laughter to slack-jawed screams. Behind the park, the midway lights glimmering on the Crystal Gardens flamed into etheric bonfires. Fiery silhouettes of salambes climbed the building's steel cross braces, seeking escape. The virulence of their emanations melted the windows in widening holes while molten glass dripped down onto the broken bodies of the crowd within. Already, the ferales were shredding the dead, claiming the corpses for their own hideous creations.

Amiri swore and spun for the ladder.

"It's not happening," Alyce said. "These passages are how hell sends evil to torture us, but not all the ways are open, not all the nightmares will come to pass. That one is dread, not truth."

Sid grabbed her arms and spun her to face him. "Are you sure? How do you know?"

The pale violet of her eyes was another window reflecting the tenebraeternum's portals of projected horror. "My demon remembers."

Once he'd touched her, it was impossible to let go. The tough resistance of the leather sleeves only emphasized the slender fragility of her under his grip. His breath faltered. "Alyce, when you said you loved me once . . ."

"Don't." She shrugged him off. "That wasn't real either. Just the last of my delusions evaporating."

He wanted to howl, some wordless cry of denial. Because what could he say now that would reach her through the demons, the threat of death, his own dumb oblivion? With every dictionary at his disposal, where were the right words?

"Look!" Amiri shouted. "It's the rest of the league."

Another altered orb dripped coagulating ether as if salivating. Between the droplets, it showed Liam, with Cyril Fane and a half-dozen others behind him, racing through the oblivious crowd. Their expressions were as uniform as their black clothes, worried and grim. Against his white shirt, Fane's expression was darker yet.

Jonah kissed Nim's temple. "Dare we hope that one is real?"

"It's not just a hope since we *did* call them," she said practically. "Let's make sure that vision becomes reality."

All around them, the orbs revealed nightmare visions—

worse, they were the passageways through the flawed Veil where hell's darkness had the chance to leach into the world. Sid pressed his fingers to his forehead. "Thorne has an angel's sword. If these portals are tuned to places and possibilities that might draw the tenebrae, the sphericanum's blessing on the sword could mask him."

"That's a problem." Nim swatted her knife through the mists in frustration. "I don't think these televisions get decent reception of the Goodness and Light Channel."

"Then he needs to feel some dread too." Sid glanced at Alyce. "Can you do it?"

"Summon the fear?" Her eyes clouded, and she nodded slowly. "I've done it before. Not with Thorne, of course."

Her icy gaze fixed on him. He was the only one she'd ever frightened off.

When he put his hands on her shoulders, her stiffness shocked him. He'd wanted to focus the aimless little Alyce who'd found him in the alley, but he'd never meant to sharpen her to this brittle point that went through his heart. Beneath his thumbs and forefingers, where the neckline of the leather bustier left her collarbone exposed, her skin was so cold.

"You did terrify me," he said softly. "But not anymore."

Her cold stare gave him no quarter. "Maybe you've just forgotten." Despite her frozen facade, she swayed with a barely perceptible shiver.

He should be focused on finding and stopping Thorne and ending the potential catastrophes unveiled in the portals. But every part of him wanted to stay in the here and now, with her. He dropped his hands and stepped back before even his demon could determine whether she'd swayed away . . . or to him.

"Thorne doesn't need to be terrified. Look at the talyan. They're just barely on the far side of freaked out. If you can inspire the same in Thorne, maybe we can get a lock on him through the verge."

"He's so much stronger than we are," Alyce said.

"Evil always is," Jonah said. "Annoyingly."

Alyce lowered her head, twisting the ring. Violet sparks burned between her fingers, and her hands flared open in surprise. "Little things," she murmured. "He won't notice the little things."

She lifted her head. When she straightened, the chevron knives along her spine flared like tiny, delicate wings. "I can find him. And the verge will take me there."

CHAPTER 26

Sid had thought he had run away from his heart. But he found it now. It was lodged in his throat. He choked on it, and Alyce was already extending her hands before he forced his voice around the objection.

"Wait," he said. "Not you."

"I'm the least," she said. "Nothing I do will distract him. Until it's too late."

Too late. The words mocked him. "I'll go with you."

She shook her head. "You can't. You're too big, too strong, too bright. It's not . . ."

"Not my place," he said softly.

She glanced away. "Not with me."

The rejection pierced him. And the regret. He must be lighting up the tenebraeternum switchboard like a disaster. Of course, he couldn't follow her. He'd never been able to give her what she needed.

She held her hands out, as Nim had, but instead of flowing toward her, the shadowy mists stilled.

"They like Nim," Alyce murmured. "They fear me." Following her shooing gesture, the ether curled backward, retreating like a wave in reverse slow motion. She pursued.

"Wait," he said.

But she didn't. The rivet flared on her finger, more violently than he'd yet seen, and she snatched at the fleeing etheric wave. The energy flared and caught Alyce in the backwash. She arched with a pained cry, eyes wide and ice blind in shock.

Her hands flung outward, as if reaching for something, anything, even the unforgiving steel table of the asylum.

Sid ran forward, reaching for her in return.

But the energy collapsed around her with a flash, like bared teeth, and she was gone.

"Alyce!"

He tripped over the place where she'd been. Beneath his nose, the ground wavered between the damp earth of the diner crypt in the human realm and an undulating gray surface. As he scrambled to his feet, his fingers closed reflexively around the only solid thing.

A ring. Alyce's ring.

He groaned. What balance she and the teshuva had regained was concentrated in the rivet, and it had been knocked loose.

Jonah and Nim were beside him, lifting him.

As soon as he steadied, Jonah gave him a shake. "Why didn't you go with her?" His voice was rough, accusing.

"She wouldn't let me."

Jonah snarled. "Never let that stop you."

Nim touched her mate's arm above the sword cuff. "It takes time."

"It's too late to take time." Jonah shook his head.

Sid refused to hear him. "How can I follow?"

"The power is hers, but you are connected."

An ugly laugh welled in Sid's throat. "We're not. I wouldn't let it happen."

"But you won't let that stop you ever again, will you?" Nim pushed him, less gently than Jonah. "Find her. Find Thorne. We'll find you."

He stumbled away from them but glanced back. "How can I — ?"

Nim swore at him. "Go!"

He ran.

He ran as his mother must have run after him that night, frightened, desperate to get to him. She'd died because no one had been there for her, and in his pounding heart, he knew *he* would rather die than not be there again.

At least he knew why he was running, and where. To Alyce. What he'd say when he got there . . .

"I love you," he whispered as the gray closed around him. He could not claim it either liked him or feared him; it was just hungry, though surely not as hungry as he. "Alyce, I love you."

She slipped sideways through the etheric winds that tore around her. Among the shadows, she surrounded herself with the twisting gray, just one of the nothing.

She remembered this. It was not so different from the electricity that had burned through her brain and silenced everything — at least for a time, before the dread demon slowly coiled in her again.

The void seemed to realize it had ingested a little irritant. The gray heaved around her, like a hanged man kicked against the noose. And the next thing she knew, the etheric winds spat her out, thus proving she was not as powerful as a rope, in case anyone was taking notes.

She rolled and came to a hard stop against a . . . pumpkin?

Her head rang from the blow and confusion. Slowly, she levered herself upright, without the teshuva's assistance.

The pumpkin was huge, its pale orange bulk curving higher than her waist. She couldn't even begin to guess how

much it must weigh, although a sign beside it said GUESS MY
WEIGHT!

She looked around. She was in the Crystal Gardens
atrium. The airy interior was decorated for the upcoming
holiday with orange tea lights, little paper ghosts dangling
from the trees . . . and a roiling storm of tenebrae circling the
panes of glass six stories overhead.

But they hadn't descended—not yet.

So much for her assurances to Sidney. Here she was,
alone again.

A small blue imp bolted around the pumpkin and nearly
bowled Alyce down. They both gasped.

"Hello," said the imp.

"Hello," Alyce said. It was a child—a blue child with
bulbous black and white eyes on top of its head and its face
peering out from the gaping maw lined in black felt, but a
child, not a tenebrae.

"You look like a princess," the child said. "Mostly. But
an evil princess."

Alyce considered. "And you look mostly like a monster.
But a nice monster."

"I'm Cookie Monster," the child crowed. "Cookies are
nice."

Alyce blinked. "Why would anyone think cookies are
monstrous?"

"Sugar," the child said promptly. "Mommy says sugar
makes me a monster."

Alyce glanced around. "Where is your mother?" Where
was everyone? The atrium was empty, though it was clear
from the burning candles and gurgling punch fountain that
the party had been in full swing.

The child waved one blue arm in a vague arc. "She's over
on the other side, watching the juggler. She told me I should
play hide-and-seek instead."

"What kind of juggler?" Alyce peered suspiciously
around the pumpkin.

"He's not very good. He has only one thing to juggle. A sword. He had some black balloons too, but that's not really juggling, is it?"

Alyce's heart pounded. No wonder her demon was still quiet. Thorne was near. "I think you should keep playing hide-and-seek."

"With you?"

"Yes. You hide. I'll seek."

"Okay. But close your eyes."

Alyce did, because the horror pulsing through her made her feel faint. All those people . . . If Thorne stripped their souls to feed the tenebraeternum, the verge would expand again, swallowing the whole pier and everyone on it: herself, the child, the crowd at the diner, the talyan, Sidney. . . .

None of them would be strong enough to stand against the verge.

When she opened her eyes, the child was gone.

With luck—and talyan—Cookie Monster would never know how close the real monsters had been.

Alyce crept around the pumpkin and scuttled to the nearest concrete planter. Palm trees—almost as otherworldly in Chicago as the demon realm—spread the serrated blades of their leaves against the gleaming steel and dark sky beyond. The threatening storm cloud of salambes drifted lower. Alyce was suddenly glad her dread teshuva was in hiding; she didn't need the tenebrae raising the alarm.

Not until some screaming might be useful, anyway.

She braced her hand on the concrete, ready to launch herself to the next barrier . . . and realized her ring was gone.

She froze.

A cold sleet of fear prickled across her skin, completely divorced from the teshuva. Divorced. She swallowed back a panicked giggle. Without the ring, she was as good as divorced from the demon. That little bit of self-control she'd focused through the talisman was lost—again.

Whispers of dark thoughts threaded through the room in the tenebrae wake, like the pale strings of fake spiderwebs spread around the Halloween decorations. The insidious murmurs wrapped her tighter than the white jackets of the asylum.

The rivet was lost. The demon was lost. Sidney was lost.

She was lost. And it hurt so much worse than before because now she remembered every precious moment.

The gray haze of the tenebraeternum was so close. So easy to sink into it, to become one with the shadows. *They* wanted her. Maybe she'd always been meant for the darkness.

A flash of golden light pierced her vision. The teshuva was dormant inside her, but she flinched from the remembered pain in her leg.

An angel's sword.

The angelic light wasn't like anything else—not like the twinkle lights, not like the candles. It was like sunlight glowing through water, maybe, yet more pure. The light was its own thing, even surrounded by the drifting tendrils of the tenebraeternum.

The shard buried in her knee had been only the tiniest piece, and it had changed her life. What could an entire sword of the stuff do?

She really didn't want to know.

That, more than anything, made her think it was no wonder the demon had taken her.

She didn't want to do this; she *couldn't* do this. She'd seen an angelic sword in action before, and the vision had been the crack in her soul that made her a flawed vessel for the teshuva. She'd spent three centuries fighting back the tenebrae, not for any righteous purpose or even a selfish one, but because she'd been too confused to do otherwise.

She wasn't addled Alyce anymore.

Except she crept one more planter forward, just to see. Where did insanity and curiosity meet?

Somewhere just a little closer to the action, apparently.

From the last planter, her view was blocked by a folding screen. The painted panels showed a monochrome parade of spooks and goblins and witches under a bloodred moon. Alyce thought it might give her nightmares. Although, considering the view it probably blocked . . .

Taking a deep breath, she peeked around the end panel.

The smaller side room of the atrium bumped out toward a patio. In warmer weather, the tables and chairs might have been a nice retreat. On a cold October night, the crowds had stayed toward the lights of the park and promenade.

No one would see what was going on here until it was too late.

Too late. Too late. Why did those words keep coming back to haunt her? Was three hundred years not enough time to get the experiment of her life right?

No, she was thinking of herself in the same way she'd accused Sidney of doing, as nothing but an interesting footnote. Small and weak—and lost and insane—she might be, but she was more than that too. She'd needed more from Sidney, and he'd been unable to give it.

So she would be that something greater. Thorne and Sidney were both in for a surprise.

She took another breath and, staying low, pushed herself out a little farther for a better view.

Thorne had herded the Halloween partyers into the side room. Pacing between them and escape, he held the sword at a low angle in front of him, as if it weighed at his arm. Or maybe the light hurt his eyes.

Alyce squinted against the gleam. What did the others see? The child had seen the sword and the "black balloons" of malice that circled around him in a constellation of evil. An artist or holy person—or asylum patient—might see the truth, but the rest would delude themselves.

As far as Alyce could tell, Thorne hadn't used the sword

against anyone. No bodies lay on the floor; no disembodied souls floated free to tempt the voracious tenebrae.

But neither did he look as if he would wait much longer.

She took a third breath—only the third of the entire time, she realized, as her head swam—and drew her legs under her to stand. What she would say . . .

From the other side of the atrium, a storm front of etheric energy swelled through the room, so potent the leaves of the palms shriveled at the edges. Curls of the rough bark spontaneously ignited, the woody slivers burning like incense sticks.

Hard-soled footsteps drummed on the tile, the boots of a dozen new intruders.

The djinni army had arrived.

Chapter 27

Wrapped around the sword, Thorne's fingers burned and blistered and wept blood and healed in ever-thickening scars that shredded under yet more blisters. He might have screamed once or twice at the unreal pain, but eventually his nerves retired for the evening.

The djinni wasn't helping much as it flooded the wounds with the etheric equivalent of bile, raging against the angelic presence. The demon didn't appreciate what he was trying to do, which might have been why the eternal battle between good and evil was taking so damn long.

But it was inevitable that eventually someone would tire of the stalemate.

By the time Carlo arrived with his good little soldati in tow, Thorne's scarred hands had stopped oozing. Maybe enough ichor had drained from him to take the edge off the djinni.

"What are you doing, Thorne?" Carlo spun on his heel, taking in the cowed crowd. When he wheeled back, the light of the sword made him squint. "Magdalena got your message and has one question for you: Are you mad?"

Thorne considered a moment. "Do you mean insane, or still angry about the scuttling of my boat?"

Carlo's left eye twitched. "She told you she would find you."

"After the first date, the man should make the next move. I'm old-fashioned that way." Thorne traced the tip of the sword in an idle pattern. A toxic droplet of birnenston sizzled off the golden edge with a stench like death.

Carlo shook his head as if he didn't realize how precariously heads were attached. "What do you want, Thorne?"

"I want my *Princess*." Thorne's voice broke across demon harmonics. Apparently not as much virulent ichor had been drained from him as the pain would seem to indicate.

"Why, when you can be with a queen?"

Thorne looked down at his mangled hands. "Queen of Spades, maybe. The black widow card. She'll dig a hole right into hell."

Carlo shrugged, calling attention to that tender curve where shoulder and neck met. "If that's where the treasure is. But she wants more. She wants you."

"I'll bring her more," Thorne promised.

He stepped over the hole the sword had scorched in the floor. Perhaps it was the flare of righteousness in his heart that made the weapon come alive in his hands.

He swung it in a tight arc, and Carlo's head never had a chance.

For a heartbeat, only shocked silence vibrated through the crowd. Then a malice shrieked, triggering the flock, and their cries soared in unholy descant to the human screams.

Sid stumbled across the atrium, half-blind and all sick as the last of the verge mists evaporated from around his feet like dry ice. The blind part he blamed on the teshuva's flickering vision. The etheric interference of Thorne's djinni was giving it fits. The sickness . . .

Why had he let Alyce leave without him?

He'd always longed for a love without provisos, without specifications. He'd wanted his father to love him despite his being a second son. He'd wanted Maureen to love him even though he had a calling she couldn't share. But when Alyce had offered him exactly that, freely, without question, he'd fled. He'd had incontrovertible proof of the existence of demons and evil, but he'd never really believed in the love he sought.

The *symballein* bond wasn't a guarantee any more than an atomic bond could prevent a plutonium neutron from being knocked askew and triggering a nuclear meltdown. It was nothing more than a chance.

He'd never been good with games of chance. But the alternative was unthinkable. He would find her, he would—

When the screaming started, he realized he'd found Thorne too.

Shite. Now they had the panic on their hands they'd hoped to prevent. The city's entire parasite load of horde-tenebrae would swarm on the pier like the least appetizing aspects of vultures, rats, and maggots combined, to feed on the emanating darkness. Worse, they'd have armed authorities backing up their terror with bullets. An unlucky round or three could bleed out a talya before the teshuva could repair the damage, especially with the interfering energy of the tenebraeternum. Even worse, there might be cameras.

But he had bigger problems—or actually, just one smaller one.

He crouched in the hazy concealment of a smoking palm tree. He'd found her.

From where he hid, her small form seemed not much more than another figure in the painted Halloween procession on the folding screen. He crept around the other side of the palm and had a clear shot to where Thorne loomed over a fallen man. Most of the crowd had drawn back in horror, hands over mouths, faces averted, but a dozen more people milled about in more active consternation.

As Sid's teshuva tried to focus, a sulfurous yellow plume billowed above the body. It was another djinn-man Thorne had killed, which meant the other people, now gesturing furiously at Thorne, were also—

Thorne swung the sword.

And missed.

The tapered edge fell far short of the djinn-men's bodies. But the light from the sword shot out and bathed them in a blue-white glow.

Two more columns of vicious yellow oozed upward, fleeing the light. Holding their hands out in front of them to block a blow that hadn't come and staring at each other in confusion, the two djinn-men remained standing.

For a moment.

Then one fell to his knees. His legs crumpled. No, crumbled. The etheric winds swirled up twin dust devils from the cuffs of his pants. He let out a thin cry before his chest caved in, and then he had no throat to cry from as he puffed away.

His empty leather jacket sagged, a thin cushion to his companion, who staggered as the years of his possession caught up with him. With no demon to hold the ravages of time at bay, his muscles atrophied and his skin spotted. He clutched at his heart with one hand, the other reaching helplessly for the uprooted djinni.

The rest of the djinn-men stepped back from Thorne.

He swung again, aiming at the freed demons. A keening cry rose from the djinnless-man, echoed by the djinni that swirled above him, as the sword seemed to stretch hungrily toward them.

Sid squinted. It wasn't the sword that lengthened, just the light that surrounded it, sucking at the darkness. The two unbound demons roiled like plasma flares and shed flickers of ether as they struggled to escape. The shrieks of the salambes above split the tenebrae cloud with etheric lightning.

But the sword's light was savagely brighter. The hunger reminded Sid uneasily of the verge.

But this worked in their favor. Fewer djinn-men meant—

Suddenly, the atrium trembled, windows shivering and steel beams creaking.

Fewer djinn-men meant scraps of their demon-shredded souls loose in close proximity to the ravenous tenebraeternum. Sid doubted that the predations of an angelic weapon would be a stabilizing influence on the verge.

And Alyce was right in the middle of it.

Not right in the middle. Sort of off to one side, but creeping closer as if she had a plan to be in the middle of it. He hoped she had a plan, because he had none, except to follow her and to never let her get away again.

And if that seemed brutally talya of him, he thought he had a reasonable explanation, what with loving her.

Now if only he'd have the chance to tell her.

The other djinn-men were done milling. Apparently wanton murder wasn't cause for too much alarm in their circle. It probably helped their calm that Thorne was pointing the sword at them as if they didn't have much choice. A handful stepped closer to him, heads bowed, and then the rest followed, a few glancing nervously at the ceiling.

Thorne lowered the sword to his side. If anything, its light was brighter. Well fed, Sid guessed. It didn't seem to care what sort of energy it subverted.

Which was very much *not* working in their favor if it helped widen the verge that was already expanding into this realm.

Sid hurried across the open space between the palm tree and the folding screen, relying on the power struggle in front of him to distract the djinn-men. Alyce had already skipped ahead to a small side table holding an array of half-empty punch glasses and a fall bouquet in the center. If she hadn't been so small herself, hiding there would have been ridiculous. As it was, the cover put her within attacking distance.

That was her plan? Sid's heart raced toward her even though there was no place for his bigger body to hide on the way. As plans went, it sucked. Even if each of her six boning knives found demon-lethal targets, she'd have a half-dozen opponents remaining.

Not to mention Thorne and that vicious sword that could strip her teshuva from her. With three hundred years behind her—she would be gone in an instant.

The atrium shuddered again, as if it felt the force of the anguished shout that tried to crack free from his throat. He swallowed it back, and it nestled in place of his splintering heart. He didn't have a plan, and he couldn't wait to think of one; he would not be too late.

Alyce's side table hiding spot was useless to him. With only open space between him and the djinn-men and their hostages, he finally understood the talyan philosophy.

To hell with it.

He tightened every muscle and hyperventilated. The teshuva coiled tighter until his bones ached with the tension. He figured he'd have a few seconds to run before the distracted djinni energy focused on him and short-circuited his demon.

Whether Alyce could come up with a plan in those few seconds . . . He hoped her plan would be to run in the other direction.

He charged.

He made it halfway before he realized he had only his human strength and a bit of momentum. He crossed three-quarters of the distance before one of the djinn-men shouted a warning.

He got seven-eighths of the way before Thorne, who obviously knew that old "What's that over your shoulder?" ploy and didn't intend to be fooled, finally turned.

Sid fired.

It was a respectable attack, he told himself, as his ears rang from the shot. Not necessarily one for the history books, but . . .

At least he'd remembered to pull the gun out. His perception wavered and time stuttered as the teshuva, angelic and djinni emanations, clashed. But Thorne raised the sword.

And the bullet panged off the blade in a radiant surge of energy.

In the sudden frozen strobe, Sid's teshuva was kind enough to show him the bullet shearing in half and the relic shard absorbed by the flaming blade. The flames danced higher.

Oh, brilliant.

Thorne's already hawk-edged features seemed whetted from darkest, sharpest obsidian, as he realized what had almost happened. His roar of rage ripped through the seething energy around the blade.

He whirled on Sid, sword at the ready.

Another bullet would only amplify the sword. Sid wondered if the sight of Red Pony's gun would give Thorne a nostalgic pause with fond memories of the fellow radical he'd apparently blown to pieces—

The djinn-man brought the sword crashing down. Sid parried outward with the gun, desperate instinct his only chance.

The blade ripped through the revolver's cheap steel without pause, shearing across the chamber. The last five of the hollow point rounds scattered in arcs of dull lead and shining gold.

At least Sid's reflexive blow had deflected the sword's blue-white holy fire upward. The salambes scattered, squalling, and left smoldering contrails across the atrium sky like undying spawn of the *Hindenburg*.

Thorne spun the sword over his head again, but instead of a smooth flow, the tip jerked down clumsily, aiming at the floor as if—as if seeking out the strewn bullets.

Sid's analytical self whirled faster than the sword as he spun away to snatch a collapsed folding chair from where it had been pushed over in the panic.

The angelic weapon had given Thorne a new power, but it had also unbalanced his djinni, just as the angel relic had crippled Alyce's weaker demon. Thorne was fighting with one hand—his djinni's—tied behind his back.

Of course, in his literal hand Thorne was still holding a very real sword. But now the sword had its own ideas about reuniting with the remnants of its fallen comrade.

It clanged with a decidedly unheavenly and bone-jarring thud against Sid's chair when they clashed again. Book-keepers had to spend a lot of time sitting, but this was not how he'd thought he'd use the tool. He dared not move back, though; that would let Thorne bring the sword's etheric disruption into play.

He remembered how Alyce moved, lithe and smooth, in an unconscious dance, without the drag of heavy thoughts.

Could he follow her lead?

He didn't have a chance to find out.

Even as he jabbed at Thorne with the chair legs, hoping to tangle the blade, a trio of heavy weights slammed into him, one, two, and the third knocked the chair from his grasp.

The remaining djinn-men had obviously decided their fate lay with Thorne's favor. Despite his questionable alle-giance in weaponry, he'd apparently won their hearts with the murder of their brethren.

They pummeled Sid until his knees buckled. He col-lapsed, stirring up a puff of the decomposed djinn-man. For a moment, he was glad they'd knocked the breath out of him so he didn't huff the dust. Another blow knocked him prone.

From his sprawl, Alyce's hiding place was directly in his line of sight. He wanted to look into those icy eyes one last time. Could he tell her without speaking, with just a glance, that he loved her?

But, once again, she was gone.

CHAPTER 28

Alyce bit hard on her knuckle to stop from crying out when Sidney raced toward Thorne. With her hand pressed against her face, it was impossible not to notice the empty spot where she had worn the ring.

When the djinn-men tackled him and struck the chair away, she thought she might never breathe again.

She wanted to run after him as the djinn-men forced him to his feet in front of Thorne. But that was stupid, terribly stupid. There was nothing she could do against Thorne alone, much less against Thorne and his new army.

Blood streamed from Sidney's nose. His teshuva would heal him, as long as it could, which might not be much longer, if Thorne's speculative glance and the impatient twisting of the angel sword in his hand were any indication.

The knowledge of her weakness—and worse, that Sidney would want her to stay away—ate through her like acid. She didn't have the power; her demon couldn't even battle malice without setting up a sneak attack. . . .

Ah.

She crabbed backward, keeping the small table between her and the violent tableau. She needed distance from the overwhelming djinn energy.

The side room was a smaller version of the rest of the atrium, encased on all sides in triangular glass panes to view the lake and city. It was tight against the weather, but not against malice. The small oozy-smoky tenebrae had crept in from all around, drawn to the huddled hostages.

The malice darted and swirled like evil starlings, gobbling up the crumbs of negative emotion and emitting a fouler mess of hopelessness and despair.

A few of the hostages wept quietly. If questioned, they probably wouldn't be sure why. Better to have something to cry about, Alyce thought.

And suddenly she was glad she'd told Sidney she loved him. Maybe that had been stupid too. But what she felt had been real, not pushed by the teshuva through the *symballein* bond.

The love had been hers and clear.

That she might not have the chance to fight for that love tore at her. The fear bled from her, from the tiny wounds her nails opened in her palms when she clenched her fists. They sank like lesser verges in her skin, opening to her darkest dreads.

The closest malice wheeled from the hostages and arrowed toward her, pursued by a handful more, and then still more. They spread as they came, making a black and crimson hollow of ether, like a mouth, more than Alyce-sized.

"I am afraid," she whispered to them. "And you are hungry. Come taste fear."

She held out her bare hands.

There were so many. They swept across her like a foul second skin. As her teshuva flared, the malice sprang into sharp relief—emphasis on the sharp. The greedy little maws reaching for her pain glistened with thousands of needle teeth. Their oily essence phased in and out of solidity to reveal claws and lashing tails that stung her, soul deep.

She drew them closer with the demon's hooks. The malice struggled, sensing their doom on the threshold of where her dread did not own her anymore and became her weapon. Too late. And this time, the words gave her grim satisfaction.

The pressure built inside her like a madness, until she thought she would explode with it and lose everything.

Perfect.

She just had to ignore the fear that she would fail, though even the wisp of the thought buckled her knees, more crippling than a thousand malice. But she had been living with her fears for hundreds of years; she would not let them stop her now. She staggered for the side room, uncaring of the hiding places that might have sheltered her. The time for hiding was past.

She nearly crumbled, though, when she saw Thorne holding Sidney aloft, with one hand wrapped around her beloved's throat. Sidney had kept his chin down and tight, and he clawed at the fingers crushing his windpipe.

That had never worked for the hanging victims she watched die.

The memory tried to sap the remaining strength from her, snatching at her last breath. She refused to stop.

Until she hit the wall of seething djinni emanations.

The conflicting flow went through her with an electric shock. Her head snapped back, and her spine arched into an agonizing bow.

And her burden of frenzied malice, desperate to escape her teshuva's presence, sprang free with a cacophony of shrieks spreading across a dozen octaves. The etheric backlash swept the confined room in a visible shock wave, rippling through the air, rippling Sidney's hair, rippling the windowpanes. . . .

The glass shattered, tearing huge holes in the metal framework that supported the windows.

Shards rained down in a glittering shower. The hostages and djinn-men alike ducked and covered.

Except for Thorne.

But as he raised his face to the glass downpour, seeking its source, Sidney swung his fist straight at the djinn-man's nose.

Thorne dropped him with a roar.

The sound galvanized the crowd. The hostages fled toward the new openings in the walls with screams to match the malice. The other djinn-men hesitated, torn between chasing their prey and rallying around their leader.

Sidney had no such hesitation. He scrambled toward her. "Run!"

But she was spent. The malice attack had left her bruised with darkness. As he came toward her, she saw only the moment he had turned away, reversed for the time being, but sure to play out again, to rip her apart again.

The teshuva wavered in her, then steeled, like a cage around her heart, around her mind. Its alien chill settled through her. She raised her head to meet Sidney's gaze.

He faltered, just one step, but it was obvious all the same. She snarled at him. No, not her. The demon. But she did not stop it.

"No closer," it hissed. "Too late."

And in another heartbeat, Sidney grabbed her hand. "I said, run."

The heat of his touch torched her, and she gasped at the shock.

As he pulled her into his arms, another shower of glass tumbled toward them, alight with reflections of the plunging salambes and amusement park outside.

She looked up, dazzled—not by the lights and sparkling shards of certain death, but by Sidney's unfaltering gaze.

"Remind me to tell you more later," he said, "but I love you too."

The words simultaneously lifted and shattered her. She reached toward him, but the glimpse of her unadorned ring finger made her falter. The demon's protective haze grayed her vision, wavering along with her conviction, too close to the verge, too close to collapse.

No—she wouldn't dread his answer. No, she never would again, not even to save herself from the truth. "I loved you from the first."

"And I'll love you until the last."

She reached up to touch his throat where Thorne's grasp had purpled the skin. "We match."

He swallowed, and his pulse raced against her fingertips. *"Symballein."*

She fainted, and the tenebraeternum—no longer held at bay—swallowed them.

"Damn," Sid murmured. That hadn't gone over quite as smoothly as he'd hoped.

He'd waited too long to proclaim his love and claim their bond, and the darkness had taken them. They were stuck suspended in the verge, the mouth of the beast, which was somewhat better than the belly of the beast, but still full of dangerous teeth.

He clutched Alyce's small body to his chest. She'd fainted before, the last time she'd taken on too many malice. This couldn't be worse, could it?

Other than the dozen roaming djinn-men, the unleashed angelic sword, and the exploding verge, of course.

Thankfully, no one was around to answer the question.

"Alyce? Sweetheart, no hiding now."

His voice fell with a strange flatness, as if the tenebraeternum had no wish for sweethearts, no place for soft words.

He held her close, struggling to breathe the warm scent

of her through his bloody nose. His heart ached with loving words, hoarded for years; words he'd never been able to say, and couldn't say here, not on the verge of damnation, when anything he said would be tainted with shadows.

The gray around them was perforated with the verge views into other possibilities. Each opening while it gaped formed a bridge from the tenebraeternum to the human realm, a myriad of unhealed scars, real and imagined, each a link to the darkness.

And a link back to the real world.

He just had to step into the right reality. Good thing he'd always had a grip on things like that.

With all his impassive analytical skill, Sid focused on each portal. But this time, he couldn't use his Bookkeeper prowess alone; he needed his demon too. Whatever he had to do, whoever he had to become, he *would* get Alyce back where he could tell her again how he loved her. He wanted that—craved it. . . .

"Alyce," he whispered.

This time, she stirred. "Sidney?"

Weirdly distorted screams—tenebrae or human?—drowned her out. Stinging shards battered his head, and he hunched his shoulder over her to protect her.

Glass. Broken window glass was tumbling through one aperture. That had to be the right portal—

Thorne pounced through the opening, still glowering, with the angelic sword raised high.

Yeah, that was the real world.

Sid swore and bolted to his feet. Alyce slung her arm behind his neck as he clasped her against his chest.

Okay, maybe he didn't have as good a grasp on realm jumping as he thought. In retrospect, it wasn't at all surprising that a bridge would go both ways.

Thorne's impressive leap carried him well within the no-man's-land that surrounded them, but then he staggered;

clearly his djinni was as unsettled on the doorstep of hell as the repentant teshuva.

Only a quick thrust of his sword into the strange shifting surface beneath their feet kept him upright.

But the tenebraeternum didn't like being poked with angel relics. The verge heaved around them. Alyce gasped in Sid's ear and held him tighter. Red, yellow, and black lightning streaked through the gray, disrupting some of the orb portals.

Including the one Thorne had arrived through. He spun back, cursing, but the rounded window collapsed into a lopsided crescent, its view to the outside world fuzzed like an old tube television losing reception.

With the djinn-man occupied, Sid let Alyce slide down his chest to her feet, though he didn't let go until he was sure she was steady, or at least as steady as one could be on the gateway into hell.

Thorne wasn't taking their precarious situation well. His scowl creased the birnenston burns on his cheekbones into a frightful mask lit by the guttering sword. The angel relic wasn't any happier than its bearer to be this close to the source of evil. "What have you done?"

Sid kept Alyce tucked close behind him. Hadn't he said exactly that to the talyan the first time he saw the verge? Not that he wanted to sympathize with this particular devil. "You shouldn't have followed us," he reminded Thorne.

"This is the last time I forget that nothing good comes of following." Thorne leveled the sword at them, but nothing happened—not even the pathetic solenoid rattle of one of Liam's junker cars. "You could die here too. Get us out."

Sid spread his empty hands. "I can't. It's up to Alyce."

She blanched when Thorne rounded on her. "I can't. . . . I don't remember what I did."

"Remember," Thorne snarled, "or I'll finish the games we've played all these years."

Sid stepped toward the djinn-man, but Alyce hauled

him back, her grip surprisingly strong. He didn't pull away; he would never willingly separate from her again. "Maybe you can *threaten* her into being yours. Since all those years she was lost and alone, and you still couldn't win her."

Thorne recoiled. He squared his shoulders again, but that first flinch of hurt had been too quick even for his djinni to prevent.

"She's yours now, Anglo. I grant you that." His tone softened. "So you make her remember, and I'll undo your possession."

Sid froze.

With her hand still on his arm, Alyce must have felt his hesitation. Her fingers trailed down his arm, and she stepped away, her gaze bleak as the coming winter when he glanced back at her.

Unbidden, his gaze slid to the djinn-man in fascination. "You can't. . . ."

Thorne waved the tip of the sword in a sinuous pattern near his feet. "I've already done it three times tonight."

"And destroyed them all," Alyce choked out.

Thorne shrugged. "Only the first one. The other two died on their own because they'd been too long possessed." He smiled at Sid. "But you . . . Your teshuva has barely had time to unpack."

As pages from league books he'd read came to mind, his life as a Bookkeeper flashed before his eyes. "It might still kill me. The flaw in my soul the demon exploited to possess me would be even more exposed when it left."

Thorne shrugged. "A risk, true. But how much worse could it be than where you are now?" A sweep of the sword encompassed the gray. "And you'd regain all you had. I'm a gambling man. Are you?"

"I wasn't before," Sid said.

Alyce made a soft sound, like the malice cry of furious despair but only a single, human octave, low and mournful. The many mouths of the verge echoed the cry, including the hazy crescent view of the talyan battling the djinn-men, no more substantial than a dream.

Or a nightmare.

Thorne smiled. "Good man. You can take that with you from your short time as talya. A parting gift."

"Go." Amidst the demented whispers, Alyce's quiet voice almost disappeared. "I think I can freeze the shifts long enough for you to slip away."

Sid searched her eyes. He saw no trace of the teshuva's fog, but just a pale sky blue down to her soul. "And what about you?"

"I can hold the verge steady on this side but not while I pass through myself." She dropped her gaze. "I'll stay."

"No bets on your surviving here," Thorne murmured. "Not even from a gambling man."

Sid glanced at Thorne. "And still you think I'd take it?"

"I'd bet the house."

"Then you'd lose your house. Again." Sid faced Alyce and forced her to look at him; he forced her to look and hopefully see what was down at the bottom of his own soul. "And you're crazy if you think I'd let you stay here."

"Crazy?" Her eyes flickered, not violet, but with the faintest hint of returning life.

"And I'd be crazy to let you go. You're my *symballein* mate, and that makes us two halves of something special."

"Especially crazy," Thorne snapped. He whirled the sword over his head. Its blessings might be twisted in this place, but the edge whistled sharply through the gray. "I'm not asking nicely."

Alyce spun on him, as graceful as the blade. "Then don't say anything at all."

She swept her hands across her body and back again in a swirl. Ether fled from her gesture in chaotic waves through the gray fog.

Thorne disappeared in the shifting madness of shadows and warped portal views as the waves expanded. His shout of rage barely reached them, lost between the jumbled possibilities.

"Interesting." Sid tapped his chin. "I didn't know you could do that."

"It's nothing, just delusion, reflected back at him. He'll fight his way through." She gazed up at him. "As you should. That's one thing he was right about, Sidney—you could let your demon go."

He reached for her, and her fingers were icy cold. "I could. I'd take the risk, but . . ."

"But nothing."

"Exactly. I'd have nothing without you."

She shook her head. "I saw those pictures in the archives of how much good my little demon can do. More than me, the league needs a Bookkeeper."

"And I'll be Chicago's Bookkeeper. It's what I am, and I don't need anyone's stamp of approval, not anymore. But not having you . . ." He tightened his grasp, willing the warmth of his skin into hers. "I need you. That illusion you seem to think I could fight my way through—that isn't a theory or a concept to unravel. That is my love."

He lifted her tight-held fist and pressed her knuckles to his throat so she could feel the vibration of his words, feel the longing pulse that sought to match itself to hers. "I love you, Alyce. I said it before, and I'll keep saying it. I'll say it in dead languages and I'll sign it in blood and ichor, and I'll keep this damn demon, so even if it takes forever until you believe me, I will still be saying I love you."

In the shifting darkness around them, the moment stretched out, until even the eternity in which they were trapped seemed about to sob out its indrawn breath.

"I do believe you," she whispered. "I do."

He rummaged in his pocket and withdrew the rivet. She smiled and unfurled her clenched hand to brush her thumb across his lips. She kept her gaze fixed on his as he slid the ring over her heart finger.

He leaned down to kiss her, slowly and gently, never mind the swirling shadows of a hungry hell and the furious djinn-man.

She tilted her face up to meet his kiss, and the shadows stilled, all the powers of darkness unable to rise between them.

But in the stillness, the delusions thrown by the unstable portals cleared. Thorne burst into view, sword high.

Alyce cried out, and Sid wheeled toward the djinn-man, yanking free two of the boning knives from behind her back.

Thorne's eyes widened, then narrowed, and he roared out a challenge. Sid never made a sound as he raised the knives in a cross to catch the falling sword.

Face-to-face with the djinn-man, he stared into the yellow-ringed eyes. There was no place for the Bookkeeper philosophy of dispassionate observation here. He would never again back away from the bonds between him and the league, between him and Alyce, who was the pale un-wavering light in his world.

Thorne strained against him, but this close to hell, the eternal darkness was a torrent of unfettered etheric energy that overwhelmed both their demons, so they fought only muscle to muscle, fury to fury.

The djinn-man did have the bigger sword, though, and he bore down with an incisor-clenched grin. "I've killed humans and angels and djinn. I've never killed a talya or a Bookkeeper. Your head will be a fine oddity for my collection."

"Who's the curiosity here? You're a djinn-man bearing an abrasax, an angel's blessed weapon. There's never been a record of such a contradiction." Sid locked the two slender knives around the heavier blade and refused to yield to sword or words. "Alyce is mine, but have you considered that maybe you are meant for something else as well?"

For the barest instant, the weight of the sword eased;

then Thorne's face twisted. "Once I kill you, I bet she forgets you before the next night falls. But maybe I'll spare your league one prayer when I wield this cursed weapon over the ahāzum."

"Bet me then. Double or nothing."

The shifting realities of the verge never quite settled, but Sid focused all his fear for the chances he'd almost lost. And still that fear was nothing compared to the love that had found him. With a furious upward shove of both slender knives against the sword, he sent the djinn-man stumbling back.

Alyce strode into the fray. Flickers of djinni yellow and blue-white angel fire played along the shine of her black leather. She had two more knives in her hands, and Sid caught his breath in dread—and in delight that she was his. Before he could shout a warning, she brought the knives slicing down.

Though the blades passed nowhere near the djinn-man, the darkness behind him gaped wide in a view too muddled for Sid to decipher.

Whatever Thorne saw made him twist from the half-open portal. But in the force of ether swirling away from Alyce, he lost his balance.

The portal swallowed, and Thorne was gone.

Sid whirled. "Where—?"

Alyce sheathed the two knives with a doubled hiss of steel. "Gone."

As if that was enough. Sid supposed, it was, for now. "Dare we hope the tenebraeternum will tear him to bits, and the sword too?"

"That I wouldn't bet on."

He sighed. "Fane will be pissed the sword is gone."

She bit her lip. "But not you?" Her tone wavered between the ghostly girl she'd been and the warrior woman standing before him.

They had time to learn each others' secret pasts and

make sense of their shared future. He gathered her close to slide the knives back along her spine. "We'll have troubles, no doubt, but I have you. And you have me. Can you get us out of here?"

She held out her empty hand to display the ring. "With you at my side, yes."

"I'll be here, always." He took her hand.

After a moment, her little smile appeared. "Maybe someday I won't keep making you say it."

He grinned in reply. "But I like to." He dipped his head again to kiss the red crescents her teeth had left on her lower lip. "Mine to love, and be loved in return. Two halves of the perfect equation. That's the *symballein* bond. Not a mystery to be unraveled, but a promise."

When he kissed her again, the verge peeled back and spat them into the atrium in a wash of etheric winds.

They stumbled across the glass-strewn floor. Archer stood atop a concrete planter, one hand braced on the palm tree, the other on his hip. He scowled at them. "About time."

Sid lifted one eyebrow. "Not too late, I hope."

Archer jumped down from the planter. "They ran, most of them. The rats. We killed a couple. Which leaves us with some awkward bones and drifts of grave dust to explain if we don't vanish right now. And we can't all pull that trick you did." He peered at Alyce. "Nice trick, by the way."

She nodded, distracted. "There was a blue child. . . ."

"Sera cleared the atrium and found one hidden Cookie Monster. Everyone's out. The talyan are hiding in plain sight, mixed with the crowd and draining malice to calm everyone. There's so much confusion, I think we can pull this off. And you two?"

"Not confused at all," Alyce said.

Sid pulled her, unresisting, into his arms and kissed her. He couldn't stop himself. He'd never get enough of the innocence, of the temptation, of Alyce.

When they paused to catch their breath, Archer was heading out through the giant hole blown in the side of the atrium. Police cruisers, the still-spinning Ferris wheel, and a lone string of lights dangling from the ruined ceiling provided the only illumination.

"I was confused," Sid admitted to her. "I thought I wasn't allowed to want; that I could only watch from the outside. But if a demon can love . . ."

He brushed a lock of her dark hair from her eyes. He stared down into the clear depths . . . and saw his love reflected back at him.

He cleared his throat. "Can I say it again?"

She touched his cheek—the ring glinting in the corner of his vision before her fingers slipped down to rest against the quickening pulse in his throat—and smiled. "Forever."

Epilogue

Nim brushed tears from the corners of her eyes, smearing her mascara. "You're so beautiful in white."

"Brides are always beautiful," Jilly said reasonably.

Sera added a happy sniff of her own. "The first *symballein* wedding."

Alyce turned slowly in front of the mirror. The neckline, wavy with lace, lay low across her collarbone. Her *reven*, quiescent, was decoration enough—except for the ring, of course. She held out her hand to admire the rivet. A thread of amethyst light, like embedded filigree, chased through the steel and matched the purple ribbons in her braided hair.

Sidney, though he called himself a traditionalist, had said she should keep the ring on before the wedding. "We're making our own traditions now," he'd said.

So she'd given him his wedding present early. The flattened band, forged with Liam's oversight from the remnants of discarded spectacles, had made Sid laugh and then kiss her. She couldn't decide which she liked more, the laugh or the kiss; she'd have to indulge in both again, often.

She turned again to check the blades tucked into the chevron sheaths down her spine. Sneaking into a church in the middle of the night on Halloween in a demon-stalked city called for a certain amount of armament.

Therese peeked in the door. "Ready? I don't think he can last much longer."

Alyce tilted her head. "He'd wait forever." When the women snorted in unison, she added, "But I don't think I can."

Jilly straightened, as if rising from a strategy table. "Let's do it then."

The women filed out, and Alyce looked at herself another moment. Something flickered in the shadows behind her, but she didn't turn. Her past was just that—behind her; though not to be forgotten for the strengths it had given her. She walked to the door with her head high.

There were no flowers; the last night of October in Chicago had begun with a hard frost. There was no music except the longing sigh of some wayward draft in the rafters. There weren't enough bridesmaids for all the groomsmen arrayed near the altar.

But there were candles, dozens of little white votives in cracked tumblers, scented of nothing but sweet wax, and all the more lovely for the darkness around them.

And there was Sidney.

She walked down the aisle alone, her gaze on his.

His smile was small, gentle, but when he took her outstretched hands, the power that surged through her was beyond everything.

A bit of metal clinked against her ring, and she looked down at the key he pressed into her palm.

"I found us a place here," he murmured. "It's small—seems talyan are paid worse than Bookkeepers—but it has a library and a roof garden with a glimpse of the river, and we can walk to work. I haven't signed yet, but it'll be ours if you like it."

"Does it have a good kitchen? I want Therese to teach me how to cook."

"You don't have to cook for me. If we're going to find Thorne, I'm guessing we'll be out most nights anyway."

"I'm not doing it just for you," she said. "It's for me. And for us." She squeezed his hands and smiled up at him. "I'll bring the knives."

They turned to stand side by side.

Liam rested with both palms planted on the haft of the war hammer propped between his feet. "I am no priest. Obviously. And words at a wedding are usually about starting a new life together. Which seems unnecessary when it's so damn clear the bride and her groom are eternally bonded, not by their demons, but by the fitting match of their souls. So I'll just wish you happiness." He stepped back and took Jilly's hand.

"And peace," Archer murmured.

"Passion," Nim countered with a wicked grin.

Sidney raised Alyce's hand to his lips. The ring warmed to his breath when he whispered against her skin, "And love."

Glossary of Terms

abrasax: An angelic-possessed's blessed weapon.

ahāzum: A gathering of djinn; forbidden since the First Battle.

ascendant: The rise of a demon within a possessed human; refers to the initial incident of possession and subsequent risings.

birnenston: Also, brimstone. A sulfuric compound leached from some demonic emanations interacting with the human realm.

***desolator numinis*:** "Soul cleaver"; a demonic weapon.

djinni: djinn (pl.): Upper echelon of demonkind; fallen angels who are content to stay fallen.

djinn-man: A human possessed by a djinni.

ether: The elemental energy of spiritual and demonic emanations.

feralis: ferales (pl.): Lesser demonic emanation encased in a physical shell of mutated human-realm material. Physically strong, but not so impressive in the brains department.

heshuka: The unknown darkness; from Aramaic.

horde-tenebrae: Blanket term for lesser demonic emanations, including malice, ferales, and salambes. Also, tenebrae.

ichor: A physical by-product of demonic emanations not compatible with the human realm.

league: Isolated clusters of possessed fighters assigned to high-density human-population areas with the mission of reducing demonic activity.

malice: Incorporeal lesser emanation from the demon realm, typically small and animalistic in shape with proto-human intelligence.

mated-talyan bond: The synergistic combination of male and female possessed powers.

reven: The permanent visible epidermal mark left by an ascended demon.

salambe: Highly emanating demonic form from the same subspecies as malice.

solvo: A chemical version of the *desolator numinis*; produces opiatelike effects in humans while splitting off the soul.

sphericanum: The realm of angels, separated from the human realm by the gates of heaven. Also used in reference to the ruling body of angelic powers.

symballein: A token, such as an engraved metal disk, that is broken into two pieces and used to establish identity when reunited; from Greek.

talya: talyan (pl.): 1. Sacrificial lamb; a young man (Aramaic). 2. A human, typically male, possessed by a repentant demon.

tenebrae: Blanket term for lesser demonic emanations, including malice, ferales, and salambes. Also, horde-tenebrae.

tenebraeternum: The demon realm, separated from the human realm by the Veil.

teshuva: A repentant demon seeking to return to a state of grace.

Veil: An etheric barrier between the human and demon realms and composed of captured souls.

And don't miss Jonah and Nim's
captivating story,

VOWED IN SHADOWS

Available now from Signet Eclipse.

Jonah knew he'd finally broken through Nim's resistance when she numbly agreed to return to her apartment to clean up and kicked up hardly any fuss when he didn't bother asking her address as they got into his car

"You followed me home," was all she said as she settled into the passenger's seat, and she sounded more resigned than angry, so he neither confirmed nor denied.

Bewildered as she was, with her new demon scarcely settled and its capabilities still unknown, he didn't want to risk pushing her. Not if he didn't have to. The soothing power of a hot shower was allowable, now that she couldn't convince herself her world was still the same.

Her teshuva had already sealed over the scrapes on her knee, and the ugly bruise on her hip was fading fast. But the streaks of blood on her tawny skin remained, and the feralis had spattered ichor on her, burning holes in her already indecent shorts.

He retrieved Mobi's case from the backseat while Nim

unlocked the security screen on the front door of the old brick building. Side by side, silent, they walked past the rows of mailboxes. He paused at the elevator, then had to hurry a few long steps to catch up with her when she opened the door to the stairs.

She smiled at him crookedly. "What? Are your legs broken?"

"You live on the seventh floor."

"Apparently, you haven't been watching me all that closely. I always take the stairs. Did you think taking an elevator gave me these legs?"

On cue, his gaze dropped to her legs, as if he had to make an assessment. Even streaked with blood, they were gorgeous. Slender ankles, toned calves, and *reven*-marked thighs that curved into well-rounded buttocks . . . not that he could see those overflowing handfuls, even with her indecent shorts. But he remembered.

Until the day some feralis took off his head, he'd never forget.

He snapped his attention to her face. "You like to do that. Make me look at your body."

She padded up the stairs, her bare feet slapping her ire on the treads. She'd refused to put on the sandals he'd retrieved from the feralis's maw. "That's how I pay the rent."

"You do it to distract." He realized he was watching the sway of her hips, back and forth, as she climbed the stairs. Distracting? Worse: mesmerizing. "You didn't like to think that I've been watching you when you weren't in charge."

She stopped so abruptly he almost collided with her. "Watching, but not closely," she reminded him.

"So you want me to watch closer. But only those parts you want me to see."

"Thanks for the analysis. Will you charge me for that, along with the orgasm?"

Though he was coming to understand her tactics, the low blow brought heat to his cheeks. "It was necessary."

"The psychoanalysis?" The wicked twinkle in her eyes dared him to disagree.

So he did. "No, the . . . orgasm." In all his years, had he ever said that word aloud? He rubbed his thumb against the base of his ring finger, ticking the band with his nail.

Suddenly, uneasily, he wondered what else he'd be forced to do. He'd only wanted a way to fight harder, to redeem himself. He hadn't quite anticipated that opening himself to another meant . . . to another person. To Nim.

She continued up the stairs. "The demon likes to fuck you? But not be fucked."

"I'm uncomfortable with your foul language." He almost winced at how prim he sounded, how outdated.

"Oh, so it wasn't the demon that was uncomfortable with what happened between us. It was you."

"I was told the most prudent method to balance your rising demon was the . . . orgasm."

" 'Prude' is right," she mumbled.

She slammed out of the stairwell and headed down the hall. He stood aside as she opened the door.

The apartment was messier than when he'd cased it previously, although the same earthy patchouli incense drifted out to tease him. He'd been surprised a stripper kept such a tidy abode. This—the magazines tangled in the folds of a blanket across the red corduroy couch, the dirty dishes piled in the sink—had been what he expected. Obviously, she'd been increasingly disturbed by the restive energies of her unbound demon.

Nice to know he hadn't been alone.

She slipped Mobi's case from his shoulder. "Okay, then. Thanks for everything. I'll call you later, yeah? Bye."

He gave her a look. Turning her back on him with an aggrieved sigh, as if that would do the trick, she went to the coffin-sized glass case against one wall and slid the snake inside. She bustled past him again to retrieve a bowl from the counter and then returned to the terrarium.

He wrinkled his nose. "Dead rat?"

"Can you think of a better use? At least this one won't morph into a monstrosity like that one you massacred." She whispered something nonsensical to the snake and placed the dish in a corner. She fussed with the water bowl before closing the lid, then slid a black sheet across most of the case.

"Praise be."

She shot him an arch glance. "That's not for your sake. Mobi doesn't like an audience when he eats. When he's done, he'll need to be left alone for a day or so."

"You dance without him?"

"Not anymore." She pointed at the framed poster above the snake's tank that showed the curves of a woman, breast to hip, body painted in tiger stripes. COMING SOON, it screamed in crimson type, VIVA LAS SHOWGIRLS INTRODUCES *BEAUTY AND THE BEAST*. "We're rehearsing for the Showgirls semifinals. I'll have to take a couple days off, but by the weekend, he'll be raring to go again."

By then, the Naughty Nymphette—like the rat—would be only a bad memory. She'd be fully immersed in the talyan world, never to return to her own. Jonah thought that could remain unsaid for now. "In the meantime, there are a few things we need to work out. The demon, when it came to you, might have felt like a dream or a hallucination. But did it leave you something tangible—a piece of jewelry, perhaps?"

She shrugged. "Maybe."

He struggled to keep his voice level. "Nim, this is important. I noticed you don't wear any jewelry when you dance." After Liam and Archer had explained how the women's teshuva had come to them bearing gifts of mutated metals, Jonah had made a point of checking Nim for jewelry throughout the week. He had looked very carefully and seen nothing.

No jewelry, anyway.

"I hocked it."

Her breezy admission snapped him back to painful reality. "What?" He took a quick step toward her, then stopped himself when she stiffened. He raked his hand through his hair. "You sold it? But you never went to a pawnshop."

"While you were staking me out, you mean? I have a neighbor who unloads stuff for me." She lifted her chin when he glared at her. "Nothing stolen. Not anymore. He gives me cold, hard cash for the cheap-ass gifts my loving customers give me. And believe me, that anklet was the cheapest-looking shit I'd ever seen."

He paced the tight confines of the room. It was that or shake her. She couldn't have known, but frustration sharpened his voice. "It was a weapon. A demonic weapon."

"It was an ugly anklet."

He coughed on a desperate laugh. "The demon should have known you well enough to at least make it shiny."

She scowled. "All I knew, I had a weird night and I woke up with some trashy jewelry lying on my floor. Could've come from anywhere." When he rolled his eyes in disbelief, she added defensively, "I have a lot of loving customers, and they tuck their gifts in a lot of places."

He held up his hand to forestall further explanation. "Which neighbor? And where does he pawn his goods?" Or evils, in this case.

"You going to chop off his head too?"

"Not before he directs me to the anklet." When was the last time he'd had to justify himself to another? The feeling chafed like the hook against his scar tissue. "I have never chopped off a human's head, and I don't plan to start. Is that answer enough?"

She crossed her arms, jaw set mulishly off-kilter.

"Nim," he said with strained patience. "If there's a demonic weapon loose in the city, don't you agree it'd be wise to find it?" With each word, his voice got louder.

"I suppose I should've asked for more money." And still she hesitated another moment. "It's Pete, down the hall in 713. But he won't answer the door for just anyone. I'll go with you."

"Clean up first. The blood on you will unnerve him more than I will." Jonah scuffed the hook along his thigh as he gave her a once-over. Just looking at her made his missing hand twitch. "After we retrieve the anklet, I suppose you have to meet the rest of the league. You should wear something . . ."

She set her arms akimbo, the tight clench of her fingers dragging the already low-slung waistband another inch past her navel. "Wear something what?"

He backpedaled mentally. "Something without ichor holes."

"Remember how you said you really liked my honesty?"

"I don't think I said that exactly."

She wrapped one long dread around the rest and tucked the edge under in a makeshift restraint and stood square to face him. "Honestly, I don't want to go anywhere else with you. I don't want to meet anyone you know. Now that I think about it—actually, I didn't even really have to think about it—I don't want to know *you*."

The scornful words grated along his nerves. "Biblically, it's a little late for that. We can't reverse this."

"Who said anything about reverse? If I really am faster and stronger, I figure I'm going to have a killer new routine worked out before the *Viva Las Showgirls* finals. I might even try fire dancing, since I'm immortal and all."

He stared at her. "You'd turn your damnation into a striptease?"

"What are you doing with it that's so much better?"

"Destroying evil." The hook dug into his leg. "Winning back my soul."

She shrugged. "That monster only attacked because you

lured it in. And you only notice your soul is lost because you're still looking."

"Wrong." He all but choked on the word. Her casual denial of what had happened to her—not disbelief, just dismissal—shocked him. "Possession wasn't a choice, and neither is what you do next. The demon chose you to fight."

"I'm a lover, not a fighter." The sharp edge to her smile belied her words. "It should've asked me first."

"It did. Not in words. Still, you accepted it."

She waved one hand. "Entrapment. It'll never stand up in court."

Frustration made his temples throb. "You've already been judged and found guilty. And sentenced."

She wrinkled her lip. "By you."

"I played no part in your possession."

"Didn't you?" A merciless glint brightened her fathoms-deep eyes. "I saw you in my dream, you know. The one where you said the demon came to me. It was you I thought I was letting in." A hint of violet lurked within the glint. "Into my body."

Startled heat flashed through him. Liam had implied that both female talyan had had premonitions of their coming possession. At the same time, their partners had been driven to restlessly roam the streets, the unbound te-shuva energies resonating with the demons already possessing them. The league leader had never said outright that the women had *seen* their ordained mates. Had been *tricked* by the image of the male talya meant to stand beside them.

He had been willing to lead the demon's unwitting quarry from darkness toward the light. But he would never have chosen to be the temptation that caused her downfall. When he told her she'd had no choice, he realized, once again, the same had been true for him. "I'm sorry."

She tilted her head. The dreads shifted across her shoulders but never obscured her far-too-perceptive eyes. "You had no hand in it—other than the hand you had in me an hour ago—yet you're here to save me, even though you hate me. Why?"

"I don't hate—" He bit off the protest. It wasn't going to convince her. He continued, each word more clipped than the last, "When my sword hand was severed, the impairment left me out of step with my demon. I need a partner to rejoin the battle."

Her gaze ticked over him, from his boots to his face. "Maybe you just need to learn another dance."

"A tenebrae tango," he agreed. "We will fight together."

"You said there are others like us? Go fight with them."

"I have. For a very long time." Bitterness rippled through him in ragged waves, the same way the teshuva's thwarted energy swirled and jammed in his gnarled scars without escape. "It was for one of them, I was maimed. And now I can't ..." The phantom muscles in his missing hand cramped, sending spasms along his *reven*. "Now I am even less than I was."

She tucked in her chin with a dubious look. "Less? Really? So you were, like, Superman before?"

"I could never fly."

"But the anklet, the demon weapon, gives you super-powers?"

"No. Without you, the anklet means nothing. But your demon is uniquely aligned with mine, in ways we can't understand."

"Can't understand?" She huffed. "You mean, 'don't want.'"

"Wanting isn't a consideration."

She peered at him. "It's always a consideration. You just have it sealed up tight. Which is bad, because when that one wanting hits you—and it will—it'll be worse than if you wanted everything."

"How very . . . voracious of you. Meanwhile, I believe together we can drive the horde into hell."

"Oh, you just *want* me to be your new right hand."

Said aloud, in her mocking tone, he realized accusing her of mercenary tendencies had been unfair. Now that his perfidy was revealed, he saw no reason to conceal the worst of what he was. "You'll be the other half of my damaged soul."

ALSO AVAILABLE
from

Jessa Slade

Seduced by Shadows
A Novel of the Marked Souls

When Sera Littlejohn meets a violet-eyed stranger, he
reveals a supernatural battle veiled in the shadows, and
Sera is tempted to the edge of madness by a dangerous
desire. Ferris Archer takes Sera under his wing, now that
she is a talya—possessed by a repentant demon with
hellish powers. Archer's league of warriors have never
fought beside a female before, and never in all his
centuries has Archer found a woman who captivates
him like Sera.

With the balance shifting between good and evil, passion
and possession, Sera and Archer must defy the darkness—
and dare to embrace a love that will mark them forever.

"Wonderfully addictive."
—*New York Times* bestselling author
Gena Showalter

Available wherever books are sold or at
penguin.com

ALSO AVAILABLE
from

Jessa Slade

Vowed in Shadows
A Novel of the Marked Souls

Once a righteous missionary, Jonah Walker now endures
immortality with nothing but a body built for battle and
a heart set on retribution. But his last devastating fight
left him wounded beyond healing—and his only chance
for redemption lies with a fallen woman whose passion
burns through the shadows...

"Dark and sexy and intense."
—*New York Times* bestselling author Nalini Singh

Available wherever books are sold or at
penguin.com